KINN
PORSCHE

KINN PORSCHE

NOVEL
01

WRITTEN BY
Daemi

TRANSLATION BY
Frigga, Onyx, Linarii

BLACK & WHITE
ILLUSTRATIONS BY
Avaritia

Seven Seas

Seven Seas Entertainment

Published originally under the title of รักโคตรร้ายสุดท้ายโคตรรัก (KinnPorsche)
Author©Daemi
English edition rights under license granted by Daemi House Limited Partnership
English edition copyright©2024 Seven Seas Entertainment, Inc
Arranged through JS Agency Co., Ltd.
All rights reserved

Interior illustrations by Avaritia
Bonus color illustration by Tamtam

Seven Seas press and purchase enquiries can be sent
to Marketing Manager Lauren Hill at press@gomanga.com.
Information regarding the distribution and purchase of digital editions is available
from Digital Manager CK Russell at digital@gomanga.com.

Seven Seas and the Seven Seas logo are trademarks of
Seven Seas Entertainment. All rights reserved.

Follow Seven Seas Entertainment online at
sevenseasentertainment.com.

TRANSLATION: Frigga, Onyx, Linarii
ADAPTATION: Abigail Clark
COVER DESIGN: M. A. Lewife
INTERIOR DESIGN & LAYOUT: Clay Gardner
COPY EDITOR: Marcelo Napoli
PROOFREADER: Ami Leh, Adrian Mayall
EDITOR: Hardleigh Hewmann
PREPRESS TECHNICIAN: Melanie Ujimori, Jules Valera
MANAGING EDITOR: Alyssa Scavetta
EDITOR-IN-CHIEF: Julie Davis
PUBLISHER: Lianne Sentar
VICE PRESIDENT: Adam Arnold
PRESIDENT: Jason DeAngelis

ISBN: 979-8-88843-760-5
Printed in Canada
First Printing: September 2024
10 9 8 7 6 5 4 3 2 1

CONTENTS

A Bad...Start

PORSCHE

WHACK! THUD!

The sound of a hard object hitting flesh caught my attention. I was stuffing a large trash bag into a green bin near the nightclub where I worked part-time, a cigarette dangling from my lips. From the corner of my eye, I saw five or six thugs beating some stupid guy to the ground. I adjusted my backpack and casually took a drag from my cigarette, ignoring the havoc in front of me.

This was a common occurrence in this alley next to the nightclub. It was quite dark, and staff only came back here to throw out the trash or pick up deliveries.

"Shit! You won't fucking give up!"

I couldn't see clearly through the darkness, but I could faintly hear the cursing. I kept ignoring them, though, studiously locking the back door of the nightclub now that my shift was over.

I worked part-time here as a server after class. Usually, the place was close to empty at this hour—and just a few customers remained, either waiting to hail a taxi, looking to get laid, or picking a fight like the guys behind me... I didn't want to be a heartless douchebag, but I also didn't want to stick my nose into other people's business.

The guy must have insulted someone in that group to get beaten up this badly...

Fine—you can call me a jerk for ignoring a guy getting his ass kicked. But what did I know? He might have done something to deserve it. And not something trivial like stealing candy from a corner store...right?

"Get the fuck off of me!"

Damn, this dude is tough. I glanced behind me and saw him spring up and hit the thugs back.

I threw my cigarette to the ground and stubbed it out with my shoe, then stretched my stiff muscles before heading to my bike in the nearby parking lot. I was ready to head home and rest...and I would have, too, if the dumbass hadn't hurled himself into my back.

I heard a faint, raspy voice.

"Help..."

I felt a tug on my university jacket. I looked behind to see a man's bruised face, blood all over his nose and mouth. He looked surprisingly handsome for someone who was so banged up. I wondered what a posh-looking guy like him did to get his shit rocked this badly.

"Get back here, fucker!"

One of the goons stalked closer and violently yanked the guy by his shirt collar. I took another look at him—something crossed my mind and made me pull his arm before the big bully could drag him away.

"Chill out, dude," I said calmly, assessing the thug's face. He had a mustache and looked way too old for me to call "dude." Why would these assholes bully a kid? The handsome guy, who I was still holding by the arm, looked about the same age as me. Judging from his clothes, he was some sort of rich kid. Were they trying to mug him or something? I pulled the guy back to shield him while staring at his attackers.

And I thought I'd just mind my own business...

"Stay the fuck out of this, I'm warning ya!"

That made me hesitate, but I was too curious. I had to ask. "What did he do?"

If this guy did something wrong, then I'd let him face his fate. But if not...I might try and be a good person for once.

"I told ya not to butt in!" the thug barked angrily before attempting to grab the handsome guy behind me. I hesitated again—this was really none of my goddamn business.

I had a little brother to take care of. Who was going to feed him if I got hurt and couldn't work? Images of my burden of a little brother flashed in my head.

I really was a callous prick—when it came down to it, I didn't want to take action without getting anything for my trouble. With that realization, I intended to move away and let the group of thugs do what they wanted with the good-looking guy...but he stopped me.

"If you help me, I'll pay you a worthy reward," he whispered.

He was trying to bribe me?! Fuck that! He really thought he could sway me with money?

...Yup! Damn straight. Money was always good motivation. "How much?" I asked.

"Fifty thousand.¹ That enough?"

My lips curled into a satisfied smile at the offer. Fifty thousand would be enough to cover the tuition fees for my little brother, Chay. I used one arm to block the goons' advance.

"If you bail, I will fucking kill you, understood?" I said. One of the thugs grabbed a two-by-four, and I immediately shoved the handsome kid out of the way to kick the thug's hand, knocking him and the plank of wood to the ground before he could clobber me.

---

1   *50,000 baht is equivalent to about 1,400 US dollars.*

I was determined not to let anyone get to that pretty man, so I called up all the martial arts skills I knew. I'd actually won a national championship title in martial arts back in high school.

I punched and kicked, taking out as many of the thugs as I could until they all turned to target me. I managed to block their strikes, countering them by yanking their hair and smashing their faces into the concrete wall. The smell of blood from their broken faces began to permeate the air.

I smirked, smug that no one managed to get the upper hand on me. I threw a couple more punches at the stubborn goons who refused to give up before hurriedly grabbing my backpack with one hand—it had somehow dropped to the ground in the fight—and the handsome guy crouching by the trash can with the other. He pressed his hand to his stomach like it hurt, but I threw his arm over my shoulder and quickly dragged him to where I had parked my motorcycle. I figured the thugs weren't going to give up easily. They kept trying to get back up no matter how many times I knocked them down.

"Where are we going?" the guy asked, his face contorted in pain and his hand still covering his stomach.

"Dunno. Just get on the bike," I said, starting the engine of my trusty motorcycle.

The guy looked unsure, but I yanked his wrist, urging him to get on the bike with me. *I'm not letting you go that quickly, pretty boy— you still owe me...* I quickly backed up my bike from the parking lot and shot out of the alley.

I saw a couple of the men run after us, but they were too late. As soon as I turned onto the main road, I revved the engine and sped off without looking back. The thugs probably ran back to their car to try and chase us.

"Thanks," the guy whispered hoarsely. I felt him slump forward, resting his head on my shoulder languidly.

"Cut that out," I said flatly. Feeling we were far enough away from the alley, I checked my side mirror. I sighed in relief, thankful that my big bike's engine was more powerful than a car's.

"I think we lost them," I said.

My passenger let out a sigh of relief as well. "Thanks again," he repeated weakly. His body sagged, unable to hold himself up. I grabbed his hand where it was resting idly on his thigh and urged him to hold onto my waist to steady himself. I was afraid he'd fall off my bike and get himself killed before he could pay me.

"Hold tight! You got a death wish or what?" I hissed as the bike soared through the wind, making my words incoherent. Still, he seemed to understand what I said and held my jacket tightly in response.

"Thanks," he mumbled again.

Is that the only word he knows? I wondered, but I decided to let it go. I kept driving, not as fast as at the beginning of our escape, but still faster than I'd usually drive.

"Fifty thousand," I reminded him tersely while checking his reflection in my side mirror. I saw him nod before painfully attempting to adjust his posture.

"Take me to my house. I'll give you the money there."

I pondered his response, not sure how much I could trust him. What if this guy was a drug dealer or a mobster or something? What if he was pissed that I'd initially planned to let those thugs beat him up? What if he didn't want to cough up the dough and decided to lure me to my demise instead? Suddenly, his promise to pay me seemed suspicious.

"Don't look at me like that. I'm not trying to lure you into some kind of trap," he said, squinting at me through the mirror with a faint smile on his face. Did I speak my thoughts out loud?

"How could I have known?" I asked sincerely.

"Look at me," he said. "Do I look like a crook?" His voice stuttered, the cuts on his lips clearly making it difficult for him to speak.

"Yeah...? Otherwise, why would you get into a fight with those thugs?"

"Ha ha..."

I decided to avoid entering his house at all costs. I was afraid he might have underlings waiting in there to beat me up. I told him I would drop him off at a gas station up ahead, and he could withdraw the money from an ATM there to pay me.

"I lost my phone and my wallet," he said when I gestured at the ATM in front of the gas station convenience store.

"You tricked me into helping you? I see how it is!" I abruptly turned to yell at him. "I'm going to fuck you up, you asshole!" I grabbed his shirt and dragged him off my bike. I was ready to kick him out of anger.

"Hmph... Here, take this. You should know that my life is worth more than fifty thousand baht." He took off his ridiculously expensive-looking watch and handed it to me. I took it, eyeing him skeptically.

"How do I know it's not a counterfeit...?"

"Then give it back," he sighed, attempting to snatch his watch back.

I dodged him. A rich kid like him wouldn't wear a counterfeit watch, right? Fine. I'd keep it, even though the watch face was covered in dirt. If this was the real deal, I could sell it for a couple hundred grand.

"All right. Now get off my bike. But remember, if I find out that your watch is some fake shit?" I pointed at his face threateningly. "I'll hunt you down and mess you up."

"Wait, let me use your phone," he said, holding out his hand. "I need to call my father," he added when I didn't respond. I was paranoid, of course. What if he took off with my phone? But just looking at the guy, I could tell that even breathing was difficult for him. I didn't need to worry about him running off anywhere.

"You're pushing your luck," I grunted, handing him my cell. *Should I charge him extra for using my phone?* I thought as I watched him input some numbers before pressing the dial.

Okay, he really did call his dad. I listened as he told his father the gas station's location so he could send someone to pick him up. I glanced at the sorry state he was in and started to have second thoughts. Should I have taken him to a hospital instead of leaving him in the middle of nowhere? His breathing was labored, and his head was still bleeding. What if I offered to take him to a hospital if he paid me thirty thousand? Would he agree?

"Thanks again for the help, you greedy bastard," he said, staying on my bike. I didn't give a shit what he called me. People should expect something in return for their labor, right?

"Anyway, I'm Kinn," he said, turning slightly toward me. "We go to the same university."

"How would you know that?" I asked, my voice flat. I wondered where he'd gotten the idea we went to the same school.

"Your jacket," he said.

I remembered then that I had my university jacket on—and that it was now covered in blood.

"Hmm..."

"What's your name?" he asked, still not getting off my bike.

I frowned at him, annoyed. It sounded like it was painful for him to speak, and I wanted to tell him to save his breath instead of talking to me.

"Why?" I asked, raising an eyebrow. "Are you gonna look for me so you can beat me up later?"

"No. It's because you saved me. So, what's your name?" he insisted.

"Why do you want to know so bad? Are you going to carve it on your bedroom wall and worship me?" I was genuinely curious why he wanted to know my name. I'd saved him, but that should be the end of it. There was no need to get to know each other.

"I won't get off your bike, then." He tried to put his head back on my shoulder, and I immediately jerked away.

"If you don't get off my bike, I'll kick you off," I said. My voice was stern, but I kept my face impassive as usual.

"Then give back my watch... You can wait to get your money until someone comes to pick me up."

I looked at the watch in my hand. Its weight and the feel of the material told me it was authentic. I sighed and finally gave in.

"Jom... My name is Jom."

His lips stretched into a tight smile, and he finally dismounted my bike without any further complaint. I looked at him waving back at me as he walked away, wondering what a guy like him did to get into a fight with those scary thugs. But it really was none of my business, so I tossed those thoughts aside and started moving my bike back into gear. I put on my helmet, which I'd forgotten about earlier, and finally drove home.

KINN
PORSCHE

Déjà Vu

PORSCHE

ACHOO!

"Dang... Who's talking about me behind my back? I've been sneezing nonstop since last night," Jom complained as he set his coffee down on a marble table in front of the Sports Science building.

I looked at him, apologizing internally. Last night, I lied and gave out Jom's name instead of my own. But who in their right mind would give out their real name in that situation? I took that guy's watch. What if he changed his mind one day and came after me to get it back? There would be nothing I could do; I'd already sold the watch to a pawn shop that morning.

I could have told him my name was Boy, Noom, Sommai, anything—but Jom had messaged me just then and I'd seen his name pop up on my phone screen, so it just slipped out... *I'm sorry, man. If something happens to you, blame it on bad luck.*

"Why the hell are you looking at me like that?" Jom asked when he caught me staring at him.

I shrugged and turned my attention to Tem, who was engrossed in correcting the group report our professor had returned.

These two guys were my best friends. Jom was notoriously loud, and Tem was a bit of a weirdo who did not live up to his name, which meant 'wholesome.' And then there was me, someone people usually tried to avoid due to my intimidating appearance. My face usually didn't show much emotion, so people could take me for cold and heartless. The full-sleeve tattoo of Japanese-style clouds and cherry blossoms covering my left arm didn't help, either. No one wanted to get involved with me except for these two.

We were in our second year at one of the most prestigious universities in the country. I would never have been able to afford to study here if I hadn't been offered an athletic scholarship. My national championship title in judo got me my full ride.

"If we finish our report, do you wanna go to Porsche's club tonight?" Jom asked while playing games on his cell phone.

"You should try helping me with the report before thinking about going out!" Tem replied.

He was right. Tem was the only one who'd been consistently working on the group report. Although I wasn't being as annoying as Jom, I wasn't helping, either. I just kept staring blankly at the assignment.

"Come on! After we finish, let's go," Jom insisted. He loved hanging out at the club where I worked. Both he and Tem came around pretty often, and they'd become good friends with the bar's owner like I was.

"Fine! We'll go," Tem said, exasperated.

Jom and I rushed Tem to finish correcting our group report. Jom kept asking every three minutes if he was done. Meanwhile, I fixed him with an intense stare, urging him to hurry up with no intention of actually helping him.

Finally, we ended up at The Root Club, owned by my boss, Madam Yok. As my two friends relaxed by the bar, I was in my uniform serving drinks. I came around to chat with them occasionally.

"Porsche, dear, can you fix me another drink?" a middle-aged woman chirped at me.

I gave her a polite smile and quickly mixed a drink for her. I was pretty good at bartending and mixing drinks, and I was popular among our female clientele. They loved giving me fat tips. Some even came here every day just to see me.

I'd hook up with customers occasionally, and we'd end up at some hotel. But they had to really catch my eye, like the woman I was about to serve a cocktail to. She had arrived with two other friends, and she was quite the looker. All the male patrons were ogling her, but—not to brag—she only had eyes for me.

"I'm Vivi. Give me a call?"

As I expected, she handed me a small piece of paper with her number on it. I grinned and stuffed the note in my pocket.

"Looks like little Chay is gonna be home alone tonight," Jom drawled. Tem handed me my drink as I came to sit next to him.

I was very close to the owner of this place, Madam Yok. She didn't mind that my friends came here occasionally.

Madam Yok was a trans woman who loved to dress as if every day was New Year's Day. The color of her qipao changed daily, which I found amusing. She was a bit flamboyant, but she had always been very kind to me. When she knew I wasn't making enough to pay my brother's expensive tuition fee, she always lent me money. She was the only adult figure in my life that I really respected.

"What's this? So early in the night, and someone's already trying to steal my precious boy?" Madam Yok purred as she sidled up to me, her arm intertwining with mine.

If this had been any other trans woman, I would've felt pretty uncomfortable. I wasn't grossed out by them, and I didn't have anything against them; I just wasn't used to being around them.

I initially felt the same way about Madam Yok, but I'd worked for her for several years and I was comfortable with her now.

Although I'd only turned twenty[2] a couple months ago, I'd been helping out at the bar for a long time now. I would come here after class to prepare the place for opening. I eventually got promoted to waiter, and the pay was better. Madam Yok said that the regulars loved me, and I could help attract more customers by showing up more often.

"You better keep a close watch on your precious boy," Tem said. "All the women here look like they want to devour him."

Madam Yok pursed her lips disapprovingly and rested her head gently on my shoulder. I just smiled leisurely and tipped back my drink.

The night was still young, so the club was quiet, with only a few customers scattered around. I'd worked here long enough that Madam Yok entrusted me to supervise all the waiters, even though some of them were older than me. She was a friend of my uncle, so I'd known her since I was a kid. She often came to our house when my uncle hosted parties. Then, disaster struck my family.

My family used to be very wealthy. My father owned several businesses, including a showroom for imported cars. But eight years ago, my parents were in a tragic car accident that killed them on the spot. We lost my parents' assets—our house, cars, everything—to bank forfeiture. One of my dad's corrupt business partners almost drained us dry.

All my brother and I had left was a ramshackle three-story townhouse. We scrounged together whatever we had left just to get by. We also had Uncle Thee, my father's younger brother. He always supported us despite his gambling problem. He and Madam Yok were the two people who had always cared for us...

---

2   The legal drinking age in Thailand is twenty years old.

"Are you really planning on being Madam's sugar baby?" Jom asked out of the blue. "I've never seen you with a girlfriend."

"He already has me. There's no place for other women," Madam Yok teased lightheartedly.

"I can't even take care of myself. How could I take care of a girlfriend?" I chuckled, taking another sip of my drink. I was happy having occasional flings with no strings attached.

"Well, look for someone who can take care of you, then," Tem said. He cocked his head, eyeing a table in the corner occupied by several good-looking men. He leaned closer and whispered, "They've been checking you out for a while."

"The fuck, man?!" I raised my foot to kick him for talking nonsense, but that fucker just dodged me.

"Or they might be checking *me* out." Madam Yok fluttered her eyelashes at them flirtatiously. Tem and Jom cracked up when the guys hurriedly looked away.

"Well, you kinda look like *the type*," Tem went on. "Y'know, the macho top with tattoos and pristine clothes..." I whacked him on the head with my ice tongs.

"You're nuts! If someone like Porsche turned gay, a buffalo would give birth to a dog with Madam Yok's face," Jom interjected, earning a smack to the head from said Madam.

"Are you low-key insulting me? You guys are no fun!" Madam Yok hushed Jom before leaving the boys to talk to other customers.

"Look! They're not paying attention to our Madam at all. They're totally into Porsche!" Tem said.

I gave those guys an annoyed glance. I really hated it when male customers tried to hit on me. Some even had the balls to catcall me or give me their numbers. There was nothing I could do except smile politely. I wasn't a homophobe, but I knew I didn't swing that way...

"Look at their outfits... Luxury brands from head to toe. If you accept their advances, you'd be set for life!"

"If you don't shut up, I'm gonna kick your ass," I replied coldly, giving Tem a death glare.

"I'm just kidding, yeesh! Oh, look—those girls are calling for you!"

I hushed Tem and went over to Vivi's table. She beckoned me over as if she wanted to order something, so I smiled at her lightly while leaning closer...

"Could you tell me where the restroom is?" Vivi whispered, her face beside mine. My lips curled up when I felt her delicate touch on my hand.

"In the back, to the left," I said, giving her a knowing smile as she caressed my hand.

"Can you show me...please?"

Everything went as anticipated. Vivi couldn't wait to pull me into a dark corner at the back of the club near the storage room. She immediately leaned in and kissed me while I pushed her slender body against the wall, hungrily devouring the taste of her lips.

This corner of the club was a blind spot where people came for a quick hookup; I was a frequent visitor myself. The area was often deserted, and being interrupted was unlikely. I'd grab a girl and come here to get off during work.

I was fondling Vivi's ample breasts with one hand and trying to unbutton my jeans with the other when a loud commotion suddenly stopped us in our tracks.

CRASH! CLANK!

"P'Porsche, we're screwed!" I heard someone yell and saw one of my colleagues approaching in alarm.

"What the hell is going on?" I asked, agitated. I tried to pull my pants up while Vivi smoothed out her dress, confused.

"Look for yourself!" he yelled. I sprinted after him to the bar and saw half the room in chaos. Tables and chairs were knocked over everywhere as customers fled from the commotion. Shards of broken glasses and beer bottles were strewn across the floor. More than ten men dressed in black crowded the bar, destroying the place without paying any attention to Madam Yok's pleas.

"Please calm down, sir! We can talk!"

I hurried to Madam Yok's side. "What happened?"

My two best friends and some waiters surrounded her, trying to stop the men to no avail. I squinted at one guy in front of me who looked vaguely familiar. He attempted to charge at me when he saw my face, but my reflexes were faster than his. I kicked him squarely in the chest, sending him stumbling backward.

Now I knew where I recognized him from. He was the guy I fought off last night. Although he and his henchmen looked pretty banged up, I was sure it was them. Now that I'd figured out why they came here, I wasted no more time and returned their punches with my friends fighting by my side.

"You are—!" he raised his fist and I caught it mid-swing.

"I'm what?" I asked sharply, my eyes glaring at him hard.

"Why did you think you could mess with us?!" he barked furiously while his underlings fought my friends and colleagues. Madam Yok also joined the fight. In a rage, she hit the thugs with a chair; she looked more like an angry hulk than her usually feminine self.

"'Cause you're a pussy," I chuckled before landing another punch to his face. The man swayed to the side, then grabbed a beer bottle and smashed it on the tabletop. He launched himself at me again, trying to stab me with the broken bottle.

In your dreams, asshole! I thought, laughing and dodging his attack, which enraged him even further.

I hadn't realized they would figure out I worked here. I was taking out the trash and locking up last night when I got caught in the crossfire. Yeah, I probably brought this trouble on myself. I wasn't afraid of them, but I *was* fearful of how much I was going to have to pay Madam Yok in damages.

"Arrogant bastard!" the man hissed, the muscles in his jaw tightening in anger. He tried several times to stab me, but I blocked him by kicking him back.

"Thanks for the compliment," I said with a mock salute, and turned to the side, trying to knee him in the gut. Suddenly, some jerk put me in a chokehold from behind, knocking me off-balance. The guy with the broken bottle, who seemed to be the boss of this gang, smirked triumphantly. I looked at him calmly as he approached, trying to find an opening to evade his attack, when suddenly—

"Stop!" someone yelled from the entrance. His loud, authoritative voice commanded attention, making everyone stop and look at him.

Some of the thugs swore loudly. "Shit! It's Kinn!"

All eyes focused on a man in a black shirt. He was flanked by a group of bodyguards in suits swarming into the bar.

"For fuck's sake!" Madam Yok shrieked shrilly. "How am I supposed to fix this mess?"

The fight started up again. I felt relieved when the primary target changed from me to the newcomer. The guy, Kinn, fought back with much more skill than he had yesterday. I looked at him while doling out punches haphazardly, confusing both parties. I seemed to not belong to any particular side, but let's just say I mainly attacked the guys who went after me first.

"Mr. Kinn, watch out!"

I turned just in time to see one of the thugs punch Kinn in the face; the force drove him backward into the wall with a loud thud.

It was five men against one, and one of them tried to stab Kinn with a knife. I quickly made up my mind and decided to fight on Kinn's side. After all, the watch he gave me last night was worth six figures. I roundhouse-kicked the ankle of the man with the knife, yanked a guy punching Kinn by his hair, and threw more kicks and punches until I'd knocked all five of them to the ground.

"Thanks." Kinn's voice was hoarse as he glanced at me.

"I'm gonna charge you for that," I said smugly before returning to the fight. *Damn, are these guys ever gonna tire out?* I thought as I tried to block the goons from getting to Kinn.

"More of them are coming," Kinn whispered.

"What?! Did you burn down their house or something?"

Kinn huffed. "I'm being hunted down."

More thugs rushed into the bar right after Kinn finished his sentence. This time, Jom, Tem, Madam Yok, and some of my colleagues decided to flee. No matter how good you were in a fistfight, even if you had ten Buakaws[3] on your side, you wouldn't stand a chance if your opponent fought dirty. The situation had taken a turn for the worse: these new guys came heavily armed with knives and guns. I figured there was a high chance we were going to get ourselves killed if we stayed here any longer.

"Let's go!" I yelled.

"Go where? We're surrounded," Kinn replied calmly. He stared down the angry mob as if he could handle them.

"Just follow me!" I didn't know why my conscience suddenly wanted me to play the saint, but I grabbed his arm and quickly pulled him away. We exited through the kitchen and into a different alley. I didn't dare escape using the same route as last night, fearing that we might not make it.

---

3   Buakaw Banchamek is a renowned Thai kickboxer and a two-time K-1 World MAX champion.

"Where are we going?" Kinn asked.

I remained silent. When I got on my bike, I realized what I had just done. I cursed at myself. Why the hell did I drag him along with me? Admittedly, some of this mess was on me, but wasn't he the one who started it all?

I pulled him onto my bike, feeling fortunate that I parked in the alley here tonight since the parking lot was full. This way, we didn't need to circle back up front. I started up the engine and zoomed into the night.

Everything seemed so familiar; it was like I'd pressed a rewind button to last night, the same events replaying. I even took the same road and saw the same gas station up ahead where I'd dropped him off last night. It felt like déjà vu.

So...how much should I charge him this time?

2

Karma

PORSCHE

"**D**ON'T TELL ME you're ditching me at the same gas station as last night." Kinn's voice was hoarse and faint. Despite the black and blue bruises covering his face, though, he was in better shape than last night. This guy was pretty tough.

"When did they start tailing us?!" I swore to myself instead of answering him when I saw motorcycles approaching fast in my side mirror. *Damn it!* Those thugs had come prepared tonight. They even had people waiting to go after us!

I revved my engine and skillfully weaved my bike in and out of different alleyways to evade our pursuers. Thankfully, I had a dirt bike, so I could easily maneuver through narrow roads.

"Take it easy!" Kinn yelled against the wind. One of his hands clutched tightly at my waist while the other held onto the edge of the seat.

"Just hold tight!" I yelled back, twisting the throttle to gain more speed. His grip on my waist tightened even further, and I felt him bury his face into my back as he used my body to shield himself from the wind.

"Am I still alive?" he muttered before carefully checking his surroundings. When I was confident that we were no longer being followed, I slowed down. I kept taking a lot of bends and turns for quite some time, long enough to confuse them and get them off our trail. When I finally pulled to a stop in front of my house, I sighed in relief. It felt like we'd just driven through hell itself.

"Where are we?" Kinn asked.

"My place," I answered. I didn't want to bring Kinn here, but on the brink of disaster, the route to my home was the one I was familiar with the most. I'd taken a final turn and arrived at my house before I even realized it.

"Well... Let me wash up a bit, then," Kinn said after letting out the breath he was holding.

"Wait!" I called out and stopped him on his way to my door. I didn't look at him as I fumbled for a pack of cigarettes from the back pocket of my pants. I took one out, lit it up, and took a long drag before letting out a puff of white smoke.

He looked at me without saying anything, raising his brows as he waited for me to continue.

"Fifty thousand," I said casually, the cigarette still dangling from my mouth. When I finally turned to face him, I put my hands on my hips.

"Hmph." Kinn chuckled in disbelief. "You took my watch yesterday—"

I gulped nervously but interjected before he could finish his sentence: "Yesterday was yesterday."

I said it shamelessly, even though I feared he would ask for his watch back. There was nothing I could do if he did. I had already pawned it and used the money to pay Chay's tuition fee, fix the broken air conditioning unit in my bedroom, and pay off our numerous debts. There was barely anything left...

"You asked for fifty thousand last night and another fifty thousand tonight. I imagine you already sold my watch. If you weren't stupid enough to get ripped off, you should've raked in at least four hundred thousand from it." Kinn pretended to be calculating as he spoke with a slight grin. Then he looked at me with an authoritative expression. "So that means I've already paid you in advance."

This was the first time I took a good look at him. He was a few inches taller than me, and he stared back at me with piercing eyes. I could sense this was no ordinary man. His facial features looked European. Despite the bruises, he was devilishly handsome, and the way he carried himself suggested that he came from a powerful family. I couldn't help worrying he might seek revenge for me threatening him to pay up.

"Just go back the way you came, then," I said flatly. I always expected something in return for my actions.

If I don't get anything out of it, don't expect me to help you out of the kindness of my heart.

"You know...you seem like a decent enough guy." Kinn looked at me with his arms crossed and sneered. "Why are you acting like a crook?"

That bastard! He was insulting me and looking down on me. That sanctimonious attitude of his was starting to get on my nerves.

"Just shut the fuck up and get out of my face!" I snapped.

The front door of my house suddenly creaked open. "Is that you, hia?"[4] my little brother called out. He was in his pajamas. "What's with all the noise?" He looked at me sleepily.

"Um...hello?" My little brother greeted the unfamiliar stranger, and that fuckwad acknowledged him with a nod.

4　*Hia means older brother in Teochew dialect.*

"Go back inside," I told my brother sternly.

"Why are you guys arguing out here? You'll wake up the neighbors. Come and talk inside!" Chay said, opening the door and beckoning me inside.

Damn you, Chay! Have some respect for your older brother!

"Well, thanks for the invitation," Kinn said. He was about to step through the door when I yanked his collar.

"*I'm* going inside my house, and *you* can go back where you came from."

I dragged him away from my door. He glared at me in annoyance, his brows furrowed, before swatting my hand off his collar. He straightened his shirt and grunted. "How dare you!"

He sounded pissed off, but I couldn't care less. I gave him a shrug and turned to leave.

"Stop! No one has ever disrespected me like this!" He grabbed my arm and squeezed hard. I shook him off, unintimidated by his threat, shoving him hard in the chest.

"So? Who the fuck do you think you are? I can do more than just grab your collar!" I looked at him furiously with no intention to step down. "If you don't get out of my sight," I continued, pointing at his face, "I'm going to beat the shit out of you!"

Chay came back outside because of the noise. "What the hell is going on, hia?" he asked.

"Nothing! Get back inside!" I pushed my little brother back inside the house, following close at his heels. I slammed the door in Kinn's face, not caring that the neighbors might curse at us.

I didn't give a damn what happened to that guy! Maybe if he got his ass handed to him again, he'd stop being such an arrogant bastard. I was no longer surprised that those thugs came after him—

he probably got on his high horse about something and pissed them off... *Ha! I'm not afraid of you, asshole.* I was only concerned that he might ask for his stupid watch back.

I finally had time to call Madam Yok and check up on her. Her voice was as chirpy as ever when she told me the police came and settled the commotion shortly after we fled the bar. She kept scolding me, thinking I had antagonized some gangsters and they had come seeking revenge. I needed to settle everything with her tomorrow and take responsibility for all the damage.

Tomorrow came, and I sulked at Madam Yok's office, listening to her talk.

"Honey, I told you not to be so hotheaded," she said. I had a feeling she wasn't going to listen to my explanation. She was already assuming that last night's fight was my fault.

"I'm sorry," I said. She heaved out a sigh and shook her head, as if saying I didn't need to apologize.

I wasn't in the wrong here. Kinn caused all the trouble! I wanted to bang my head on the table in defeat. I didn't get his money last night and I was probably going to end up paying for all the damage caused by the thugs who came after him. If I'd known it would turn out like this, I wouldn't have helped him in the first place.

"Don't worry about it. Let's clean up. The new furniture will be delivered in the afternoon," Madam Yok told me.

"How much?" I asked quietly, afraid of knowing just how expensive it would be.

"What?" said Madam Yok, looking confused.

"The damage... How much?"

"Tsk, tsk! You wouldn't be able to afford it, darling," she teased, fluttering her Chinese folding fan delicately in front of her face.

"I've got some money," I said. Although I wasn't the main culprit, I'd feel terrible if I didn't take some of the blame.

"We're lucky that Mr. Kinn took care of everything... Otherwise, I could not imagine how long it'd take you to pay for everything," Madam Yok said.

"Kinn?" His smug, handsome face and piercing eyes popped into my head.

"That's right. Mr. Kinn said those thugs were his enemies as well as yours. He saw them causing trouble here and felt he had to aid us."

Hmph! That conniving bastard! I could admit I was money-hungry, but I always minded my own business. Now, all of a sudden, I had made an enemy. I presumed Madam Yok hadn't seen that Kinn and I escaped together, since she was busy fighting off those goons with her kung-fu skills.

"All right..." I gave her a slight smile.

"It's funny, now that I think about it," she said. "It looked like the cops came to shut down an illegal brothel. It was chaos!"

I chuckled and replied, "You do look like *that* kind of madam."

"Yeah, I was about to run when I saw the cops. Then I realized they came to help!" She put her hand on her chest and belted out a hearty laugh. "Really, we are lucky that Mr. Kinn knows some higher-ups in the police department. Everything was settled before it even hit the news. The police came to get some footage from the CCTV cameras this morning. Ah...I still shiver every time I think about Mr. Kinn."

"Why?" I asked.

"He's gorgeous! How can someone be that handsome? It should be illegal! Talk about husband material!"

I listened to her ramble about how handsome Mr. Kinn was for a while, and then I went to help clean up the place with the other employees. Blood splatter, glass shards, and broken furniture littered the floor.

We were lucky no one got fatally injured in last night's altercation. Still, some waiters needed to be treated at the hospital, and the others sported bruises and cuts all over. They jokingly said they took all the hits for me, since I got out pretty much unscathed. I told them I'd treat them to meals later to pay them back. Although I didn't get any money from Kinn, I didn't end up having to pay for the damages—buying dinner was the least I could do for my coworkers.

We kept the bar closed to the public tonight, but most of the crew came as usual to help clean the place up. At nine o'clock, everything started to settle back to normal, so I decided to take a smoke break. I went to sit on a giant cooler in the alley behind the bar and took a steady drag of my cigarette, letting the nicotine clear my head.

Stomp. Stomp.

Curious, I turned toward the sound of footsteps. The back alley of the club was very secluded, so I rarely saw anyone walking past this dingy and narrow passageway.

"Hey..." The footsteps stopped a few feet from me. I frowned and glared at the group of men in black suits who wanted my attention. The man at the front, who looked like the head of this entourage, scoffed at me. I looked at him intently through the shadows, then hopped down from the cooler once I realized who it was. I threw my cigarette to the ground in annoyance and stubbed it out with my foot.

"What?" I flatly asked Kinn, who came to a stop right in front of me. I rested my hands loosely on my hips and glanced from side to side, checking to see if his enemies had decided to tag along. I couldn't stop myself—every time this guy showed up, chaos followed, and I didn't want him to instigate another brawl. Madam Yok would cuss me out for sure.

He still hadn't uttered a word. "Is someone on your ass again?" I asked.

"I need to talk to you," Kinn rasped before he fell silent again. I felt my heart pound in anticipation.

"What?" I asked, my face remaining neutral as I buried any emotion.

"Come with me."

"Where?"

"We have a lot to talk about," he said casually, his hands in his pockets. He focused his piercing gaze on me, but I couldn't figure out what he wanted.

"I don't have anything to talk to you about," I replied tersely, still nervous.

I tried to go back inside the bar when he suddenly yanked my arm, pulling me to face him again.

"Well, I do!" Kinn said sternly.

"But I don't!" I quickly shook him off and forcefully shoved him back before heaving some of last night's broken furniture to clatter between us. Kinn quickly dodged it, but his subordinates rushed to his aid and tried to attack me. I kicked and punched, knocking everyone down before anyone could reach me. Kinn grew irritated and tried to approach me himself. I raised my fist to punch him, but he caught my wrist with an iron grip, stopping it in midair.

Oh, he thinks he stands a chance against me? I moved to kick him in the gut instead. He evaded me, so I jabbed him with my other hand, and he caught that, too. He twisted both my wrists, forced them behind my back, and used his body to press me against the wall. I couldn't believe he managed to get the upper hand tonight when he got his ass kicked so badly earlier.

"Let go of me!" I growled, turning away when he leaned closer, his handsome face brushing next to mine. He used his weight to pin

me down, relentlessly gripping my wrists as I struggled to free myself.
He was practically hugging me. *Damn it!*

"Hey! I just want to talk," Kinn said patiently. He was so close that
I could see his defined cupid's bow moving as he spoke and feel his
warm breath against my face.

"I don't want to!" I barked back, still trying to squirm away from
his uncomfortably close face.

"Pfft! I thought you'd be better at this," he chuckled.

His insult stung. I roared and jumped at him, biting into his neck
with all my might. The pain startled him, his grip loosening as he
pushed me away.

Ignoring his scream, I ducked into the bar through the back
door. I quickly locked it and scurried to the staff room to get my
bag. My coworkers eyed me in confusion.

"What's the matter?" asked P'Deaw, one of the older staff members.

"Tell Madam Yok I'm leaving early. She can deduct it from my
wage for all I care!" I yelled back. Truthfully, I was scared of Kinn.
Not of him trying to beat me up—but of him asking me to return
his watch.

That night, I quickly got on my bike and sped back home, my
mind consumed with thoughts of the wristwatch. I couldn't think
of a reason Kinn would come looking for me with his subordinates
except to get his belongings back. He might remember that his
watch was worth five...six...no, *seven* hundred thousand baht!

I got up at six and went to the market to get breakfast for Chay.
I hadn't slept a wink last night. I kept worrying about Kinn and
when he was going to come for me.

"Looks like someone's loaded right now," Chay said, glancing between me and the bounty of food on the table.

"Just eat and get your ass to school," I chided him while absentmindedly pushing around the shrimp in my rice porridge with a spoon. Our breakfast was indeed fancier than usual. We usually only had rice with a fried egg or porridge with pork. But today, we also had toast, butter, jam, fresh milk, orange juice—the whole shebang.

"Can I have my weekly allowance?" Chay asked.

I took six one-thousand baht notes out of my wallet and handed them to him.

"Wow!" Chay's eyes widened in disbelief.

"Let's just say I'm giving you your allowance for the whole month in advance," I replied. I decided it would be better if I spread the money around. This way, I couldn't repay Kinn even if he wanted me to.

"Where did you get all this money?"

"I've been saving up," I said. My little brother clearly didn't believe me one bit. He kept staring at me skeptically until I shooed him away.

"Go to school! And don't spend it all in one place!" I yelled at him. I watched my little brother leave the house in his prestigious high school's uniform.

Once he was gone, I sighed. The tuition fee for my brother's high school was costly. Still, we should be able to cover at least four semesters with the money I got from pawning the watch.

You might wonder why I still let him attend such an expensive school. He'd been attending this school since kindergarten, and I didn't want to uproot his life. It was my school growing up, too. I didn't want him to transfer to any school that wasn't as good as his current one.

Chay often told me he didn't care what school he went to, but as his older brother, I wanted to provide the same life for him now as our parents did when they were still alive. I didn't care if I had to work hard. I would do anything to take good care of my brother.

I locked the door and was about to drive my bike to university as usual when it suddenly hit me that Kinn knew where I lived. *Crap!*

"Auntie Ooy!" I called for my neighbor. She was a kindly lady who fought with her husband from time to time. I often heard them shouting through the thin wall between our houses.

"What?" she yelled back.

"If anyone comes looking for me, tell them I moved."

"Who's looking for you?" she asked, curious.

"Just...if anyone asks, tell them I moved to a border town," I told her dismissively. After she nodded in agreement, I quickly brought in the stuff I had lying outside, like the shoe rack, my umbrella, helmet, and spare bike tires. I tried to make the house look like it was abandoned. Luckily, we didn't have a lot of stuff in the first place, so it didn't take me long to put everything away...

❦

We went to the cafeteria after class. Tem stared at me for some time before finally asking me, "Why are you so restless today?"

"What do you mean?" I retorted.

"You keep looking around nervously. Is someone out to get you again?"

"Tem's right. You're acting skittish." Jom looked at me skeptically for a brief moment before he continued, "I won't help you again. We barely got out of there alive last time."

They both had managed to get away from the fight without getting seriously injured. Since then, they'd berated me over the phone and in our group chat for getting them caught in the crossfire. I gave no excuses and let them believe it was my fault.

"It's nothing," I said, idly playing with my food. I managed to keep my emotions at bay, but I had been on guard since I arrived today.

"Nothing, my ass! Are you afraid those thugs will show up here? I doubt they'd try," Jom said incredulously.

"So, what did you do to piss them off?" Tem asked.

"Ha! I bet he just looks at them with that annoying face of his. That'd piss anyone off," Jom interjected before I could reply. I shrugged, too lazy to explain myself.

"Jom!" A yell came from P'Ohm, a third-year student in our department. "Your dad's[5] looking for you!"

We greeted him as he approached our table.

"My dad?" Jom asked.

"Hell if I know. But that guy said he has to talk to you," P'Ohm said.

Jom looked flabbergasted, so P'Ohm insisted, "He really said that!"

I gulped at P'Ohm's words, wondering if it was Kinn who was asking for Jom. I *did* tell him my name was Jom. *Shit...*

"What does he look like?" I asked nervously.

"Jom's dad? He's fine as hell! I didn't think someone that good-looking would be related to someone so hideous."

"Seriously, man! Who is he?" Jom cried out.

P'Ohm chuckled. "He really said he was your dad and that he wanted to talk. He's wearing our uniform with the business school's pin. Min said he's very popular. His name is—"

"Hey! Let's go see a movie. My treat." I cut P'Ohm off before he could finish his sentence. Everyone turned to me in confusion.

---

5   Joking about someone's dad or mom like this is a form of insult in Thai culture.

"What the hell is wrong with you, Porsche? You're awfully talk-
ative today." Jom eyed me suspiciously.

"Come on! Let's take Tem's car. I'll leave my bike here," I said,
nudging Tem's arm. Both of my friends were utterly perplexed.

"Fine! We'll go to the movies, but first let me take a good look at
my *handsome dad*." Jom stressed his last words with a pointed look
at P'Ohm.

"Suit yourself, shithead!" P'Ohm cussed and walked off toward
the soccer field.

"I'd smack you if you weren't my senior!" Jom yelled at the departing figure.

"Let's go," Tem said. He picked up his backpack and headed to
the school entrance.

"Guys! Movie!" I said in a firm voice.

"I got it! But let's swing by the entrance first so Jom can see his *dad*."

"I won't treat you if you don't come with me," I tried to threaten
them, getting more anxious by the second.

"Of course we're going with you. I just want to check who *my
dad* is."

"Really, what the hell is wrong with you today, Porsche?" Tem
asked.

"I don't want to go near the entrance," I said, not budging.

"Wait for us at the car, then? We'll be quick." Tem handed me his
car keys before taking off with Jom.

Phew! I'll pay you back, Jom, I told myself in case anything happened to him.

I was on my second cigarette, patiently waiting for my friends to
return. I wasn't really worried that Kinn would do anything to them;
I was more afraid that Kinn had come after me for his watch. I could
fight him, but he'd still force me to return it.

What should I do?

"P'Ohm, you fucker! Is he messing with me?"

I immediately looked up at Jom's loud voice. I heard him before I saw him.

"So? Did you see your *dad*?" I asked Jom, who looked visibly irritated.

"There was nobody there! What a waste of time!" Jom spat.

I sighed in relief and chuckled. "P'Ohm likes to mess with us like that. Let's just forget about it."

Tem and Jom nodded and took out their cigarettes for a quick smoke. Then, we drove to the movie theater near our university in Tem's car.

"Has anyone come looking for me, Auntie Ooy?" I asked loudly when I arrived home.

"Yes!" she replied. "What did you do? Those guys look like the mafia."

I pursed my lips nervously. "What did they say?" I asked.

"They asked for Jom, the house's owner. I didn't know who that was. So, I told them there was no Jom here—or anyone else."

I nodded. "When did they come?"

"Around noon." She looked at me in puzzlement, but didn't press me for more. We rarely talked—this was probably the first time in years I had spoken this much with her.

"Can I park my bike at your place?"

"Fine!" Ooy agreed to my request, then began to rant at me: "Don't get yourself into trouble, Porsche. Think of your little brother."

I simply nodded at her, thinking it was good that they came when Chay wasn't home. I reminded myself to warn my little brother not to open the door to strangers. More anxiety crept into my head: what if Kinn decided to pay me fifty thousand and ask for his watch back?

No way! That watch was worth seven hundred thousand! I won't trade it for anything else.

KINN
PORSCHE

3

Hunt

KINN

I LOOKED AT MY REFLECTION in the mirror, the bite mark on my neck vividly visible as a small trail of blood trickled from the wound. The skin around the mark had turned ugly shades of purple and yellow. I tilted my head slightly to the side, letting my close subordinate tend to the wound with a cotton swab.

"Are you really going to hire someone like that as your bodyguard, Mr. Kinn?" Big asked. He sounded slightly disapproving.

I hissed from the sting of antiseptic on the open wound. "Why are you asking?"

Big looked at the wound on my neck and the bruises adorning my body. He let out a heaving breath. "Look what he did to you! I'll hunt him down and knock his lights out!"

"My father would not be pleased," I said, matter-of-fact.

"I don't understand your father, either. What made him so interested in this guy? He ditched you twice. He even bit your neck last time. How can we tame a viper like that?"

I glanced at my subordinate in annoyance, and Big realized that he had said too much. He shut his mouth and went back to treating my wounds without another word.

In truth, I didn't want a guy like Jom to be my bodyguard or my subordinate. I wholeheartedly agreed with Big—he was not a good choice. Judging from our encounters, I could see he was driven by greed. He could easily change sides if it was more profitable for him. One could hardly hope for loyalty from a guy like that.

But what could I do when my father had taken a real interest in Jom after he saw the security footage from The Root Club? My father had been trying to figure out who had kidnapped me for the past three days. Instead, he saw a guy who came to my rescue two days in a row. My father didn't know that Jom had asked for money in return for his help. He didn't help me out of the kindness of his heart.

"Get him on our side before our enemy does! We're screwed if he ends up with them."

My father's words echoed clearly in my head. He seemed very impressed by Jom's flawless fighting skills—he could effortlessly take down men twice his size. At first, I'd also wanted to find him right away and offer him a deal. But now I just wanted payback for the bite. No one had ever done anything like that to me!

At the university.

"A bandage on the neck? Oh my god, which of your lovers is a sadist?" Time shrieked loudly when he saw me approach the table.

"You can go," I told Big, who'd accompanied me to the university today. I usually drove to school alone, but my father insisted I take some guards with me today, considering how unsafe things had been lately.

"I'll wait for you at the usual spot," Big told me.

"Wait! Don't forget to check out the place I told you. His name is Jom," I reminded Big of my earlier order.

"What happened?" Tay asked.

"My father wants me to look for a guy."

"Someone from your family's Minor Clan? Is that why you were gone for three days, because you got kidnapped again?" Tay asked. He turned me to the left and right to check if I was badly hurt.

"Yeah, but the guy I'm looking for isn't from the Minor Clan."

"And who is he, exactly?"

"He's the one who did this to me!" I exclaimed, irked. I peeled off the bandage covering my neck to show the wound underneath.

"Ouch!" Time, Tay, and Mew cried in unison.

The bite still hurt this morning. Every time I felt a twinge of pain, I resented this Jom guy even more. What if he had rabies or something? But I couldn't care less about that. All I could think about was how much I wanted to punch him in the face.

I told my friends everything that had happened. These three had stuck by me since high school, so they knew everything about me. I wasn't friends with anybody else, nor was I interested in making new friends in university. I wasn't a friendly person. Tay said that whenever I looked at someone, I looked like I was insulting their father—not to mention how people feared me when they found out who *my* father was.

"You know a ton of people, don't you?" Mew asked Time. "It shouldn't be hard to find Jom from Sports Science."

It was lucky that guy was wearing his school's jersey that day, with "Sports Science" embroidered near the hem. That was how I knew where he might be.

"What? I don't know anyone from Sports Science!" Time protested and glanced nervously at Tay, who smiled coldly.

"Why don't you just tell Mew that you like a guy from Comm Arts more?" Tay stared hard at Time, his voice aloof.

Tay and Time were lovers, and Tay must have recently caught Time messing around with someone from the School of Communication Arts. Time was a handsome playboy who loved to sleep around, while Tay had the heart of a saint. He always forgave Time for his infidelity, no matter what.

"It's nothing!" Time said, looking incredibly restless. He tried to change the subject. "I'll take you there after class."

I nodded at him.

"Come on! Let's get to class, then. I made copies of the handouts for you guys," Mew said, giving out the papers. Mew was the most reliable guy in our group. He was the nerdy one who consistently scored the highest and threw off the grading curve for everyone else. And when I missed classes, he was also my savior.

After we finished our classes, Time drove us to the Department of Sports Science as promised. This was my first time coming here, and I was at a loss for where to start.

"P'Time! What are you doing here?" A cheerful voice made Time jump in surprise. I wondered if he really *was* sleeping with someone in this department.

"Oh, Min! Hi!" Time's smile faltered slightly as a cute guy with a thin frame—Min, apparently—smiled broadly at him.

"Didn't you say you don't know anyone here?" Tay growled through gritted teeth, his voice low. He gripped the back of Time's shirt tightly. He was visibly angry because Min was obviously Time's type. A guy who was more cute than handsome—just like Tay.

"Don't look at me like that. I know P'Time because my dad works for his dad," Min explained pleasantly.

"I told you..."

Tay smiled politely at Min, but hissed at Time: "Just wait, I'll catch you!"

"So, what's a popular trio from the Business School doing in my building?" Min finally asked.

"Oh, right! Do you happen to know a guy called Jom?" Time asked.

Min replied instantly. "I do! P'Jom, in second year, right?"

"I don't know. Is he?" Time turned to ask me.

"I don't know," I said.

"Well, I only know one Jom," Min said.

"Can you take us to him?"

Min raised his eyebrows.

"We need to talk to him," Time added.

"You need to talk to P'Jom? Has he done something to you? He can be annoying..."

"Come on."

"Well, I'm not sure where he is," Min said, taking a look around.

"P'Ohm!" Min shouted at a nearby student with tan skin.

"What's up?" Ohm replied.

"Have you seen P'Jom?"

"Not sure... I just saw Tem in the elevator, but not Jom."

"Classes are done for the day, so they could be anywhere," Min said with a shrug.

"I'm going to the cafeteria now," Ohm said. "Jom might be there."

"If you see him, can you tell him to meet us here?" Time asked Min and Ohm.

"Who do I say is looking for him?" Ohm asked when he came closer to us.

"Umm... Say that his *dad* is looking for him!" Time said with a sneer. Min and Ohm were taken aback, but they nodded nonetheless.

While waiting for them to return, I called Big to check if he'd found anything. It turned out that people in the neighborhood didn't know anyone named Jom, and the homeowner had moved away. I didn't understand why Jom was so afraid of me that he had to avoid me like this.

Rrrring!

The caller ID on my cell showed my father's number, and I picked it up immediately.

"Yes, Father. I'll be there right away." I checked the time on my phone, then looked at the Sports Science building and saw no one I was looking for. Since my father wanted me to return immediately to meet an important guest, I decided to quit looking for Jom today. I told Time to walk me to the entrance, and I waited there for someone to pick me up.

Just wait until I finish my business... I'll hunt you down!

"Thank you, Mr. Vichian," I told my father's business partner as I walked him to his car after dinner.

After that, my men and I were called to an urgent meeting in our grand hall.

"All of you are fucking useless!" my father cursed loudly, his voice so harsh that everyone practically jumped out of their skin in fear.

"This month, Khun was attacked twice, Kinn got kidnapped, and someone stalked Kim. Do you think their lives are replaceable?!" My father lit a cigarette. I took a quick glance at him as he pulled in a long drag. He was obviously furious.

The silence was deafening. Everyone kept their heads down to avoid my father's murderous gaze, not daring to utter a sound. I crossed my legs and casually poured myself a glass of water. I was used to this.

"What kind of bodyguards are you to let this shit happen over and over again?!"

My father kept ranting. I understood why he was so pissed off; he'd been under a lot of stress lately. This month, his business partners had been constantly trying to provoke him. Then, I got kidnapped, and my brothers hadn't fared much better. Khun, my older brother, probably had it worse than me. He'd been abducted upward of ten times since his childhood. The trauma was starting to mess with his head.

"Pete, Big, Nont! As my sons' lead bodyguards, what exactly are you planning to do? Answer me!"

The three men looked nervously at each other and stayed silent. Their faces were red and swollen from the beating they'd taken from my irate father.

"We're deeply sorry, sir," Pete, Khun's bodyguard, finally answered. "We'll do better."

"I'm tired of your excuses! Look at the bruises on Kinn. And what about Khun—he's bedridden!"

We knew that the people chasing us down wouldn't dare to do anything more than rough us up. They were our rivals, or people who owed us money. But even if we knew damn well who they were, we were helpless to do anything; the one behind all of this mess was someone very close to us. He happened to be my father's younger brother, who headed the Minor Clan. However, we had no solid proof.

Our families—the Major Clan and Minor Clan—had been business rivals for decades. My agong gave my father the shares of his casino and real estate businesses and made him the company's president. My father's younger siblings, Zek-Kant and Gou-Gim, became vice presidents. My grandfather's actions had spurred conflicts between the families that continued to this day.[6]

"I apologize, sir. We tried to gather the evidence as you requested, but the Minor Clan always hires someone else to do their dirty work," Big tried to explain.

"Are you saying they're smarter than us?" My father's cold voice made Big audibly gulp in fear. He lowered his head in surrender, letting my father continue to angrily berate him.

It wasn't like our hands were completely tied in this situation. My father just wanted us to collect all the evidence first so he could get rid of Zek-Kant once and for all. This was a challenge, considering my uncle was just as cunning as my father and not afraid to get his hands dirty. Our families took turns attacking each other in a seemingly never-ending fight.

"If anything happens to my sons again, I'll fire all of you!" my father shouted at them before turning to me. "Kinn, have you found out who that guy is?"

I shook my head no, knowing full well that my father wanted to recruit new, more competent bodyguards.

"Hurry up!" he exclaimed. "I'm offering a new casino lease soon, and the Minor Clan won't stay quiet about it."

"Is there anything I can help with, Mr. Kinn?" asked P'Chan, my father's secretary. "I don't want us to lose this young man. He's such a skilled fighter that I'm worried our rivals will try to recruit him."

P'Chan seemed equally concerned that those thugs would tell their boss about the anonymous martial artist who came to my rescue. If they knew about Jom, they'd try to recruit him to join their side, like they did with our other guards.

---

6   The words used here are terms of address for family members in the Teochew dialect. "Agong" means grandfather, and "Zek" and "Gou" are used to refer to the younger brother of one's father and the sister of one's father respectively. See the Appendix for more details.

"I'll take care of it," I replied bluntly.

P'Chan nodded and turned to look at my father.

Then, a guy who looked like a younger version of me—despite being three years older—abruptly entered the room. "Hey! Did you enjoy your vacation?" he asked. His voice sounded overly cheerful amid the stressful atmosphere.

"Not a vacation, asshole," I answered my older brother, irked. Due to his insolent behavior, my younger brother and I never addressed our older brother with respect.

I hadn't seen either of my brothers since I came back after being held hostage for three days. I'd heard that Khun was so sick he couldn't get out of bed, but here he was, standing in our meeting room with a cold pack stuck to his forehead.

"Don't be crude," my father warned us.

Khun ignored him. Instead, he tilted my face left and right to check out my bruises. "Wow! You got a lot of *souvenirs*!"

"Get lost!" I snarled, swatting his hand away.

He simply smiled at me with no remorse. He then plopped down on the sofa and turned on the television like nothing had happened. My father shook his head without saying anything—Khun was his favorite son.

I actually felt sorry for my older brother. Life had never been easy for him. He'd been kidnapped and attacked more than any of us for over ten years, and he'd been acting strange lately.

"Just bring me that fighter as soon as possible," my father told me with a sigh, and I nodded.

"What's your plan?" the golden child casually asked our father while unwrapping a piece of chocolate he'd pilfered from one of the jars of sweets placed all over the house.

"I'm looking for a new bodyguard for Kinn," our father replied. Big, my current bodyguard, glanced at me.

"Aww... What about me?" Khun said sweetly, turning up the charm.

"What about you? You already have Pete," my father said, glaring at Pete, who stood with his head low.

Khun turned to look at Pete and grimaced. "Pete is stupid. I like the smart ones."

Pete rolled his eyes. In truth, Pete was an excellent bodyguard. We'd hired him after we fired Khun's old bodyguard. Since then, Khun's kidnappings had reduced significantly.

My father tried to appease his oldest son. "If he lets you get beaten up next time, I'll find you a new one."

Who said the youngest child was the one who always got his way? In my family, it was the oldest son who always got what he wanted. He had everything handed to him on a silver platter, while my younger brother and I were left to our own devices.

"What about me?" a deep voice asked.

Another figure with a cheeky grin on his face appeared in the doorway. I rolled my eyes at my younger brother, who looked wildly similar to me. He was practically my clone.

"Who the hell are you?" Khun asked incredulously, pointing at our brother as he stood beside a large wooden door engraved with a dragon design.

"Are you nuts?" Kim asked, leaning against the door with his arms crossed over his chest. The guards started to walk out of the room after Kim arrived, leaving only us and our exhausted father.

"Me? Nah... Did you suddenly remember where you live?"

Kim narrowed his eyes in disdain at his older brother. But Khun was right; it was a surprise to see him at home. He was gone so often that no one would notice if he was kidnapped.

"Having all of you at home makes me think there's a storm in the desert," my father muttered.

"Well, it's because you only care about Khun. I ran away to get your attention," Kim said as he sat next to our father on the sofa.

I knew what he said was all bullshit. He'd probably left because he was infatuated with another lover of his again and stayed at their place.

"You shouldn't have come back! Father said he would give all his inheritance to Kinn and me," Khun said, biting back at Kim. My brothers always argued whenever they were in the same room together.

"Papa! How did you let your oldest son lose his mind like this?" Kim pointed accusingly at Khun, who just swatted his finger away. "Can't you see he's talking nonsense?!"

"That's enough!" my father warned. "You're all giving me a headache!"

Meanwhile, I just channel-surfed the TV. It was far better than listening to them squabble.

"Anyway, since all of you are here, why don't you go check the accounting documents at the factory for me?"

My two brothers visibly deflated when they heard our father's order.

"Can't one of your men do that?" Khun cried out.

"You three will take over my business in the future. Maybe it's time to get off your ass and start helping. Don't disappoint me! Especially you, Kim. Be home for once." My father left the room after giving his final order, leaving Kim to start another spat with Khun.

"I shouldn't have come back!" Kim swore loudly.

"Yes! This is your fault!"

"Why don't you act like a responsible older brother? We always have to pick up your slack!"

Khun didn't give in. "How dare you! I've helped Father more than you, dipshit!" he exclaimed, continuing to harass his little brother.

Who would believe that this was our *older* brother? He not only looked young, but he acted the most childishly out of the three of us. People often mistook me for the oldest child instead, due to my calm demeanor. But despite looking immature, Khun had already graduated with a bachelor's degree in Business Administration. He'd gone to the same university as me. Our father tried to take him to work as an assistant so he could learn about our business, but Khun said he wanted to take a break first. It had been two years already, and it didn't look like he'd get his shit together anytime soon.

Kim was also a business student. He was in his second year at a different university. My younger brother might have seemed stubborn and ignorant, but he was really something when he got serious. He was witty, clever, and self-sufficient, so I didn't need to worry about him.

I left my two brothers to their argument, and went to look for my subordinates to tell them to keep their eyes on Jom's house and The Root Club.

I didn't like what I heard from my men the following day. They said people at the club and around that house did not know anyone named Jom. They insisted the person we were looking for was not here, and that got me thinking...

I was watching TV in my office when Big started to talk to me in a serious tone. "Trust me when I say I remember his face, Mr. Kinn. Last night, I didn't see him at The Root Club. My men stayed around his house all night, and they didn't see him either. Everyone seemed genuinely confused when we asked if they knew Jom. Is Jom even his real name?"

I agreed with everything he said. Then, I suddenly remembered that I had Jom's number!

I immediately went looking for my father.

"Father," I called out when I found him sipping coffee in the living room. "Can I borrow your phone?"

"What for?" my father asked, but he gave his phone to me anyway.

I reviewed my father's call history until I found one incoming call from four days ago. I checked the time to ensure it was the one I was looking for. Then, I quickly added the number to my phone.

"Thank you." I returned the phone to my father, who looked at me curiously.

"I'm hunting down that guy for you," I explained.

"You still haven't found him after all this time?" he grunted.

"It's not that easy! This isn't any ordinary man," I complained, before I went back to my office to make the call.

The phone rang briefly before I heard a familiar voice pick up: "What?"

"Hi..." I said calmly.

"Who is this?!"

The corners of my lips curved into a sneer at the hostile reply. This guy seemed to be worse at communicating with people than I was.

"And who are you?" I asked.

"Don't you know who you're calling, shithead?"

"Jom... Is this Jom?"

Beep...beep...beep.

The way my call suddenly disconnected made me confident I had finally found him. *Hmph! You dared to fool me?!*

"Big! Bring Jom, the second-year student from Sports Science, to me!" I barked the order at my subordinate.

Is this really how you want me to find you? Fine!

I let Big look for the guy named Jom while I went to check the factory with Khun and Kim. My brothers dozed off as soon as they got into our driver's fancy van. My father would be depressed to see his sons so uninterested in his family business.

We finally arrived at our factory, a company affiliated with the Theerapanyakul Group. This factory, which specialized in crafting caramel-filled chocolates, had been near the brink of financial loss since its establishment, but my father had tenaciously kept the operation going for over five years without being able to scrounge up a profit. He only kept this place going because Khun loved the chocolates.

The packaging for our chocolate was absolutely hideous, featuring a realistic drawing of three boys wrapping their arms around each other and making funny faces with their tongues out. Evidently, the inspiration for this peculiar design came directly from the image of the owner's three sons. The brand's name, "Mr. 3K," was equally off-putting.

All three of us, dressed in suit and tie, greeted the factory's employees, who seemed happy to see us. We checked the income and expense records and briefly visited the production department. The business seemed stagnant; not growing, but not losing any more money, either. It had been like this for a while now.

This chocolate factory was our family's only source of clean money. The majority of our income came from casinos and real estate. My father was a loan shark as well as a legitimate lender, a weapons smuggler, and a landlord who leased his properties to be used as casinos in other provinces. Our businesses experienced significant growth and success, so much so that people were visibly jealous of us. It was a shame that no one wanted to buy a share of our chocolate factory so I could change the packaging. It really was an eyesore.

"Have your men pick you up after lunch, all right? I have some business to attend to afterward," I told my brothers. We were sitting in a Hyundai van with Pete as our driver and two other subordinates as passengers.

"Where are you going?" Kim asked.

"None of your business. Have you chosen where you want to eat yet?"

"I want to go somewhere with a good view... Why don't we go to Vanista?" Khun suggested. Vanista was an Italian restaurant atop a skyrise building with an equally sky-high price.

"I don't want to go somewhere that fancy! I just want a simple meal. Hey Pete, take us to that department store up ahead," Kim ordered. He put on his earbuds with the volume blasting to the max to block out all of Khun's complaints.

Once we arrived, I strolled around aimlessly, waiting for Khun to choose a place to eat. Then, I caught sight of two tall figures who appeared to be siblings. Khun also saw them, but he was not pleased with this encounter. He quickly approached them, and Kim and I almost had to run after him.

"Hey, Minor Clan," Khun sneered at the two men. They were around our age, and also happened to be our cousins. They looked up in surprise from the menu they were reading and smiled back.

"Hello, P'Kinn," Vegas, the eldest brother of the Minor Clan greeted me.

"Hi, P'Kinn," Macau followed. He was Vegas's younger brother, currently attending high school.

"There's three of us, and you only said hi to Kinn?" Khun grumbled.

Ignoring my brother, I casually asked my cousin, "You here for lunch?"

"Yes. You too?"

I was unsurprised that I was the only person Macau was civil with. We never directly confronted each other face to face. We knew damned well who was behind the kidnappings and the attacks my brothers and I were forced to suffer. I tried not to get involved in our parents' problems, but it seemed I was the only one who thought that way. Since they were young, Khun and Kim had picked on Vegas and Macau whenever they had the chance.

"Yes, sir."

"Kim, let's go somewhere else for lunch. The vibe here is depressing, and it's making me uncomfortable. It's like there's evil spirits around," Khun turned to whisper to Kim, who nodded in agreement. This was the only thing those two saw eye to eye on.

"Really? Everything was fine when it was only Macau and me here. Maybe *you* brought the bad vibes," Vegas retorted. He had been on the receiving end of Khun's harassment since he was a kid. But he was a man now, more mature—so he was bolder and unafraid.

"Ha! The Minor Clan didn't teach you any manners, I presume?" Khun scoffed. He looked at them disdainfully, his arms crossed over his chest.

"You think you're better than us, Major Clan?" Vegas did not let the subject drop.

"Both of you, that's enough! Let's just go our separate ways!" I exclaimed, tired of them being at each other's throats.

"P'Kinn, your eldest brother started it," Vegas said, pointing at Khun.

"What? I can't just say *hello* to my cousins?" Khun asked.

"Come on. Let's go." I dragged Khun away by the arm, and Kim chuckled and followed me without any further complaint.

"You should put a muzzle on him the next time you take him out, P'Kinn!" Macau's shout could be heard in the distance, but I hurriedly pulled Khun away before things could escalate further.

I found an ordinary-looking Japanese restaurant and shoved an agitated Khun inside.

"Why did you get in my way?" Khun shouted at me.

"C'mon, don't pick on children," I dismissed him and started browsing the menu.

"Those twerps will never learn their place! I hate them!" Khun said, pouting. He always sulked when things didn't turn out his way.

My father was solely responsible for raising Khun to be such a spoiled, arrogant brat. He'd divorced our mother, who was half French, when we were young. We never asked him why. I knew he loved us very much. Sometimes even too much...

"And how old are you?" I retorted.

"Are you my family or theirs?"

"Both."

Khun didn't like my answer and became more aggravated. I couldn't imagine what it was going to be like when he became leader of the Major Clan. It was sure to be disastrous.

After lunch, we casually strolled around the mall while we waited for Khun to do some shopping. Our bodyguards trailed us at a distance, but they were more there to carry Khun's shopping bags than to guard us. I caught a glimpse of a suspicious-looking man who appeared to be heading toward us as my older brother selected a watch worth nearly a million baht.

"Sir! Please help me, sir!"

A middle-aged man in filthy clothes approached us. The mall crowd quickly moved away in disgust, and before I realized it, he'd sidled up to me. My bodyguard promptly pulled me away as soon as the guy grabbed my arm.

I frowned at the man being carried away by my bodyguards. All three of us brothers stayed silent.

"Please listen to me, sir! I beg you, let go! Sir!" he cried. He desperately tried to plead with me and escape my bodyguards' hold at the same time.

Curious about his behavior, I walked over to him and told my men to let him go.

My subordinates looked at me briefly and did as they were told. The old man looked visibly relieved and started to approach me again.

Pete cut him off. "Say what you want, and don't move!" he said sternly.

"Mr. Tankhun, please speak to your father for me," the old man said.

I frowned at him and turned to look at the real Tankhun, who'd gone back to check out a watch without any interest in the commotion.

"You're mistaken, old man," Kim said with a chuckle. "This guy is Mr. Anakinn."

As I mentioned before, I was often mistaken for the oldest brother in our family because we looked so much alike. Even people at the office thought I was Khun sometimes.

"What do you want?" Khun asked without looking at the man.

"Sir, please help me. My name is Thee. I used to do business with your father ten years ago. Now I'm in debt..."

"Lost everything to gambling, I assume?" Khun's voice was disinterested, like he was discussing the weather.

"B-but I used to work with your father..."

"Get to the point." Khun cut him off as he handed his credit card to the sales assistant.

"I...I owed your father five million. He gave me three days to pay back my debt. Otherwise, he..."

"He'll give you a pair of cement shoes," Khun finished his sentence.

I also lost interest in him and turned to check out the watch Khun had just purchased. This man's plight was nothing new to us. We were accustomed to such matters, and we knew our father would undoubtedly follow through with his threat.

"P-please! I'll pay your father back, but it's impossible to do it in three days. Please give me more time to find the money. Please tell your father to change his mind. I'm begging you, sir!"

Khun ignored him and walked away. "I'm in the mood for some ice cream. Let's go."

I followed my older brother quietly. The man tried to follow us again, but our bodyguards kept him at bay. We had never been involved in the casino business, leaving that to our father's judgment. We never questioned his decisions, and believed he knew what he was doing.

"Mr. Tankhun, please help!"

I could still hear his shouts as a couple of mall security guards came to extricate the old man from the building. I knew why these people tried to approach us; they thought we would be able to help them negotiate with our father. But they were wrong. We would not help them.

Some might have thought they could just run away. But that wasn't possible, either. My father would always find them, even if they ran to the ends of the earth.

I stayed at the mall a while longer until it was time to leave. We stood at the entrance waiting for our van to pick us up when I caught sight of the same old man sulking by the side of the road. What caught my attention was the familiar motorcycle parked right next to him. I squinted at the two figures; my lips curved into a smile when I saw the man I'd been searching for attempting to pull that old man over to his bike.

Gotcha! I didn't think he'd show up this easily after all this time. Maybe fortune had finally smiled upon me.

Now it's my turn!

Pressure

PORSCHE

I RODE MY TRUSTY BIKE, now with a passenger in tow. He looked so depressed that you'd think the world was ending.

I was surprised to get a call from Uncle Thee out of nowhere. He didn't answer any of my questions, just asked me to pick him up and begged me to take him home.

"Get off the bike," I told him. He obediently did as he was told, but his brows furrowed as he watched me kill my bike's engine and slowly push it into a bush behind my house. His brows furrowed further when I hauled myself over the back wall.

"What the hell are you doing?" he asked in confusion.

I offered my hand to help him climb the wall. "Shh! Be quiet!" I shushed him. "And hurry up!"

Uncle Thee grabbed my hand, and I pulled him up on top of the wall with me. Then, I lowered myself to the other side as quietly as possible.

"Why do you have to sneak into your own house?" he quietly complained. However, he followed me when I beckoned him to come down. I looked around cautiously before I opened the door, trying not to make a sound.

Relief washed over me once I let myself in. "Phew! That was close!" I said. My uncle followed close on my heels, and went straight for the light switch.

"Hey! Don't turn on the light!" I warned him.

"What?!" He looked at me, puzzled.

I lit a candle with my lighter. The wax had already burned down by half from when I'd used it last night.

"Don't ask!" I scolded him.

He looked at me in bewilderment when I opened a drawer, took out a woven fan, and handed it to him.

"Use this if you get hot. Don't turn on the AC!"

"Did you not pay the electricity bill or something?" Uncle Thee asked.

I ignored him and walked to the window. I lifted the curtain slightly and saw two men dressed in black staking out my house on their motorcycles.

How long are they gonna keep following me?

These men had shown up at the bar and my house for two days straight, and it was starting to get on my nerves.

I'd told Madam Yok I'd be absent for a few days, and she replied by telling me someone came looking for Jom every night. I felt incredibly apprehensive when she insisted that I ask Jom to apologize to Mr. Kinn.

"Tell Jom to apologize to him at once! Mr. Kinn is not someone to be trifled with!"

I had never been this freaked out before. People were out looking for me, believing I was Jom. I came to the realization that Kinn would not give up hunting me so easily.

"Did you piss off the mafia?" Uncle Thee asked as he came to peer through the gap in the curtain with me.

"That's none of your business!" I told him. "What about you? What have you done this time?"

I couldn't tell him I'd extorted money from Kinn, and that he'd sent his men after me—probably to get back what I owed him. If Uncle Thee found out about this money, he'd ask me to share it.

My uncle sat on my old sofa and heaved out a breath without asking any more questions.

"Are you back, hia?" Chay asked as he came downstairs in a tank top and shorts, furiously fluttering the woven fan in his hand and sweating profusely in the heat.

Uncle Thee nodded when Chay greeted him. "You're here too, Chay?"

"Yes," Chay replied, before turning to me. "Hia, I'm gonna sleep at my friend's place tonight."

"Why?"

"I'm tired of sneaking into my own house! I can't turn on the air conditioner or do anything! I can't even turn on the goddamn lights. All I *can* do is charge my phone. This is ridiculous! What have you gotten yourself into, hia?"

I quickly covered his mouth and shushed him. "Quiet!" He frowned at me and tried to pry my hands away. "Fine, fine! You can go to your friend's place. Call me once you get there, okay? And don't forget to go out through the back!" I insisted.

After I let him go, my brother rolled his eyes at me and went back upstairs to pack his things.

"Porsche! Do you owe someone money?!" Uncle Thee asked, his face perplexed.

"No! It's nothing. Anyway, what about you? What happened?" I turned the question back on him, my voice serious. I put my hands on my hips as I awaited his answer.

"I... I... I need money," he said.

I sighed. This was not the first time I had heard about his plight, and it was getting tiresome. Uncle Thee had been in debt more than ten times over the past year. I couldn't help him—I was just as broke as he was.

"I don't have any cash, you know that. I pawned my mother's gold to get you out of debt last time," I said, dismissing him and going to the kitchen to get some water.

"But you have to help me this time!" my uncle cried, pulling at his hair like a madman. "I don't know what else to do!"

"How much?" I asked.

He bit his lip, glancing at me nervously, before speaking in a tiny voice. "Five million," he admitted.

I choked on the water I was drinking straight from the bottle, coughing violently. "What?!"

"It's different this time. He's definitely going to kill me. I need you to help me, Porsche!" he pleaded hysterically.

"Are you crazy? Where am I supposed to find you five million baht?"

I was telling him the truth. All of his previous debts had been a couple hundred thousand, and we could usually scrape together some money from selling some of our remaining possessions to pay off what he owed. I'd thought the last time would be the end of it, but I was wrong. I had no idea how I was supposed to help him this time.

"I don't know, but you've gotta help me out!" He anxiously paced back and forth, muttering gibberish to himself until something he said alarmed me: "Damn it! I already put up the house as collateral! What do I do?!"

"Wait! Which house?" I asked, remembering that my uncle's house had already been seized to pay off other debts. He'd been spending all his time at the casino lately, and he only visited me here occasionally. "You mean *your* house, right?"

When he gave me a guilty look, a sinking feeling took hold in my heart.

"Um... Well... I-I'm sorry. I didn't know what to do," Uncle Thee said.

I stared at him in disbelief, unable to fathom what I had just heard from my own uncle. I rushed toward him, desperately hoping that I had misheard him. "Don't tell me you—!"

"Yes! I put up *this house* as collateral!" he finally confessed. "He'll seize it if I don't repay him in three days." He pressed his fingers hard against his temples, as if trying to calm his nerves.

My knees almost gave out. This house was mine—the only remaining inheritance my parents had left for me. I couldn't believe my uncle would do this to me. I tried to pull myself together and walked straight to the drawer where I kept the ownership documents. When I saw an empty folder, I glared at my uncle in fury. I was too angry to speak.

I'd just turned twenty, so this house would be legally passed down to me soon. Uncle Thee had been our legal guardian, taking care of us and our inheritance until I reached adulthood. He sold a lot of our stuff, but he promised never to touch this house. It belonged to my little brother and me. But now...

How could he do this to me? My own uncle!

"I'm sorry," he said quietly.

I really wanted to punch him for what he'd done to me. He was the only relative my brother and I had left. He should have been a man I could rely on—but he was nothing but trouble.

"Three days..." I repeated his words, reminding myself I only had three days left to live in my own house.

"Um... In three days, I need to find money to pay off my debt and reclaim the house. The total is about five million..." he rasped, looking at the floor in defeat.

Bang! Crash!

The silence that had fallen over us was shattered by the loud noise of someone bashing the door with something hard. I whipped my head around at the sound, and my eyes widened at what I saw.

"Shit!" I yelled.

A group of men in black suits stormed into my house, followed by a familiar face. His tall figure exuded power and confidence.

"Mr. Anakinn!" my uncle cried. He jumped off the sofa, equally shocked to see him. I stood still, too stunned to do anything when the man I had been avoiding suddenly appeared in my home. With all the shit that kept happening to me lately, I had no clue what to do now.

I tensed up, glowering at him. "How... How did you get in my house?!"

"Hmm... It'll be *my* house in three days, though," he replied in amusement.

I glanced at my uncle to confirm that Kinn was the one he was indebted to. My uncle simply nodded.

"Hia, what's with all the noise?" Chay asked as he came down the stairs. He looked at the strange men in our house and frowned. "Who are these people?!"

"Go back to your room," I told my little brother sternly. I was not ready for him to learn the details of the current situation.

Chay refused to do as I said, approaching me and demanding an answer. "Why? What's going on?"

I kept my eyes locked on Kinn. He stood languidly with his hands in his pockets, entertained by the scene unfolding in front of him.

"Get back to your room!" I roared.

My brother's face faltered. "Will you be okay, hia?" he asked nervously.

"Just go. I'll be fine," I said. I watched my younger brother slowly retreat to his room, waiting until his door was closed before returning my gaze to Kinn.

I was still in shock. Everything had happened so fast—I couldn't comprehend the situation.

"Well...um..." Uncle Thee mumbled when no one spoke up. "Why did you come here, Mr. Anakinn?"

"Why can't I come? Half of this place belongs to me, doesn't it?" he quipped. His callous attitude made me clench my fists in anger.

"Well...could you give me more time?" my uncle tried to bargain.

"Three days," Kinn sneered. "Five million baht. If you want to reclaim your property deed as well, that'll be six million and two hundred thousand in total..."

My heart sank as I heard the numbers. Talking about my house like it meant nothing had me itching to punch him right in the face. His arrogance pissed me off so much that it rendered me speechless.

"But, Mr. Kinn..." Uncle Thee pleaded.

Kinn lifted his broad hand, stopping my uncle midsentence. "I have an alternate offer," he said.

My uncle's eyes lit up, looking at Kinn expectantly. "What is it? Tell me! I'll do anything if you give me a chance!"

I was dumbfounded when Kinn suddenly pointed his finger at me.

"You!" he exclaimed. "Come work for me!"

Work? For *him*?

"If you work for me, I'll extend his payment term to two years."

I stared at Kinn, but I couldn't figure out his intentions.

"Work?" my uncle asked.

"I want this guy as my bodyguard. If he agrees, I'll talk to my father about your terms of payment," Kinn told my uncle.

I took a deep breath, trying to wrap my head around everything I'd just heard. In the end, I scoffed. "Who do you think you are? Are you really someone so high-profile that you need a bodyguard?" I wanted to laugh in his face. Was he really that delusional? Did he think he was in a mafia movie?

"Quiet!" my uncle hissed at me.

"What?! This is your problem. Don't drag me into your mess!" I snapped.

I was completely fed up with my uncle; I wanted nothing to do with him anymore. I couldn't figure out how I got into this messed up situation in the first place. Not only did Kinn want me to work for him, but he also wanted my house! *What the hell?!*

"Then you can say goodbye to your house," Kinn said.

"This is my parents' house!" I spat through gritted teeth, my body shaking with anger. With my hands curled into fists, I launched myself at Kinn. My eyes burned with rage when two of his bodyguards immediately blocked my advance.

"It'll be my father's house soon!" Kinn replied with a smirk. This asshole knew exactly what to say to piss me off!

"Fuck you!" I yelled.

"Stop it! If you want to keep this house, just do as he says!" my uncle tried to warn me.

"But this isn't my problem! Why do I have to work for him?"

"Hmm? What are you afraid of?" Kinn asked.

"What am I afraid of?!" I yelled. "Are you insane? Who in their right mind would want to risk their life for you? You want someone to do your dirty work, yeah? And by 'bodyguard,' do you mean someone who takes the beating for you? Or do I have to threaten people who owe you money—like what you're doing to me right now? What would my brother do if something happened to me?!"

That was probably the most words I'd said at once in years. I'd never wanted to get involved in shit like this—it wasn't worth the risk. I knew my life would be in danger if I decided to go down that path, and I had my little brother to worry about too.

"You have three days. If you can't do it, leave!" Kinn reminded me.

"Argh!" I roared and hurled myself at him again, knowing I'd never get past his bodyguards. They came after me all at once.

"I'll get my house back, you hear me?!" I screamed in frustration.

"Just stop! Don't be a fool!" my uncle shouted as he tried to block me from reaching Kinn.

He shoved me hard, driving me backward until my back hit the wall with a loud *thud*. I scowled at my uncle, silently cursing him for everything he'd done to drag me into this mess. I screamed and yanked at my hair, all the while wondering how the hell I was going to get my house back.

Everyone quietly stared at me. I glared back before I finally spoke: "If I just want my house back, how much do I have to pay?"

"How much?" Kinn turned to ask one of his men.

"One-point-two million, sir," the man replied.

"Hey!" my uncle yelled. "Don't do this to me. If I can't pay him back in three days, I'll die! Go work for Mr. Kinn, I'm begging you!"

"No way!" I said. "I only want my house back!"

"And where will you get the money?"

"I have a job," I told my uncle. Then I turned to Kinn. "Give me some time, and I'll get my house back."

"Very well," Kinn replied.

"What about me?! What about my debt?!" Uncle Thee cried.

He shook my arm in a hopeless attempt to beg for mercy. "Please think about it! There's no way you can make a million baht that fast. At least working for Mr. Kinn, you'll get paid *and* get your house back."

I shook off his grasp. "I don't want to be involved!" I yelled. "I hate this! I'm worried about my brother!"

I exhaled audibly. Ignoring my uncle, I tried to walk over to Kinn again, but I stopped when his guards refused to move out of the way.

"Give me one year," I said. "I'll find the money and get my house back."

"And where will you and your brother stay during that time?" my uncle interjected.

"That's none of your business!" I shouted back at my uncle, who looked like he had lost his mind. I could rent an apartment just for Chay and me and work until I saved enough money to get our house back. That way, we'd still be able to earn our keep.

"Suit yourself. But the five million still needs to be paid in three days." Kinn shrugged and left with a menacing grin.

Once Kinn and his men were gone, my uncle finally snapped. He started destroying everything in his reach, shouting, "What the hell have you done?! Don't you know they'll kill me if I can't repay them in three days? They'll *kill* me!"

"That's your problem!" I yelled back at him. "Sort it out yourself and leave me out of it! I value my own goddamn life too, you know?"

"If I die, it's because of you!"

"And isn't my life a disaster right now because of *you*? How can you be so selfish? You sold my parents' fortune to save your own ass. Now you're using *me* to bargain for your debt?! Why? Is my life worth nothing to you?!"

Uncle Thee glared at me heatedly as I yelled at him. I never blamed him for selling our family fortune to pay off his debts, not even once. But this was different. This house was the only remaining thing my parents owned that belonged to me. Now, in the blink of an eye, it had been ripped from my hands.

"Fine! Call me a selfish bastard," Uncle Thee replied. "But don't you have a conscience? I'm your father's brother. Why won't you help me? There's a way to save this house *and* me, but you won't do it. Who cared for you all this time? Who paid your high school tuition? Me!"

I clenched my hands tightly, shaking with anger as I listened to my uncle harp on about all the favors he'd done for me. It was true that he'd helped me a lot in the beginning—but he hadn't suffered from a gambling addiction back then. His problems were nothing but trouble for my brother and me, and this time, it was far worse than anything that had come before.

I took a moment to think. I wondered whether or not it was worth risking my own life to work for Kinn just so I could clean up this mess and keep my brother and uncle out of harm's way.

Should I...?

"Please don't...*hic*...don't do it, hia!"

I looked up at the sound of my younger brother sniffling loudly as he hurried down the stairs. Chay threw himself at me and hugged me tightly, burying his face in my chest. My heart ached to see my little brother so vulnerable.

I fought hard to hide how weak I felt, to push it down to the deepest and darkest corner of my heart, as I lifted my hand to gently stroke Chay's hair. Chay had probably heard everything and figured it all out...

When I remained silent, Chay begged me in a shaky voice, "Please don't take the job! It's too dangerous! I can't lose you, hia!"

This was the only reason why I would not risk my life. I could not die and leave my little brother alone in this world. Chay had already suffered enough. Everything I did was to protect my little brother and keep him safe. I loved him more than anything—more than my own life.

"It's okay if we lose this house. We can stay anywhere. Just don't leave me, please!" Chay continued to plead. His arms tightened around me even harder, as if he feared I would disappear.

"Okay..."

"Hmph! Listen to me, punk," Uncle Thee interrupted us. "Your older brother won't die that easily. He fought all the time in high school, and here he is, alive and well. Don't tell me you're a coward now, Porsche!"

I clenched my jaw and glared at the man I was loath to call my uncle. I could not believe my father's brother, who said he loved Chay and me like his own children, would tell me to risk my life for a bastard like Kinn.

I reflected on the last two days of getting mixed up in Kinn's business. The men hunting Kinn down weren't afraid to use knives and guns. It was unlike any brawl or fistfight I'd been in, and there was no doubt in my mind that I should stay the hell away. I would not put my life on the line for Kinn. I could never risk causing Chay any more pain. I cared for my little brother more than anything in the entire world. *No! I won't do it!*

My brother and I quickly packed only the essentials and went straight to Tem's apartment. I couldn't stand being in the same home as that man anymore, and I couldn't respect him as my uncle, either.

Uncle Thee was still shouting at me when I left. He kept alternating between blaming me for ditching him and trying to convince me to take the job as Kinn's bodyguard. I tried my best to stop myself from hurting the only family member we had left.

"Come in, man. Have a drink," Tem said when we arrived at his place, pouring a glass of water for me and Chay.

"Thank you," Chay said softly.

Tem turned to me, his face full of concern. "What happened?"

"Sorry for bothering you," I mumbled, staring off into the empty space of Tem's balcony.

"Bothering me? Cut the bullshit! You're my friend. You know you can come here anytime!" Tem insisted. "So...what's wrong? Anything I can do to help?"

I felt his hand squeeze my shoulder and turned to look at his handsome face. He was looking at me with genuine concern.

"My house was seized," I finally replied.

"What?!" Tem hissed in shock and confusion. "What happened?"

"Uncle Thee put it up as collateral for his gambling debts..." It pained me to say my uncle's name. It hurt to even think about him.

"Shit," Tem swore. He and Jom knew what my uncle was like, so I didn't need to explain any further. He could fill in the rest.

We sat quietly for a while before Tem asked, "So, what's your plan?"

I shook my head. Everything happened so suddenly—I still had no idea what to do.

"I'll only trouble you for tonight," Chay told Tem, breaking the silence. "Tomorrow, I'll stay with a friend."

"You can just stay here, Chay. Both you and your brother," Tem said seriously. "It might be a bit crowded, but you can both stay as long as you like."

"Thanks, but I'm okay," Chay said, politely declining Tem's offer. "I'll stay with a friend tomorrow. My brother can stay with you."

"I told Chay I'd find a room for us. I promise I'll be out of your hair soon, but for now..."

"Oh, shut up!" Tem cut me off before I could finish. "Don't act like we're strangers. You can stay here. I want to help you, Porsche."

Although my life had taken a drastic turn, it seemed like I still had good friends I could count on.

"Thanks, man," I said sincerely.

"By the way, have you told Jom about all this?" Tem asked.

"I was going to go to Jom's place at first," I said. "I called him a few times, but he didn't pick up. He's probably asleep."

"Yeah, I've been trying to reach him since earlier in the evening, and he still hasn't texted me back. Maybe he got laid?" Tem joked, trying to lighten the mood. He was a good host, turning on the TV and bringing us snacks and drinks to cheer us up. "Make yourself comfortable, yeah? Wanna use the shower? You two can sleep in my bed tonight. I'll take the sofa."

"No, I really don't want to impose. Chay can share the bed with you. I'll take the sofa," I insisted. Tem and Chay agreed without protest.

It had been a really long day, and I was exhausted. I couldn't work at the club, my house was seized—my entire life had turned upside down. Hopefully, I could get back on my feet tomorrow and start working again. I had to save up to buy my house back from Kinn.

The next day...

"What the hell is wrong with Jom?!" Tem swore. He'd called Jom for the umpteenth time with no answer. Our afternoon classes had finished, but Jom had yet to show up. Nobody had been able to get hold of him since yesterday. Jom usually left a message in the group chat if he was sick or absent, but this time he'd gone completely MIA on us, like he'd been kidnapped.

Tem and I stopped trying to reach him, thinking he'd return our calls eventually. I went back to Tem's apartment and started looking at listings online for cheap rooms nearby. I jotted down a couple of places that I could afford. Then, it was time for me to get dressed and head to work at Madam Yok's.

"Eek! Not again!"

The moment I secured my bike's kickstand in the parking lot, I heard a loud scream. Alarmed, I whipped my head toward the source of the familiar voice. The sight of an anxious crowd gathering at the entrance of the club gave me a bad feeling.

I pushed through the crowd and entered the club. "What's going on?" I yelled. I quickly looked around to see upended furniture and broken glass littering the floor. It looked like war had broken out in here.

I came across a familiar figure dressed in a qipao. She was weeping, collapsed on the floor.

"Porsche! We need to talk!"

I flinched when Madam Yok yelled at me. Her voice sounded deep and masculine, completely different from the higher pitch she usually used. Right now, she looked like a man wearing his wife's dress. Madam Yok got up and forcefully dragged me to her office.

Shit! What did I do this time?!

"Aah! This is driving me crazy!" Madam Yok screamed, knocking her forehead against the wall repeatedly.

"Wh-what happened?" I stammered.

"Who the fuck did you pick a fight with?"

I cringed at Madam Yok's strong choice of words. She had never spoken this harshly to me before.

"What do you mean?" I asked, trying to remember if I had offended anyone recently. I couldn't think of anything besides the issue with my house.

Madam Yok glared at me for a moment, and then she began to loudly weep. "Didn't I tell you not to get into trouble?" she sobbed.

Her voice had returned to its typical feminine pitch. She fussed over me while dabbing at the corner of her eyes with a Chinese silk handkerchief.

"I didn't..."

"Hush! What did you do to offend Mr. Kinn?"

I eyed my boss skeptically at the mention of Kinn's name. I couldn't recall if I had done anything to offend him. He had already taken my house—and the debt of five million baht was my uncle's problem, not mine. I thought we'd reached some sort of agreement before he left yesterday. He didn't ask me to return his watch, either. Not knowing what else Kinn had to be mad about, I stared blankly at Madam Yok.

"I came to open the bar this afternoon and found one of Mr. Kinn's men waiting. He asked if a guy named Porsche still worked here. When I said yes, he hit me with a club and knocked me out! When I woke up, my bar was trashed. Porsche, what did you do? Huh?!" Madam Yok exclaimed, her voice growing more hoarse and masculine toward the end. It was as if she could no longer maintain her composure.

"I didn't do anything!" I insisted.

"Don't bullshit me, Porsche! That guy even told everyone that he and his men were going to come back and knock some sense into us until we fire you."

What the hell?!

"Wait. What the hell is going on?" I said. I usually remained unflappable, but right now I couldn't help gaping at the absurdity of it all.

"I should be asking *you* what the hell is going on," Madam Yok spoke tersely, but then her voice softened. "I'm so sorry, Porsche. But will you please stop working here?"

She did not look angry with me anymore, but instead looked stuck in an awkward predicament.

"No... You can't fire me!" I begged her. How was I going to save up the money to buy my house back from Kinn if I didn't have a job?

Kinn, what the hell did you do?!

"I can't keep fixing up the place every day..." Madam Yok said between sobs.

"But you can't just fire me! I need money," I replied truthfully.

"I need money to repair this place, too. I don't even know where to get the funds for it this time," she said.

I looked through the tinted window separating the office and the bar. The place was a trash heap right now, and some of my colleagues were beaten up badly. I felt terrible about it.

"I really don't know why he's so mad at me," I sighed. I was pretty confident I wasn't the one who'd started this fight. But I couldn't stop blaming myself for all the chaos that had unfolded here.

"I'm begging you, Porsche. Please quit."

I silently stared at Madam Yok. The past two days had been hell. I didn't know what to do or what to feel anymore.

"Don't look at me like that, darling. You know I love you, but... I have to love my own life, too..."

I understood her reasoning: I'd brought trouble to this place two days in a row. I couldn't blame her for wanting me to quit.

"You can still come back to me anytime. I'm willing to help you with anything—except money. For right now, anyway..."

"All right, then... Could you put in a good word for me to Mr. Q?"

"Mr. Q, the guy who owns the bar in the next street over?" she asked, raising her brow at me.

"Yeah, him. Can you ask Mr. Q if I can start working at his place tonight? I really need the money."

"Are you sure Mr. Kinn won't send his men to wreck Q's place as well?"

I really had no idea if Kinn would keep sending people after me. I couldn't figure out what his problem with me was.

"All right. I'll give Q a call. Wait just a second." Madam Yok pulled out her phone and went outside her office to have a chat with Mr. Q.

I knew Madam Yok was furious with me for what happened to her bar. Seeing her still trying to help made me believe she really did care about me.

"It's settled. You can start at his place tonight," Madam Yok said when she returned to the office.

She told Mr. Q that her place would be closed for the foreseeable future, and she needed a temporary place for her staff to work. That was what she told me, anyway, and Mr. Q seemed to accept it without question.

"Um... Thanks. Do you need me to help clean up before I go?" I asked.

"Nah... Just go. Q is waiting for you." Madam Yok shooed me away with a wave.

I nodded to her and left, heading to the bar where I would work from now on.

"Good luck, Q," Madam Yok muttered to herself.

I needed to find a job and make money right away—I couldn't afford to waste any time. I was in over my head, and I didn't have time to wonder why everything had turned out this way. This could just be a big misunderstanding. It was possible that the people who trashed Madam Yok's place weren't Kinn's men, but those thugs I'd pissed off the first night.

My first shift at Mr. Q's bar went without a hitch. Mr. Q's seemed to have more customers compared to Madam Yok's, so working there was exhausting. I also had to learn a completely new routine and adjust to working with a different crew.

Being a newcomer didn't come easily to me. In fact, nothing was easy for me right now. I was depressed. I kept blaming myself, the gods, and even bad karma for all the shit I had been through recently. Nothing seemed to be going my way.

I got distracted by a man and a woman groping each other obnoxiously near the entrance to Tem's apartment, and it made me enter the wrong combination to unlock the door.

The man looked up at me in annoyance and tried to pick a fight with me. "The hell are you looking at?!" he barked.

"Oh, hell!" I swore under my breath. *I didn't want to look at you, asshole! You were feeling that woman up in public—I just happened to be here!*

I stood my ground and glared back at him. The woman pulled the man into their room before we could start a fight.

My life seriously sucked right now. I was only trying to get into my friend's apartment, and some random guy tried to pick a fight with me. I considered asking Tem to visit a temple with me tomorrow to give an offering to a monk. Maybe it'd help get rid of my bad luck.

I finally got inside Tem's place. My life got more demanding with each passing day, and I was totally drained. I tried maneuvering around the room as quietly as possible, figuring Tem would already be asleep. But when I got out of the shower, I saw my best friend standing wide awake in the middle of the room, staring daggers at the wall.

"Did I wake you up?" I asked him, curious.

"It's not you. It's my fucking neighbor!" Tem nodded at the white wall. Through it, I could hear rhythmic thudding and the loud moans of people in the throes of passion. I realized it was the same wall that separated Tem's apartment from that of the couple I saw earlier.

"Earth, can you quiet down?!" Tem shouted at the top of his lungs. "I'm trying to sleep over here!"

Tem hit the wall with his fist, making me jump, but the moans just seemed to get louder. Visibly irritated at this point, Tem stomped over to his balcony. He yanked the glass door open so hard that it crashed into the wall with a loud *bang*. Then, he leaned outside and shouted into the room next door, "If you're gonna fuck, do it quietly, damn it!"

"Sorry, man!"

I was perplexed. I hadn't expected a reply from Earth, the guy next door. I looked at Tem as he slammed the door—now I remembered he had complained to me about this a while ago.

"Is this the guy who likes to have loud sex with women and wakes you up all the time?" I asked, recalling how Tem had said he wanted to move because his next-door neighbor was always making a racket.

Tem went to the kitchen to pour himself a glass of water. "Yeah, that's the one," he said. "It's not only women he sleeps with, though. Sometimes it's men," he said. "I fucking hate the guy. I can't stand him!

Screw you, Earth!" Tem shouted at the wall, sticking up his middle finger. However, his plea went unheard; Earth and his girlfriend were going at it louder than ever.

I figured Tem was having a stroke of bad luck like I was. It would be good for us to visit the temple for once. We really needed some good fortune.

In the car...

"Should I move with you?" Tem asked on the way to the temple. "I'm so fed up with Earth being a dick."

I was not a spiritual person, nor did I believe in karma. However, all my recent misfortune made me rethink my beliefs. Maybe I could even become a monk to escape these problems as a last resort...

"Why don't you turn on some music to drown out the noise?" I asked.

"I'm a light sleeper. Even the faintest sounds wake me up," Tem said, exasperated.

We kept making small talk as Tem drove around the university to an entrance on the other side. We'd remembered there was a temple nearby. We almost reached that entrance when Tem's mobile phone began to ring.

Rrrrring.

"Oh, look! Your *dad* is calling." Tem flashed the screen at me. The caller ID showed Jom's name.

Tem turned the phone on speaker. "What's up, man?! Glad to know you haven't forgotten about us."

"He...help...help me," a faint, feeble voice replied.

Tem slammed hard on the brakes, bringing his car to a screeching halt. He looked at me. We were both equally shocked—Jom sounded like he was in pain.

"Where are you?" Tem asked hurriedly. "Are you hurt?!"

"Help... I'm behind the uni," Jom gasped out, then started coughing.

Tem quickly made a turn and headed in Jom's direction. A horrible feeling washed over me as we searched for him.

"Don't hang up! Tell me where you are!" Tem shouted into the phone as we searched for Jom. We spotted a group of people hovering above a man sprawled helplessly on the sidewalk. Tem put on his hazard lights and stopped his car in the middle of the street.

The crowd moved away when we yelled that we were friends of the fallen man. We dashed toward him and gasped. "Shit! Jom!"

I was horrified at the state Jom was in. He lay on the sidewalk with his head propped haphazardly against a utility pole. Bruises covered his skin, and his white shirt was stained with dirt and footprints.

"Hey, guys," Jom said weakly, trying to give us a smile even though his lips were bloody and one of his eyes was swollen shut. He tried grabbing us as we crouched down next to him.

"What happened to you?!" I asked.

"I dunno... I was buying some grilled meatballs from a snack stall when a guy approached me and asked if I was Jom, a second year in Sports Science. When I said yes, he said Mr. Kinn sent me his regards. Then, he hit me and dragged me into a van. He beat me up until I passed out. When I came to, he beat me again..." It was clearly difficult for Jom to speak. His voice was very raspy, and his breathing was labored.

I clenched my fists and gritted my teeth as I listened to him struggle. Fortunately, he didn't seem to have any critical injuries.

Still, I was pissed at Kinn for beating up my friend, and for hurting Madam Yok. It finally dawned on me that Kinn was pressuring me to work for him by using my friends' safety as a bargaining chip.

I quickly scrolled through my cell phone's call history. I remembered the last two digits of Kinn's number, so it didn't take me long to find it. I pressed the call button; it rang twice before he picked up and greeted me with an icy chuckle.

"Hmm?"

"What the hell did you do to my friend?!" I angrily shouted at Kinn.

"What? I didn't do anything to *your friend*," he said.

"Don't give me that bullshit! You beat up my friend, you dickhead!"

"Oh?! Then it was my mistake. I only wanted my men to say hi to you, *Jom*. I don't know why they would pick on your friend," Kinn replied, his voice overly amused.

"Fuck you! My name is Porsche!" I yelled. "What the hell do you want from me?"

"Oh... Your name is *Porsche*. I get it now—my men went after the wrong guy."

I vibrated with fury. Kinn was laughing like he enjoyed screwing with me. How would he not know by now that my real name was Porsche when he was sending his men after me at Madam Yok's club?

"Stop messing with me and tell me what you want," I snarled.

"Come work for me," he said.

"I. Will. Not!" I angrily stressed each syllable.

"Hmm. By the way, is your little brother called Porchay?" Kinn asked. "I don't want another unfortunate mix-up."

I snapped when I heard him mention Chay. "Leave my brother alone!"

"Well...I'd love to. But just so you know, your brother's high school is very close to my house..."

"Damn you, Kinn! Just tell me what you want!"

"Meet with me."

I hung up and waited for Kinn to send me his location. I was furious with this man. He intentionally threatened Madam Yok to fire me and he terrorized the people around me. He was doing everything in his power to make me bend to his will. I had to endure all this shit just because he wanted me as his bodyguard? *Screw you, Kinn!*

KINN
PORSCHE

5

The Choice

I SAT WITH MY LEGS CROSSED on a large leather sofa, my arms leaning leisurely on the armrest. My eyes were fixed on the dragon carving on the large wooden door as I patiently awaited my guest's arrival—I particularly enjoyed messing with this special guest's head.

"He's here."

Big, my bodyguard, announced his arrival, and moments later, a tall, lean figure appeared at the door. He wore a simple white T-shirt, revealing his prominently tattooed forearm. I couldn't help but take a quick glance.

Porsche looked around nervously before he finally settled on glaring at me.

"Sit!" Big barked at him, pushing him to sit on a sofa opposite me.

The room was dead silent as we glared at each other, each waiting for the other to yield.

"What do you want?" Porsche finally broke the silence. His eyes darted to my bodyguards looming behind him. I had never seen him look so uncertain and afraid before.

"Work for me," I said calmly.

"No!"

Just as I expected, he promptly declined my offer. I chuckled a little. "Hmm? You're more stubborn than I thought."

I looked at the man in front of me. Porsche was aggressive and strong-willed. He always acted tough, like he had something to prove. He was prideful to a fault and would never bow to anyone so quickly. Although I was only in my early twenties, I had been through enough to see right through someone like Porsche. I knew how to handle him.

"Why are you doing this?" he asked.

I smiled at him slightly. "Doing what?"

"Why are you messing with the people around me? Are you doing all this just to get me to work for you?" Porsche demanded. His face remained neutral, but I could feel the anger in his every word.

"Yep," I said.

"You intentionally trashed the club where I work just so I would lose my job," Porsche said. "You hurt my friend, even when you know full well that Jom isn't me!"

"I hurt Jom to teach you not to play games with me," I said with a shrug.

"Leave my friend alone!"

"If I had, would you have come to me willingly?" I sneered, watching his body shake with fury. I knew what made men like him tick, so it was easy to manipulate Porsche to fall into my trap. I couldn't target him directly—he would have fought tooth and nail to resist me. But by targeting the people he loved...I had backed him into a corner, and he had no other choice but to help me.

Don't blame me for playing dirty. I tried negotiating with him politely, but he refused to listen. His bad luck was my good fortune, and it gave me the upper hand. I took no pleasure in it, but a stubborn man like him had to be taught not to screw with someone like me!

"Why me? Why do you want me to work for you so badly?" he asked, still visibly irritated.

I grinned when Porsche glowered at me. "Because I always get what I want," I said.

I spoke the truth. My family was very wealthy, and my father was a formidable man. I'd grown up surrounded by loyal servants and bodyguards who catered to my every whim. I always got what I wanted. The greater the obstacle to my desire, the fiercer I wanted what lay beyond it—just like I wanted Porsche.

"Why should I do what you say?"

"Because I'll make sure you know what happens if you don't."

Porsche exploded. "Who the fuck do you think you are? How can you be so full of yourself?!"

He tried to attack me, but my men quickly surrounded him. Alarmed, his eyes darted between the looming bodyguards, and he reluctantly returned to his seat. Porsche's martial arts skills were admirable, but he couldn't take on ten men simultaneously. He was on my turf now. He stood no chance.

"Porsche." I called his name as I leaned forward, resting my forearms on my knees. "I know you don't like being told what to do. I only want you to work for me because of your exceptional fighting skills. That's all."

"I won't work for you," he stubbornly refused.

I turned to my men. "Leave us," I said. There were some details I wanted to negotiate with Porsche that I'd prefer my other bodyguards not to know about yet. I didn't want them to think I favored Porsche's skills over theirs.

"But Mr. Kinn..." Big started, but he snapped his mouth shut when I glared at him.

"All right, sir..." Big bowed to me before turning to Porsche, pointing a finger at his face in warning. "If you lay a finger on Mr. Kinn, we'll kill you!"

Porsche kicked the sofa beside him in frustration and yelled back at the retreating figure. "Come fight me one-on-one, you coward!"

Big scowled back, but said nothing as he closed the door to leave me alone with Porsche.

"Hmm... Your bravery is impressive." I smiled and shook my head at him. He was behind enemy lines, but showed no sign of backing down.

"Allow me to repeat myself: I want you to work for me. You may also ask for compensation." I made another offer. With how financially minded he was, I knew I could persuade him if cash was on the table.

"...I want a million a month," Porsche said. "Can you afford that?"

I looked at him in disdain and sighed. I knew he was only saying it to provoke me. "That isn't funny," I said. "Be more realistic."

"I am being realistic! If you want me to work for you, you've gotta pay me one million a month. It's like a soccer team buying a new player for ten million baht, yeah?" Porsche's tense demeanor completely relaxed when discussing money. Did he think he had the upper hand now?

"You are not a soccer player," I reminded him. "Did you think you could work for me for a month, get paid a million baht—which happens to be what you need to repurchase your house—and then quit?"

Porsche tried to stay calm, but his face betrayed him. He seemed surprised that I could read him so easily. *He should know better than to try tricking me again!*

"Then I won't do it!" Porsche exclaimed.

"How long would it take to save up enough money to repurchase your house from me? You're a bartender making minimum wage, after all. Ten...maybe forty years, I figure?" I said triumphantly.

"I'd have done it my way!" Porsche butted in.

"Fine." I pulled out my cell and called Boy, one of my men I had scouting Porsche's new workplace. *Don't you realize I know where you work now?*

I stared at Porsche's confused face. "Do it," I said into the phone.

"What are you doing?" Porsche asked.

"Wait and see," I said, getting up from the couch.

I walked over to the shelf where I kept my coffee maker and leisurely pressed a button to brew a cup. The room was quiet now. I glanced between the clock on the wall and Porsche, my lips curling up slightly when I noticed him fumbling with his phone.

Rrring!

Porsche's phone rang. He quickly answered, "Yes, Mr. Q?" before a deafening shout exploded from the speaker.

"You're fired!"

Porsche stared at his phone in disbelief for a moment, and then he leapt up from the sofa. I smirked at him as he stood there, his body quivering with rage and his eyes glaring daggers at me.

"Screw you!" he yelled.

He hurled his phone at me, catching me off guard. The unforgivingly hard object hit me squarely on the temple. It had broken the skin—my anger intensified as I felt the warmth of blood beginning to seep from my forehead. I closed the distance between us without hesitation, one of my hands instinctively making its way to his neck as I forced him against the wall with a resounding *thud.*

Despite his attempts to shake me off, I managed to pin him down with the sudden surge of adrenaline that accompanied my rage.

"H-hey?!" Porsche yelled. He'd slipped—not because he was weaker than me, but because I managed to catch him by surprise.

"I tried being nice to you!" I hissed. My eyes only saw red as I continued to crush his neck. Porsche began to look terrified. When he stopped resisting, I eased my grip but did not release him. Porsche coughed.

"I wouldn't be this angry if you hadn't tried to play me," I said.

"I...did...nothing..." Porsche struggled to speak, his voice hoarse.

I gave him the list: "You told me your name was Jom. You avoided me when I only tried to be civil with you. You *bit* me." I swore I hadn't wanted it to end like this, but I was fed up with him trying to play games with me when I looked for him at the university and the club where he worked. He also bit my neck when I hadn't done anything to him yet.

"*Tsk!* You deserved it! And...don't think you can make me your little underling!"

Porsche spat in my face. That was the last straw. I roared, shoving him against the wall again as I felt his saliva dripping down my cheek. I wiped it away with the back of my hand as I choked him. I couldn't care less if I strangled him to death.

"No one dares disrespect me like this!" I growled through gritted teeth. My grip around his neck tightened as I nearly wrung the life out of him.

"Mr. Kinn! Mr. Kinn, stop!"

I didn't notice people had rushed into the room until I felt P'Chan attempting to pry my hand from Porsche's neck. A few other bodyguards surrounded me, trying to get me to back down.

I finally let go and Porsche crumpled into a helpless pile on the ground, gasping for air like a fish out of water.

"What on earth do you think you're doing?!" my father shouted at me from the doorway.

I shook off the men holding me, looking anywhere but at my father.

"You all right?" I heard P'Chan quietly ask my nemesis as he helped him onto the sofa.

"I told you to bring him here to be your bodyguard, not to kill him!" my father said, exasperated. "Go outside and take a breather. I'll handle this."

PORSCHE

I TOOK SEVERAL DEEP BREATHS, still shaken by what happened. The way Kinn glared at me with such animosity terrified me like never before. His menacing stare made me feel like Death himself had come for me. I was paralyzed, standing frozen as time came to a standstill. This Kinn was not the same man I'd met a few days ago...

Someone helped me get back up and sit on the sofa. I touched my neck as the dread finally faded and was replaced by intense pain. It felt like I was drowning when Kinn choked me. Each breath I took now was a painful struggle for air.

"I don't know what is going on between you and Kinn, but let me apologize on his behalf," the older man said, his voice deep and authoritative.

I looked at the man sitting in front of me. He seemed to be in his fifties, and he exuded an air of power and sophistication. My oxygen-deprived brain still strained to comprehend the situation, so I remained quiet.

Another man in a crisp black suit politely put a glass of cold water in front of me. "Have a drink," he said.

I gladly took a sip—my throat was raw from all the coughing. I closed my eyes slightly, letting the cool water soothe the soreness in my throat.

"I hear you do not want to work for me," the older man said.

I opened my eyes to look at him again. With his confident posture and manner of speech, there was no mistaking that this man was Kinn's father.

"Yes," I croaked my reply.

"Why?"

"I...did not want to risk my life. And...I want nothing to do with him," I said. What Kinn had done inspired such hatred in me that I couldn't even bear the thought of him.

"Your life has been in danger since the day you decided to help my son," he said, observing me calmly. "Did you think those men would leave you alone? They could have done much worse to you than what my son did."

"What do you mean?" I asked. I still couldn't see why I had to risk my life for someone like Kinn. Kinn had fucked up my life, and it pissed me off.

"They will not let someone who can go head-to-head with the nation's most elite fighters fall into the hands of their enemy."

I didn't know who that *someone* was or who *they* were. But I knew Kinn's father was trying to persuade me to work for him.

"No... No way. I still won't do it," I repeated.

"I hear Thee is your uncle?"

I stayed silent.

"His life will be spared if you accept my offer," Kinn's father said.

"I don't care what happens to him," I said. I no longer wanted anything to do with the man I used to call my uncle. Offering to ensure his safety had no effect on me. *You can forget about it,* I thought.

"I figured his useless life means nothing to you," he chuckled, relaxing on the couch.

Kinn's father had reminded me that Uncle Thee was yet another reason my life was so screwed up!

"I'm leaving... Tell Kinn to stop harassing the people around me," I stressed, standing up to leave. However, the ensuing response from Kinn's father stopped me in my tracks.

"If it isn't Kinn, someone else will continue to harass you regardless. You might fare even worse... You have a little brother, yes?"

"Leave my brother alone!" I hissed, glaring furiously at the older man.

"Oh, I wouldn't do something like that," he said with a laugh. The way Kinn's father chuckled reminded me so much of Kinn, and I was pretty sure that my hunch was correct.

"Take my offer, and I'll pay you fifty thousand baht per month. That will be enough for you and your brother to live comfortably, right? Or do you want him to struggle?"

There was a clear threat in his words, contradicting the softness in his eyes as he looked at me. I was at a loss for what to do.

"I don't want to take your offer because I don't want my brother to suffer," I finally confessed. I had already brought enough suffering down on the people around me.

"With your skills, you would not die so easily," Kinn's father said. "I suggest you focus on providing a better life for your little brother rather than dwelling upon your fear of being killed. Additionally, if you accept my offer, I assure you that I will take excellent care of your brother. You won't have to worry about his safety or his school tuition any longer."

I still couldn't grasp why Kinn's father would do so much just to get me to work for his son. Were my fighting and self-defense skills really that remarkable?

"I am proposing this offer because I require your talents," he said. "Is it not enough? Is there anything else you want?" He gestured with his arms open, suggesting he would consider any request I made.

"My house," I said. "I want my parents' house back."

I knew what I wanted was impossible. I did not expect Kinn's father to even consider it. To my utter shock, he said, "All right. I will return the house to you."

I could not believe this intimidating man would accept my outrageous demand. I wasn't sure whether it was delusional to think that Kinn's father was merciful—it certainly was contrary to his ruthless appearance.

"Anything else?" he asked.

"My compensation. I want...one hundred thousand a month," I pushed, trying to see if I could ask for anything. I was totally unaware his persuasive tactics were starting to sway me.

"Whoa, that's a bit much!" he said, bemused. "How about eighty thousand?"

I pursed my lips together. The pressure and worry began to melt away, leaving only the sensation of comfort and relief. This man reminded me so much of my own father: the way he talked, the way he looked at me, the way I felt in his presence.

An image of my father and Porchay, my little brother, suddenly crossed my mind. I was reminded of my parents' funeral—I'd made a solemn vow at my father's grave to look after my brother the best I could. But now? I couldn't even save our house!

The generous offer Kinn's father had made already made me reconsider my initial decision. However, when I looked at Big—Kinn's bodyguard who'd threatened me earlier—I came up with another condition I wanted from this arrangement.

"I get to be their leader," I said.

Big's jaw dropped open. He was about to say something, but a piercing gaze from Kinn's father silenced him instantly.

"Ha ha! That was my intention," the older man laughed.

I smirked as Big stood flabbergasted, his body trembling with anger. That was a small victory.

"I won't wear that stupid suit, either!" I said. "I'll wear my normal clothes."

Kinn's father burst out laughing. "Did you think you were going to be a bodyguard, or a CEO? Ha! I like this man!"

I felt more relaxed around him, so I prodded further. "Well? Can I?"

"Fine! But only at home, all right? Do me a favor and wear a suit when you go outside with my son. Otherwise, it'd look unprofessional."

"Uhh..."

"Is that all?" he asked.

I suddenly remembered something: he wanted me to be *Kinn's* bodyguard, right?

"What if Kinn kills me?" I asked.

"I won't let him do that," he promised.

"How do I know you really mean it? That my brother will be safe, and you'll return the ownership of my parents' house to me?" I asked.

"Hmph! You should already know who I am," Kinn's father said. "I have been in this business long enough to know better than to risk my reputation over such trivial matters. I'm a man of my word."

He did not sound like he was simply bragging. His words reassured me, and I could not find any further reason to decline his offer as I had initially intended.

"If ensuring the safety and well-being of your brother means putting your life at risk, as appears to be the case now, then consider accepting my offer. I've already accepted your conditions, and I have never been this generous with anyone else."

"...I'll think about it," I told him.

I needed more time to carefully consider everything. Admittedly, I was already inclined to accept his offer. However, my mind kept flashing between the image of my brother being happy in the future and the memory of him in tears these past few days. Without a doubt, this was a tough decision to make.

"When can you give me the answer?" Kinn's father asked.

I paused as another thought arose. Although I no longer wanted to consider Uncle Thee as part of my family, he was still someone my dad had cared for very much.

"I want to ask for one more thing," I said, and waited for him to nod before I continued. "If I accept your offer, please spare my uncle his life and extend his payment term."

"As you wish."

"Then, tomorrow... I'll give you my answer tomorrow," I said.

After our negotiations, I rode my motorcycle back to Tem's apartment. I kept mulling over the decision I had to make. It was a critical choice; my entire life would hinge on this. If I accepted the offer to be Kinn's bodyguard, my brother would be taken care of, and my uncle's life would be spared. Otherwise, I needed to find a new job to repurchase my house. I would also sever ties with my uncle. Our lives would be difficult, but at least my brother and I would have peace of mind...

Which option should I choose?

[A CONVERSATION BETWEEN BOSS KORN AND CHAN]

"Why did you agree to all of his requests? Isn't it a bit too much? We should just let him go. He's not the only good fighter out there."

"I did consider that. I didn't want to waste my time with such a nuisance."

"Then why...?"

"Because I know who his father was..."

KINN
PORSCHE

6

Right or Wrong?

PORSCHE

I LOOKED AT THE DOCUMENT in front of me, my eyes poring over every line under the scrutinizing gaze of the judicious man I'd first met yesterday. Another tall figure sat opposite me with his arms crossed over his chest, turning his sulking face away from me: Kinn. His arrogant attitude irritated me so much that I wanted to grab the vase from the table in front of me and smash it over his head.

I finally gave in to Kinn's father and accepted his offer—he was very persuasive. He was eloquent and respectable, and I could tell he was an exceptional businessman. Mr. Korn—Kinn's father—understood precisely how to buy my cooperation. So here I was, back in the same house as yesterday.

Their house was enormous, with luxurious decor adorning every space and men in black suits constantly buzzing about. I'd realized my initial assumption about Kinn was far off the mark. I'd originally assumed his family was a run-of-the-mill gang that just owned a gambling house or some sports betting sites, but from what I was seeing now, they were probably big-time casino owners or even international arms dealers.

"If you agree with everything, just sign here," Mr. Korn said.

Just thinking about what I was about to do made me queasy. I looked over the contract one more time. It was very thorough—it even specified who my beneficiary would be in the event of my death. The contract also covered the terms and conditions: the times I could access this house and the times I could leave it, security measures for checking weapons, and the contract's duration.

The current contract specified that I must work for at least one year. There would be a penalty fee of two hundred thousand baht for a premature termination of the contract. I was entitled to two days' leave per month, and I could work any day of the week as long as it added up to five days a week in total.

The work schedule was the part that I had a problem with.

"About my work schedule... I'm currently a university student, so I can't fulfill this arrangement," I said calmly, pointing my pen to the relevant section of the contract.

"That's not a problem. You can work night shifts."

"I can choose the time?" I asked.

"The bodyguards here work around the clock. The morning shift is six a.m. to six p.m., and the night shift is six p.m. to six a.m.," explained P'Chan, Mr. Korn's secretary.

Damn! Was this a bodyguard job or a convenience store gig? I hadn't realized this work would be in twelve-hour shifts. It was absurd to think Kinn needed a bodyguard around the clock. Was someone gonna break into this place at night to assassinate him in his sleep?

"If I work nights and go to classes during the day, when will I sleep?" I said, matter-of-fact. I was only human—I needed time to rest!

"So fucking fussy," Kinn spat.

I glared at him. He thought it was that easy? *Show me how you do it, asshole!*

"Kinn said you were a bartender, yes?" Mr. Korn asked.

"I worked only from seven at night to two in the morning. I got to go home and sleep before class the next day," I explained. Madam Yok's place was never overly busy, and we usually closed up around two. Not to mention I only worked there from Thursday to Sunday. The rest of the week, I got to relax at home.

"When do you usually have a full day of class?" Mr. Korn asked.

"Monday to Wednesday. On Thursday and Friday, I only have class in the afternoon." I answered Mr. Korn politely, because I felt a bit intimidated by him. I was telling the truth, though. Tem was the one who'd registered me for all my classes. He said I should rest on the weekends, so he made me take most of my courses from Monday to Wednesday.

"Then you can work from Thursday to Sunday."

"Father..." Kinn looked at his father with slight disapproval. "You don't need to cater to him."

When Kinn turned and shot me a hostile look, I stared straight back at him.

"Just listen to me first," said Mr. Korn. "You can work Thursday to Sunday. But I want you to work from ten a.m. to midnight on the weekends to make up for the lost time."

I contemplated his offer for a moment, trying to figure out if there was a catch. I actually preferred to work nights, since it ought to be less of a hassle. Kinn wouldn't be out and about at night that often, right?

"Still need to think on it? I'm already willing to pay you handsomely, considering I'm on the losing end of our bargain."

"What exactly do I need to do as a bodyguard?" I asked. I still couldn't see what was expected of me after reading through the contract. Did they want me to follow Kinn around and give anyone who dared to get close to him a menacing look? Did I just need to tag along, no matter where he went?

"You need to be with him at all times to make sure no one can harm him," Korn's secretary explained. "You may need to assist him at home once in a while."

I furrowed my brows in confusion. "Assist him? How?"

"Help him look through work documents, make sure he eats, help him get dressed, help him with his university assignments, fetch him what he wants, that sort of thing."

"He's still in school? I figured he was ripe for the retirement home," I snickered.

Suddenly, it dawned on me. Although tailing Kinn for protection seemed like a typical bodyguard gig, the rest of my responsibilities made it seem like I was his personal attendant!

"Am I a bodyguard, or a *servant*?" I blurted out before I could stop myself. Mr. Korn chuckled, while his secretary cleared his throat and gave me a disapproving look. I knew I'd said the wrong thing.

"Stop being so demanding!" said Kinn. "Father, just get rid of him. I've had enough."

"Fine! I didn't want to do this in the first place!" I retorted, equally annoyed. I ignored his heated glare and dropped the pen on the contract, then leaned back with my arms crossed over my chest.

"This is giving me a headache," Mr. Korn said with a heavy sigh. "You specifically asked to be Kinn's head bodyguard. Naturally, that comes with more responsibilities."

What is wrong with these mafia people?! Are they a bunch of help-less pissbabies? Why do they need an army of lackeys to wait on them hand and foot? Do I need to wipe Kinn's ass for him, too?!

"It's not that bad. Your main task is to keep Kinn safe and look after him an appropriate amount."

I still couldn't work out how much servitude was *appropriate*. I felt like I was getting tricked into being Kinn's butler. The bodyguard thing seemed like it was actually nothing more than a fancy title.

Silence fell over the room as I sat there, deep in thought. All eyes were on me, awaiting my answer—except for Kinn, who stared so intensely at the wall he looked like he might burn a hole into it.

"Here. Your property and mortgage deeds."

My eyes widened when another secretary sitting at the corner of the table pulled out a thick folder and placed it in front of me.

"Mr. Korn will return the deed to your house after you agree and sign the contract," he said.

I had to admit the deal was tempting. I kept looking back and forth between the mortgage deed and the binding contract. In the end, I gave it one last thought before surrendering. I sighed and picked up the pen I'd dropped earlier to sign my name on the paper. With every stroke of the pen, I told myself I had to be making the right decision.

I looked up after I was finished signing and was met with smiles from Mr. Korn and his secretaries. The older man took the document, finalizing it with his signature before returning everything to me. One thought popped into my head once I had the property deed back in my hands: *if I run away now, will they hunt me down and kill me?*

I was pulled back from my errant thoughts when Mr. Korn plucked the contract from my hands to examine something.

"Pachara... It means diamond, right?" he said, looking from the paper to me. "You have a good name and good facial features."

"What are you, a fortune teller?"

I hadn't meant to rile him up. Still, the indifferent tone of my voice and my blasé manner made it seem like I was trying to provoke him. All eyes turned sharply toward me as if I had done something unforgivable. In reality, I was merely curious.

"Have some manners!" his secretary said, eyeing me with a severe expression. "Mr. Korn is your boss now. Watch your mouth."

What the hell? Were these people so high and mighty that you had to walk on eggshells around them?!

"Hah, forget about it. You can start tomorrow," Mr. Korn said with a chuckle.

"What? Tomorrow? That's so soon," I protested.

"Do you need your father to perform a ribbon-cutting ceremony first or something?" Kinn said, sounding sour.

"Go to hell," I growled under my breath as I locked my eyes with Kinn's.

"Chan, show him to his room," Mr. Korn told his secretary. "Maybe if I relax for a minute this goddamn headache will go away."

With that, Mr. Korn left with Kinn.

I gulped. I was now alone with this man named Chan, who looked several years older than me. He remained silent as he urged me to follow him through the house.

"Umm... Where are you taking me?" I asked P'Chan as I tried to keep up with him, holding the folder containing my property deed at my side. The size of this place was impressive—it featured a magnificent foyer, a spacious dining room, various offices, and a number of mysterious rooms with no discernable purpose. We'd been walking through this house for what felt like an eternity, but there was still no sign of reaching the end.

P'Chan finally stopped and turned to answer me. "I'm taking you to your room," he said.

"What room?"

"The room where you'll stay."

"Is that really necessary? Can't I stay at my place and show up here when I have to work?" I asked. The notion of staying here made me feel even more like a servant. Were these people fucking with me? Was the whole bodyguard gig just an elaborate ruse?

"Every guard here has his own quarters. It means you can head straight to university with Mr. Kinn after your night shift."

I rejected that idea outright. "Huh?! Who said I'd do that?"

"Didn't you go to the same university as Mr. Kinn?"

"Dunno," I replied. I vaguely remembered something about that... Still, I didn't see any reason why I had to go with him.

"Anyway... Just sleep here when you work. Try not to cause any trouble. We don't appreciate nuisances around here," P'Chan said; his tone of voice and the set of his eyes told me he was serious.

If I hadn't been outnumbered here, I wouldn't have put up with being glared at like that. *Hell, was this place a house or a prison? Why were there so many rules?*

"Fine. But I won't stay here on my days off," I grumbled.

"Suit yourself." P'Chan shrugged me off, his indifferent demeanor becoming more irritating by the minute. My frustration built up to the point where I felt like unleashing chaos in this place. Geez!

I would've continued my staring contest with P'Chan if we hadn't been interrupted by someone calling P'Chan's name.

"P'Channn... Where are you going?"

"Master," P'Chan replied, bowing gracefully to a tall, lean man in casual clothes. He smiled broadly as he drew closer. He bore an uncanny resemblance to Kinn, except that this man looked younger—and, quite frankly, friendlier.

"Who's this?" the newcomer asked, pointing in my direction. He looked more cheerful than the solemn bodyguards trailing behind him.

"This is Mr. Kinn's newly appointed head bodyguard," P'Chan replied politely before turning to me. "Porsche, meet Mr. Tankhun, Mr. Kinn's elder brother."

I raised my eyebrows in surprise before scrutinizing the appearance of this man named Tankhun. If no one had told me, I might have mistaken him for the younger brother. It seemed Kinn just looked way older than he really was...

Tankhun rushed to grab my tattooed arm. "Whoa! This is so cool! He even has tattoos! So badass!" he exclaimed in awe. I stood there utterly dumbfounded as he raised my arm, turning it left and right to inspect my tattoo from different angles. *What the hell?*

"Aww, man, this is so dope! I want my guards to get tats, too. It'd make them look handsome as hell!" Tankhun said excitedly. With a serious expression, he turned to his bodyguards. "Hey! All of you, go get tattoos tomorrow. Get one exactly like this. I like it!"

I saw the color drain from his bodyguards' faces at the absurd order. This dude was crazy!

"Master..." P'Chan warned, his voice firm and low. Tankhun released my arm immediately. He muttered something to himself and walked away, his entourage trailing behind him. What the fuck just happened?

"Come on, let's go," P'Chan told me. He let out an audible sigh of exhaustion before continuing to lead the way.

We exited through the back door of the main residence, where we were met by a series of townhouses that served as living quarters for the bodyguards. The structures appeared freshly constructed and well maintained, surrounded by towering trees that provided ample shade. Were these people really that invested in the well-being of their lackeys?

P'Chan unlocked the house at the far end, and I stepped through the door after him. I was surprised by how spacious the place was. It was similar to a student dorm, featuring an attached bathroom, a bed with a metal frame and a simple mattress, and a slightly worn-out dresser. There were no pillows or bedding yet, but what the room did have was an air conditioner!

"I don't believe it," I muttered to myself in amazement. I thought I'd be sleeping in a shabby room with just a blanket, a pillow, and an old standing fan, like something out of a movie.

I put the folder containing the deed to my house on the mattress before continuing to check out the place.

"You're lucky that the previous owner installed an air conditioner," P'Chan added.

"Where is he now?" I asked.

"Dead."

His answer shocked me. I studied his face, trying to work out if he was joking, but he remained indifferent. Shit! Did he really expect me to sleep in a room that belonged to a dead man? I swallowed hard, a slight chill creeping down my spine. I was afraid of ghosts.

I attempted to ignore what P'Chan had just told me. The room didn't seem haunted. *Fuck it,* I thought, *I can sleep here.* I wouldn't be staying overnight that often anyway.

P'Chan tossed the key for the room on the table and signaled for me to follow him back outside.

"Big!" P'Chan yelled, scowling. Big grudgingly made his way over to us. I wondered if anyone working here ever felt happy. They all seemed perpetually sullen, as if someone was constantly hurling shit their way. Maybe there was a rule banning bodyguards from smiling.

"Yes, P'Chan?" Big asked. He glanced at me as he waited to see what P'Chan wanted from him. His attitude pissed me off—he threatened me with the same shitty demeanor yesterday. *Hmph! Just wait, it's your turn next!*

"I want you to show Porsche around. Get him familiarized with the place. I'll go check on the boss..."

"I ain't interested. Go bother someone else," Big blatantly refused, sneering at me. I snorted in response. I understood why he hated my guts—I did just take over his job.

"This guy is my subordinate, right?" I casually remarked, prompting a glower from Big.

"Yes! This is Big, one of Mr. Kinn's trusted bodyguards. You should really get to know each other. How about I leave you two alone for some bonding time?" P'Chan said with a touch of sarcasm, before making a swift exit.

I stood there smirking contentedly with my arms folded confidently over my chest. Big glared back at me, his tenacious gaze unwavering.

"What the hell are you staring at?" he snapped.

I maintained my smirk, offering no response.

"Don't assume we'll accept you as our leader just because it's what Mr. Korn wants!" he declared, striding forward until he was a hair's breadth away from my face, but I stood my ground and stared at him. "We won't submit to the likes of you. Don't get too cocky!"

"Pfft! What's your point?" I scoffed.

"You're not welcome here!"

"Yet here I am," I shrugged, well aware that my nonchalant attitude would only piss him off more.

"I know that you will never be loyal. Sooner or later, you're gonna betray my boss. Rest assured, I'll make sure to get rid of you before then!"

"Oh, I'd love to see you try..." I leaned forward, my tone dripping with mockery, "...and fail!"

I saw his body tremble with anger, his hand clenching into a fist. I scoffed at him. Maybe he'd forgotten that his boss wanted me to work for him so badly that he'd turned over every rock to find me. I couldn't be knocked down that easily.

I deftly evaded the incoming punch. The momentum of Big's swing sent him off-balance, and he stumbled forward in frustration. He roared and tried to hit me again. Seizing the opportunity, I raised my foot to deliver a powerful kick to his gut, sending him skidding backward until he collided with the wall. I crushed my foot against his chest, preventing him from making any further moves.

"Screw you!" Big yelled.

"No wonder Kinn needs a new head bodyguard," I said. "You're pretty mediocre."

Big managed to break free from my grasp and tried to lunge for me again, but I swiftly blocked his punch and twisted his arms behind his back, forcing him down. I kept him firmly pinned to the ground with my knee as he thrashed and swore loudly. With my free hand, I leisurely retrieved a cigarette from my jean pocket, lit it up, and indulged in a long drag.

Big kept shouting curses at me. "Damn it, get off me! Just wait until I break free. I'll kill you!"

"Please, go ahead and try," I scoffed, casually enjoying my cigarette until it burned out. I flicked it to the ground, stubbing it out with my foot and standing back from Big. I was ready to walk away, thinking I had taught him a lesson. I couldn't have been more wrong.

The sound of rapidly approaching footsteps from behind me caught my attention. I ducked quickly as a whooshing sound went past my ears. Big staggered forward, brandishing a thick piece of wood. Apparently, some lessons were hard to learn.

I sent him stumbling to the floor with a forceful kick, following it with a punch that left his mouth bloody. I straddled him, unleashing a barrage of blows with no intention of relenting. I'd been planning to let him off the hook, but it looked like we were past that point.

I was blinded by rage—I would have killed him if someone hadn't stopped me. Chaos erupted as forceful hands tried to pry me off of Big, whose face was now swollen and bruised.

"Stop! What the hell is going on?!"

The bodyguards who'd witnessed the entire incident were shouting in my direction. A few of them rushed to intervene, separating me from Big before dragging us to another location.

They swung open a large wooden door and forcefully ushered us into the room. There was no need to guess whose room it was. I saw a familiar imposing figure lounging on the sofa, engrossed in his TV.

"These two got in a scuffle, sir," one of the bodyguards reported. I wrenched free and shot Kinn a piercing glare. He glanced at us with indifference before returning his attention to whatever show he was watching.

"Mr. Kinn, he picked a fight with me..."

My head snapped toward Big as he fumbled for words. It wasn't surprising to discover that he wasn't just a sore loser, but a snitch to boot.

"Causing problems before you even start?" Kinn asked under his breath, not even bothering to look at us.

"Coward," I muttered directly to Big, whose face contorted in agony as he clutched his stomach. What kind of man tried to shift the blame by pointing his finger at someone else?

"Go to hell!" Big snapped back.

"Put a lid on it. You never know when you might need that extra energy," I jeered.

Clang!

The noise of Kinn flinging his remote control at the coffee table made me jump. My hands rested lightly on my hips as I watched him stand up and approach. His steely gaze reminded me of yesterday, when he'd stared me down and squeezed his hand tightly around my neck. I averted my eyes. I could admit to myself that I was afraid of him. His intense gaze seemed like it could overwhelm me.

"We don't tolerate disruption here...and this is no place for you to be a show-off."

"I wasn't showing off! Your guy started it."

Kinn looked skeptically between the two of us—Big was disheveled, while I was completely unruffled.

"Do you know what I'll do if you disregard my warning?" he said, his voice cold.

I gulped, unease settling in as his eyes darted to my neck. The fingerprint bruises he'd left and the lingering pain there served as a stark reminder of what had happened yesterday. I maintained a stoic silence.

"Don't forget who I am," Kinn said. "You should know to speak to me with respect—"

"Why should I?" I shot back. "I'll speak to you however I like!"

Kinn took a step forward, and I instinctively retreated. "I'm warning you!" he grunted.

"Why don't you just fire me, then?" I retorted. Despite my fear of Kinn, my sharp tongue managed to get the better of me.

"Nah...I won't let you go that easily. You'll work for me..." Kinn said, closing the distance between us until our faces were mere inches apart, "...until I'm thoroughly satisfied."

I turned my face away so Kinn wouldn't notice my nervousness. "What are you going to do?" I asked.

"Get here on time tomorrow," Kinn said, smirking.

I struggled to swallow the lump in my throat as I watched him saunter away. "Screw you!" I muttered under my breath at his retreating figure.

Damn it! I despised his arrogance. I hated how he looked down on everyone. Unable to endure the oppressive atmosphere any longer, I stormed out.

Had I made the right decision?

I went back to my quarters for my property deed before rushing to my motorcycle parked next to the house. Hopping on my bike, I sped off to fetch Chay from his friend's place. There was another challenge I had to face today: I had to figure out how to tell my younger brother how I managed to get our house back.

As we stepped into our home, Chay asked me right on cue: "Hia, how did you get our house back?"

"Um, well... I borrowed some money from Madam Yok, Tem, and Jom," I lied, not ready to tell him the truth just yet. I knew he'd pitch a fit if he knew.

I flicked on the light and proceeded to tidy up the things scattered all over the floor. I hadn't returned to our place since the incident that night.

"Hia," Chay grumbled, his voice low and full of caution. He stared at me with his arms folded over his chest, attempting to get my attention.

"What?" I responded, still making a big show of cleaning up, putting everything back in its place. I had a hunch that my brother might have seen right through me...

"The two of us are all we have..." Chay started.

I sighed in defeat. I waited for him to continue, focusing on tidying up our living room.

"You and I are close," he said. "You know I can tell when you're lying to me."

I closed my eyes, taking a deep, calming breath before turning to face him. My gaze met Chay's as I attempted to conjure up an explanation for my decision that wouldn't upset him.

"You did it, didn't you?" Chay's voice quavered, a look of disappointment sweeping across his face. "You took their offer."

"Yeah," I mumbled, confirming his suspicions.

"Why would you do that?!" he shouted, his hands abruptly gripping my arms and squeezing them tightly.

"Chay... Everything I did was for you."

"If that was true, then you would've listened to what I said!"

The sight of tears welling in Chay's eyes, his trembling lips pressed together, shattered my heart. I felt so ashamed that I'd let my brother down.

"Listen! We are all we have. What will I do if something happens to you?" Chay's voice softened, tears finally trickling down his face.

A weight settled in my chest as I listened to him, burning my heart with guilt. My brother, the person I cared for the most in this world, was distraught because of me.

"I'm sorry... I promise you I'll be okay," I whispered, attempting to place my hand on Chay's head in tender reassurance.

My brother swiped my hand away. "I'll be so angry if anything happens to you... I won't forgive you, and..."

I pulled Chay into a tight embrace before he could finish speaking. He'd never shown this kind of vulnerability to me before. While we didn't really express our affection openly with each other, we both understood how much we cared for each other. After all, we were all we had in this world.

"I swear I'll be okay," I said. "I won't die that easily."

His fist struck my back with a resounding *thud*. His other hand clutched my shirt tightly. "Don't do it," he sobbed. "Please..."

I avoided his eyes, struggling to conceal my emotions. I didn't want my younger brother to see that I felt just as torn up inside as he did.

"Chay...I'll never leave you. Trust me. Please?" I hugged him tighter, desperately hoping that my brother could hear the sincerity in my words. I wouldn't let anything take me away from him. I would always remain by his side.

A silence enveloped us, and I continued embracing my brother until I felt a light nudge from him. Chay looked up at me, his eyes puffy and tinged with red—a sad sight on my beloved brother.

"You really have to do it, then?" he asked.

"Yeah..."

"If you die, I'll dig you up just to tell you off again. I won't burn any offerings for you. You'll go hungry in the afterlife, and your spirit won't be able to move on..."

A smile crept across my lips as I listened to my younger brother sternly threaten me.

"I know," I replied. "Mom always said that I have strong luck— I won't go down that easily. You don't need to worry. I'll stick around, working and making money for you to burn until you're sick of me." I tried to crack a joke to lighten the situation, playfully ruffling my brother's hair. Despite his persistent pout, I could sense that he wasn't upset anymore.

"You swear?"

"Yep!"

"Then...can I snag some money for online gaming?"

"Geez! You little shit!" I snorted, gently jostling his head out of fondness.

I really appreciated him joking back at me even as his face still shone with tears. I pledged not to let anything harm me and to never cause my brother pain again. I promised I would do anything, no matter how challenging, to ensure Chay's happiness. I would not give up, and I would not die!

[THURSDAY]

I let out a sigh. I was beginning to second-guess my decision to take this job. After finishing class for the afternoon, I got on my bike and headed to the grand residence I'd visited two days in a row now. It seemed I would be a frequent guest here from now on.

I rode around the premises at least three times, trying to work up the nerve to face Kinn.

I knew the path ahead would not be easy.

I still couldn't decide...had I made the right or wrong decision?!

7

First Day

I SPENT A CONSIDERABLE AMOUNT of time lamenting the tragic loss of my freedom before I finally approached the massive golden gate. The security guard checked my name in the log before directing me to the employee garage nestled along the perimeter of the property. I sighed wearily at the sight of all the men in sleek black suits scattered around the area. I began to contemplate the nature of Kinn's family business. Why did they need this small legion of bodyguards? It seemed, to say the least, kind of over the top.

Being the only guy wearing a university uniform amidst a flock of black suits made me stick out like a sore thumb. I glanced at them and, feigning disinterest in their obvious hostility toward me, strolled forward to the main building.

"Ah, you've finally arrived," P'Chan greeted me as I entered. Balancing a set of documents in one hand and cradling a steaming mug of coffee in the other, he inclined his head, gesturing for me to follow him to one of the rooms. I looked around cautiously, still adjusting to the unsettling atmosphere of this place.

"Come in."

I followed him into what appeared to be a meeting room, complete with a meticulously arranged array of desks, chairs, and a projector.

"Mind your manners with your superior," P'Chan reminded me as he arranged some boxes on the desk.

"Hello...sir," I said, promptly putting my palms together and bowing[7] slightly. I had forgotten how to act appropriately; I was nervous as hell and I wasn't used to this kind of work environment.

"So...you got into a fight with Big yesterday?" P'Chan asked.

"He initiated it," I replied truthfully.

"Try to keep your nose out of trouble, will you? Go with the flow. Don't aggravate Mr. Kinn."

I frowned at P'Chan's words. Was Kinn some all-powerful god not to be provoked by mere mortals?

"Sit," the older man said when I didn't reply to him, gesturing at a chair with his hand. "Here are your knives and firearms. Carry them when you accompany Mr. Kinn. You do know how to use a gun, yes?"

I nodded. In my youth, I'd had a fondness for toy guns. Shooting had eventually become my favorite pastime alongside judo.

"Good... Remember, you must keep Mr. Kinn safe at all costs," P'Chan said, sliding the black box containing the weapons toward me.

"Am I gonna end up in jail if I unintentionally kill someone?" I asked bluntly. He'd just handed me a gun like it was a piece of candy. I wanted to know if Kinn would shield me from legal consequences if I killed someone for him.

"Everything this family does is above the law," P'Chan replied.

Did that mean Mr. Korn had the cops in his pocket? Damn, that man was the real deal. Now I *really* wanted to know what he did for a living. Being like him someday seemed like a worthy goal.

"Could you tell me who it is exactly I'm meant to protect Kinn from?" I asked.

---

7   The act of putting your palms together in a prayer position and slightly bowing your head is called "wai." The wai is commonly used in Thai culture to greet others, especially when showing respect to elders and those in higher social positions.

"Anyone who wishes him harm..."

Well, that probably includes me, I chuckled inwardly.

"There are many individuals who pose a threat to Mr. Kinn—those who owe him money, his rivals...even his business partners," P'Chan continued, nonchalantly reading the document in his hand as he sipped his coffee.

At this point, I found myself genuinely intrigued by Kinn's family. Why did they need such stringent security? They didn't exactly appear to be good people—law-abiding citizens didn't tend to accumulate so many enemies with deadly agendas.

"Mr. Korn's family controls various businesses, such as casinos, moneylending, arms trade, and port operations," P'Chan explained as if he had read my mind. *What a know-it-all,* I thought—then wondered if he could read that thought, too.

"Stop staring at me," P'Chan said. "Mr. Kinn has returned from his university classes. You should go to him."

Reluctantly, I nodded and stood up, taking the case of weapons with me.

"Where's that dude's room, anyway?" I asked as I headed out. I got a disapproving glare in response.

"Mr. Kinn is not your friend," P'Chan stated firmly.

I rolled my eyes at his pedantic response. P'Chan behaved as if Kinn was royalty, and we, his obedient servants, had to worship the ground he walked on. Didn't they realize that King Rama V abolished slavery in Thailand over a century ago?

"So, where do I need to go?" I reiterated, careful not to mention Kinn this time.

"Second floor, last room on the left. And let me be clear: if you try to pull any tricks—or even *think* about betraying him—the consequence is death!"

I knew he was just trying to intimidate me, but I still felt a bit nervous. These people seemed to have no compassion; they treated other people like mere pawns in a game. P'Chan in particular was incredibly stoic, as if emotions were a foreign concept to him.

I followed P'Chan's directions, clutching the case of weapons in my hand. The other bodyguards shot me disapproving looks as I passed by, but I ignored them. I made my way to a room that felt oddly familiar, as if I had been here just yesterday. A bodyguard sitting on a couch in front of Kinn's room glanced up at me as I came to a stop in front of him.

"There you are. Mr. Kinn wants to see you," he said.

I shot a sardonic expression at the three or four men stationed outside Kinn's room, finding their presence somewhat excessive. Hell, this place was as bustling as a busy Likay[8] stage. Something about it was hilarious to me. I had a feeling that things were about to get interesting.

As I reached for the doorknob, the same bodyguard abruptly warned me, "No weapons are allowed in Mr. Kinn's room!"

I wearily rolled my eyes, wondering if anyone else found these rules absurd. "All right, I'll go put it away," I said, retreating from the door, planning to place the case in my room. However, he stopped me again.

"Hold on! Leave it outside. Don't keep Mr. Kinn waiting."

Sighing heavily, I placed the box on the floor beside the door and stepped into Kinn's room.

I paused, observing the people inside. My presence seemed to have caused an abrupt halt to their animated conversation.

"Don't you know how to knock?"

---

8   Likay is a type of Thai folk drama and performance arts equivalent to musicals or operas. Likay troupes usually set up a temporary stage to perform at temple fairs or other events.

The voice was one I recognized well. His expression shifted from joyful to sullen in an instant. I found it odd to see Kinn in his university uniform; I was used to the all-black attire that made it seem like he was constantly in mourning.

Knock, knock.

I knocked on the door twice in an attempt to get under his skin. "Now I know," I said. I looked at the other men in the room. They wore the same university uniform, so I figured these people might be Kinn's friends. They stared at me in confusion.

"Who the heck is this?" one of them asked Kinn.

"My new bodyguard," he replied casually, his gaze fixed on me.

"What?" I asked, crossing my arms over my chest and glaring at him in disregard.

"You sure he's your bodyguard and not your dad?" his friend asked with a snicker. This seemed to make Kinn frown even harder.

"Go get me some refreshments," he said.

Kinn's sudden order left me dumbfounded. I stared at him with a blank expression, not quite comprehending his request. "Refreshments? What refreshments?" I asked.

"He looks confused," one of his friends whispered, loudly enough for me to hear.

"Fetch me refreshments from downstairs!" Kinn repeated, his tone growing more authoritative. I frowned at him. Why did I have to bring him refreshments? I wasn't his fucking servant!

"I'm not your butler!" I blurted out, earning surprised looks from his friends.

"Damn! This one has a spine," one friend exclaimed.

"Porsche! What did I tell you?!" Kinn yelled. Everyone jumped at his raised voice except for me. I took a deep breath, trying to push down my anger.

"Go downstairs and bring me my refreshments!" Kinn ordered again.

"If you want something, go get it yourself!" I replied, cold as ice.

"Porsche!" Kinn sprung from the sofa and reached me in an instant. His hand violently seized my arm, yanking me forward before I could fight back. The intensity of his grip conveyed his seething fury.

"Are you trying to challenge my authority?!" Kinn growled through clenched teeth, his gaze turning as lethally sharp as it had the other day. I firmly shoved at his chest, and he released his hold on me.

"Fine!" I huffed, stomping out of the room with a scowl. Had anyone ever dared to stand up to Kinn, or was he completely spoiled rotten? I wanted to see someone confront him head-on!

And how was I supposed to figure out where to get Kinn his snacks?! I had no idea where the kitchen was. This colossal house might as well be a palace.

The bodyguards I passed were not exactly the friendly and helpful type. Their expressions were constantly sour and sullen. Every time my eyes met theirs, they shot back with murderous glares. As I descended the stairs, I spun halfway around, pointedly searching for the kitchen and thinking about where I should be headed.

"Looking for something?" a man in a black suit asked, his voice neutral.

"A kitchen," I replied.

"Head that way and take a left," he said, indicating the direction with a wave of his hand. I walked away without looking back to gauge his reaction, my irritation reaching boiling point.

The kitchen was exactly where he said it was. Four maids milled about until one of them noticed me.

"How may I help you, mister?" she asked.

I took a deep breath, making an effort to temper my frustration before replying politely. "Some refreshments...please?" This woman was much older than me, and I needed to speak with respect. I didn't want to offend her.

The elderly woman looked at me from head to toe and said, "Are you a friend of Mr. Kinn or Mr. Kim?" Her words were polite, and she had an amiable smile on her face.

"Nah...I'm that guy's...I mean," I corrected myself quickly, "I'm Mr. Kinn's new bodyguard."

The maid gave me another quick once-over. "Oh, Mr. Kinn's new bodyguard?" she asked, her voice curious. "Why haven't you changed into your suit?"

I sighed. "I'm just here to fetch his refreshments, ma'am." I repeated my request, intentionally deflecting her question.

"All right, give me a moment. Are Mr. Kinn's friends here, too?"

I nodded. She returned to hand me a tray loaded with snacks and tea.

"By the way, this plate is for Mr. Tay. Tell him I made it especially for him," she said.

I rolled my eyes, wondering why she wasn't the one bringing this stuff upstairs in the first place. I cursed to myself as I carried the hefty tray back to Kinn and contemplated spitting in his tea. I wanted to get back at him for being an arrogant bastard, but I could only amuse myself with the thought. With this many bodyguards patrolling the area, my actions would absolutely be noticed. They would have immediately shot me in the gut.

"Can you open the door?" I asked the men sitting in front of Kinn's room when I returned, hoping they would help me get inside their boss's room. Everyone seemed to deliberately ignore me and kept reading their magazines.

"Hey!" I called out again. Still no response. *Fine!* I bent down to put down the tray on the floor so I could open the door, but one of them yelled at me.

"What are you doing?!"

"Opening a door," I said sardonically.

"You can't put Mr. Kinn's food on the floor!"

Sheesh! Was Kinn royalty or something? I planned on putting his food on the floor, and I would have nudged the tray around with my shoe, too! I straightened myself up with the tray in hand as one of Kinn's men grumbled, rapping on the door and seeing me in. It turned out these animals had some manners after all.

I saw Kinn and his gang engrossed in a discussion about a school report and decided to step right into their circle. I carelessly dropped the tray on the table, the clatter of it echoing through the room. The tea inside the cups sloshed slightly. Kinn's friends rapidly withdrew their papers from the impending mess and quickly reached for some tissues. All eyes stared at me in disbelief.

"Shit! Did it get on our report?" a member of Kinn's clique inquired.

I scoffed. How would the report get dirty when the mess was only on the tray?

"Porsche!" Kinn hissed, his voice low. His eyes flashed with anger. I looked at him out of the corner of my eye, trying to play it cool.

"Come on, just let it slide," his other friend interjected, guiding Kinn back into his seat with a firm push on his shoulder. A faint smirk played on my lips as I saw Kinn close his eyes, obviously trying to suppress his rising anger. I started to exit the room, figuring my task was completed, when Kinn's voice stopped me:

"Who said you could leave?"

I turned around to glare at him.

"What now?" I grumbled.

"I want coffee," he demanded.

I sighed for what seemed like the millionth time, wondering why he hadn't just asked before and spared me the multiple trips. I turned around again, intending to go fetch his coffee from the kitchen downstairs.

"Where do you think you're going? Didn't you hear what I said?"

"I heard you loud and clear," I replied, turning to face him again. "I was on my way to fetch that coffee for you, Your Highness."

"The coffee machine's over there," he said, gesturing toward a corner of the room where a fancy machine sat next to some coffee mugs. For fuck's sake! This rich bastard had his own personal coffee machine. It seemed like this family knew no hardship—they were surrounded by amenities that catered to their every whim.

I headed toward the counter, staring blankly at the modern machine with its myriad of buttons—utterly clueless about how to use the damned contraption.

"I want a hot americano," Kinn said blandly.

Damn it! How could I make an americano when I didn't even know how to turn this thing on?

"Wanting coffee in the evening, what a pain..." I muttered under my breath as I fiddled with the "ON/OFF" and "START" switches on the machine. I stood there awkwardly with no sign of any coffee appearing. Wondering if I needed to press more buttons, I pushed my finger on the red button labeled "HOT." Still nothing. I tried another button with a coffee mug symbol, which also yielded no results. Perhaps this machine was like a kettle, and you needed to wait for the water to boil before pouring it over coffee grounds...

I stared at the machine for a while, assuming it was in the process of boiling water. Contrary to its hi-tech appearance, the machine turned out to be nothing more than an electric kettle.

In the meantime, I took a moment to survey the room. The interior design mirrored the elegance of the rest of the house. The color scheme was predominately brown. A chandelier hung overhead. There was a sizable work desk, a bookshelf against the wall, and a black sofa in the middle of the room. A centerpiece displayed a bundle of lengthy dried twigs, which looked rather lifeless and stupid.

There was another room attached to this one, roughly the size of a small office. It had a glass door, but the view was obstructed by black curtains. I couldn't figure out the purpose of the room, but the curtain suggested it wasn't a bathroom. A bedroom, maybe? My lips twisted into a sneer, and I felt a pang of jealousy at this family's lavish wealth.

Kinn's room was well furnished, resembling some kind of lavish condo suite. However, the decor had a mature, dull vibe, much like its owner...

"Anyone smell something burning?" someone blurted out.

"Yeah...it's like the smell of burnt metal."

I could smell it too, I realized. I looked in their direction while searching for the source of the acrid odor. Was someone trying to torch this place? They had so many enemies that it seemed plausible.

"Porsche!" Kinn shouted, rushing toward me in alarm.

"What?"

"The fucking coffee machine is on fire!"

I shifted my attention back to the device as a plume of black smoke erupted from it. I'd assumed it was steam from boiling water. I stared with my jaw dropped in shock, at a loss for what to do. A spark flashed near the back of the machine. I was so screwed!

"Damn it, quit standing around! Shut off the power!" Kinn barked at me. He darted out of the room to inform the other bodyguards to turn off the main switch in the breaker box.

Where was the off switch? The smoke was so thick that I couldn't see a damned thing.

"Where the hell is the switch?!" I frantically searched for the power switch while trying to wave away the smoke in front of me. Kinn's three friends were in similar states of panic, running around and shouting chaotically.

"Cough...cough..."

"Time, check on them!" Kinn screamed. "And you! Have you found the switch yet?"

Fucking hell, can't you see I'm as freaked out as you are? The smoke made me cough so violently that I was afraid I might choke to death. I couldn't see which part of the machine was on fire—I didn't know what was making this much smoke.

"Where is the goddamn switch?!" I yelled back at him.

"Shit! Watch out!" Kinn shouted.

Boom!

I heard Kinn yell just before the explosion erupted. I was forcefully pushed to the ground, shielded by Kinn's body. Then, the electricity in the entire house went out.

"Mr. Kinn, are you hurt?" one of the bodyguards asked, rushing inside.

"The breaker has been shut off," another man reported.

A look of relief washed over Kinn's face. He allowed a bodyguard to help him up and guide him to the sofa. I remained where I was, sitting up on the floor. I was still processing what had happened. It had all been so sudden that I was caught totally off guard, unable to react.

"Kinn, are you all right?" his friends asked when they returned, accompanied by more bodyguards who proceeded to open all the windows and doors in the room to air the smoke out.

"Don't just sit there like an idiot. We could use a hand!" someone angrily shouted at me.

I huffed. *Can't you see I'm in shock?!* Nevertheless, I stood up and went to help clear the smoke while the other men unplugged the malfunctioning machine and took it away.

This wasn't my fault! Kinn was the one who ordered me to make the damn coffee in the first place!

After everything settled down, Kinn called me over. He glared at me, his eyes burning with lethal fury. His friends had left, leaving only me and a line of bodyguards behind me.

"Were you trying to burn my house down?" Kinn asked, his voice just as sharp as his gaze.

"I didn't mean to," I replied, sincere.

"We're lucky this place has an emergency shut-off system. Otherwise, it would have burned to the ground," one of the pissed-off bodyguards complained.

Fuck off. Kinn being angry at me was enough. Why did this guy have to butt in?!

"Are you blind? Couldn't you see there was no water in the machine?" Kinn badgered me, still glaring daggers.

"I didn't know. I don't know how to use that thing," I replied.

It turned out that pressing the "HOT" button with no water in the machine caused the heating coil in the back panel to overheat and explode.

"Why didn't you say something?" he pressed.

I rolled my eyes. I hadn't said anything because I assumed it operated like any other kettle! I maintained a blank stare, unwilling to argue any further. Why did my first day here have to turn out so draining?

"You should've asked. Don't be a smartass when you don't know shit!" Kinn cursed.

"Screw you! I'm here to be your bodyguard, not your butler. If you want someone to make you coffee, hire a barista next time," I snapped, no longer able to hold back. My hands rested lightly on my waist as I glared defiantly at him.

"Porsche!" Kinn yelled, slamming his fist on the glass tabletop with a loud *clang* and making all the bodyguards in the background flinch in fear. He pointed at me threateningly. "I've made it clear who I am and who you are. Know your place—and don't ever cross me again!"

I continued to stare at him without voicing any response.

"This is your final warning. If you fuck with me again, there will be consequences!"

I glanced at him disdainfully at his arrogant command, earning a scowl in return.

Knock! Knock!

We were interrupted by a knock at the door and the arrival of one of Kinn's bodyguards.

"Mr. Peem is here," the bodyguard announced, stepping aside to reveal a beautiful man in his twenties. The man smiled pleasantly at Kinn before sitting by his side. It seemed like Kinn had a lot of friends over.

"All of you can leave," Kinn declared.

About time! I'd wanted to get out of here ages ago. I spun around and made a beeline for the door before the other bodyguards even had a chance to react. Sadly, I stopped short when Kinn suddenly called my name: "Porsche, wait!"

What was the matter with this guy?!

"Kom, give him the keys," Kinn told a guy I assumed was Kom, before turning back to me. "You know how to drive, right?"

I nodded scornfully at him.

"Take Mr. Peem back to his house at two a.m.," Kinn continued. "You're dismissed for now."

His order left me with a bunch of questions. Why me? And why at two in the morning? His friend should stay overnight if he was planning to be here that late.

Kom handed me a key fob engraved with the logo of a luxury car brand.

"Where to?" I asked, not knowing where I had to take Mr. Peem later on.

Kinn looked like he was fed up with me, but he showed me the address on his phone.

"Okay," I said, handing the phone back to Kinn and leaving without looking back.

I noticed that Kinn's bodyguards were not eager to converse with me. Perhaps it was because I had kicked their superior's ass yesterday. To think about it, I hadn't seen that guy at all today. Did I really knock his lights out?

With no other plan in mind, I strolled down a dimly lit walk-way, hoping to find a spot to smoke. I recalled seeing the other bodyguards smoking near a garden when I first arrived here in the evening, so that became my destination.

"Hey..."

A man puffing on a cigarette greeted me. I recognized him as the guy who gave me directions to the kitchen earlier. I gave him a small nod as I retrieved a pack of cigarettes from my back pocket. I pulled one out, lit it up, and smoked in silence.

"First day on the job?" he asked with a smile. It was probably the first smile I'd gotten in this house that wasn't hostile.

"Mm-hmm," I answered him with a hum.

"My name's Pete."

"I'm Porsche."

"Cool name! But why the long face?" he asked, lighting up another cigarette as he kept the conversation going.

"I'm tired," I answered truthfully.

"How come?! I heard you're Mr. Kinn's bodyguard. Your job should be easy," he said, blowing out a puff of smoke.

Easy, my ass! I hadn't had time for a breather since I arrived, and it was already midnight.

"What do you mean by *easy*?" I asked him to elaborate.

"Mr. Kinn seems strict, but he's the easiest one to work for," Pete said with a smile.

"Are you shitting me?" I muttered, looking at Pete suspiciously.

"Hah! Don't look at me like that. Trust me, you're lucky," he insisted.

"And who do you work for?" I asked.

"I'm under Mr. Tankhun," Pete said, letting out a heavy sigh.

I recalled meeting Mr. Tankhun yesterday, and he seemed like a friendly guy. "Why the long face?" I fired Pete's question right back at him.

"The three sons in this family are all polar opposites. Especially Mr. Tankhun—he's very demanding. His mood is so unpredictable that I've got a constant migraine working under him. But he's still better than Mr. Kim."

Mr. Kim?

"Who?"

"Mr. Kim! Boss Korn's youngest son! Well, it's not surprising you don't know if it's only your first day. And Mr. Kim is hardly ever home. He's like a missing person," Pete said with a hint of humor.

"What do you mean?"

"Mr. Kim has traumatized everyone. He doesn't like being followed by bodyguards, and he doesn't like coming home. He constantly manipulates his bodyguards and stirs up trouble," Pete explained. "P'Nont is exhausted from looking after Mr. Kim. And P'Nont is the one Boss Korn holds responsible when something goes wrong with his youngest son... Oh, P'Nont is Mr. Kim's head bodyguard."

Ah...so many names to remember. Meeting Pete felt good, though. He felt like a friend; it was like hanging out with Tem and Jom. *At least my life here wouldn't be too depressing.*

"Mr. Kinn is the most reasonable of the three. Everyone wants to work for him."

I scoffed immediately at Pete's words. Kinn? *Reasonable?* It was more likely a buffalo could give birth to a dog.

"I don't believe it," I said.

"Anyway, why aren't you wearing a suit?" Pete asked, eyeing my attire.

"I'm too lazy to change," I replied dismissively, not wanting to explain myself further.

"See? If I wore that in front of Mr. Tankhun, he'd scream my ears off."

Zzzzt!

A buzzing sound came out of nowhere. Pete sighed audibly and picked up his walkie-talkie. "Just listen to this," he said.

"Hey, Pete! Where the hell are you?" A voice came from the two-way radio. "Come up here this instant!"

Pete stubbed out his cigarette on the ground, looking exhausted.
"You've got a radio?" I asked.

"Yeah. Mr. Tankhun gave one to all his bodyguards, and he's been calling us all day! Anyway, I gotta go watch a TV show with him now."

I started to speak, but Pete ran off into the house before I could ask what he meant by watching a TV show. At least I'd met one friendly person in this place, even though we worked for different bosses. He appeared to be around my age, too, and that was somewhat comforting.

It occurred to me that I'd forgotten to ask Pete where the bathroom was. This place was massive—I needed to take a leak, and I didn't want to go all the way back to the one in my room.

"Porsche! Mr. Kinn wants to see you!" one of Kinn's bodyguards said, his expression souring when he found me.

I felt irritated that the bastard kept summoning me. I also needed to pee real bad. Damn it! I was in a jam. Going back to my room would take too much time, and the bodyguard who came to get me didn't wait around for me to ask where the toilet was.

Argh! I scanned my surroundings, desperately hoping to spot a restroom. I hadn't used one since I arrived here earlier in the evening. Nobody had paid me any attention. There was no orientation, and no one cared enough to show me where things were.

I was left with no other choice. I didn't want to show up late and get another reprimand from Kinn. I had to make do with the last option available. I approached the wall on the far side of the garden.

It was pretty dark, with plenty of trees shielding the view. There was a murky pond that I assumed was part of a septic system. The situation was urgent... After all, a man didn't really care where

he pissed, and this spot was right on the border of the property—
it wouldn't bother anyone, right?

I pulled down my pants, relieved myself as quickly as I could, and
hastily ran back into the house.

One of the guards stopped me as I was about to push the door
open. "You don't need to go in."

I turned around, finding him holding out a pile of papers.
"What?" I asked.

"You have to arrange these according to the table of contents.
Then, check Mr. Kinn's class schedule. If there are any papers on his
desk, it's your duty to identify each document accordingly. These are
crucial details that you need to stay on top of," he said. "Additionally,
you need to ensure that his work is accurate and organized. You
need to be prepared to jot down notes for him when he attends to
business matters."

I took the paper from him with a shocked expression.

"Why do *I* have to do it?" I asked.

"You wanted to be his head bodyguard, didn't you? It's your
responsibility," he said, lowering himself onto the sofa.

I looked at the papers in my hand with disdain. Since I got here,
I hadn't done a single thing I'd expected I would be doing. My tasks
were menial and borderline stupid!

I took a seat on the sofa opposite him. There was already a man
occupying it, but the moment my ass touched the seat, he abruptly
stood up and walked away. Jerk! One day, I'd make them pay—each
and every one of them!

These papers appeared to be Kinn's homework. That guy went
to the same university as me, but he was part of the international
program at the Business School, and all the text in his report was in
English. How did he expect me to read it? I knew I was a brute with

no book smarts, and I got accepted into this university by sheer luck. I usually relied on Tem to complete our class reports. I hoped Kinn wouldn't blame me if I screwed up his paper.

[2:00 A.M.]

I kept rearranging Kinn's report until it was time to give his friend a ride home. I didn't know if they were roughhousing or what in Kinn's room, but Mr. Peem looked utterly exhausted.

As soon as Mr. Peem settled into the back seat, he rested his head against the window. He looked like he could doze off at any moment. Though I couldn't get a good look, I thought I saw bruises on Mr. Peem's neck and arms. I couldn't recall whether they had been there before and I just hadn't noticed. Or perhaps he annoyed Kinn, and Kinn had lashed out at him like he did with me. Regardless, it was none of my business.

"Just let me off here," Mr. Peem said, getting out of the car as soon as I stopped at the designated location.

Now that my task was complete, I had the urge to drive around town for a while—I didn't want to go back to that hellhole. However, I could only fantasize about it. I had no idea if there was a GPS tracker in this car, and I didn't want to listen to a lecture from Kinn if he found out I'd taken a joyride. It pissed me off!

I returned to the same old sofa outside Kinn's room, noticing that some of his men were either falling asleep there or playing games on their phones. Kinn was probably asleep, as he was nowhere in sight.

I felt a bit sweaty, and I figured I could use a shower... I waited anxiously for morning to come so I could change out of these clothes. I was beginning to feel exhaustion creep in. However, I resisted the urge to rest, preferring to wait until I was home before I relaxed. I couldn't let my guard down here, in case these guys decided to jump me.

The night seemed to drag on longer and longer, and I just wanted it to end.

Throughout the night, I alternated between sitting down and pacing until morning finally arrived. I didn't wait for anyone to tell me my shift was over, just hurried to my room to stow away my weapons and take a shower. Then, I headed straight to the garage, and I would have run straight home if I hadn't been interrupted by a loud commotion.

"Who pissed in my koi pond?!"

An ear-splitting scream pierced the air, prompting everyone to turn to the source of the outcry. Then, another anguished wail followed:

"No! Elizabeth! Sebastian! Wake up! Wake up!"

I saw a group of bodyguards frantically hurry to the source of the scream. In the midst of all the chaos, I spotted a familiar face and grabbed his arm before he could pass by me. It was Pete.

"What the hell is happening?" I asked him.

"Some jackoff pissed in Mr. Tankhun's koi pond. All the fish are dead! Fuck! What a headache. First thing in the morning, too." Pete cursed vehemently and dashed off.

I swallowed thickly, a chill running down my spine. I deftly mounted my motorcycle and sped away from the scene. I was so screwed!

8

Forgotten

I CLUNG TO THE EDGE of the pool, my brow furrowing as I pondered my dilemma. The feeling of being dragged underwater made me unable to focus on today's test. I was haunted by the thought of the koi I'd killed the night before, uncertain what repercussions awaited me.

Honestly, I was scared. Rather than confronting the looming issue, I contemplated the idea of succumbing to the water and meeting my ultimate demise like those poor fish. Unfortunately, I wouldn't drown quickly—I was a good swimmer. And I wasn't as sensitive as those delicate koi that perished at the slightest change in their environment.

"What's wrong? You've looked tense this entire class," Tem said, swimming toward me. Jom, still nursing his injuries from his recent beating, crouched down beside me at the pool's edge. The instructor had exempted Jom from today's swimming test, permitting him to submit a report for credit instead. Both my friends looked at me in concern.

"Yeah, what's the matter? Your pace was bad. I just saw the instructor deduct points from your score."

I heaved out a sigh, which just confused them more. Expressing emotions was rare for me unless I was stressed beyond my breaking point.

"I'm stressed out," I admitted, pulling myself out of the pool to sit next to Jom.

"Wanna talk?" Tem asked. "Maybe we could help." He glanced at Jom and me as he floated in the water. His orange swimming cap conjured up the image of those koi in my head. Damn it! I wouldn't be this worried if I had killed any other fish—but these had belonged to a mafia member who could easily ensure *I* was sleeping with the fishes.

"What am I supposed to do?" I groaned, wearily scrubbing a palm over my face. Tem and Jom exchanged a startled glance. This was probably the first time either of them had seen me this vulnerable.

"What happened?! What did those mafia fuckers do to you? I'll kick their asses!" Jom snarled.

"Dude!" Tem cut in. "Look what happened to you! Don't get cocky."

"Hey! They caught me by surprise! Let's see what happens one-on-one," Jom huffed. He still bristled every time that incident came up.

I had already explained everything to Jom, and apologized for using his name. He was obviously pissed at me, so I countered by offering to buy him lunch for the entire month. That got me back on his good side.

Both of them knew that I'd started working for the mafia. Tem was totally against it, but I'd explained that it was for Chay and my home, and the offer was too good to pass up. While my friends did not fully agree with my decision, they respected it.

"Tem, can you take off your cap?" I asked. Seeing him swimming around in the pool with that orange thing on his head made me nauseous.

"Why? I picked my lucky color so I'd get a good score on the test," Tem grumbled, but he took off the cap eventually. He hoisted himself up to sit with us. "What's wrong?"

I closed my eyes and confessed: "I killed Elizabeth and Sebastian."

"What the hell, Porsche?!" Jom shouted. "They made you kill people on your first day? We need to call the police! I'm friends with a murderer. A murderer!"

I smacked Jom harshly on the head, never mind that he was already covered in bruises.

"Damn! Do they really treat people's lives like that? You should quit," Tem said, inching away from me. He looked horrified.

"It's someone's life!" Jom kept on shouting.

I had to intervene before things escalated any further. "They're not *people*!" I yelled.

My friends abruptly snapped their mouths shut, waiting for me to clarify.

"They were *fish*!"

A wave of relief washed over their faces, and they scooted closer to me again.

"Phew... That's a relief!" Jom exclaimed. "What kind of fish have names, anyway? What was it again? Eliza-something?"

"Since they have names, I figured they must be adorable!" I said.

I proceeded to recount the entire story to Tem and Jom, and both of them burst out laughing. It wasn't funny to me—I kept on sulking. Frustrated, I considered calling off work today, not ready to face the impending shitstorm. I could already tell an unfortunate fate awaited me.

Tem urged me to quit, warning me that what I feared might be inevitable. But quitting was not an option—I'd already signed a one-year contract. I didn't have the money to pay the premature termination fee!

I got up from the pool and made my way to the locker room. Glancing at my phone, I noticed eight missed calls from Kinn's number. I hadn't even saved it in my contacts yet. A weary sigh escaped me as I contemplated my life choices. I decided to follow my friends' advice and face the consequences; there was no escape for me.

I arrived at six p.m. on the dot. As I removed my helmet, I prayed to the Triple Gem,[9] hoping Buddha would protect me from harm. When I hopped off my bike, some bastard approached me with a scowl.

"Mr. Kinn is summoning you."

I sighed. There was a saying that each sigh was a stolen breath, and too many stolen breaths could shorten a life. At this rate, my life was almost over.

Dragging my feet, I trudged up the stairs to Kinn's room. I looked at the enormous door, mustering my courage before slowly opening it. The room was dead silent when I stepped inside.

Kinn was not alone. His older brother, Tankhun, sat next to him with his arms folded tightly over his chest, glaring at me spitefully. I glanced at Kinn, trying to avoid making eye contact with Tankhun. However, Kinn's heated gaze told me he already knew I was the culprit.

Tankhun cursed loudly when I came to a stop in front of them. "Murderer!" he cried. "Why did you kill my koi?!"

Initially, I'd been planning to confess—I had no idea they'd already figured out I did it. Looking down at my feet, I remained silent and waited for the rest of the reprimand.

Kinn huffed. "Just apologize to Tankhun," he said, his voice neutral. When I remained tight-lipped, not knowing what to say, Kinn arched an eyebrow. "Or are you denying that it was your fault?"

---

9   The Triple Gem, or Ti-ratana, are the core foundations of Buddhism: the Buddha, the Dharma, and the Saṅgha.

"How could it be anyone else?! You can see it in the security footage—it's definitely him!" Tankhun exclaimed, using his fingers to zoom in on a picture on his tablet. "At first, I got mad at Time because I thought he did it. But it turned out to be you!"

There it was: a picture of me pissing into the pond. That was undeniably my face.

"I'm sorry," I whispered when I realized Tankhun wasn't going to let this slide.

"What did my koi ever do to you? Why did you piss on them? Why?!" Tankhun wailed, his voice quavering with a combination of fury and despair. He sniffled. "Teach this guy a lesson! Next time, I'll piss on you so you know how it feels! Let's go!"

I almost cracked up at the sight of Tankhun trying to cuss me out while holding back tears. Despite the tense situation, his reaction struck me as absurd.

The door slammed shut with a resonating crash as Tankhun left with a herd of bodyguards. I was relieved that things didn't turn out as badly as I'd feared...but I started to suspect I might be wrong about that when I saw the disdainful look Kinn gave me.

"Have you realized your mistake?" he asked, crossing his legs and folding his arms over his chest, annoyance etched into his expression. I glared back at him in defiance.

"Why didn't you use a toilet like a normal person?" Kinn continued to scold me sternly. "Don't act like a savage in my house."

"I didn't know it was a koi pond. It looked murky, and I thought it was some sort of a septic system or sewer drain," I explained with a vacant expression. Still on edge from the previous confrontation, I dropped onto the couch opposite Kinn.

The moment my ass touched the cushion, Kinn shot me a pissed-off glare. "Who said you could sit?!" he snapped.

"I'm tired!" I retorted, baffled that Kinn wouldn't let me sit down.

"I don't even know where to begin with you—the fish, your remarks, or your audacity to act like my equal!" Kinn shouted. "Get up! That's not your seat."

"Who the hell do you think you are?" I grumbled, reluctantly standing up. Who would have thought sitting on the sofa would be such an issue? I was fed up with Kinn acting like he was better than everyone else. I didn't step on his toes when I sat down, did I?

"Here's another thing," Kinn said, getting up to retrieve a stack of papers from his desk and haphazardly throwing them in my direction. The sheets flew everywhere. What gave him the right to treat people like this?!

I scowled at him. "Asshole!" I growled.

"Don't call me that! Do you even realize what you've done?" Kinn yelled, stepping into my space.

I didn't back down. Kinn shouldn't assume he was the only one who could get angry—or that I was going to roll over and take it!

"What? What did I do?!" I yelled back.

"How dare you raise your voice at me!"

"Why not? It's what I always do, isn't it?" I scoffed, confidently brazen. I wouldn't be here if I didn't have the guts to stand up to him.

"Oh, I'd love to see you keep it up!" Kinn retorted sarcastically, shoving my chest with considerable force. My back slammed against the wall, knocking the wind out of me.

Bastard! I quickly regained my balance, lunging back at him with an equally violent push. Caught by surprise, Kinn stumbled and nearly fell back onto the sofa.

"Porsche!" Kinn roared, seizing my wrist. I staggered forward, and Kinn took the opportunity to throw me onto the couch and straddle me, pinning me flat against the cushions. His rage was evident in his furious gaze and clenched teeth.

My arms hurt from the strength of Kinn's hold, and the pain increased as I made a futile attempt to break free from his viselike grip. I knew that I should have been able to fight him off, but Kinn's strength seemed to increase with his rising anger.

"I'm warning you," Kinn snarled. "What you did today was unforgivable!"

"What?! Let go of me, damn it!" I shouted back.

I remembered our first encounter—how Kinn got the absolute shit kicked out of him by that gang of goons. In this moment, he was an entirely different man.

"Why did you organize my report like that? It was in the wrong order from the very first page, you dumbass! You were trying to fuck with me, weren't you?!" Kinn continued shouting at me.

"Let me go! I can't breathe!" I cried out, struggling to escape. Although I momentarily succeeded in pulling my hands free, his weight on top of me rendered me immobile.

Kinn snatched my wrists again. "I'm going to kill you!"

If Kinn thought he could get the better of me, he was mistaken. I managed to lift myself up, pushing against him repeatedly with my foot until I finally wrenched myself out of his hold. After shoving Kinn against the armrest on the other side of the sofa, I promptly stood up and regained my composure. Kinn always tried to catch me off guard, and it pissed me off. If he had the gall to fight me, he should have faced me head-on!

"Hell, I don't know what to do with you anymore!" Kinn said, refraining from approaching me. He angrily pounded his fist against the back of the couch.

"Up for a one-on-one match?" I taunted him. I was aware that we were similar in strength, but I knew I could outmaneuver him in a fair fight.

"You just never learn," Kinn sighed, exasperated. His expression went from fury to frustration.

"And you never play fair," I muttered, glaring as Kinn massaged his temple.

"I'm afraid I might end up killing you one day," Kinn said.

Ignoring Kinn's remark, I turned around to leave, sensing that our little talk was over.

"Who said you could leave?!" Kinn shouted.

I stopped in my tracks, wondering what else he could possibly want with me. "What now?!" I asked.

"Go change your clothes. I'm going out," Kinn barked.

I looked at him, baffled. "My clothes?"

"I won't have you following me in that outfit," Kinn said, giving me a once-over.

I'd gone home earlier to change into a black T-shirt and jeans— the most respectful outfit I owned—before coming here.

"No," I declared, crossing my arms over my chest in defiance.

"You! Must! *Change!*" Kinn emphasized each word loudly.

"Then I won't go!"

Kinn stood up and quickly strode toward me. I anticipated this, and I would not let him gain the upper hand. However, he caught my punch and dragged me toward the door.

I resisted his attack, shouting, "What the hell?!" before yanking my hand from his grasp.

"Are you going to follow me without causing a scene, or do I need to have my men drag you outside?" Kinn yelled, pulling me along with him. Eventually, he succeeded in hauling me to the door.

The bodyguards outside had probably overheard our fight, but they quickly pretended to be busy pacing back and forth or reading a book.

"Are you going to leave willingly, or do you want my men to take you by force?" Kinn repeated.

Looking at the bodyguards glaring at me with hostility, I reluctantly shook off Kinn's grasp and complied with his order.

"Fine! I'll go with you," I answered, trailing behind him while swearing under my breath. If Kinn didn't have his entourage backing him, he'd be no better than anyone else. If he ever managed to slip up one day, I'd give him the beating of a lifetime. I'd like to see him get so cocky after that!

Kinn led me to a room downstairs. "Has Father returned?" he asked a man standing by the door.

"Yes, he has," the man responded.

Kinn immediately opened the door and ushered me into a room where Mr. Korn and P'Chan sat behind a desk. This appeared to be Mr. Korn's office.

"What's the matter?" Korn raised his brow in confusion before suddenly bursting out into laughter. "Hah! What did you do to Kinn this time, Porsche? He looks like he's about to explode!"

I shook my hands from Kinn's grip and placed them together over my chest, greeting P'Chan and Mr. Korn with a polite wai gesture.

"Father, I won't let him wear this when we go out!" Kinn complained.

"Ah...I see." Mr. Korn turned to me. "I heard you tried to burn down my house last night?"

I didn't respond.

"Father! He's not dressed appropriately. You know I have to meet Mr. Krit tonight." Kinn gave me another disapproving once-over.

"You kids will give me a stroke one of these days. Tankhun came blubbering here earlier," Mr. Korn mumbled, wearily putting his face in his palm. He then patiently addressed me. "Remember our deal, Porsche? While you can dress as you please here, I ask that you wear a suit when going out."

I sighed. Mr. Korn shot me a somewhat disappointed look, a silent reminder of our agreement. Defeated, I nodded my assent. I would never have agreed to follow Kinn's order if I hadn't made that promise to Mr. Korn earlier!

"Look. Go get changed and be at the front door by eight," Kinn said with a disinterested tone, though his dour face told a different story. Kinn left the room without waiting for my response. I swore under my breath. Kinn should be proud of himself, making a quiet guy like me curse so much!

Mr. Korn ordered P'Chan to provide me with a couple of black suits. Once I had them, I returned to my room to clean up and change. As I shrugged on the suit, I wondered if I had killed Kinn in my past life, and he was here to haunt me in this one.

I remembered P'Chan's order to carry a gun every time I went out. I grabbed the weapon from its case and made my way to the designated meeting spot right at the appointed time.

I wasn't used to wearing a suit; it felt itchy and uncomfortable. The other bodyguards snuck curious glances my way, and a few audibly snickered at me like I was some kind of freak. *Hmph!* I vowed to remember each of these moments and wait patiently for an opportunity to settle the score. The day would come when I could punch every one of these bastards in the face!

Kinn arrived shortly after, decked out in a sleek navy suit. He quickly appraised my appearance, the corner of his lips lifting into a faint smile, before gracefully entering a luxury car parked nearby.

I followed behind him, but I came to an abrupt halt after Kinn sat in the back seat. I was unsure where I was supposed to sit. Kom was in the driver's seat, and another bodyguard occupied the passenger seat next to him.

"What the hell are you waiting for?" Kinn called out as I hesitated. "Get in! Do you need an invitation?"

I took the only available seat—the one next to Kinn—as I entertained the thought of smashing his face in. I slammed the door shut behind me, disregarded Kinn's disapproving look, and scooted away from him until I was pressed against the side of the car.

No one uttered a word, leaving the car in total silence. Kinn sat with his legs crossed, preoccupied with whatever was on his tablet. As I observed him, I reflected on something Pete had told me about Kinn: compared to his brothers, he was a meticulous person.

Pete was probably correct, considering Kinn's appearance. His suit was flawlessly tailored, and his crisp white shirt was buttoned up all the way. He wore a pocket square folded neatly in the breast pocket of his suit jacket, and the hem of his slim-fit pants perfectly grazed the top of his polished dress shoes. Even his hair was meticulously styled. He looked handsome, though perhaps a bit too mature for his age.

"Why are you looking at me?" Kinn asked without sparing me a glance. I quickly averted my gaze to watch the scenery outside of the window. I'd only taken a look at Kinn to confirm that he dressed way older than he needed to.

The car stopped in front of an elegant hotel building. I'd only seen this place from a distance before—it looked way classier than my usual haunts. Kinn briskly instructed the three of us to stay close but maintain a discreet distance, and to stay aware of our surroundings.

I followed closely behind them to the elevator, still not knowing what we were doing here. With the push of a button, it transported us to a rooftop bar that exuded the same sophistication as the rest of the hotel. The music playing in the background set a pleasant mood as Kinn greeted his associates.

The patrons of this fancy joint were dressed just as impeccably as Kinn was. The men were in suits and ties, and the women wore gowns so long I was afraid they might trip and fall. I nervously surveyed my surroundings, realizing this was my first encounter with the luxurious realm where the affluent sought the pleasure of alcohol...

"Don't let Mr. Kinn out of your sight," one of Kinn's men told me.

"What about you guys?" I retorted.

"We'll be watching him as well. And you better not start anything!"

I walked away without acknowledging his order and sat down at the bar. Kinn had instructed us to maintain a discreet distance, and I figured this should be discreet enough. This was a pretty great joint, actually, especially considering most of the female guests were exactly my type: fair-skinned Asian women with delicate facial features.

I returned flirty smiles to the women checking me out. Soon, a waiter approached me with a drink. He placed the glass in front of me and gestured toward a woman smiling brightly in my direction. I gave her a nod, raising the glass in acknowledgment, before downing the amber liquid in one go. The expensive whiskey tasted far superior to the bottom-shelf stuff I'd had before. It was robust yet smooth, unlike the cheap shit that just tasted sour and left your throat burning.

I exchanged flirtatious looks with every woman who cast her eyes my way, fully aware that I looked even hotter when I was a little buzzed. I was on my third glass now, courtesy of the beautiful women generously buying me drinks. Each glass tasted unique—these drinks were stronger and more delightful than anything I'd tasted before.

"Can I join you?" a sweet voice asked, bringing me out of my thoughts.

I responded with a subtle smile, indicating my approval. The woman extended her hand and introduced herself. "I'm Prim."

I worked as a bartender long enough to know what it meant when women approached me in a bar. "Porsche," I replied, shaking her hand and playfully brushing my thumb across her skin.

"Oh, our names have a nice ring to them. Let's drink to that. How about I get you another one?" Prim smiled sweetly at me before turning to place her order with the bartender.

My eyes lingered on her graceful figure, perfectly curvy in all the right places. I couldn't help finding her attractive—she was just my kind of woman. I had a feeling I might get lucky tonight!

There was a nagging feeling in the back of my mind that I'd forgotten something important. However, the line of shots in front of me, and Prim's insistence that I drink them, was infinitely more appealing than remembering what it was. So I brushed it off and thought, *Fuck it, let's drink!*

A wave of dizziness hit me, but I wasn't totally hammered yet. The combination of the gorgeous woman and the liquor had my mind pleasurably preoccupied, keeping me from dwelling on whatever it was I'd forgotten.

"Porsche, what the hell are you doing?!" came a shout from one of Kinn's men. He tried to violently yank me off the barstool. In my intoxicated state, I glared at him in annoyance. *Jackoff!*

I scoffed at him while glancing at the terrified woman behind me. "What?!"

"It's Mr. Kinn! He's been attacked in the bathroom!"

My eyes widened as the realization hit me. I knew what I'd forgotten now. *Kinn!*

"Why aren't you helping him?" I yelled, jumping up to hurry after him, but I felt the room start to spin.

"I am! That's why I came for you!" he shouted back, rushing to the bathroom. Something told me I should run after him. I crashed into tables and chairs along the way, scaring the other guests. When I reached the restroom, I saw Kinn fighting off three strangers with his other bodyguard. I launched a flying kick at the man who was about to lunge for Kinn.

"Ow! What the hell are you doing?!"

It seemed like my aim was slightly off, and my foot made contact with Kinn's torso. He yelped in pain but quickly returned to the fight. Without any further hesitation, I strode over, grabbed a man by his hair, and began throwing punches.

It looked like we had the upper hand. Kinn's attackers were soon sprawled out on the floor. As I observed the fallen figures, their numbers mysteriously multiplied from three to six. I shook my head slightly, trying to pull myself together before getting back in the fight. I continued kicking the men down until I lost track of time and accuracy in the flurry of kicks.

Kinn glared at me sideways. "Are you drunk?"

I glanced back at him, hearing the irritation in his voice. As I watched, Kinn split into two identical people... I shook my head before replying. "No..."

"Kom, call our people at home. Tell them to come and take care of these guys," Kinn ordered his driver.

I waited until our reinforcements arrived to round up the attackers and load them into a van. Afterward, I got back into the same car that had brought us here. Kinn maintained a brooding silence throughout the entire ride home. He looked pissed as all hell, leading me to wonder if my actions were the source of his anger—the main action being the one that left a noticeable imprint of my shoe on his once-pristine white shirt. I wanted to yank my hair out at my carelessness.

The pounding in my head intensified as the alcohol seemed to finally kick in. I didn't usually get this drunk this fast. With the expensive drinks those women kept buying me, I probably ended up consuming more alcohol than my body could handle.

When we got back, Kinn stormed into his room while barking orders at me to follow suit. I grudgingly trailed behind him, mentally preparing to block out his yelling along the way. After opening the door, I saw Kinn standing with his back to me, his hands on his hips.

Knowing that I was in the wrong this time, I decided to speak first. "Well...m'sorry," I slurred.

"What the hell do you think you were doing?!" Kinn snapped.

I scratched my ears slightly, oblivious to his shouting.

"I'm 'pologizing to you now, aren't I?" I said, struggling to keep my eyes open as Kinn turned to confront me. My eyelids grew heavy and warmth flooded my body. The suit was suffocating me. Unable to stand it any longer, I shucked off the black slacks, leaving me in my boxers. I hoped Kinn wouldn't mind my half-dressed state—we were both men, after all. I was just too fucking hot in this suit...

"What now?" Kinn's exasperated sigh flew past me. I couldn't keep myself upright any longer, and I collapsed on Kinn's forbidden sofa.

"Let me sit. My head hurts," I groaned.

Kinn's voice softened. "Do you feel even a *little* guilty?"

I looked up at him in confusion to see that his gaze was already set on me. The fury burning in his eyes had been replaced by a cool intensity. I'd expected Kinn to rant until my ears fell off—it was a shock to see him so silent and composed.

"What're you lookin' at?" I mumbled as Kinn kept staring at me. It occurred to me that he might be waiting for an answer to his previous question. "Yeah, I feel guilty. And my head hurts..."

He smiled faintly at me. "Since you're feeling warm," he said, "why not take off everything?"

It was a struggle to determine Kinn's emotions—I wasn't sure what kind of face he was making anymore.

"I can? Why didn't you just say so?" I immediately stripped off my black suit jacket, loosened my tie, and undid the first three buttons of my shirt. "Phew!"

I noticed Kinn still watching me. I wondered why he was being so oddly kind to me right now.

"You look...quite good," Kinn whispered, his handsome face suddenly drawing near. I jumped. *When did he get so close?*

"Huh? Whaddya want from me? M'not making coffee!" I muttered, shaking my head nervously at his remark. What did Kinn want? That coffee machine incident still haunted me, and I was kind of sloshed right now.

"No...I won't ask you to make coffee anymore," Kinn whispered softly.

I closed my eyes for a moment. When I opened them again, Kinn's face was unexpectedly close to mine—so close that I could feel his warm breath ghosting over my forehead. I met his piercing gaze, and I wondered why he was able to stun me every time he fixed his eyes on mine.

I felt a gentle tickling sensation against my cheek, like a delicate insect skittering across my skin. Irritated, I swatted it away. *Argh!* I didn't know why I felt so warm, annoyed, and...

"I need to take a leak," I mumbled blearily. "Hey, can I go piss?"

I heard an exasperated sigh in response. Then I was engulfed in darkness, and I wasn't conscious of anything anymore...

9

Exhausted

MM...

A low groan escaped my lips as I struggled to wake up. The first thing I felt upon regaining consciousness was a throbbing headache. I squinted my eyes against the harsh light in the room, trying to piece together what had happened last night.

I remembered accompanying Kinn to some fancy rooftop bar. I'd been downing liquor like water... I had a hazy image of Kinn being attacked in the bathroom—*damn, is Kinn okay?!*

My eyes snapped open as the memories flooded back, and I panicked at the sight of an unfamiliar ceiling. I looked around, taking in my surroundings, and discovered I'd passed out on the couch in Kinn's office. Holy shit!

"Fuck!" I swore loudly. Kinn would never let this slide. I hoped to hell that he got his ass killed in that bathroom so he wouldn't be here to berate me.

"You're awake?" A bone-chilling voice came from behind me. I swallowed hard, my parched throat protesting. I turned around, expecting to meet Kinn's wrath, only to find his face entirely void of emotion.

"Umm... I..." I faltered, staring blankly at him. My heart pounded with trepidation as guilt threatened to swallow me whole. I was desperate to get the hell out of here.

"Since you're up, go shower and change. Your shift today starts at ten, does it not?" Kinn continued impassively, returning his focus to his computer screen.

Glancing at the large clock in the room, I saw it was already past nine a.m. I immediately leapt up from the sofa, ready to get out of there in a hurry, before realizing that my bottom half felt unusually exposed. Huh? Why was I in my underwear?!

"What happened to my clothes?" I muttered under my breath.

Kinn managed to hear me. "You took them off yourself," he replied.

I looked down, noticing last night's outfit scattered across the floor. *Shit, what did I do?!* Swearing, I hastily picked up my clothes and tugged them back on. I stole a glance at Kinn, who had yet to scold me... Was he feeling okay? I was sure the Kinn I knew would have screamed his head off and choked me out by now. Who the hell was this guy?

"Wait!" Kinn's voice stopped me just as my hand reached the doorknob. I glanced back, waiting for him to continue.

"Wear the suit today. We have guests coming," Kinn said bluntly.

I stood there, mystified.

I finally decided to ask the question that had been nagging at me since I woke up. His indifference was incredibly unnerving—the entire situation baffled me. "Um...well...about last night," I said. "Aren't you gonna say something...or yell at me?"

"What would that accomplish?" he asked.

"Well...usually, you—" I began, but my words were cut short by Kinn's response.

"It doesn't matter how much I yell. Someone like you will never feel remorse," Kinn stated without looking in my direction, his finger rapidly clicking at his computer mouse, preoccupied with some game on the screen.

EXHAUSTED **163**

I had never witnessed Kinn behaving like this before. Come to think of it, I'd never seen him in a simple T-shirt, either. Every other time we'd interacted, he'd been wearing a dress shirt. My eyes lingered on him for a little too long.

He looked back at me and raised an eyebrow. "Do you *want* me to yell at you?"

"No," I replied tersely and exited the room, still groggy.

Closing the door behind me, I was met with a hostile glare from a man I hadn't seen in a while: Big.

"What the hell are you doing in Mr. Kinn's room so early?" he snapped, his anger palpable. I pulled my suit jacket tightly around myself under his scrutiny. Glaring back at him, I focused my eyes on the bruises covering his body—the ones I gave him.

"Answer me!" Big raised his voice when I stayed silent. Finding his behavior ridiculous—and wanting to piss him off—I ignored his demands and walked away.

Snatch!

Big yanked me by the arm. I promptly pulled away from his grasp, shooting a pointed look at his bruises as a warning. It was an unspoken threat: *There's more where that came from if you don't let go, asshole.* Big's eyes darted away, and he finally released me.

Back in my quarters, I washed my face and studied my reflection in the mirror above the sink. The events of last night still eluded me; I couldn't figure out how I'd ended up asleep on Kinn's couch in just my T-shirt and boxers.

However, the most disconcerting thing was Kinn's uncharacteristic calm. It was downright bizarre. He normally flipped his lid whenever I even dressed casually around him, so his impassiveness just now had left me thoroughly confused. While this seemed like a positive development, I couldn't shake off a lingering sense of unease.

I thanked myself for remembering to buy toiletries earlier. I'd packed them in my bag along with a spare set of clothes. These things were meant for emergencies, and what happened last night definitely counted. I wasn't planning on staying here permanently. I wanted to be home with Chay as much as I possibly could.

I quickly showered and changed as Kinn had instructed. I hated how tight and restrictive the suit was—I was practically suffocating. How did people manage to wear these damn things all day?

It was almost ten a.m., and I was getting hungry. I stepped out of my room, scanning my surroundings for any sign of where people could get something to eat around here. That was when I spotted Pete, wearing casual clothes and beaming brightly in my direction.

"What's up, man? Looking for trouble again?" he quipped.

I frowned at him but decided to ignore his remark. "I'm starving," I said.

"Ahh, you have a morning shift?" Pete asked, and I nodded in response. "Walk to the end of the hallway," he said, "and you'll find the staff mess hall. You can grab a bite there."

"Thanks, man. You're not working today?"

"It's my day off! I need to get out of here as soon as possible!" He tightened the strap of his backpack, waved a quick goodbye, and hightailed it to the front gate.

I looked at him incredulously. He seemed agitated, like he was trying to run away from something.

"What the hell?" I muttered under my breath.

As I was about to head to the mess hall Pete had mentioned, a bodyguard approached me.

"Mr. Kinn needs you," he told me.

For fuck's sake! I checked the time on my phone. I still had at least ten minutes before my shift was supposed to start, and I couldn't fathom why he was in such a hurry.

I hesitated. I was hungry, and it wasn't time to meet Kinn yet...

"Hurry up!" the bodyguard snapped. "Don't make Mr. Kinn wait."

"My shift hasn't started yet. I'm going to eat first," I replied brusquely, earning an annoyed glare from the bodyguard.

"Don't be so difficult! When Mr. Kinn calls, you have to go!" the man said before swiftly walking away.

I kicked the ground in frustration. *Fine! Whatever!* I probably wouldn't have made it in time if I'd gone to eat first, anyway.

Kinn's persistent summons were beginning to get on my nerves. Irritated, I raked my hand through my hair and headed to his office. I opened the door to find it deserted—Kinn wasn't at his computer desk where I'd left him this morning. Placing my hands on my hips, I looked around the space and frowned.

"Why summon me if you're not even here?" I grumbled.

My eyes landed on a peculiar jar in the room. I'd noticed other jars like this one scattered throughout the house and wondered what they were.

Curiosity got the better of me. I approached for a closer look and reached inside to find what appeared to be some kind of candy. Each piece was wrapped in gold-colored foil and featured a hideous green logo.

I read the label: Mr. 3K Caramel-Filled Chocolate. I scowled at the three goofy-looking boys standing side by side in the logo. I wondered who designed this atrocity, and whether it was the same person who came up with the brand name—it sounded more like a bathroom cleaner than candy.

I was starving. Groaning, I gave in to my hunger and unwrapped a piece of chocolate. Hopefully one of these would help quell my appetite. I popped the piece in my mouth, praying no one would get angry at me for eating it. After all, they seemed to have plenty of these sweets lying around.

The chocolate left a distinctly unpleasant taste in my mouth. Did they actually *like* this crap? It felt like I was eating dirt, and the caramel was as sticky as glue. I pushed past the awful taste, though, and ate five more, thinking these would be able to keep me somewhat satiated. If Kinn wouldn't let me have breakfast, then I was going to eat his chocolate!

After a while, Kinn finally emerged from the glass-walled room that I figured was his bedroom. He was dressed as immaculately as ever in his customary black button-up and slacks. He looked at me curiously as I attempted to hide the empty candy wrappers behind the jar. I maintained a stolid expression, staring back at him and trying not to look suspicious.

"What are you doing?" he asked dismissively, his attention split between me and his tablet.

I deflected his question. "Why did you call me?"

"Look over these documents for me and put the pages in order," he commanded. "And don't screw it up like you did with my report!"

"That report was in English. How was I supposed to know what order it was supposed to be in?"

"I didn't realize you were stupid," Kinn remarked, placing a stack of papers on the coffee table.

"Like you're so smart," I muttered under my breath.

Kinn signaled me to get to work, so I leaned down to look at the papers. I sighed in relief when I saw they were in Thai.

As I started spreading papers across the table, Kinn interrupted me. "Why don't you sit?" he asked.

I glanced at the sofa, recalling the reprimand I got last time I sat on it.

"I'm allowed to sit?"

Kinn scoffed. "Why do you have manners all of a sudden? You slept on it last night," he pointed out, taking a sip of his coffee as he walked back to his desk.

"Fine!" I muttered.

As I settled into the couch, the constricting feeling of the slacks I was wearing became increasingly irritating. Everything seemed fine while I was standing, but as soon as I sat down, the pants and the belt tightened uncomfortably. It made it hard to breathe.

It reminded me of my freshman year of university, when I had to wear a full uniform. Back then, the pants had to be formfitting, and the shirt had to be neatly tucked in. Fortunately, the university relaxed its uniform rules for the upperclassmen. I gladly swapped the tight pants for looser jeans, and I hadn't been forced to deal with constricting clothes since—until now.

"What's the matter?" Kinn asked, his eyes still fixed on his computer screen.

"Why do you make me wear such tight clothes?" I complained. "I feel so constricted."

Kinn's lips curled into a smile as he leisurely drank his coffee. I suspected the suits P'Chan gave me were a size too small—they were uncomfortably tight everywhere! I seriously considered unbuckling the belt and unclasping the slacks. I needed to ask Kinn.

"Hey, is it okay if I take off my pants?" I asked. I was wearing boxers underneath, so it wouldn't be that indecent if I took my pants off. I wore boxers around Jom and Tem all the time, and they didn't care.

I assumed Kinn wouldn't care either—we were both guys. "They're uncomfortable. I'll put them back on when we leave."

Kinn remained silent, with his eyes still focused on the screen, but I could see him grinning. I took his lack of objection as permission and swiftly kicked off my pants, then folded them neatly over the back of the sofa. I felt no shame. After all, this was still within our agreement: at home, I was free to dress as I pleased.

I saw Kinn steal another glance at me. There wasn't even a hint of disapproval on his face, just a pleasant smile playing on his lips as he leaned back in his chair.

It was a welcome relief. Kinn was being unusually generous today; he hadn't yelled at me a single time. I hoped he understood that guys liked to dress comfortably around their friends. And although Kinn wasn't exactly my friend, I still wanted to be comfortable.

"My uncle is visiting this afternoon. I want you to take these papers and follow me to the meeting room," Kinn announced.

I gave him a perfunctory nod. "What time is he coming? Can I get something to eat first?"

Kinn glanced at the clock before replying. "Finish organizing the pages, and then you can go," he said. "Meet me in the conference room on the ground floor at one o'clock."

I concentrated on the task at hand and finished putting the documents in order. After pulling my slacks back on, I headed to the staff mess hall. I grumbled, wondering why Kinn couldn't have let me eat before I had to organize his documents. Was he deliberately screwing with me? His behavior this morning was entirely out of character. Usually, he'd find something trivial to yell at me about. But he said nothing when I took off my pants in the middle of his office today. I knew it was inappropriate, but Kinn was the one who made me wear this tight suit in the first place, so he could endure the sight of me in my underwear!

I followed the directions Pete gave me and found a compact dining area on the ground floor. All the bodyguards present shifted their attention toward me when I entered but, sensing their obvious hostility, I ignored them as usual.

I headed straight to the buffet line to see if there was anything I wanted to eat. I liked simple stuff like omelets. However, the dishes served here looked full of weird vegetables and spices—the kind of thing that didn't sit well with my stomach. Tem used to joke that people who looked as badass as me should be able to eat a wild boar or a cobra with no problem. I'd told him to fuck off. I wasn't that kind of man! I could barely tolerate even slight spiciness, and my go-to foods were eggs, fried pork, and fried chicken.

I had only taken three bites of my meal when a loud yell disrupted the peace of the small mess hall.

"Kom! Fix your face. Do you want to start trouble or what?"

My gaze instinctively shifted to the source of the commotion. There they were, sneering in my direction. I understood at once that those words weren't meant for their friend Kom, but for me.

"What's on the menu for today?" another bodyguard asked, having just arrived.

"Omelets!" the first bodyguard replied. "But I'd advise against eating one. You might get cocky and act like your boss's equal—you could completely forget your place. You're better off with tom yum soup like me!"

I put down my spoon and took a deep breath, trying to suppress the anger welling up inside me. I shot them a brief, intense glare before returning to my meal. Bastards!

"Huh? What the hell are you guys talking about? I'll just go grab my food," the newcomer responded, confused.

"Yeah, just go with whatever's on the menu. Being too picky might get you in *trouble* someday," the first guy continued, deliberately emphasizing the word as he locked eyes with me, mocking me with a raised eyebrow.

Asshole! I thought to myself with a grunt. It looked like I wasn't going to eat in peace after all.

"Are you a dog?" I asked bluntly, leaning back in my chair and crossing my arms.

"Who are you calling a dog?!" he shouted, slamming his fist down on the table. The mess hall went dead silent.

I smirked in response. "I sure hear a lot of barking," I said.

The group at the table immediately rose from their seats. Several pairs of eyes glared at me, outraged.

"Are you lookin' for trouble?!"

The threat didn't faze me. Unperturbed, I took a sip of water and stood up to return my dishes. I turned to face the group.

"You really are a bunch of dogs," I remarked. "Only brave enough to fight in a pack."

"Fuck you, Porsche!"

I felt a jolt at my arm, and in the same instant, a fist hurtled toward my face. Instinctively, I dodged to the side, causing the assailant to lurch forward. I took the opening to deliver a forceful kick to his flank. The man staggered backward and crashed into tables and chairs, knocking over trays of food and sending them scattering across the floor.

The rest of the pack quickly closed in, pulling me into a body lock and punching me in the face over and over. Despite my attempts to defend myself with kicks and punches, taking on five men single-handedly while hungover proved a daunting task.

The man I'd kicked to the ground earlier regained his balance. "You son of a bitch!" he yelled, smashing his fist into my face. I contorted in pain, but I would not surrender. I struggled to break free from their hold, twisting and kicking out blindly. It frustrated me to no end—these bastards wouldn't have the upper hand right now if they hadn't swarmed me all at once!

"Enough, all of you!" someone shouted, but the scuffle persisted. I stumbled, taking hits and delivering my fair share of them in the chaos.

"If you don't cut it out, I'll tell the boss!" one of the kitchen aunties yelled, prompting some of the other bodyguards to step in and separate us.

"Fight me one on one, you cowards!" I yelled at them, blinded by anger. My feet hovered slightly above the ground as someone held me back, and I kicked wildly as the other bodyguard dragged me out of the room.

I could still hear their shouting and cursing as I was forcefully ushered upstairs. My rage began to dissipate when I realized where I was being taken. I shook them off as they pushed me inside, and my eyes met Kinn's. He was looking away from his computer to stare harshly at me.

"Mr. Kinn, your bodyguards are fighting again," someone said. I whipped around to the informant with a murderous glare. Moments later, the men I'd just fought with were thrust into the room alongside me.

"I just let you off, and you're already causing trouble?" Kinn said with a huff.

"They started it!" I snapped, glowering at my adversaries, who stood with their heads lowered.

"Can you go one day without causing a fuss?" Kinn complained, his irritation evident. He remained focused on me, disregarding the other men in the room.

"Tell that to your men! I did nothing!" I argued, annoyed that Kinn was singling me out when I wasn't the one who started the fight.

"I've told you not to cause trouble, Porsche! We don't tolerate that kind of behavior!"

I couldn't believe Kinn was still singling me out.

"Fine! It was all my fault! Your other bodyguards are such upstanding citizens!" I shouted in frustration. I'd lost count of how many times Kinn had refused to listen to me. He continued to blame every disturbance in the house on me, and I hated being blamed for shit that wasn't my fault! It wasn't fair!

"You can leave," Kinn said, dismissing the rest of the men from his office. I rolled my eyes.

"Damn it!" I swore once we were alone, kicking Kinn's couch so hard it crashed into the wall.

"Porsche!" Kinn admonished me, slamming his fist on his desk. He stood up and shot a sharp look in my direction. I glared back at him with the same fiery intensity.

Kinn pointed his finger in my face. "You're testing my patience!" he shouted. He was finally starting to act like the man I knew he was.

"You're so fucking stupid!" I retorted. "Is this how an effective boss behaves? Don't you realize your men are playing you?!"

Kinn lunged forward, his hand grabbing my collar and yanking it hard, pulling me closer to his raised fist. Our eyes locked. His face was a portrait of rage, but it didn't scare me at all. I clenched my hand into a fist, ready to strike back if necessary. However, before our fists could collide, a knock on the door interrupted us.

A man opened the door, stopping in his tracks when he found us about to exchange blows.

"Mr. Kinn," he said, "the Minor Clans have arrived."

We released each other. Kinn took a moment to compose himself, taking a deep breath before addressing me. "If you don't watch your mouth, I'll kill you!" he spat. Smoothing out his clothes, he headed toward the door, but stopped to glance back at me. "Bring the documents and follow me!" he said, his voice cold.

The door slammed shut behind him. My nerves still frayed, I punched the wall hard to keep myself from going crazy. My seething rage toward Kinn drowned out the physical pain.

"Shithead!" I cursed. "Do you think I'm scared of you?!"

I closed my eyes and forced down my anger. I let out a heavy sigh and went to retrieve the documents from Kinn's table.

Exiting the room, I saw Kinn's retreating figure and briskly followed him downstairs to the grand hall. Two older adults were waiting for us there; Kinn greeted them with a wai gesture before acknowledging a greeting from two good-looking teenagers seated across from them.

"Your father isn't home today?" one of the older men asked as Kinn settled into his seat. I assumed my position behind him alongside the other bodyguards.

"He'll be back in half an hour," Kinn replied. "Have you eaten anything yet, Zek-Kant?"

I observed the interaction in silence, my resentment still simmering beneath the surface. Tuning out the ongoing conversation, I dwelled on the earlier events and Kinn's lingering resentment toward me.

After conversing with his guests for a while, Kinn turned to me. "The documents, please."

I haphazardly tossed the stack of paper onto the table in front of him with a loud thump, making Kinn snap his head to shoot me a disapproving look. He turned back to smile politely at the older man—his father's younger brother, apparently—as he handed over the documents. I hadn't even registered how hard I threw those papers against the table; my anger had momentarily robbed me of self-control.

"Excuse me, sir. May I offer you some refreshments?" a maid asked from the doorway. She beckoned me over to take the tray from her. I looked at her in confusion until one of the other bodyguards nudged me forward.

"Take the tray to Mr. Kinn," he instructed.

I sighed, reluctantly walking over to accept the tray. I placed it on the table, and all eyes shifted from me to the tray. The same guy as before gave me another nudge.

"Serve them."

I closed my eyes, trying to suppress my irritation.

Kinn glanced at me briefly. "Both of my uncles will have tea," he said, "Mr. Vegas will have juice, and I'll have an americano."

Kinn returned to organizing the documents in front of him without acknowledging me further. I picked up the hot americano from the tray, planning to place it in front of Kinn. However, as I looked at his stupid face, my ire boiled over. I harshly dropped the cup and saucer, spilling hot liquid onto the cuff of Kinn's dress shirt and the papers in his hand.

"Shit, ow!" Kinn yelped as the heat burned his skin. He glared angrily between me and his startled guests.

"Porsche! What the hell are you doing?" he hissed.

"My bad," I admitted, realizing that my lack of self-control made me act like an ass in front of the guests. Guilt started to edge out my displeasure.

"You are testing my patience," Kinn growled, maintaining eye contact.

"I'm sorry! What more do you want from me, huh?" I said calmly.

The guests began to chuckle, drawing our attention back to them.

"Well... Is this how this house trains its bodyguards? I didn't know they could talk back to their bosses. Kinn must be so well respected."

A burst of laughter erupted. Kinn's smile faltered as he looked at his extended family. He stood up and bowed slightly. "Excuse me while I get changed," he said. "Please let my men know if you need anything. My father will arrive shortly."

Then, he turned to me. "Follow me!" he ordered.

I started to get nervous under Kinn's penetrating glare. The hatred behind his eyes was palpable—even stronger than the time he'd choked me. If looks could kill, I'd already be dead. I sighed, obediently trailing behind him to his room.

As the door closed behind us, Kinn whipped around to face me, furious.

Smack!

The forceful blow from Kinn's open hand struck me with jarring force, making me stagger and almost fall. A numbness spread across my cheek and I felt metallic liquid fill my mouth. I brushed a hand over my face, struggling to regain my composure, before giving Kinn a forceful shove onto the sofa.

"What the hell are you doing, Kinn?!" I yelled. Kinn pushed himself up and lunged at me, his hands gripping my forearms so tightly it was impossible to break free.

"What the hell are *you* doing?!" Kinn fired back, still grasping my arms with unrelenting force. "I don't care how deplorably you act when it's just me, but you are *not* allowed to behave like that in front of guests! You humiliated me in front of the Minor Clans! I've warned you about your language, but you don't seem to care. I've had enough of you!"

Kinn slammed my body against the wall with an audible thud, the force of it knocking the breath out of my lungs.

Bracing myself, I stared back at him. "What about you?!" I shot back, my frustration flaring. "You blamed me for all kinds of shit in front of your bodyguards when it wasn't my fault. Have you ever listened to me? I'm not trying to act like an asshole. I know who you are, and I know what my position entails. But you've never even given me the chance to explain myself. When your men started a fight with me, you said it was my fault." I jabbed a finger at Kinn's face. "You want to know why you haven't earned my respect, Kinn? You've never been fair to me!"

It was like a dam had burst. I was practically exploding with pent-up anger. Damn it! I was sick of the blatant injustice. I knew I'd fucked up, but maybe if he'd treated me with basic respect, none of this shit would've happened.

"Even if you think I'm in the wrong, I'm still your boss. You have to do as I say." Kinn glared at me, still furious. "No questions asked."

"And you think slapping me will make me listen to you? *Respect* you?!" I shoved him hard again, but this time he managed to grab my arms and shake me off.

"If you can't accept the rules, then quit! If you want to stay, you have to stop acting out with me in front of guests!" Kinn said, pushing me back.

I stumbled backward. I didn't want to talk to Kinn anymore.

Did he think being the boss meant he could do anything he wanted? I was a person, too, damn it!

I stormed out of Kinn's room, slamming the door shut behind me. I couldn't stand to keep looking at him. I didn't push the issue, not because I couldn't handle arguing with him, but because I didn't want to be in there for another second.

Our unresolved issues just kept piling up. We might end up killing each other one of these days. How was this my life? I hated being constantly belittled—despised feeling so insignificant, so helpless!

I stormed out to the garden, a lit cigarette between my fingers. I took a deep drag to calm myself down. I had the urge to hop on my motorcycle and get out of this hellhole, but the thought of that premature termination fee in the contract held me back. My frustration surged and I kicked the ground, sending pebbles scattering. I wiped my lips with the back of my hand. It came back bloody. What gave Kinn the right to treat me like dirt?

I flicked a second cigarette to life, futilely seeking solace in the nicotine. I wanted to set this entire place on fire. With my free hand resting loosely on my hip, I surveyed my surroundings with a scowl until I noticed a high school-aged boy holding a comic book. He was peering directly at me with wide, innocent eyes.

"What're you looking at?" I spat. "Want me to pop your eyes out of your head?" I didn't care who this boy was—maybe he belonged to one of the household employees. I needed an outlet for my anger, and I was about ready to smack him for his blatant ogling. He stared right back at me with terrified eyes before hastily stashing his comic book into his bag and darting back toward the house.

Calm gradually started to settle with my third cigarette. I could admit that I was in the wrong for talking back to Kinn. He shouldn't have treated me like that in the first place, though.

I was halfway done with my smoke when I heard someone calling me.

"Porsche! Mr. Kinn is summoning you!"

I wanted to yank my hair out in frustration. Instead, I flicked my cigarette to the ground and stomped it out with my foot, imagining it was Kinn's face.

I followed the guy who'd called me and ended up back in the grand hall. I'd figured they wanted me to resume my position in the meeting. However, I was greeted by familiar faces in the hallway—Kinn, his guests, Tankhun, and even Mr. Korn. All of them were glaring at me in disapproval, with the eldest man among Kinn's guests looking the most pissed off. I felt my stomach drop in anticipation when I noticed the boy from the garden hugging the older man beside him.

"Papa! This is the one who said he'd pop my eyes out!" the teenage boy exclaimed, pointing directly at me. I gulped. Shit!

Tankhun chuckled and grinned at me when a stern Mr. Korn asked, "Is this true, Porsche?"

I lowered my head, silently accepting the blame.

Mr. Korn sighed. "Please apologize to Mr. Macau."

Sighing, I turned toward the boy called Macau, who was still giving me the stink eye.

"Sorry," I muttered.

"Show my son some respect!" Macau's father shouted. All eyes in the room focused on me, compelling me to yield to the man's demands. I conceded and put my hands together in a wai gesture.

"I apologize," I said.

"Watch your tone!" he snapped, clearly dissatisfied with the sincerity of my apology.

I guess my expression conveyed my annoyance and discomfort

with the entire situation, because Mr. Korn finally intervened. "All right, that's enough. Porsche has apologized." He then turned to me. "You're dismissed."

"Enough? Hia, that man wanted to hurt Macau!"

"I'll take care of it. Porsche, get out."

I nodded. Despite the tense situation, Tankhun flashed me a bright smile and gave me a thumbs-up on my way out. He looked so delighted that Mr. Korn had to tell him to tone it down.

"We're going to my office," Kinn said. He caught me off guard—I hadn't realized he was following me. He tugged on my sleeve, pulling me along with him, and as the door to his office shut behind us, the air grew heavy with tension again. Everything that was happening today was going to drive me insane.

Kinn perched on the edge of the table, crossing his arms tightly over his chest before letting out a frustrated huff. Though he was clearly still irritated, it wasn't as bad as it was earlier.

"On your first day, you nearly set my house on fire and killed Tankhun's fish. The second day, you got drunk and let me get attacked in a bathroom. Today, you embarrassed me in front of my relatives and even threatened my cousin. Hell, I don't know what to do with you anymore. You've only been here three days, and you've managed to make trouble every single day..."

I grunted in response. These three days on the job had been hell for me as well. As Kinn continued his diatribe, I found myself itching to escape. It was all just so exhausting. I wanted to die peacefully in my sleep so I never had to face this shit again.

"Why don't you just fire me?" I asked him, weary.

"Why can't you show me some respect?" Kinn countered, raking a hand through his hair. There was no hostility in his voice, only vague frustration.

"You haven't *earned* my respect. Have you forgotten what you did to me and my friends? Because I haven't!" I said, recalling the underhanded methods Kinn used to force me into submission. How could I possibly show respect to a man like him?

Kinn snorted. "So, what is this—your revenge?"

"You're an asshole egomaniac who never listens!" I exploded, then huffed in exasperation and crossed my arms.

"You're the one provoking me."

"Me? Provoking you? Yeah, right! Nothing is ever your fault, is it, shithead?!"

Kinn took a deep breath before standing up from the desk and stalking toward me. "I told you not to challenge my authority," he hissed, yanking me toward him. He caught me by surprise when he shoved me flat on my back onto the sofa and swiftly straddled me, his tall figure pressing down until I could barely breathe.

"What the hell are you doing?!" I thrashed violently, trying to free my arms from his grip and buck him off.

"Teaching you a lesson!" Kinn growled, his face coming incredibly close to mine. I shut my eyes tightly and tried to turn away from him. Hot breath ghosted over the nape of my neck, and then I felt Kinn's nose pressing against my skin there, inhaling deeply. I yelped in revulsion, a cold shiver racing down my spine.

"What the fuck, Kinn?! Let go of me!" I tried to pull away from the ticklish sensation on my neck, but Kinn managed to hold me in place. His soft lips grazed against my neck, and he started to suck and nip at the sensitive skin there.

I lay there in shock. I had no idea what the fuck Kinn was doing. Hundreds of questions raced through my head. I shuddered as I felt his wet saliva on my skin, followed by a sudden sting of pain.

"Ow! What the hell, man?!" I yelled as Kinn sank his teeth into the meat of my neck, hard enough to break the skin. I writhed in pain, desperate to shake him off.

Finally, he looked down at me and let go. I immediately touched my neck where he had bitten me and found blood.

"Are you a goddamn dog?!" I cried. Kinn's lips curled into a smile, and he went back to sit at his desk, hands casually tucked into his pockets.

"I merely did to you what you've done to me," he said, unable to hide the smug satisfaction on his face.

"You bastard! Are you fucking with me?!" I shouted, reaching for a nearby vase with the intent to hurl it at him.

Kinn promptly pointed his finger at my face in warning. "Try that, and I'll bite you again."

I forcefully slammed the vase back down, ready to unleash a string of curses at him, but I was stopped short by a resounding bang at Kinn's door.

"Don't you know how to knock?" Kinn asked as his older brother barged into the room. Tankhun smiled brightly, dragging a sulking Pete behind him.

"You should've locked the door if you wanted privacy," Tankhun retorted, yanking Pete forward by the wrist.

"Master..." Pete started.

"What's this about?" Kinn frowned, looking between Pete and his brother.

"I want to make a trade," Tankhun explained. He gestured toward me. "I like this guy. I want him."

I jumped up from the sofa, pointing at myself in bewilderment. *Me?*

"Didn't Porsche kill your beloved koi?" Kinn's voice remained neutral.

"He said he'd pop Macau's eyes out of their sockets! I forgive him," Tankhun declared, clapping his hands together and circling me with a pleased expression.

What the fuck?!

"Come on! Let's go," Tankhun said, seizing my wrist and leading me toward the door.

"Mr. Tankhun, don't joke with me like this," Pete protested, though there was an amused glint in his eyes that contradicted the tone of his voice.

"I'm not joking! I want Porsche as my head bodyguard, not you. You're stupid, Pete. I specifically ordered you to harass Macau, but you never did, you ungrateful piece of shit!" Tankhun huffed, releasing me and marching over to Pete. He plunged his hand into Pete's jacket and retrieved a two-way radio.

"Here! This is yours," Tankhun said, handing me Pete's walkie-talkie. I accepted it, still bewildered by this entire situation.

"Mr. Tankhun, do you really mean it?" Pete's tone was somewhat sad, but his expression told me otherwise. I looked skeptically at Pete, remembering him mentioning that it was his day off today. I wondered why he'd even shown up.

"I mean it! I want Macau to get a smack upside the head for once," Tankhun answered Pete. Then, he turned to me, saying, "Don't worry, Porsche. I've got your back."

Tankhun grabbed my wrist again and led me toward the door.

"Wait!" Kinn shouted, stopping us before we could leave.

"What? Don't try to stop me," Tankhun protested. "You have to make sacrifices for your big brother!"

"I just want to let you know that I don't accept returns," Kinn smirked smugly in my direction. Pete stood behind him, grinning broadly and shooting me a peace sign.

"Fine!" Tankhun replied.

I let Tankhun drag me away, still grappling with what the hell had just happened to me—or why the last three days seemed so exhausting. Fucking hell!

"What should we do, Mr. Kinn?" Pete asked.

Kinn shook his head. "Just wait for the inevitable disaster," he replied, a faint smile tugging at his lips.

Change

I GRINNED AS TANKHUN swapped Pete for Porsche, making Pete my new head bodyguard. The mere thought of Tankhun and Porsche teaming up was ridiculous, but I knew it would end in chaos. My older brother was known for his eccentricity. Pairing him with an impudent troublemaker like Porsche was a recipe for disaster.

"Um... Mr. Kinn, is Big your night bodyguard today?" Pete asked respectfully.

"Yes... Why?" I asked, seeing hesitation on Pete's face.

"Actually, today is my day off..." Pete mumbled, averting his eyes.

I glanced up from the game I was playing online with Time, Tay, and Mew. "Oh! Why are you here, then?"

"When Mr. Tankhun heard Mr. Vegas and Mr. Macau were going to be here, he gave me a call and nagged me to come back. He wanted me to torment them while they were here," Pete replied, weariness etched into his expression.

"Ah...you must be exhausted." I chuckled, shaking my head in amusement. This house was hectic enough with Tankhun's antics; bringing Porsche into the mix just added fuel to the fire. "You're excused," I told Pete.

"You're staying in today, then, sir?"

I nodded, already feeling calmer now that Porsche was gone. The past few days had wreaked a whirlwind of havoc in my room, and now I could finally have some peace and quiet.

"Would you like me to stay until Big starts his shift?" Pete asked.

"No need," I dismissed him. "I'm going to rest today."

Pete gave a slight bow before exiting the room. I let out a long sigh and settled back into my seat. Today had been utterly draining. I knew I tended to lose control when I got angry, and I'd ended up hitting Porsche today when I hadn't meant to. I'd never done anything like that to any of my subordinates, and I felt somewhat guilty.

Porsche's resentment toward me was obvious. It had surprised me to see someone usually so stoic lose control like that. He took offense at my persistent scolding, claiming that I never listened to him and that I unfairly blamed him for starting fights. While I did see him as a troublemaker, I realized that I had gone a bit too far in my reaction to his behavior.

To an extent, I could understand Porsche's reluctance to show respect. My repeated attempts to corner him must have pissed him off. Admittedly, I had been intending to provoke him. The more Porsche resisted or defied my orders, the stronger my desire grew to assert my dominance over him.

Porsche was the first person who had aroused such intense emotions in me. I found myself frustrated, both with him and with myself. I couldn't figure out why I lost all restraint nearly every time I saw his face.

It wasn't like I had a crush on him or anything. Although Porsche's handsome features and impressive physique made him undeniably attractive, he just wasn't my type. I did find men more aesthetically pleasing than women, but I wasn't interested in Porsche that way at all. Seriously. Even if I found my gaze lingering on him…

Porsche had proved even more captivating when he was drunk. His plump lips took on a richer shade of red, and his eyes became even more alluring as he lazily scanned his surroundings. For a fleeting moment there, I found Porsche sexy. I'd even been a little pleased when he spontaneously took off his pants in front of me last night.

I allowed Porsche to sleep on my sofa after he passed out. I didn't take advantage of his inebriated state, but I appreciated the unexpected visual. It was against my principles to force myself on an unconscious person. Besides, Porsche really wasn't my type—even if his athletic body was nice to look at! It was merely a nice surprise to see a handsome man undress.

I was dressed in a black bathrobe watching TV on my sofa when I heard Big's voice. "Mr. March has arrived."

I turned around and smiled at my visitor, who beamed back at me and came over to embrace my arm.

"I've missed you," March said, planting a gentle kiss on my cheek. He nestled closer, playfully rubbing his head against my chest. I wrapped my arm around his waist, caressing it gently. Now *this* was my type—a slender man with an adorable face, affectionate, eager to please—the type of guy who knew exactly what he was doing…

"Let me quickly take a shower. Wait for me, okay?" March said sweetly.

March was not my boyfriend; he was merely a casual sex partner. I had no intention of being in a serious relationship, preferring the thrill of a new lover each night.

The men I chose to share my bed with tended to look like March. Some willingly joined me for the night, no questions asked—while others, often up-and-coming actors seeking to be a rich person's boytoy, expected a token of gratitude in return for their company. March fell into the latter category, but he was worth every cent.

Soon, the room resonated with passionate moans and the sounds of two bodies moving together. The naked man in front of me really knew how to turn me on. Out of all my favorite activities, sex had made its way to the top of the list: it offered a challenge, exhilaration, and relaxation all at once.

"P'Kinn, don't bite me!" March pleaded between breathy moans. "I...I have to be on set tomorrow..."

I moved from nibbling March's neck to sucking on the skin below his collarbone, where any mark could easily be concealed by clothing. I hadn't meant to bite March. I couldn't get the memory of biting Porsche's neck out my head, and it made me forget where I was.

I couldn't shake the memory of Porsche's intense glare, either. There was an oddly endearing quality to it that stirred up something savage within me. The skin at the nape of his neck had carried a distinct, enticing scent that made me bury my nose into him and inhale, making me temporarily forget my intention to bite Porsche in the same place he had bitten me. Porsche's undeniable magnetism had led me to act impulsively around him, even though he wasn't my type.

"You were aggressive tonight," March purred when we were finished, twining his arms tenderly around my neck. He was already back in his clothes, ready to leave after fulfilling our arrangement.

"And I'm usually *not*?" I teased with a playful smirk, leisurely cupping his ass through his jeans.

"You were...more aggressive than usual!" March giggled. I felt a soft peck on my cheek before March pulled away from my embrace. With a cheerful smile, he waved goodbye and left.

I typically didn't let my lovers stay overnight at my house, a rule that bodyguards knew well. They understood my preferences, and made sure to send my lovers off after we'd finished our activities.

I collapsed on my bed, feeling spent after going two rounds with March. While I tended to be assertive in bed, the presence of bruises and bloody bite marks on March's body told me I might have gone a little overboard. Lying there, I contemplated if fighting with Porsche today was what got me so pent up...

I scheduled a study session with Time, Tay, and Mew at my place the next morning, fully aware that their real agenda was just to play games together. Once everyone arrived, my room erupted into an uproar.

"Kinn, my man! You did it again!" Time exclaimed enthusiastically.

"What?" I replied. I had nothing on my agenda, so I'd been playing computer games all day.

"I heard your men saying you had N'March over again?" Time whispered in my ear so that Tay wouldn't overhear him.

"Yeah, so?" I shrugged.

"I want him too!" Time whined, stomping his feet like a child throwing a temper tantrum. His loud voice prompted Tay to turn around.

"What do you want?!" Tay demanded, curious.

Time jumped at his lover's voice and swiftly pointed at my screen, pretending to be interested in the game. "I, uh, want a new hero character like Kinn's."

I snickered at his lame excuse, glancing up to find Time smiling sheepishly at Tay. It was only fair for Tay to be suspicious. They were lovers, after all.

"Then...buy one?" Tay said.

His naïve answer made me understand why the two had managed to stay in a relationship for nearly four years. Sometimes I felt bad for Tay; Time was always playing with his heart.

"Hey, Kinn!" Time whispered at me again. "I'm looking at this guy..."

He discreetly showed me a picture on his phone of a cute boy around high school age. We both preferred the same kind of guy. I'd even considered hitting on Tay once upon a time, but Time had beaten me to it.

"I've already fucked him," I said casually.

Time was irritated. "Fine! I don't want your sloppy seconds, anyway."

"You're such a piece of shit, Time!" I muttered with a slight shake of my head. "I really pity Tay."

Tay was entirely aware of his boyfriend's penchant for fooling around, and he seemed willing to accept it—as long as he remained Time's only openly acknowledged lover. While I didn't particularly approve of Time's infidelity, considering they were both my friends, I opted not to take sides. My role was limited to cautioning Time if his behavior crossed the line and offering comfort to Tay when he was hurt.

"Has anyone worked on the presentation for Professor Vichian's class?" Mew interrupted us. As always, he was the only one being productive.

"Let's play some games first," said Time, who often found Mew's seriousness annoying. "Come on! Put that away. Don't tell me you've got schoolwork open on your screen."

Mew sighed wearily, then gathered his laptop and settled on the carpet, ignoring Time's order. Stubbornness seemed to be a common trait among all of us—we'd all grown up in affluent families that lavishly spoiled their children. Time's family owned several gold shops[10] and other enterprises, Tay was heir to one of downtown Bangkok's most luxurious hotels, and Mew's father owned a prestigious private school. Their upbringings meant they were accustomed to having household staff around, and they easily made demands without a second thought.

"I'm hungry..."

Tay went outside, trying to see if he could order one of my bodyguards to bring us something to eat, as usual. This was a prime example of my friends being demanding.

"Where are all your men?" Tay turned around to ask me.

"They're on a break, I think," I said. Tay frowned at me before poking his head outside of my room again.

"Hey!" Tay called out to someone before stepping outside. I didn't pay much attention; I knew that Tay was as familiar with my house as his own. He returned to my room shortly after, heading to me with his arms crossed and a scowl on his face.

"What's the matter?" I asked, still focused on my computer screen.

"Tsk! I saw that new bodyguard of yours coming up the stairs, so I told him to fetch some drinks for me. He said he's not your lackey anymore, and I can't order him around. Then he walked away—just like that!" Tay complained before unceremoniously plopping onto the couch next to me.

"That's just how he is," I replied, glancing at Tay. Then, I got up, abandoned the mouse I was clicking, and headed toward the door. Stepping into the hallway, I spotted Porsche on his way to Tankhun's room.

---

10   In Thailand gold, particularly 23 karat gold, is popular as both jewelry and as an investment. Gold shops may sell either gold jewelry, bullion, or both.

"Porsche!" I hollered at him. Porsche turned to glare at me, clearly annoyed.

"Come here!"

"No!"

I smirked slightly at his immediate denial. It seemed like we were incapable of civil conversation.

"I said, come here!" I repeated, trying to compel him with a stern look.

"What makes you think you can order me around?" Porsche said.

I sighed, feeling fed up with Porsche's habitual defiance. "Fine." I strode toward him purposefully.

Porsche stood there with his hands on his hips until I was nose-to-nose with him. "I'm not your subordinate anymore," he said, his expression stoic. "You can't force me to do anything."

I studied his face. He exuded brash self-confidence as he glared back at me. However, his disdainful stare wavered slightly when I lowered my eyes to the large bandage on his neck. I smiled at the sight of my masterpiece, a mirror of what Porsche had done to me.

"Fetch some drinks and snacks for my friends," I ordered him calmly.

"You have feet. If you can walk to me, surely you can walk to the kitchen," Porsche muttered under his breath before looking away and sighing.

I raised my voice. "Just do as I say!"

"No!" Porsche stubbornly insisted.

"Do it! Don't piss me off!" I began to yell, not because I was angry with him, but because I wanted to see him yield to me.

"Tell your men to do it!" Porsche retorted, still not afraid of me.

"I'm telling you... Do. It!" I stressed each word, my brows furrowing in annoyance.

"What's with all the noise, Mr. Kinn?" P'Chan asked as he came to the top of the stairs. His face remained neutral when he turned to look at Porsche. "Porsche, what did you do to Mr. Kinn?"

"Great," Porsche sighed. "It's my fault again."

"Go fetch my drinks and snacks now!" I shouted to his face.

P'Chan backed me up. "Porsche, do as Mr. Kinn tells you."

Porsche swore loudly but proceeded to do as he was told. I noticed that Porsche seemed to be more courteous when he was dealing with my father and with P'Chan. He never listened to anyone else.

I returned to my room with a smug smile, feeling pleased with myself. I loved making Porsche lose his cool. It felt like a triumph to see a closed-off person like Porsche reveal his true self.

Shortly after I sat down at my desk and resumed my game, I heard a knock on the door. I was surprised: Porsche usually barged into my room like an animal.

"Enter," I said, but the door to my room remained closed. I frowned slightly, wondering what his problem was this time.

"Come in!" Tay yelled. Still, no one entered. Tay frowned, equally confused, and went to open the door himself.

"Does that guy think we're guardian spirits[11] or something?" Tay grumbled, bending down to pick up the snack tray on the floor in front of the door.

Porsche was nowhere to be seen. I shook my head disapprovingly. I was entirely fed up with him.

Tay dropped the tray on the table with a loud clang.

"What the hell is wrong with him? Does he have no manners?" Tay complained. "What a shame! He's so sexy. He even has a cool tattoo!"

---

11   In Thai and Chinese-Thai culture, people pay respect to gods and spirits by offering them food and drinks.

"Hey! Make up your mind!" Time interrupted his boyfriend. "Are you complaining about Porsche or admiring his looks? Don't make me jealous!"

Tay giggled. Porsche did look like the type of man he liked—from behind, he even kind of looked like Time. Tankhun had initially mistaken Porsche for Time when he'd checked the security footage to see who killed his fish—Time had been utterly bewildered at the angry phone call he got that day. Of course he refuted Tankhun's accusation, insisting that a handsome and educated person like him would never do such a thing. Tankhun almost didn't believe him until I confirmed that the person in the footage was indeed not Time. I recognized Porsche with a single glance.

"Heh, I'm just kidding!" Tay said, offering Time a drink to distract him.

"I know you meant it!" Time feigned being angry at Tay, but he was preoccupied with a game we were playing on our phones.

I played two more rounds before finally settling on the floor next to Mew, who was sprawled on his stomach with no concern for getting his clothes dirty. It was about time I helped him work on the report for tomorrow's class. I felt somewhat ashamed to take advantage of Mew, but he happened to be the hardest worker among the four of us.

Monday arrived, and I went to class as usual. The only thing out of the ordinary was Tay's insistence that we visit our university's outdoor market. I rarely ventured very far from the business building. We were part of an international program, so we didn't usually engage in any intra-university activities like people in the regular programs did.

I recalled my freshman year, three years ago now. Some up-perclassmen from our program had asked the four of us to be contestants for the King and Queen of the fresher's party. I found it ridiculous and categorically declined, and nobody had dared to bother us since.

"I've studied here for three years, and Time's only taken me to the market once. I didn't know there were so many food stalls!" Tay exclaimed excitedly, his eyes darting between the plethora of food stalls crowding the outdoor market.

The rest of us quietly followed Tem, not exactly thrilled to be in a crowded outdoor market with the sun glaring brightly overhead. I couldn't remember the last time I'd visited the market, if I'd ever been there at all...

I sighed for the umpteenth time. Time and Mew were no different. The only one who seemed to be enjoying himself was Tay. He looked so excited about everything, as if Time had been keeping him locked up in a cage this whole time and it was his first time outdoors. Meanwhile, I was starting to feel irritated. I hated being in crowded places and getting gawked at by strangers.

"Tay, are you done?" Time asked his boyfriend, his eyebrows scrunched up. "It's hot out!"

"What? I don't get to visit the market that often! Can't you just let me check everything out?" Tay complained with a pout. All three of us agreed that Tay looked adorable when he begged like a little kid, and we often ended up giving in.

"All right, let's look over there. I saw something that you'd like."

It wasn't Time who'd said that—the person who liked to spoil Tay the most was actually Mew. He put his arm around Tay and led him over to a snack stall. Time and I shared a glance and sighed in unison as we watched the two of them happily choosing snacks together. I still didn't know what Tay found so damn exciting about this market.

Soon, his hands and ours were filled with bags of food.

"Mew, stop spoiling him! It's hot outside, and I'm bored!" I blurted out. I was never interested in the food here—or the market itself. It was hot, tedious, and crowded!

"Come on! We only do this once in a while!" Mew said, giving me a reassuring pat on the shoulder. Seriously, Mew coddled Tay more than his actual boyfriend did.

"Hey, Mew, doesn't that guy look familiar?" I heard Tay say as he and Mew waited to order a crepe.

"Oh, right. He looks like your husband," Mew said, scoping out the guy Tay had mentioned.

"I'm right fucking here!" Time interrupted, obviously irked.

"It's Kinn's bodyguard!" Tay exclaimed. "That hot guy who's super rude!"

I hadn't been paying much attention to their conversation, but Tay's words made me look up instantly. I turned in the direction he and Mew were looking and spotted a familiar tall, brooding figure in the crowd. He seemed to be waiting for a friend to finish buying something.

I smiled to myself. It seemed I had finally found something interesting at this market.

"Hey! Where're you going?" Tay called out as I started walking away from them.

I heard Time yelling back at my other friends as he hurried after me. "I'm gonna go with him. You two come find us when you're done, okay?"

Porsche hadn't noticed me yet. I quickly approached him. *Meeting him here of all places—what are the odds?*

"What the hell is all this food? I said I'd treat you to lunch, not buy out the whole market!" Porsche complained to his friend, who was buying a box of french fries. His voice was impassive as always, but he seemed to speak more freely around his friends.

I watched Porsche pay for his friend's food. It surprised me that a guy like him could be so generous. Porsche eventually noticed me as I drew closer, just when he was about to leave the stall. His footsteps faltered and his brows furrowed into a scowl.

One of his friends, who was sipping a red syrup drink, nudged him. "Why did you stop?"

Porsche looked surprised to see me, so I decided to be the first to break the silence. "Hey," I said.

I casually put my hands in my pants pockets and stared directly at him. However, Porsche turned away and didn't look at me.

"Huh? What's the matter?" Porsche's friend asked.

"Wait up. What's the hurry?" I asked sternly, grabbing Porsche's arm to stop him. Porsche immediately shook me off. His reaction drew the attention of some of the crowd, who turned to look at us in interest and caution.

"What do you want?" Porsche asked tersely.

I wanted to push his buttons. "Buy me something to drink," I said casually, looking straight at him.

"No! I'm not your lackey today," Porsche replied.

"Who is this guy?" one of Porsche's friends asked, eyeing me with suspicion.

"Buy me something to drink!" I repeated, harsher this time.

"What's your problem? Why does my friend have to buy you a drink?" Porsche's friend butted in, giving me an accusatory glare.

I glanced at him. This must be Jom; I remembered Big sending me his photo after capturing him. He still had some leftover bruises.

"I won't!" Porsche yelled at me and turned away.

I yanked his arm, pulling him closer to me. Maybe I was going crazy, but riling him up was so satisfying. My initial displeasure had shifted into delight.

"Porsche! Do you want me to cause a scene?" I hissed, squeezing his arm tightly. Fortunately, Porsche didn't yell or threaten to punch me in the face like yesterday. He glanced at the passersby as he pried my hand off his arm.

"Let him go!" Porsche's other friend chimed in, stepping closer to help Porsche break free from my grip. "What makes you think you can order my friend around?"

I took a glance at the newcomer. He was cute, with a pretty face and a great body; just as attractive as Porsche. I suddenly realized why Time had been quiet this entire time. He must've been checking this guy out instead of paying attention to me.

"Porsche, who is this?" said Jom, rolling up his sleeves. "Hey! You wanna go?"

I ignored Jom and repeated my order to Porsche. "I gave you an order. Didn't you hear me?"

My eyes swept from Porsche's face to his neck, noticing that he had bandaged his bite wound like yesterday. Porsche's gaze wavered slightly.

"Really, Porsche. Who is he?" Jom asked, relentless.

"Kinn," Porsche replied.

Jom looked taken aback. I observed him more closely, taking stock of the still-healing bruises all over his body. He gulped nervously, straightening his posture and staring back at me. Apparently, he knew very well who I was.

"Hurry up," I demanded. "It's hot out here. Don't piss me off."

Porsche closed his eyes and heaved a sigh of frustration. "I'll buy you one drink, that's it," he muttered. "What a pain..."

I watched him walk away. He probably just wanted to get it over with without making a scene in the middle of a busy outdoor market. I went to sit on one of the market's benches for customers to sit and eat. If I hadn't wanted to provoke Porsche so badly, I never would have sat in a hot, cramped place like this.

"Whoa, Porsche's friend is freaking *hot!*" Time remarked as he joined me on the bench.

"Who? Jom?" I teased him back.

Time's eyes gleamed and he gave me a pleading look. "His name is Jom?"

Jom's name was getting a little too popular. I felt the need to clarify. "The one eating french fries is Jom," I told Time. "I don't know who the other guy sucking on a straw is."

"He should try sucking on something else," Time said salaciously as he watched Porsche and his friends.

"You can suck on your wife's foot," I grumbled. "Here they come."

Time quickly straightened himself up and pretended to look casual. Tay returned Time's wallet and dropped bags loaded with food all over the bench before sitting down. He fanned his face with his hand, attempting to find some relief from the heat. "It's scorching! What are you guys waiting for? Eat!"

"You knew it'd be hot, but you insisted on coming," Time scoffed, snatching a cold drink from Tay's hand and taking a sip.

I waited for Porsche to bring me my drink. Before long, he returned with his other friends, as stoic as ever, and shoved a reddish-orange smoothie in my face. I looked up at him in confusion.

"What is this?" I asked.

"A healthy smoothie," Porsche said flatly.

"Aww... I didn't know you cared about Kinn's health!" Time joked, eyeing the oddly-colored drink in suspicion.

"Enjoy," said Porsche. "I'm leaving."

"Wait," I called out before Porsche could leave. He grunted, turning around to glare at me in disdain. He looked like he wanted to ask what the hell I wanted from him.

"You drink it," I said, handing the drink back to Porsche. He looked puzzled. "I said, you drink it!" I waved the smoothie in his face.

"Not gonna. I don't like vegetables." Porsche turned away, avoiding eye contact.

"Ugh! Stop bothering my friend," Porsche's other friend cut in. "Come on, Porsche. Let's go. You don't want to miss the tryouts."

That caught my interest.

"What tryouts?" Tay asked, voicing my thoughts aloud.

"None of your fucking business," Porsche snapped.

There was a loud bang as Tay hit the bench hard with his fist, glaring at Porsche like he was ready to pick a fight.

"Hey! I asked nicely!"

Porsche ignored Tay and turned away, clearly intending to annoy him.

"Where do you think you're going?!" I said.

"None of *your* business either. Am I dismissed?" Porsche said, ready to leave. I tugged his arm to stop him without saying a word, but he shook away from my grasp. Our silent exchange went back and forth for a while until I noticed Porsche's cute friend pick up his phone. He said something into the speaker before turning to Porsche.

"Hey, P'Ohm is nagging us to hurry up. There's already a bunch of people at the pool," he said. He looked pretty agitated.

"You can't leave until you drink this," I insisted. I knew Porsche wouldn't just buy me a healthy smoothie out of the kindness of his heart. His initial reluctance to buy me a drink and how quickly he changed his mind made me suspicious.

"Ugh! Come on, I'll drink it myself!" Jom snatched the smoothie from my hand and took a big slurp, ignoring his friends' horrified looks. As soon as it hit his tongue, he spat it out, sending the drink spraying everywhere—but mostly all over Mew.

"Shit, I'm a mess!" Mew yelped as he jumped up from the bench, using his shirt to furiously wipe the smoothie off his face.

"Porsche, what the hell is in this smoothie? It tastes like shit!" Jom turned to yell at his friend, who smiled sheepishly back at him. I'd been right to think that Porsche wouldn't play nice with me.

"What's wrong with you?! It's all over my shirt and my face!" Mew confronted Jom, visibly angry and ready to fight.

"Come on, hurry up!" Porsche's other friend pulled at his shirt and jumped up and down like a squirming child. It was pretty adorable, to be honest—I was sure Time thought so too.

"I'm sorry!" Jom apologized to Mew. "I don't have any water with me, and it's too far to go buy a bottle." He then turned to hiss at his friend, "Tem, don't rush me!"

Jom turned back to Mew. "Can I take you to wash up at the pool? It's really close, and I need to take these two over there for tryouts, anyway." He was getting more agitated by the second as his friends kept hounding him to get going.

Mew nodded begrudgingly before turning to me. "You guys can wait here," he said. "I'll be right back."

Time nudged me a few times. I immediately knew what he was thinking.

"Let's all go together. Get up!" I said. My friends complied straight away. Tay and Time picked up their bags from the bench and the three of us hurried after Porsche and his friends.

I took a couple of long strides to catch up with Porsche, until I was right behind him. "I'll make you pay for trying to mess with me," I hissed.

Porsche huffed. "Sorry, I'm not your lackey anymore. Tankhun is my boss now!" he spat back through gritted teeth.

"Tsk! Do you think you can get away with it?"

Porsche picked up his pace, trying to avoid me. I snickered, watching as he drifted farther and farther away from me.

After we arrived at the university's pool—not too far from the market—Mew broke away and headed to the showers with Jom, who'd promised to take responsibility for his earlier blunder. Mew hated getting dirty; even his own sweat made him want to shower.

The rest of us stood by the stadium with our arms crossed, watching people jump into the pool for swim tryouts. I glanced around, feeling nowhere near as excited as the people cheering loudly in the bleachers seemed to be. I'd never watched sporting events at university before—I hadn't known things got this lively.

"Damn!" Time said, nudging me to get my attention as he pointed at something by the side of the pool.

I looked over and saw the prominent tattoo on Porsche's left arm. He was bare except for his swimming trunks, revealing smooth skin from head to toe. His body glistened in the afternoon sun, wet from the water he'd poured over himself before entering the pool.

Porsche's face was handsome, with a prominent nose and plump lips that suited him quite well. He raked his hand over

his undercut—I was surprised to find such an ordinary action so attractive. Then, he flexed his lightly-muscled body, twisting his tapered waist and revealing a glimpse of his six-pack abs. A loud cheer erupted in the stadium as Porsche continued his warm-up stretches.

I really should have been gawking at the guy next to him instead, but for some reason I couldn't tear my eyes off of Porsche for a second. Time was certainly busy ogling Porsche's cute friend. He barely blinked as he took in the sight of the young man's lithe body and his pale skin that practically glowed. He'd had the sense to hand Tay his phone earlier, ensuring Tay was engrossed in a mobile game and didn't notice his boyfriend checking out another guy.

"I heard his friends call him Tem," Time whispered in my ear. "Don't you lay a finger on this one! I want him for myself!"

Time probably assumed I had my eyes fixed on Tem like he did, when in reality, I couldn't stop staring at Porsche's body.

"Don't make me tell Tay," I teased him, still watching the man on the starting platform. A roar erupted from the stands as he got into position to push off. It was quite the sight to see Porsche concentrating on something other than picking fights with my bodyguards; I was surprised to see him taking something so seriously, especially a university activity.

As the sound of a whistle pierced the air, Porsche plunged into the water. He was fast, but not much faster than the other contestants. My lips curled up slightly as I watched him compete, wondering when I'd started to take such an interest in Porsche's body.

Before the match finished, Mew finally came to join us. He was soaking wet.

"That's it! I'm going home! That jerk poured water all over me!" Mew complained, pulling me away from the pool. I glanced back just in time to catch the sight of Porsche and Tem heading to the showers in the back.

I silently thanked Tay for dragging us all to the outdoor market with him today—I got to see Porsche in an entirely different light. Porsche was actually so fucking hot...

PORSCHE
[THURSDAY]

I HEAVED A SIGH, lazily checking the screen on my phone. Although I hated working for Kinn, I'd discovered that working for Tankhun wasn't really that different. The moment I stepped foot in the house, Tankhun immediately called me over the two-way radio. I barely had time to catch my breath before I was summoned to his room with a few other bodyguards.

He forced us to sit on a sofa facing an enormous TV screen and watch some shitty rom-com series. We needed to pay attention to the story in case Tankhun suddenly decided to ask for our opinion. If we couldn't answer him, all hell could break loose!

The couch in Tankhun's room wasn't off-limits like the one in Kinn's room, so I could sit freely with Tankhun's other bodyguards. They acted differently from Kinn's men. When I started my first shift on Sunday, one of them asked me if I had eaten yet, and when I said I hadn't, they were kind enough to switch their work shifts with me so I could grab a bite to eat. We called our work shifts "punishment" because we were forced to watch terrible TV shows with Tankhun. Just like what was happening right now!

I felt like I'd been locked up in a mental institution. My crazy boss did absolutely nothing important all day long. I often found him playing board games or singing karaoke. Tankhun's other body-guards told me that he'd been obsessed with TV shows lately, and he could spend hours watching them without moving from his spot on the couch. He visited his business occasionally, but he was usually reluctant to leave the house for fear of getting attacked or abducted. When I thought about it, his eccentric behavior made sense—he'd probably gotten hit in the head one too many times.

"Do you think he's gonna die?" Tankhun asked with a sniff. The rims of his eyes were red from crying.

I was leaning on an armrest, resting my face in the palm of my hand as my eyes flickered between the screen and Tankhun. Working with Tankhun was not as physically strenuous as working for Kinn, but the mental toll was the same.

Click.

Tankhun pressed a button on the remote to pause the show. The four of us bodyguards immediately straightened up and turned our eyes to him. *Here he goes!* I wondered what Tankhun was going to ask us. He would yell at me if he found my answer unsatisfactory. I couldn't believe this was my life now.

"Do you think he'll die in the end?" Tankhun repeated his question.

I exchanged glances with the other bodyguards, trying to urge someone else to take the lead and answer our boss.

"Um... I don't think the protagonist is going to die. If he did, then what would happen to his lover?" P'Jess, one of the other bodyguards, spoke up. I felt kind of sorry for him. He looked about fifty—he was way too old for this shit.

"How about you, Pol? What do you think?" Tankhun turned to a different bodyguard.

Pol looked around nervously for help. Then, he took a deep breath and answered, "I don't think so... Looking at the bullet's trajectory, I think the bad guy missed his vital organs."

Tankhun nodded, seemingly satisfied with these answers, before pressing play. All of us let out a sigh of relief. Tankhun loved haranguing us with questions out of the blue. It was driving me crazy. I wasn't sure if he or I should be sent to the psych ward—one of us belonged there, anyway.

"Yay! It's over!" Tankhun gleefully exclaimed. "You guys were right. He didn't die!"

We forced some cynical smiles before Tankhun continued: "Porsche, what should we watch next?"

This was a shock. I checked the time—it was almost midnight. Did Tankhun plan to sleep at all tonight? Sometimes, I hoped someone would abduct him and beat him into a coma. Then at least Sleeping Beauty wouldn't be our problem anymore.

"Anything is fine..." I replied wearily.

Tankhun turned to look at me. "Come here! Sit next to me and choose what to watch," he said. "Let's celebrate your new position as my bodyguard. We'll watch TV all night!"

I reluctantly went to sit next to him, taking the remote to browse through the list of TV series on the screen.

"But Mr. Tankhun," P'Jess objected feebly, "you already threw Porsche a welcome party on Sunday."

"Why not do it again? I can celebrate as many times as I want. I can celebrate all year long!" Tankhun said, sounding like a spoiled child who always got his way.

I couldn't believe that Tankhun was the eldest son of the family. He acted like a spoiled brat. I wanted to slap him upside the head with a flip-flop to teach him a lesson. With the way he looked and the way he acted, I wondered what woman would be crazy enough to be his wife—or how fucked up his children would be when they grew up.

A wild idea popped into my head. "I don't find any of these that interesting," I said, handing the remote back to Tankhun, who gawked at me. The other bodyguards sat there petrified, shocked that I would dare defy our basket-case boss. But before Tankhun could yell at me, I added, "I think we should switch from rom-coms to something a little more exciting."

Pol nudged my back. "Porsche, what are you doing?" he hissed.

"Just leave it to me," I replied to Pol under my breath. "If you want to stop watching these boring soap operas where the girls just fight each other for a guy, then do as I say."

Tankhun pouted at me for complaining about his choice of TV show. "What do you mean?" he asked.

I rolled my eyes slightly at the titles of Tankhun's favorite series: My Stupid Cupid, The Flower Garden of True Love's Sorrow, or The Clumsy Love of Mr. Klutzy. All of them made me want to throw the remote out the window.

"I promise, it'll be exhilarating." I pulled out my phone to connect it to the giant smart TV.

"Really? If it sucks, I'll smack you," Tankhun said, crossing his arms and leaning back on the couch. His eyes were fixed on the TV screen as I went into the web browser on my phone and found my favorite tab.

Arm leaned over to see what was on my screen. "Oh gosh, Porsche! Don't!" he exclaimed, his eyes widening in shock.

"Come on," I said with a shit-eating grin. "Don't tell me you guys don't want to watch it."

"Well...I do. But...it's a bad idea!" Pol tried to stop me from completing my mission.

I gave them a pointed glare. "Do you want to keep watching those stupid soap operas?" I muttered. "I'm trying to help!"

Their faces fell at my words. They went back to their seats and watched me with worried expressions. I bet someone as naïve and sheltered as Tankhun would never have seen anything like this! I couldn't wait to test just how innocent he was.

Once I saw my phone had connected to the TV, I pressed play, and the intro music began. Tankhun paid very close attention to the TV, increasing the volume even more when he found the sound to be too low.

I got up from the sofa and went outside to call the other body-guards to join us. They looked rather sullen as they shuffled their way inside. Then, their eyes went wide as saucers at the image on the screen of a Japanese woman walking to her office in a super tight uniform.

"What's going on? Is nobody going to say anything? Why are they just walking?" Tankhun asked, upping the sound another notch.

I leaned against the wall behind the sofa with my legs crossed, smiling in amusement as I looked from the TV to Tankhun, who was engrossed in the action onscreen.

"Mr. Tankhun...I'm afraid this might get too loud," one of the bodyguards warned as Tankhun continued to increase the volume. The story was still unfolding, and it hadn't yet reached its climax. I looked at Tankhun's rapt expression as he watched the screen and came to the hilarious realization that someone like him was too naïve to know about these kinds of movies.

"Why is he tying her up like that?"

All of the bodyguards and I struggled to hold back our laughter at Tankhun's question. The movie I'd decided to show Tankhun was a Japanese porno about an office lady getting tied up by her boss.

[FIFTEEN MINUTES LATER]

All eyes were glued to the screen, especially Tankhun's—his face was nearly flush with the monitor.

"Ah... Ahhh... Kimochiii... Mmm—!"

The sound reverberated throughout the room, and it seemed no one wanted to lower the volume. Thanks to Tankhun's expensive home theater system, the continuous moaning made it feel like we were right there in the action. I felt a twisted sort of pride in my choice of movie—everyone seemed rapt. After all, this particular porno was my favorite.

I was so absorbed in the events onscreen that I didn't hear the pounding on the door. When no one answered, the man outside barged into the room.

"What the hell are you all doing?!"

A thunderous yell from behind made us jolt up immediately. When we turned around to see Mr. Korn standing there, we all looked down in shame, with one exception: Tankhun. He continued watching, ignoring his father's arrival.

"Khun! What on earth are you doing?!" Mr. Korn demanded. I saw he was not alone. P'Chan and Kinn stood behind him, watching the situation unfold with great interest.

"Shh... Be quiet, Father!" Tankhun shushed Mr. Korn without even turning to look at him.

"Seriously? Do you know how loud this is? You nearly gave me a heart attack!" Mr. Korn said with a pained sigh, clutching his hand to his chest. "Just turn the volume down, would you? I don't care if you want to watch porn. But...is it really something you should watch with other people?"

"Ugh, Father! Be quiet!" Tankhun cried out in annoyance, but he eventually reached for the remote to lower the volume.

Kinn was leaning against the doorframe. "Just let him do what he wants, Father. It's good he's finally showing interest in this sort of thing," he snickered. "He might even be able to give you grandchildren soon, eh?"

Mr. Korn just shook his head at Kinn and left without another word. I noticed Kinn smirk in my direction. Then he simply followed Mr. Korn and left, closing the door behind him. Now that the brief commotion was over, nobody wanted to leave. The rest of us stayed to watch the video all the way through.

I let the smoke escape my lips, my head tilted up slightly to allow the cool night wind to gently brush my face. Once he finished watching my favorite movie, Tankhun had started feeling sleepy, so we were dismissed from his room.

I was finally able to take a breather after a long day. Tankhun was a highly demanding and irritating boss—although at least he didn't nitpick me all the time like Kinn did.

Speaking of Kinn, that had been the first time I saw him after the incident at our university on Monday. I wasn't sure if Kinn was my boss or my nemesis—he insisted on tormenting me both at home and at school.

I knew he was trying to rile me up at the market. I really wanted to slug him, but I knew it was a bad idea. If I got into a fight on university grounds, my scholarship would be revoked. That was why I tried to sneak my revenge on him with the smoothie, but he managed to sniff me out. That man was as stubborn as a dog!

"Hey, Porsche! Lookin' good!" Pete greeted me cheerfully, pulling a pack of cigarettes out of his pants pocket as he approached.

"Yeah, I'm feeling good," I replied.

"I'm glad you're happy," Pete said with a laugh. He didn't look as miserable as he had when I first met him, and now I knew why.

"What about you?" I asked. "How's everything going?"

"Oh, it's heaven on earth! I can finally see the light at the end of the tunnel!" Pete gushed.

"Don't be so dramatic!"

I looked around aimlessly as Pete and I sat in companionable silence, enjoying our cigarettes. Then, I noticed Kom, Kinn's driver, emerge from the front door of the house. A young man followed him to a car idling in the driveway. Wondering who he might be, I turned to Pete.

"Hey, who's that?" I asked, gesturing at the unfamiliar figure leaving in the car with Kom.

"Mr. Kinn's guest," Pete replied.

It seemed like Kinn had a lot of nighttime guests. I'd never seen this one before.

"Kinn has lots of visitors," I mused. "Why does he look all roughed up? Did Kinn slap him around?" I continued.

Pete frowned at me. "Huh? It's not like that," he said. "You *do* know what they were up to, don't you?"

I stared blankly at Pete, not sure what he meant by that. The only thing I knew was that Kinn loved kicking my ass. I wondered if Kinn liked beating up his friends, too. Just how screwed up was this guy?

"What do you mean, do I *know*?"

"That man was his lov—"

Bzzzzt!

A buzzing sound from my two-way radio interrupted Pete before he could finish his sentence.

"Porsche!" came Tankhun's voice from my walkie-talkie. "Where are you? Come to my room!"

I looked at my radio in disbelief. I thought Tankhun had already gone to bed. I stubbed out my cigarette in the garden's ashtray, forgetting to ask what Pete was about to say.

"I gotta go!"

I rushed back into the house, wondering what my crazy new boss wanted this time. From Kinn to Tankhun—I'd gone out of the frying pan and into the fire.

KINN
PORSCHE

11

Nervous

"**P**ORSCHE! I don't want to watch the kinds of movies you showed me last night anymore!"

"You didn't like them?"

"No! There's nothing but sex!"

I smirked at Tankhun, who kept changing the TV channel without looking at me. I wasn't sure if he was embarrassed about last night or if something else had happened, but the other bodyguards told me that he was quieter than usual today. I wondered how a guy his age could still be embarrassed about sex. How was he this naïve? Was he born on the back of a unicorn and raised in a lavender field? Had he even had sex with a woman yet? It would be ridiculous if he was still a virgin.

After he'd shooed us away last night, Tankhun summoned us back a bit later and asked us to show him two more porn videos. He said they were exciting and unlike anything he'd seen before. The other bodyguards and I had forced our eyes open until it was nearly four in the morning. We watched porn with Tankhun until he eventually decided to call it a night. Our initial excitement from watching porn quickly turned into exhaustion when he kept bombarding us with questions: why was he restraining her? Why were they having sex under the table? Why was she tied up? He went on, and on...

"Do you really want to watch this, Mr. Tankhun?" Arm asked, nudging me repeatedly like he wanted me to do something.

The four of us were in our usual seats in Tankhun's room, bracing ourselves to watch a show called "Falling in Love in a Sugar Cane Field by the Woods." The title alone made me roll my eyes.

Since Tankhun had given us a preemptive warning that he didn't want to watch porn again, I was running out of options to get us out of this. I wondered if he ever planned to do anything else with his day. I was hoping I'd get to do some typical bodyguard activities, at least, like fighting and beating up would-be attackers—not being tormented with garbage TV!

The truth was plain to see—Tankhun was just lonely!

"Ah... Mr. Tankhun," I whispered. I addressed him as politely as the other bodyguards did, even though I really wanted to call him a moron. I didn't feel the need to disrespect Tankhun like I did with Kinn, because Tankhun had never gone out of his way to piss me off. That was why I reluctantly tried to be polite with him.

"What?"

"Don't you want to go out?" I asked. I was really starting to feel cooped up in this room. My life had become so damn boring. Day in and day out, all Tankhun did was watch TV. Didn't he want to experience the nightlife?

"I didn't have anything to attend to outside," Tankhun replied innocently, looking at me with his big, round eyes.

Kinn and Tankhun had a striking resemblance to each other, but Tankhun looked like Kinn with rainbows and butterflies coming out of his ears. Let me put it this way: he looked like the idiot version of Kinn.

"So, Mr. Tankhun, don't you want to...um—"

"Are you guys bored?" Tankhun cut me off before I could make my suggestion.

I glanced at the men next to me; their faces paled, as if afraid Tankhun might go berserk on us.

"Um..."

Tankhun didn't wait for an answer. He turned off the TV with the remote in his hand and announced, "Let's sing karaoke, then!"

There was a chorus of sighs from the other three bodyguards. I wanted to scream!

"That's not what I meant, Mr. Tankhun. I think you should experience the excitement of nightlife," I said casually, watching as he took microphones and a home karaoke system out of a cabinet.

"Going out?! No way!" Tankhun didn't bother to look at me. "I'm tired of getting abducted!" He busied himself with connecting the microphones to their cables, and a couple of the other bodyguards went over to help him out.

"What about going out for a drink? Do you not like bars?" I asked, hatching a plan so I wouldn't be stuck here feeling bored. I could go out and do things that I liked—my every day used to revolve around vibrant nightlife. Right now, it felt like I was being held prisoner by a maniac.

"Nope! I'll get jumped if I go to a bar," Tankhun said with a shake of his head.

I figured the bar he had in mind was someplace similar to where Kinn visited last time: a bar full of rich people. I wouldn't be surprised if he bumped into his enemies there; the place was full of wealthy elites.

"Then we won't go to those bars," I insisted. "Let's go somewhere new, somewhere fun. Somewhere you won't run into your enemies."

Tankhun turned to look at me, his brows knitted together in confusion. I felt like my communication skills had improved a lot lately—it was a skill I needed to survive in this place.

"Where?" Tankhun inquired.

"It's somewhere fun with lots of people. I guarantee no one will hurt you there," I said with a smile.

Pol scooted closer to me. "What the hell are you doing?"

"Don't you want to go out and have some fun?" I whispered back.

My statement seemed to spark something within him. Pol smiled brightly at me and nodded. "Of course! Anything other than watching these shows or singing karaoke."

I turned to look at Tankhun's back, a wicked smile creeping across my face. *I'll show you a whole new world.*

"Come on, Mr. Tankhun. It'll be safe, I promise!" I repeated, trying to reassure him. It wouldn't be difficult to persuade someone as gullible as him.

Tankhun stood up, staring at me nervously with his arms crossed over his chest. "Are you sure no one will try to attack me?"

"I'm sure!" I said. "We just need to blend in. We'll have a great time!"

Tankhun gave me a nod, but he still looked rather doubtful. "If I get assaulted or have a bad time, I'll tell my father to kill you!" he told me.

I nodded wearily. The other bodyguards knew where Tankhun's enemies hung around. Why couldn't they just look for a different place? It wasn't rocket science.

Tankhun turned to bark an order at his men. "You guys, let's go!"

"Wait! You can't go out like this," I stopped him. He looked at me questioningly.

The other bodyguards still looked hesitant. "We've got to blend in. We need to change into something less formal. Trust me!" I insisted.

All eyes turned to look at Tankhun for confirmation. He still seemed reluctant, so I pressed on. "We don't want to stand out," I explained. "Nobody will pay us any attention if we blend in. I swear, you'll have a great time!"

Tankhun finally gave in. "Fine! We'll go! If it's not fun, you'll pay for it," he said, stomping off to his bedroom to get changed.

I smiled, looking forward to the night about to unfold. Finally, something exciting!

I instructed the other men to change out of their suits. Then, I knocked on Tankhun's bedroom door. "Wear something casual!" I shouted. "Don't wear a suit unless you want your head bashed in!"

Tankhun yelled back that he understood. I grinned. Maybe I could work with this guy.

The fancy bars these people frequented had hot women, sure, but they were no match for the women at the bar I intended to take them to.

We piled into one of the swanky vans that Tankhun's family owned. The rest of the staff in the house eyed us in suspicion, probably wondering what the hell we were up to—they'd just witnessed us change into T-shirts and jeans and follow our dipshit boss into a van.

Tankhun had eventually decided on a white shirt and simple jeans. Initially, he put on black slacks, and I immediately told him to change. I didn't want the bouncer to mistake his outfit for a university uniform and deny him entry. Luckily, he had a pair of jeans in his closet—admittedly, jeans that cost nearly a hundred grand, but at least he could change into something that made him look like a normal guy.

The van finally came to a stop in front of a familiar place that I used to frequent on an almost daily basis. Tankhun's bodyguards looked so excited that I felt sorry for them; their lives must have been insanely boring. Tankhun himself seemed fascinated by the alley where the club was located. This place was the heart of local nightlife, filled with clubbers dressed to the nines. Loud, lively music blared from each establishment as if they were all competing to be the noisiest on the block. I walked to the place I knew best, with its vibrant lights in front that beckoned guests to come inside.

"Holy shit, it's Porsche! Madam, Porsche brought his gangsters to wreck our place again!" someone shouted as I stepped inside. I watched as he ran to Madam Yok's office and knocked on the door. Madam Yok immediately emerged, dressed in her usual qipao. Her eyes widened as she saw me, and she came barreling toward me.

"What the hell are you doing here? I just reopened this place a week ago!" Madam Yok shouted like a maniac, frantically shaking my arms.

"Madam, no one is wrecking your place tonight!" I tried to calm her. "I brought you a VIP customer!" I pried her off me and nodded to the man behind me, who was looking around in awe.

"A VIP?" Madam Yok repeated, snapping her paper fan open as she checked Tankhun out. "Aww, he's so handsome! But...why does he look familiar?"

"He's also *loaded*," I whispered. "Get me a good table."

Madam Yok nodded and instructed the waiters to prepare a table for our group. Once the table was set, I led Tankhun to sit right in front of the stage. Madam Yok had mentioned there would be live music tonight.

I ordered the most expensive whiskey in the house—Jack Daniel's—along with water, soda, and Coke. I was pretty sure Tankhun had never tasted anything like this before, since the bar I'd gone to with Kinn had served drinks that probably cost more than ten thousand baht per bottle.

"Do they have wine?" Tankhun asked me.

"They don't, but trust me, the drink I'm gonna make you tastes much better than wine," I said as I put some ice in a glass. Mixing drinks was my specialty—I used to be the number one bartender in this club. He'd love it for sure!

"I'll become a monk[12] for you, Porsche!" Arm praised me. "Shit! We owe you big time!"

"It's nothing," I replied. Working for Tankhun was depressing, and I figured this was the least I could do to help them out.

Everyone looked around eagerly, handing me their glasses so I could make them drinks. I passed a glass of whiskey and Coke to Tankhun, who was sitting across from me and bobbing his head to the music.

"I've never been anywhere like this!" he told me, taking a sip of the drink. He paused for a moment, looking surprised at the unfamiliar taste, before taking a couple more sips. "This is good!" he exclaimed, smiling brightly at me.

I knew it! A guy as sheltered as Tankhun really never had experienced a night out like this.

"Porsche, I love you!" Pol proclaimed, throwing his arm over my shoulder as he gulped down his drink. I smiled at him, feeling pleased that my idea to go out was proving a hit.

"What's this song? It rocks!" Tankhun said as his body started to sway to the upbeat rhythm of a Luk Thung song[13] reverberating through the club.

Oh, welcome, ladies and gentlemen!
Oh, welcome, ladies and gentlemen!

12   This is a common expression for showing gratitude, stemming from the belief of Buddhist men in Thailand that becoming a monk is a form of expressing great gratitude, especially to their parents for raising them.
13   Luk Thung is a genre of Thai country music.

Hurry up! Don't wait up, pretty lady.
Anybody wanna have some fun?
Get up and shake, shake, shake, shake, shake, shake, and make your
way over here![14]

All of us tried our hardest not to spit out our drinks in laughter as Tankhun shook his shoulders energetically. I wasn't sure if Madam Yok had decided to have a Luk Thung night at her place tonight or what, but Tankhun seemed to really dig the music. He danced enthusiastically, throwing his arms up in the air and loudly shouting nonsense. I'd only made him two drinks, but he already looked wasted. The rest of his bodyguards began to dance along to the music, too, laughing at our boss's weird dance moves.

"Pol, come dance with me! Go ahead and have fun, guys. Tonight is on me!" Tankhun shouted while beckoning Pol—who was dancing just as hard as he was—over to him.

After ensuring that everything was going smoothly, I slipped away from the table to greet my acquaintances around the club. Some customers who knew me rushed over to give me a hug or buy me a drink. I caused quite a stir, seeing as I used to be the most popular bartender here. I also knew that I looked sexier after I'd had a couple of drinks. I wasn't trying to brag—everyone told me I did.

After a while, I returned to Tankhun's table to see how things were going. It seemed that even P'Jess, who was pushing fifty years old, had joined in dancing to the Thai Cha-Cha-Cha music. They looked like drunk partiers dancing wildly during Songkran.[15] Other bar patrons cheered loudly, urging them on. I saw Arm and Pol

---

14 The song's name is Ma Kat (Bit by a Dog), a famous song by Ekachai Srivichai with ambiguous lyrics that sound sexual and suggestive but are innocent in context.
15 Songkran is a Thai New Year festival that is celebrated on April 13th, known for its water fights and wild parties.

trying to teach Tankhun the infamous 'catching the stars'[16] dance.
I shook my head, amused at them and their annoying dance moves.
I wouldn't be surprised if they ended up pissing someone off with
their rowdy dancing.

"Are you kids already drunk?" Madam Yok asked as she approached our table.

Tankhun, extremely flushed from the alcohol, stopped dancing
and turned to gawk at the approaching figure.

"Ah, it's a kathoey!"[17] Tankhun shouted, pointing at Madam Yok.
"I've heard about kathoeys, but I've never seen one!" He added a
weird sing-song melody to his last sentence. It was obvious he was
drunk.

"Shut your mouth, you little shit, or I'll slap you! I'm a woman!"
Madam Yok exclaimed, readying to take off her high heel and chuck
it at Tankhun.

"Don't mind him, Madam! He's an idiot!" I said, slipping my
hands into my pockets.

I looked at Tankhun and his men again. They were doing a
Ramwong dance[18] around the table now, walking three steps forward
and four steps back—it was kind of stressing me out!

"What a shame. He's so handsome," Madam Yok said, still looking
annoyed at Tankhun, "but he's a dimwit!"

"Don't mind him," I told her.

---

16 A dance move featuring exaggerated pulling downward movements accompanied by excessive
hip-swaying. It's popular among teenagers, especially motopunk boys and girls.
17 Kathoey (sometimes translated as "ladyboy") is an identity used by people in Thailand,
Cambodia, and Laos. Some self-described Kathoey identify themselves as effeminate gay men, while
others are transgender women—however, not all transgender women identify as Kathoey. This term
can carry derogatory connotations, as in the case here.
18 Ramwong is a Thai folk dance where the dancers dance in a circle to the rhythm of percussion
instruments. Today, Ramwong has also become a popular form of entertainment during festivals,
where festival-goers dance with Sao Ramwong (female Ramwong dancers belonging to a Ramwong
band) to uplifting music played by a live band.

"Who is he?"

"Kinn's older brother. You know Kinn, right? The guy who wrecked your place?" I answered.

Madam Yok immediately clutched her chest, clearly terrified. "Oh my god! Why didn't you tell me sooner that he's in the mafia? If I knew, I'd have treated him better. Oh, maybe I should sing for them." Madam Yok lifted the hem of her long qipao and scurried to the stage.

Tankhun looked pissed when Madame Yok shooed the current singer away and stopped the music. He glared at her, irritated.

"Get back down here, ladyboy! I want to dance!" Tankhun shouted, and a burst of laughter erupted in the club.

Madam Yok gritted her teeth, attempting to hold back her anger, before speaking into the microphone in a high pitch.

"Tonight is an extraordinary night—we have a VIP guest! I'd like to give him a warm welcome by dedicating this song to him. Let's give our guest a round of applause!"

I stood with my arms crossed, curiously watching Madam Yok onstage. Then, the music started, and Tankhun and his bodyguards resumed dancing. I had no idea Tankhun would enjoy this kind of music so much. Maybe next time I should take him to a Mor Lam[19] concert in the countryside, like Valentine Band.[20] He'd love it.

I can't sleep. My heart is restless, mad with fever.
I've been scared for so many nights,
Startled by a man with a gun every time I close my eyes.
He stands there, he stands here,
Pointing his gun to shoot me there,

---

19 Mor Lam is a kind of traditional music in Isaan (North-Eastern Thailand) and Laos, known for its distinct vocalizations.

20 Valentine Band is a famous performance group that plays Luk Thung and Thai pop music at festivals. The group consists of various singers, dancers, and Coyote Girls (female dancers who dance in a sexually provocative manner).

Pointing his gun to shoot me here,
Cocking his gun to shoot me there,
Cocking his gun to shoot me here.
Aah! I'm startled awake![21]

I rarely laughed, but I was cackling now at the sight of Tankhun dancing to the music. I wished his father could see his son pretending to point a gun at Pol, who played along by trying to duck away. Then, when Madam Yok sang the last part, Tankhun chased his bodyguards around the table.

"Porsche! Come here! Dance with me!" Tankhun called me over. I walked over to him, still laughing. He put his arm around me, and we continued dancing to the upbeat music. All the while, I made sure his glass stayed full.

"This is great! I love it!" Tankhun shouted, downing the contents of the glass in one go. "This's a magic glass! Why can't I ever finish m'drink?" he slurred. The drunker he got, the crazier his dancing became.

"I think we should call it a night soon. Mr. Tankhun looks ready to pass out," P'Jess said as he came over to me, still panting from all the dancing.

I pulled out my mobile phone to check the time. It was almost two in the morning, and the club would close soon. I glanced at Tankhun, who had passed out on a sofa, and then looked back at P'Jess and nodded.

Pol and I each held one of Tankhun's arms to lug him toward the parking lot. After we pushed our unconscious boss into the van, the rest of the bodyguards chatted away about how much fun this night had been, praising me like I was some kind of hero.

---

21 *Nong Non Mai Lab ("I Can't Sleep") by Apaporn Nakornsawaan, a famous female Luk Thung singer.*

When we arrived home, Arm and Pol helped Tankhun to his room and I trailed behind them. Pete appeared from the opposite side of the house, looking surprised when he saw us.

"Why is Mr. Tankhun in such a state?" Pete asked.

"I took him out for an eye-opening experience," I replied, amused at his confusion. Then I noticed the car keys in his hand. "Where are you going?"

"I'm driving Mr. Mile home."

I looked behind him and saw a young man in his late teens coming toward us. He was in a similar disheveled state to the guests of Kinn's I'd seen last night and the night before. Frowning slightly, I turned around to ask Pete about him, but he just followed Mr. Mile without saying goodbye. I shrugged and decided to continue on my way to Tankhun's room when I heard someone speak.

"Where have you all been?"

I turned and saw Kinn walking toward me, wearing only a black bathrobe.

"None of your business," I snapped at him.

"None of my business?! You reek of alcohol! Where did you take my brother?" Kinn said, leaning closer to me. I quickly took a step backward when he started sniffing near the nape of my neck.

"Just leave me alone," I muttered, too tired to start an argument with him. I was dizzy and my head was pounding. I'd had too much to drink. Tankhun had ordered two bottles of whiskey tonight and ordered everyone to drink up—he'd threatened to smash the whiskey bottle over the head of anyone who dared to defy him.

"Who said you could leave?!" Kinn hissed when I turned away from him. He grabbed my arm and wrenched me forward, sending me crashing into his broad chest.

"Let go of me, asshole!" I yelped, trying to struggle free from his viselike grip. Kinn dragged me toward his room while his bodyguards looked on, not interfering. The door slammed shut behind me before I could throw him off.

"What the hell?" I glared at Kinn, still trying to pry his hand off my arm.

Kinn frowned, his hands on his hips. "I heard people say Tankhun and his bodyguards changed into casual outfits and went out together. Tell me where you've been."

I closed my eyes and tried not to puke, holding back anger and dizziness. Kinn harassing me was not helping in the least. Figuring he was only trying to set me off, I went to sit on his sofa, propping my elbow on the armrest and resting my head in my hand before looking up at him.

"What do you want from me?" I asked, my voice flat.

"Psh! You're drunk." The corners of Kinn's lips lifted slightly as he approached me. "Every time you're drunk, you're just..." He trailed off, his eyes roaming all over my body.

I pushed at Kinn's stomach when he got dangerously close, intending to stop him, but I ended up pulling the sash that tied his bathrobe loose. The silk band dropped to the floor, and the front of his bathrobe fell open. Kinn only wore boxers underneath, revealing a muscular torso and well-defined abs. Kinn's near-nakedness didn't trouble me; we were both men. I was merely startled that I'd accidentally opened his bathrobe. I quickly averted my gaze, fearing he might scold me for my actions.

"Heh... I didn't know you wanted to see me naked," Kinn said.

I looked back up at him, confused at the innuendo.

"Why would I? I have the same equipment as you," I retorted.

Maybe I would have been excited if he had a nice pair of boobs to look at.

"You're the one undressing me," Kinn said with a grin.

Huh? Why isn't he pissed at me? What the hell is he smiling about?!

Kinn leaned closer. "What's wrong with you?!" I yelped, trying to scramble off the sofa, but he trapped me in the bracket of his arms. What had gotten into him?!

"Get off me!" I insisted, pushing at him, but Kinn seized my wrists and pinned me down with his body. I fell flat on my back on the sofa, his heavy weight settling on top of me.

"What the fuck are you doing?" I demanded, lifting my knee to shove him off, but he managed to press my arms down onto the couch.

"Answer me," Kinn said, his face dangerously close to mine. "Where have you been?"

I turned my head from side to side, trying to avoid the hot breath ghosting over my face.

"Let go! What are you doing? I only took him clubbing! He wanted to go. Kinn, let me go!"

Kinn's actions were baffling, especially when he pressed his nose below my jaw. I made a futile attempt to twist away from him. What the hell was going on?!

I heard Kinn chuckle, the sound a deep rumble from his throat. Although I was confident in my strength, he'd managed to wrestle me into a difficult position, and I couldn't manage to throw him off of me.

"What are you doing?" I thrashed wildly. "Don't you dare bite my neck again!"

Kinn's nose slowly swept from my jaw to my neck—the unbitten side. I tucked in my chin to avoid his contact, but it gave him instant access instead. He immediately pressed his nose to my neck and inhaled.

I was left dumbfounded by Kinn's actions. I felt a shiver running down my spine as he started to nibble and suck at the skin of my neck, and my heart skipped a beat at the twinge of pain.

"Kinn, don't you dare bite me!" I screamed at him, feeling a sort of déjà vu. I was apprehensive, bracing myself for the inevitable bite, but it never came.

"Let me go!" I felt hot, moist breath on my neck as Kinn kept nudging me with his nose, like he was trying to inhale my scent. My mind went black and I started to feel lightheaded, and a strange, unknown feeling bubbled up within me. My resistance started to falter, until a sudden buzzing noise brought me back to the present.

Bzzzt!

"Hello, hello. Testing, testing. Porsche! Where the hell are you? Mr. Tankhun threw up. Come help us clean up the mess!"

I recognized Pol's voice coming from my walkie-talkie. I thrashed against Kinn with all my might, but just then, he released me. I quickly stood and moved as far away from him as I could.

"What the fuck were you doing?!" I yelled in his face, feeling both confused and furious about what he'd done. I could only conclude that Kinn was trying to mess with my head. He'd been looking for a chance to bite me again, but Pol had interrupted him before he succeeded.

"Hmm... I shouldn't have let Mile go so early," Kinn muttered to himself, closing his bathrobe like he was trying to hide something. I eyed him skeptically as he bent down to grab the sash on the floor and tie it around his waist.

I didn't wait around to see what he'd do next. I stormed out of his room, kicking the sofa along the way. It seemed that Kinn thrived off tormenting me, as I heard him burst into laughter, so I turned around and gave him the middle finger before slamming his door shut.

Why did that psycho love making me suffer? Was he looking for a chance to draw blood? Damn it! One day, it would be my turn to make that bastard bleed.

"What happened to your neck?" Pol asked me as he wiped off Tankhun's vomit.

I immediately touched the side of my neck and went to check the mirror in the bathroom. Reddish bruises had begun to bloom on my skin. I frowned, stomping out of the bathroom.

Screw you, Kinn! You're trying to embarrass me, aren't you?

"Did you sneak away at the club to make out with some chick? Did she give you those hickeys?" Arm teased, putting clean pajamas on Tankhun.

"It's just my shrimp allergy—it always gives me a rash!" I answered him, flustered. I would've been pretty smug if I'd gotten these hickeys from a woman. Instead, it was that asshole Kinn, trying to set me off.

Arm and Pol looked at me dubiously. I ignored their attempts to poke fun at me, turning my attention to the man sleeping spread-eagle in the middle of his enormous bed. I had no idea Tankhun was such a loopy drunk. He even pushed my hand away when I attempted to clean him with a damp cloth, throwing his hands into the air and singing something incomprehensible. It was seriously annoying!

I was on shift the next morning, but Tankhun slept all day, leaving me and the other bodyguards with nothing to do. We strolled around the house and chilled out, smoked cigarettes, or played games on our phones. I'd grown close to Tankhun's bodyguards by now, and they stood up for me every time we ran into Kinn's bodyguards. They didn't like Kinn's men either, especially Big. They said that Kinn's men liked to gang up and bully others, always acting like they were better than the rest of them.

[6:00 P.M.]

The rest of Tankhun's bodyguards and I returned to the main residence after having dinner in the staff mess hall. Suddenly, I heard a commotion break out; alarmed, we rushed to the source of the noise.

"Pointing my gun to shoot him there!" came Tankhun's singsong voice.

I saw him pulling a gun out of the waist holster of one of the bodyguards and pointing it at him.

"Cocking my gun to shoot him there!" Tankhun sang, and pointed the gun at another bodyguard, who quickly ducked down to take cover. P'Jess, Pol, Arm, and I tried to stifle our laughter.

"Cocking my gun to shoot him here!"

A group of his lackeys, who happened to be nearby, quickly put their hands behind their heads and ran away frantically, yelling for mercy.

"Aah! I was startled awake!" Tankhun dropped the gun to the floor, yelling the last line of the song and running around until he stopped in front of his father, who glared at him from the door of his office.

"What the hell are you doing?" Mr. Korn demanded, looking sternly at his eldest son. Tankhun giggled gleefully. "Where were you last night?"

Tankhun ignored his father's questions and beckoned us over to him, still singing the famous Valentine Band song, much to his father's dismay.

"Hey mister, hey mister, my name's Khun, and I'm here with Porsche and Arm! La, la, la—!"

P'Jess smiled as he answered the big boss. "We took him clubbing last night, sir."

"That's good. He should get out of the house more," Mr. Korn remarked before returning to his office. He probably couldn't be bothered to keep trying to speak with his son.

"Let's go again tonight! I love it there!" Tankhun exclaimed, shaking my arm excitedly.

I nodded at him and then looked at Pol and Arm, who gave me a thumbs-up.

"Where are you guys going? Let me come with you," came a familiar voice. I quickly turned around to see a smiling Kinn walking in our direction. He glanced at me briefly before turning his attention to his elder brother. I glowered at him, wanting to sock him squarely in the face for all the bandages on my neck and the questions everyone kept asking about them. *Screw you, asshole!*

"Yeah, come with us!" Tankhun said. "It was superb!"

"All right!" Kinn smirked and walked away while I cursed him inside my head.

"I'm mafia, I've never helped the clan," Tankhun sang to himself as he headed toward the kitchen. "My men know, my father knows, even the house spirits know. Tankhun means freedom. I'd never bow down to anyone because I'm Thai. I'm proud to be Thai and a slave to no one!" Either this guy was insane or I was. I didn't understand Tankhun at all!

We headed to Madam Yok's club at around eight, with Kinn and Pete joining our entourage this time. They both wore casual clothes like the rest of us. Pete seemed very excited about the club, having heard about it from Pol, and said it was like a dream come true to go out with us tonight. I was happy that Pete was coming—it was Kinn I was dreading hanging out with. He wore his typical all-black outfit that gave the impression he was in mourning, and he gave off his usual nonchalant air.

I'd called ahead to make a reservation with Madam Yok and informed her there would be more guests than last night. I asked Tankhun if I could invite my friends to come along, and he said yes—the more, the merrier.

"Tem and Jom are waiting for you at the table," Madam Yok said when she saw me. She then turned to greet the other guests. "Good evening, Mr. Tankhun! Oh, you came too, Mr. Kinn? Please, come in!"

I had no idea when Madam Yok had gotten on such good terms with Kinn, considering he was the one who'd wrecked her club last time.

"Evening, kathoeyyy!" Tankhun greeted back.

"Kathoey, your ass!" Madam Yok swore under her breath before flashing a smile back at Tankhun. I held back my laughter and gave her a pat on the shoulder in consolation.

Madam Yok's service was top-notch, with drinks already waiting at our table without us having to ask. Tankhun insisted on the same music as last night, and Madam Yok gladly complied with his request.

"Why didn't you tell me there'd be so many people? I'm nervous!" Tem hissed at me as he greeted Tankhun and Kinn. He looked frightened at the group of bodyguards trailing after them. These men had come out with us not because they were worried about Tankhun's and Kinn's safety, but because they wanted to have fun.

"Come on, it's gonna be fun," I replied, smiling at Tem before I glanced at Kinn, who plunked down beside me on the sofa.

"Go sit somewhere else," I said.

"Why? I want to sit here."

"Well, I don't want to sit next to you!" I snapped.

"I can't believe you've brought Tankhun to a place like this," Kinn said, casually lounging on the cushions. "What if something happens to my brother?"

"It's safer than the places *you* go," I replied, feeling annoyed that he kept staring at me.

Kinn turned to give an order to Pete. "Pete, can you meet Mr. Time and Mr. Tay at the entrance and show them to the table?" The rest of the bodyguards seemed to know what was expected of them, and began to mix drinks for everyone at the table.

I looked at Kinn. His eyes were scanning the place, trying not to show his nervousness. I could tell that he wasn't used to places like this. Tankhun, on the other hand, jumped onto the dance floor as soon as the music started. Then he shoved his glass in front of me.

"I want Porsche to make my drink! His drinks taste so good!" I nodded at him and did as I was told.

"Is this really Kinn's older brother? He seems nuts," Jom whispered. I laughed at him while mixing Tankhun's drink.

"It's just the way he is," I said with a shrug and handed the drink to Tankhun, who was dancing with Pol and Arm like a bunch of young, rowdy punks.

"Fix a drink for me, too," Kinn said casually with his arms crossed, the corner of his lips quirked in a sinister smile.

I couldn't be bothered to argue with him, so I took a glass to make a whiskey and Coke for him.

"You look used to this," Kinn remarked.

I shrugged and looked up to see his friends approaching our table. They seemed slightly taken aback to see Tankhun and Kinn in this kind of place, which annoyed me. I wondered just how high and mighty they were that they couldn't visit a normal club like this.

When Time and Tay came over to the sofa where Kinn and I sat, I got up to give them my seat. However, a large hand grabbed my wrist—Kinn pulled me back down and scooted closer, pressing himself against me so his friends could sit on his other side.

"Pete, go sit over there," Kinn said, then addressed me: "You stay where you are."

"Why do we have to huddle so close together? Let me get more chairs," I complained, trying to pull my hand away from his grasp.

"I told you to stay here and make drinks for me," Kinn ordered.

"I'm not your host boy, asshole!" I snarled at Kinn, who kept smiling at me. Eventually, he let go of me, and I went to sit on the other sofa with Tem and Jom.

"Such a smart mouth," Kinn muttered.

I ignored him and deftly made drinks for everyone at our table.

"Tay, Time, come dance with me!"

Tay's and Time's faces paled when they heard Tankhun calling for them. They turned to look at Kinn, as if asking whether he really wanted to stay here. I side-eyed Kinn, displeased at his friends' behavior. They didn't seem to care what I thought, though, and in the end Kinn's tall friend just went over to Tankhun without kicking up a fuss.

Our group took the largest table in the club and became the center of attention for every patron in the place. It was partly due to how good-looking we were, but the majority of the attention was on Tankhun and his bodyguards' dance moves. They let it all out, as if they hadn't been allowed to dance in ages. It made me wonder if their parents had never taken them to Mor Lam concerts when they were kids. In any case, this was the moment they could finally let go.

Soon after, Tankhun made Jom and Tem join him on the dance floor as well. I told my friends to just humor him. I didn't want Tankhun to throw a temper tantrum here; that would be a disaster, so they were obliged to join in with Tankhun's crazy dance moves.

Ngad-tang-ngad-tang-ngad-tang-ngad
Ah, ngad-tang-ngad-tang-ngad-tang-ngad
Ngad-tang-ngad-tang-ngad-tang-ngad![22]

We had already finished two bottles of whiskey. The lively music continued, and everyone kept on drinking and dancing—except for Kinn and me. Kinn refused to join the festivities, instead just staring at me as I refilled everyone's glasses.

I glowered at him. "What the hell are you looking at?"

"Do you realize how sexy you are when you're drunk?" he said with a smirk, leering at me.

I frowned at him. "Fuck off!" I tried to ignore his intimidating gaze, focusing my attention on refilling empty glasses with ice.

"Hello, boys! I brought a special drink called B-52 for you to try," Madam Yok said as she came around with a tray of shot glasses. "Porsche, you take care of it, okay?"

I counted almost twenty shots on the table, each glass layered with dark liqueur at the bottom and white cream on top. Madam Yok handed me a lighter, knowing that I knew how to serve this particular cocktail.

"Wow! This looks tasty!" Tankhun exclaimed, his eyes widening as he leaned closer to look at the rows of shots on the table.

---

22 This song is Ngad-tang-ngad by Toey Athibordin, a male Luk Thung singer.

"I'm gonna set the top layer on fire, and then you drink everything at once with this straw," I explained. "All right, Mr. Tankhun?"

Tankhun nodded eagerly. I gave him a straw, placed a shot glass in front of him, and lit it up. Tankhun immediately sucked the cocktail through his straw. He looked extremely pleased with the drink and asked me to light up another shot for him.

"These shots are pretty strong. Take it easy, Mr. Tankhun," Pete warned, seeming to know this cocktail and its effects quite well.

"Shut up!" Tankhun snapped at Pete, slurping his third shot.

"Up to you, then..." Pete went back to dancing.

"That's enough for now. Why don't you dance for a couple of songs before taking another shot?" I cautioned Tankhun when he handed a fourth shot to me to light. He seemed to put more stock in my advice than Pete's, because he returned to the dance floor.

"I want to try it, too," said the man next to me. Kinn was like a ghost that kept haunting me. I sighed, but took one shot glass from the tray and put it in front of him along with a straw.

"Drink it all at once," I instructed him before lighting the cocktail on fire. Kinn made a surprised face as he finished the drink, and quickly took a sip of water.

"Give me another one," he said.

I did as he asked, placing another shot glass in front of him and setting it ablaze. He leaned down to suck it up with the straw and turned to me when he'd finished the last drop.

"I want you to drink, too," he said, downing a glass of water.

I brushed him off. "I'll drink in a bit."

"Come on! I want to set it on fire," Kinn insisted.

Tonight was going well, and I didn't want to start an argument with him, so I handed the lighter to Kinn. Placing a B-52 shot in front of me, I leaned in with a straw between my lips. When Kinn lit the drink on fire, I sucked it all up with the straw, a familiar sweet, chocolatey taste flooding my mouth. I knew very well that this cocktail was pleasant to drink—and that it could easily knock you on your ass before you even realized it.

"Here, have another one," Kinn said, placing a second shot in front of me.

I was never one to turn down a drink, so I slurped up the shot Kinn gave me. Kinn seemed to really enjoy setting the cocktail on fire, and before I knew it, I had already drunk a fifth shot. I was starting to get dizzy.

"Have some water," Kinn said, handing me a glass.

I was already buzzed, so I took the glass without really looking. I knocked it back and almost spat it back out—Kinn had handed me whiskey instead of water.

I swallowed the amber liquid before chugging a bottle of water. "Fuck you, Kinn! Are you trying to get me wasted?!"

Kinn just chuckled at me. I was starting to see double; I shook my head a little to make it go away. I knew that mixing whiskey and cocktails was a bad idea, and I was already seeing the effects.

The rest of our group showed interest in the flaming B-52 cocktails, lining up to do shots. As the night progressed, the music grew louder and livelier, and Tankhun got even drunker and bolder. Pol ended up carrying Tankhun on his shoulders and parading him around. At the same time, Arm had him place his palms together in front of his chest, imitating a Hae Nak procession.[23] Pete, P'Jess, Kinn's friends, and my friends all joined this impromptu ceremony, singing and dancing along shamelessly. Even strangers from the bar decided to join the parade.

---

23   The Hae Nak procession is a colorful ceremony where a Nak (a man about to be ordained as a Buddhist monk) is carried on the shoulders of his friend, or rides a horse, cow, or elephant, to the temple for his ordination. Lively music and dances accompany the procession.

Oh, my fair lady. Phi-Nak requests one bottle of booze, half a bottle of booze, or just one bottle of booze each day. No need for soda![24]

When the band saw the guests starting the Hae Nak procession for Tankhun, they immediately began playing a song called *Nak Sang Sika*. I took more shots, smiling and laughing as I watched the antics unfold. It was like everyone in this place decided to come together and dance in Tankhun's procession.

"I didn't know you were capable of making other facial expressions," Kinn remarked before returning his attention to his older brother. I shot him a look. He was one to talk—he couldn't hold back his laughter at the scene his brother was making, either.

"Fuck off!" I stopped smiling and took another shot. Although the liquor was starting to give me a headache, it didn't stop me from drinking more.

"Here, have another," Kinn said, placing yet another shot in front of me.

I heaved out a sigh, shaking my head at him. I knew how much worse things could get. "I'm not doing any more shots," I said.

"You're drunk already? What a lightweight," Kinn snickered, leaning back on the sofa with his arms and legs crossed.

I scowled at him. *Huh?! You callin' me a lightweight? Let's see who's really a lightweight!*

"Who're you calling a lightweight?" I shot back. "Let's see who's the real lightweight—match me shot-for-shot." I hated when people claimed to be better than me at something, especially when I was drunk.

I didn't realize I had walked right into his trap. Kinn quickly placed shots in front us, sneering at me while holding a straw

---

24   *Nak Sang Sika* ("Nak's request to a woman") by Tossapol Himmapan, a famous Luk Thung singer.

between his lips. I lit both drinks on fire, and we drank up. On the fifth shot, my head started to spin. I felt like I might puke, but Kinn looked completely at ease. I squinted at him in suspicion. The way he was leering at me made him look like a fucking psycho. I was starting to wonder if he was just as crazy as his brother.

"Oh hell, Porsche! Are you drunk?" Tem exclaimed, handing me a glass of water.

"Nah...I'm okay," I replied, trying my hardest to concentrate on my friend, who seemed to be sweating profusely. "Did you finish the Hae Nak procession?" People were returning to their seats now, and they all looked exhausted.

"Stop! I'm cutting you off!" Jom walked over and took the whiskey glass from my hand before Tem could reply. I straightened up, trying to shake off the dizziness.

"Let's go wash your face," Tem said, pulling me up and leading me to the bathroom.

I felt much better after splashing cold water on my face. I stood with my arms resting on the edge of the sink, muttering to myself to stay sober for several minutes before Tem took me back to our table. The pounding in my head began to subside, and my vision got less blurry.

"We should go back soon. Our bosses have passed out," someone said.

I looked at Tankhun where he lay draped over the sofa. Pol and Arm were trying to keep his head up. Kinn was also sprawled on the couch, unconscious. That surprised me—he hadn't seemed that drunk earlier.

"What happened to Kinn?" I asked Pete.

"He had a B-52 drinking duel with Mr. Tankhun. It knocked them both out," Pete said, before calling me over to help carry Kinn.

"Now who's the lightweight?" I snickered as I helped Pete drag Kinn to the parking lot.

"Are you all right, Porsche?" Tem asked, after we'd managed to load Tankhun and Kinn into their vans. "You look a little unsteady." He wasn't wrong: I'd made Kinn wince several times because I kept stumbling on our way out and making him hit his crotch against the corners of the tables.

"I'm fine. How are you guys getting home?" I asked Tem and Jom.

"P'Time and P'Tay will give us a ride," Tem replied cheerfully. "They said they'd drop us by the university. Jom is staying in my dorm room tonight."

I had no idea when they'd gotten so close with Kinn's friends, but I nodded at them before getting in the van myself to head home.

"You help Pete look after Mr. Kinn. We'll take care of Mr. Tankhun," P'Jess said as we tried to carry them upstairs. The other bodyguards seemed surprised to see their bosses blackout drunk.

I dragged Kinn to his bedroom, where I slid the glass door open and dropped him onto the bed. I wanted to just throw him onto the bed and leave, but Pete stopped me. He turned to address Kinn's bodyguards, who had followed us inside. "You guys can leave. Porsche and I can handle this," he said. The others weren't happy, but they left nevertheless.

"Why me and not them?" I asked, frowning at Pete. "I should go check on Tankhun."

"I can't stand them. Come on, give me a hand," Pete said, arranging Kinn's body on the bed so he could sleep comfortably.

I kept looking at them without moving from my spot. I didn't want to touch Kinn at all.

"Don't just stare. Help me!" Pete cursed. "Or you can grab a washcloth and a tub of water from the bathroom."

I sighed and headed to the bathroom as instructed.

"You can leave, Pete," Kinn said, opening his eyes.

Pete was shocked to find Kinn fully conscious and coherent. "Um..."

"Just leave," Kinn insisted.

Pete seemed to finally understand Kinn's intentions. He glanced at the bathroom with a knowing smile before leaving as he was ordered.

"Pete! Where the hell are you?" I returned from the bathroom to find only Kinn. Pete was nowhere in sight. I put the tub of water next to the bed and looked around.

"Damn it! He ditched me," I grumbled, returning my gaze to the sleeping man. My eyes lingered on his tall frame and handsome face, which looked slightly European. His shirt was unbuttoned halfway down.

"Maybe I should splash him with water and suffocate him to death with a pillow," I said out loud. Kinn wouldn't hear it; he was out cold. "Pete, you piece of shit! My head hurts, and you left me to deal with this crap alone."

I looked between the washcloth in the basin and Kinn's sleeping form and decided to be a good bodyguard for once and take care of Kinn. It was too much trouble to get someone else to help me, and I was so drunk that I might pass out in the process.

I slowly unbuttoned Kinn's shirt all the way and carefully removed each of his arms from the sleeves. My eyes roamed over his bare torso, and I found myself appreciating how fit he looked. Kinn didn't seem to exercise much, but he had a six-pack and very well-defined muscles. His skin was pale and flawless. I gazed at him with a twinge of envy—I had to work out like crazy for my abs to show.

"You're a good-looking guy," I muttered. "Why do you like provoking me so much? Are you a psychopath or something? Should I just pour water all over you?" I felt tempted to dump the entire basin of water on him.

I dampened the washcloth and started wiping Kinn's arms and shoulders. Once both arms were clean, I wrung out the cloth and wetted it again before continuing to rub him down. My thoughts drifted to Kinn's muscular physique, making me seethe with jealousy. When I realized I'd probably spent too much time cleaning Kinn's torso, I quickly dropped the cloth back into the tub of water.

My hand went to the zipper of his jeans. I pulled it down halfway before stopping. *Do I really need to do this? Isn't cleaning his upper body enough?*

I eventually decided to remove his jeans, thinking that it would be uncomfortable for him to sleep in them. I wasn't sure why I gave a damn about his comfort, but before I could have second thoughts, I already had Kinn down to his boxers.

"Let me make it clear: I'm just being a good employee!" I declared right in his sleeping face before continuing to wipe down his thigh all the way to his calf. After finishing with both legs, I threw the cloth back into the tub. I giggled when I realized I hadn't even wiped his face yet.

"I'll wash your feet before your face, then," I said.

As I was about to put the washcloth on him, Kinn abruptly grabbed my wrist, yanking me down onto the bed and straddling me. Everything happened so fast—I didn't have time to react. My body hit the mattress with a loud thud, making my head pound even harder.

"What are you complaining about?" Kinn said. He sounded entirely sober. I stared at him, confused, before realizing that I was flat on my back with Kinn on top of me.

"What the hell are you doing?" I yelled, pushing hard at his chest. He didn't budge, and that was when my body stopped cooperating. My vision blurred.

Seeing Kinn with two faces, I wondered if it was those ten shots of B-52. That cocktail was lethal. You didn't feel it at first, so you thought you could handle it, but you were drunk by your fifth shot.

"You're drunk. You lose," Kinn said, smiling as he held both of my wrists in a death grip, pinning them down roughly against the mattress.

"Let go of me!" I snarled, trying to push Kinn away. However, the more I resisted, the more my vision swam. I'd thought I was sobering up, but it turned out I was only just now starting to feel the full effects of the alcohol. I shut my eyes tightly against the dizziness.

"You lost, so you should be punished," Kinn said with a chuckle, leaning into me with all his weight. His laugh made me want to yell at him.

"Punished? That wasn't part of th'deal. M'not even drunk!" I protested, trying to throw him off me, but my body just would not cooperate.

"You're drunk!" Kinn jeered. "Just listen to yourself!"

I frowned at him, thinking my speech sounded normal. "Lemme go!"

"You splashed water all over my bed," Kinn said, "and the way you sloppily wiped me down... *Fuck*, it turned me on!"

I didn't understand what Kinn meant. I wasn't being sloppy! All my movements were thoughtful and intentional!

"Get off me!" I yelled, trying to put all my strength into resisting Kinn, but it was a feeble attempt. Hot breath brushed over my face, and I felt something hard bumping against the tip of my nose. Then, a gentle touch that faintly tasted of alcohol brushed across my lips before pressing tightly against them. Somehow, it felt amazing.

Running out of breath, I gasped for air, which allowed something wet to slide into my mouth. It prodded around like it was searching for something. My mind started to go blank, my heart fluttering wildly from the thrilling sensations coursing through my body. Without thinking about it, I reciprocated Kinn's actions, sliding my tongue against his to chase more pleasure.

My body relaxed, and Kinn let go of my wrists. I threw my arms around his back, pulling him into a tight embrace that brought our bodies closer together. I didn't notice the bandage on my neck was gone—the feeling of Kinn kissing my cheek and my jaw was too good. Something warm and wet pressed into the nape of my neck, causing a shudder of arousal to course through me as Kinn began to suck and bite.

"Mmm..."

I let out a loud moan, a thrill running through my entire body. It felt so good that I didn't want him to stop. However, a different feeling quickly took over the pleasure. I hastily shoved Kinn out of the way and threw up with a loud retch.

"Fucking hell, Porsche...!"

I heard an emphatic sigh as darkness swallowed me up.

After that, I didn't know anything anymore...

KINN
PORSCHE

12

Question

ITH A GREAT DEAL OF EFFORT, I managed to roll over. As I pried my heavy eyelids open, I was struck with a pounding headache. Fucking booze! This happened every time I drank. Why did I still feel like throwing up? Damn it!

The headache kept intensifying, like there was a boulder knocking around in my skull. I slowly pushed myself up, and slowly peeled a blanket off me.

Hold up! Blanket? On a king-sized bed? This big room looked familiar, too. *Shit! Where am I?!* I looked around the room, trying to recall what had happened last night.

I could remember bits and pieces. We'd gone out to Madame Yok's bar. When we got back to the house, I helped Pete bring Kinn to his room, and I gave him a sponge bath.

Shit! Don't tell me this is Kinn's room! I looked around and saw that I was alone. My eyes caught sight of a framed photo of Mr. Korn and his three sons, which confirmed my suspicions: this was definitely Kinn's room. I pulled at my hair in frustration. I couldn't believe this. Fuck!

The headache subsided quickly as new memories began to emerge: I remembered feeling really good last night. Warm breath, soft lips... I could recall with perfect clarity exactly how it had felt. *No! It's not... No way. Why would Kinn kiss a fucking guy?!*

Even though I'd been drunk, I'd still been conscious. I remembered everything. The person on top of me last night had been none other than Kinn. *Holy shit!*

I was about to get out of bed, but the smell of something awful stopped me. I glanced at the floor next to me and swung my feet back onto the bed. Gross—it was my own puke. Right. Obviously.

I couldn't remember anything after I'd thrown up—my memory cut off right there.

Ugh... The sensation of being kissed, followed by the image of Kinn's face... Damn it! My heart dropped just thinking about it. Why the hell would Kinn kiss another man? Maybe he planned to embarrass me—the kiss was another way for him to rile me up. Screw you, Kinn.

I got down from the other side of the bed and checked the clock on the wall. It was already past nine, which meant I had to clock in less than an hour from now. This was eerily similar to the time I passed out on his sofa. Everything felt the same! I stood with my arms crossed, glaring at the glass door before opening it.

The sound of the glass door sliding open caught the attention of Kinn, who was lying on the couch under a blanket and playing around on his phone. He turned to me, his face as impassive as ever. He didn't utter a single insult. That surprised me—it seemed like Kinn got annoyed at me less and less lately. I missed our verbal sparring matches.

"Why didn't you wake me up?" I asked in my usual tone, but then my voice got softer as I wondered, "And what the fuck are you doing here?" I felt guilty seeing him on the couch like this. I'd taken over his bed.

"Clean up your vomit," he said, without looking up from his phone.

"Yeah, I know. You didn't wake me up," I said, walking back into the bedroom. Bending down to clean up my puke with a tissue, I felt a returning wave of nausea. I was still wearing the same clothes I'd passed out in, and the stench of alcohol and vomit made me dizzy. It was a good thing I hadn't scattered all my clothes on the floor like last time, or else I would have felt even guiltier. I was lucky he didn't shove me out of his bed to sleep on the floor with my puke.

I wiped the floor one more time with a damp cloth. Then I stripped the comforter off the bed, planning to get it cleaned. I wasn't going to do it myself, though; I'd go ask Pete where the maid was. It reeked of alcohol. Ugh. I carried it through the bedroom, planning to leave, but stopped when Kinn opened the door and walked right into me.

"Leave the duvet. The maid will come collect it," Kinn said, leaning against the doorframe with his arms crossed. He looked at me with a vacant expression. I immediately let the blanket drop to the floor.

"Can't you put it in the corner?" Kinn asked with a chuckle.

"She'll find it easier here," I said. I was just going to leave it in front of the door. I wanted to get the hell out of here.

There were so many questions racing through my head, but I didn't have the courage to ask any of them. I was afraid that I might have been so drunk that I'd imagined everything. I *hoped* I'd imagined it all.

"Wait!" Kinn's hand blocked the doorway when I tried to step out. I didn't know what he wanted from me. This entire situation was stressing me out.

"Wh...what?" I asked, barely louder than a whisper.

"What did you do to me?" Kinn asked.

Shit! I hadn't even figured out what happened last night yet. Everything was still a jumble in my mind. *Now what?*

"What did I do?" I echoed, trying to face him head-on as usual but finding it difficult. I averted my eyes.

"You knocked me against the table," Kinn continued. It was unclear from his inflection if it was a question or a statement.

"When?" I asked.

"Last night. When you carried me out of the club," he said.

My head started pounding. There were so many things I couldn't remember. "Wh-what did I do?" I stuttered, unsure.

"It still hurts," Kinn said.

My heart pounded in fear and guilt. *Shit! Stop that.* Sleeping in his room was one thing, then puking on his floor, then that nasty mental image of what we did—I was going to go crazy!

"What? What hurts?" I asked.

"You bumped me into the table last night. Right here. It still hurts!"

Kinn snatched my hand and pressed it against his crotch. Only the thin material of Kinn's flimsy pajamas separated my hand from his dick. Kinn's hand held mine in place. I froze, my eyes widening as I felt him start to get hard.

I quickly pulled back. "What the fuck are you doing, you shit-head?!" I pushed away his arm blocking the doorway and scrambled out of there. I heard laughter ring out behind me, but I didn't bother turning around. That bastard! Fuck! What the fuck was that?!

I slammed his door shut. All of the men standing guard in front of his room flinched. Big whipped around to face me, his eyes full of questions, but I didn't want to stay there any longer than I had to, so I headed straight to the stairs.

"Wait!" Big yelled, yanking my arm.

I tried to shake off his hand. "Let me go!" I cried out. Irritated, I turned to face him.

"Why were you in there?" Big demanded, his face furious and his voice stern.

"None of your business," I snarled. Fuck! Kinn was annoying enough, and now this?

"Porsche, you little shit! Why were you in there?!" he shouted in my face.

"Like I said, none of your business!" I wanted to walk away, but Big held my arm in place. I had to shake him off multiple times.

I couldn't take it anymore. I closed my eyes, trying to push down the overwhelming urge to punch this bastard in the face.

"Answer me," he insisted. "And what happened to your neck?"

I didn't understand why Big was being so damned nosy. I reached to my neck and realized that the bandages were gone. Shit!

"If you have so much free time, why don't you stop sticking your nose into my business and go do something useful?" I said, annoyed. The hickeys—I wasn't sure if Big meant the old ones or the new ones—supported my suspicion that my memories of last night were real.

"Porsche! I'll kick your head in if you don't answer me right now!" Big shouted, raising his fist. I wasn't afraid of this guy, so I rolled my sleeves up, hoping for the opportunity to take out my anger on him.

"Why do I hear a dog barking this early?!" Pol's voice came from behind me. He walked up to me, put his arm around my shoulder and pulled me back.

"What? Stay the fuck out of this!" Big yelled.

"What's up with you? Forgot to take your chill pill? Getting crazy this early in the morning?" Arm said, moving to stand beside me.

"You all want a piece of me, huh?" Big seemed furious. Judging from his expression, he was ready to fight.

"Hah! Come on! I'm not scared of you!" Pol said. "But I think we should go, Porsche. Better not waste your time on that little bitch."

Pol urged me to keep walking. I took a glance over my shoulder and saw Big trying to lash out at us, but his men held him back. His frustrated shouting followed us down the hallway, but we didn't pay it any mind. Pol and Arm dragged me all the way to the staff cafeteria, where we found Pete in his casual clothes, eating.

"Big being an asshole—what a way to start the day," Arm said as he placed a bowl of rice porridge in front of me. "Don't mind him. Just let him seethe."

"Thanks," I said, picking the vegetables out of my bowl.

Pol turned to me. "Porsche?" he asked. "I thought your shift ended at midnight. How did you end up in Mr. Kinn's room?"

I stayed silent, unsure how to answer. *Yeah, Pol, I got drunk and ended up crashing in his room. For the second time this week. Man, talk about déjà vu.* I glanced at Pete, who was smiling mischievously, and suddenly remembered what he did last night.

"Damn it, Pete! You left me, you bastard! Why didn't you get me out of there?!"

"Don't blame me. I was drunk. I don't know anything," Pete said with a smirk, like he was hiding some big secret.

"Damn it! How could you leave me there?!" I was kind of offended. Pete was still playing innocent, which irritated me.

"You got another hickey!" Pol exclaimed. "Shit, Porsche! I told you to count me in if you found some hot chicks. What girl gave you that?"

Pete, who was eating his own bowl of rice porridge, burst out into giggles. *What's his deal today? He's acting fucking weird.*

"What is it, Pete? Why are you laughing?" Arm asked.

"Nothing, nothing. Food's too hot," Pete said. I looked at him, trying to figure out why he was acting so suspiciously, but he shook his head like he knew nothing.

"Man, I wish I was born with a face like Porsche's. Get drunk and get a girl every time. But no, here I am, trying to put on my best look and I'm still trash. No girl has even spared me a second look," Pol complained. I didn't know how to respond to that, so I wolfed down my food and went to my room to get ready.

"Pooorsche! The boss is going out today. Don't forget your uniform!" Arm shouted after me. I turned and nodded at him, then went straight to the bathroom.

Shit! That's a new hickey! Shit, shit, shit, shit, shit! So my memories of last night *were* real. I wanted to ask Kinn why he kissed me, but I was too afraid. And what the hell happened this morning—was he gay? I wasn't sure. He had that bad boy look that girls loved, so it'd be a shame if he was. But he'd been acting weird lately, so he could just be fucking with me.

I let out a heavy sigh, confusion building up inside my head. I didn't know if Kinn was gay, but *I* sure wasn't. I wanted to punch him in the face for what happened this morning. Holy shit! If he did kiss me last night, I'd kick his ass!

I had to admit that it had felt good. But it was only because I was drunk. If I had been more aware that I was kissing a guy, I definitely wouldn't have responded like that.

What the hell was Kinn doing?!

I quickly took a shower and got dressed, then went to Tankhun's room. One of my duties was to drag him out of bed—he had partied a little too hard last night.

Pol and Arm told me I'd be going to a shooting range around noon. Mr. Korn wanted Tankhun to practice shooting regularly so he could better defend himself. Pol wouldn't be joining us since it'd be after his shift. Good thing I still had Arm to keep me company; it was a relief to have a friend around.

Tankhun's daytime bodyguard and I helped haul him to the bathroom. He was as heavy as a corpse. We put him in the bathroom and knocked on the door from time to time, making sure he didn't pass out in there.

Tankhun's guards on the day shift were all pretty nice people. They even talked about our night out at the club, saying that they wanted to join us next time. They offered to swap shifts someday, which I was fine with. I was willing to bring them with me, but it depended on whether Tankhun wanted to go out again or not.

"Porsche, please help him hit the target," Mr. Korn said with a knowing smile. "I hear you're a competitive shooter, yes?"

I nodded. Mr. Korn walked to the front gate to see Tankhun off. Tankhun was still sleepy, and it looked like he might pass out at any second. He couldn't even walk straight. It was embarrassing. I struggled getting Tankhun in the car—it felt like taking care of a toddler.

Kinn and a handful of his men also emerged from the house.

"Take care of your brother," Mr. Korn told Kinn, then headed back to the house. I realized this meant Kinn would be joining us for the day, taking the van parked behind us. I didn't even want to see his face. I didn't know why, but I hated him even more right now.

A little distracted, I got in the car. Once I sat down, I took a look at Tankhun, who was in a pretty damned pathetic state. He was out cold, head flopped to one side, his body limp against his seat. He looked lifeless, like his soul had left his body.

Man, Tankhun. If you don't need our respect, at least have a little respect for yourself.

[AT THE SHOOTING RANGE]

"Mr. Tankhun, I'm going to get us some coffee," I said. I couldn't stand watching Tankhun doze off anymore, so I went to order him some coffee. I had no idea how he liked it, but he was falling asleep with his face smushed on the table. I had to do something.

Tankhun lifted his sleepy face up and squinted at me. "Mmmm. Let's hang out again tonight," he said.

"Sir, you're not even sober yet," I told him plainly. *Man, you really need to look at yourself right now.*

"I am, I am. Please. Tonight," he pleaded, trying to open his eyes wide.

"Well, since you're sober, sir, then get up. It's time for training." I looked through the window. At the range, the other bodyguards and Kinn were having a blast shooting targets. It was just me and a few others who'd been left in charge of looking after Tankhun. My fingers were itching for some trigger action, but I couldn't leave this hungover idiot to his own devices.

"Nope. It's too loud," Tankhun said, planting his face back on the table.

"Okay, sir, then we won't go out tonight. Since you haven't sobered up yet," I said, crossing my arms and pretending to ignore him.

"Don't patronize me!" Tankhun snapped, lifting his head up immediately to shoot me an offended glare. He looked much more alert than before.

"I'm not patronizing you, sir. If I take you out in this state, Mr. Korn is going to rip me a new one," I said, my expression cold. He gave me a bratty look before springing up from his chair and walking to the range. He grabbed a pair of noise-canceling earmuffs from one of his bodyguards and hastily put them on. I let out a sigh.

Arm walked up and threw his arm around my shoulder, smiling broadly. "You've got some balls, man," he said. "Ordering the boss around?" He patted my back before handing me my own set of earmuffs. I quickly took them and went after Tankhun.

The shooting range was closed for our private use today. Arm said this facility was one of the many businesses owned by the family. On regular days there were a lot of visitors, but whenever any members of the clan wished to use it, it would be closed for privacy. What a cushy life. If I were a member of this family, I would be here every single day.

"You go keep an eye on the boss. That guy's never hit a target in his life," Arm said. He walked to his firing lane and deftly aimed his gun, furiously blasting the target like he was releasing weeks of pent-up anger.

I approached Tankhun, who couldn't even figure out how to load the magazine or turn the safety off. I stood right behind him, trying to guide him with gestures. I couldn't instruct him with my voice because we both had soundproof earmuffs on. Ugh.

Life did feel a bit more exciting today, though, considering I could finally work for real. It was better than being stuck in Tankhun's room doing fuck all.

I hadn't noticed at first, but I saw through the glass partition that Kinn occupied the lane next to ours. He glanced at me and smirked. I turned away from him because I didn't want to get distracted thinking about the crazy shit that happened last night.

Tankhun held his gun and aimed at a man-shaped wooden target. I gestured at the safety and guided him to cock the gun. With his finger on the trigger, he narrowed his eyes and fired. Damn! I sighed. He didn't even graze the target. I held my hand out, telling him to try again.

This time, I held his hand in place and locked my eyes on the target. I tapped his finger, telling him to fire. The bullet hit the target, but it could've been more centered. I readjusted his angle and posture, and he complied without resisting. I guess he wanted to get this done quickly because he still had a hangover.

Bang! Bang! Tankhun's score kept improving as I kept guiding him from behind. As soon as the magazine ran out of bullets, he put the handgun down and walked past me, leaving the firing lane. I watched him go, seeing him take off the earmuffs and plant his face on the same table as before. I sighed. I'd hoped that he'd show interest in his family's business.

I was going to turn back to the range, but Kinn caught my eye. He was leaning his shoulder against the glass partition and glaring at me. The scene from this morning flashed through my mind as I glared back. He pointed at my muffs, gesturing for me to take them off. I frowned. *I'm not doing that, asshole!* I was ready to get back to shooting, but he grabbed me and mouthed slowly: "Don't. Ignore. Me."

I shook his arm off, knowing he was just messing with me. I ignored him and moved to turn around again when he did something unthinkable: he pointed the gun in his hand at my head. I was taken aback. That was a real gun—that thing could fucking kill me.

I stared at him in stunned silence, my body frozen in place. What the fuck was he doing?

"Scared?" he asked, breaking into a grin. After taking a moment to collect myself, I straightened my back, took a deep breath, and stepped forward. The barrel was now inches away from my forehead. Kinn narrowed his eyes at me, then grinned even wider.

"I'm. Not. Scared. Of. You," I said slowly. My eyes locked on Kinn's. I wasn't afraid of anyone. If Kinn thought he had the balls to shoot me, then he should go ahead and do it.

Because I had more guts than he thought.

"Great," he said as he lowered his gun. I knew that fucker was just messing with me. As soon as he holstered the gun, he reached his hand out to take off my earmuffs, then his.

"The hell...?" Did he *want* to ruin our hearing?

I felt dozens of eyes on me. All the bodyguards at the range had left their firing lanes to watch us. Arm, who had tried to approach me but was stopped by Big's men, sighed in relief when he realized Kinn wasn't going to shoot me. Kinn's stern gaze shifted to the other bodyguards, prompting them to go back to their training.

"You're good," Kinn said, his eyes still on me. He must have watched me coach Tankhun earlier.

"So?"

"Let's have a shooting match... Or are you scared?" he asked, mocking me.

I huffed. "I'm not scared of you. Bring it on!" I stared daggers at him. *What a shithead. Don't go crying to your daddy if you lose!* I was a professional. Why would I be afraid of a spoiled brat like Kinn? All he was good at was giving orders.

"But there's a catch," Kinn said, his smile turning dark.

"What do you mean?"

"We'll judge it shot by shot. Loser has to strip off one item of clothing," Kinn said. He had a look on his face that I'd never seen before, a sort of brash, teasing expression. His words almost made me want to punch him in the mouth.

"Hell no!" I shouted. I would've gone at him right there if I hadn't seen Big and his men angrily glaring at me.

"Oh, are you feeling shy?" Kinn said, moving his face closer to mine, his voice laden with ridicule. "Feel free to note your score. You can strip down in my room later."

That pushed me over the edge. I shoved him against the glass wall of another firing lane. The bodyguard on the other side looked taken aback. He quickly took off his hearing protection and looked ready to defend Kinn.

"I'm fine," Kinn said, straightening himself out and waving the guy off. The bodyguard gave me a dirty look, but I didn't care. Kinn wasn't done messing with me, and I wasn't done fighting back.

"You've got balls. Better watch out!" Kinn said. I wanted to shoot his smug face right then and there.

"I'm not into that, you freak! Go ask your dad or something!" I shouted. I put the noise-cancelling muffs back on, then opened fire at the target, imagining it was Kinn's head. I didn't give a shit what kind of face he would make or what sort of taunt he would throw at me next. The only thing I was focused on was blasting at the target's lethal zones. My points were through the roof. *Kinn, you shithead. What the hell is wrong with you? Are you gay for real?!*

Arm walked up to me and lit his cigarette. "Are you okay?"

We were in the designated smoking area outside the building. Various bodyguards who were done with their training stood around, chatting and playing games with each other. Kinn was finished as well—I saw him go into the VIP room to have lunch with his brother.

"I'm fine," I said, my voice neutral. In my head, I was still conflicted about Kinn—about what had happened last night and his shitty words from earlier. I wanted to ask Arm for advice, but I was afraid it might sound like I was condemning his boss.

"What was with you and Mr. Kinn back there? Seriously, both of you... You cause a scene every single time," Arm said with a shake of his head, clearly fed up with us.

I had an idea—a way I could finally get some damn answers. I looked left and right. The other bodyguards had finished smoking and were heading inside, leaving only Arm and me.

"Hey," I said. Quickly, I reached my hand out and grabbed Arm's crotch. He flinched, gave me a dumbfounded look, then batted my hand away.

"What the fuck was that?" he asked, startled.

"How do you feel?" I asked him.

"Confused. You grabbed my junk out of the blue... Are you high or something?" Arm looked amused now, a soft huff of laughter escaping his lips.

"Shit... Well, when I grabbed your crotch, what did you think?" I asked.

Arm frowned. "Are you gay?"

I frowned even harder, because Arm was thinking exactly what I was when Kinn did it to me.

"But a guy like you, gay? If you are, your boy must be a cute little feminine thing," Arm said. "Or were you just messing with me?" There—he read my mind again. Was Kinn gay or just fucking with me?

"Yeah... Guys don't really joke around like this, do they?" I said, throwing my cigarette butt into the trash can. I still couldn't get this shit out of my head.

"Are you kidding me? Do *you* ever joke around with your friends like that?" Arm chuckled before putting out his cigarette as well.

"Yeah..." Shit, he was right. Tem, Jom—none of us did that.

"What's the matter? Do you...*like* me? You think I'm cute?" Arm asked, teasing me. "All right, I'll give you that. You're handsome, too."

Fucker. I chased him all the way to the front of the VIP room, where the other bodyguards watched us with curiosity.

Big glared at us. "This is not a playground. Have some respect for the boss."

Arm quickly threw his arm around my shoulder and shot Big an insolent look. "Who said it wasn't?" He smirked at Big. "This is a park, as far as I can tell. It looks like someone just let their dog out."

Big jumped up from his chair and rushed over to us. "Who are you calling a dog?!"

Arm and I weren't threatened by his aggression at all. We glared back at him.

"I hear someone barking right now," Arm said. He put his hands in his pockets and whistled.

"Fuck you, Arm!" Big shouted. He began to raise his fist, but then the door to the VIP room opened.

"The hell is going on out here?!" Tankhun said. "Damn, you're fighting like a bunch of bitches."

Arm howled with laughter. Big drew back and straightened his posture as Tankhun made a beeline for me.

"So, you'll take me out tonight?" he said, clinging to my arm like a child begging his parents for a new toy. I glanced at Big, who wouldn't stop grumbling.

"Sure," I said, and made a face at Big.

Tankhun led us to the parking lot, with Kinn following soon after. He didn't pay any attention to me, the same old cocky expression on his face as he walked past me to the van, getting ready to leave.

Suddenly, a loud sound erupted in the air. Everyone—me, the bodyguards, Tankhun, and Kinn—dropped to the ground.

Bang! Bang!

Gunshots! As soon as it went quiet, the bodyguards urged Tankhun and Kinn to get into the cars. Before they could do anything, a nondescript van sped through, blocking their path.

"They've got guns! Protect the boss!"

I hurried over to Tankhun, but I was too slow. A group of men in black shirts and ski masks emerged from the van. I hit one of them with a flying kick before he could reach Tankhun. Tankhun was almost in the car, but the door couldn't close because those bastards kept yanking him away. It looked like the situation was the same at Kinn's van as well.

"Let me go! I don't wanna go with you!" Tankhun kicked and screamed as the men wrenched his hand back. I quickly sent each goon to the ground, slamming my fists into their faces one by one and kicking and jabbing with my elbows and knees. The martial arts I'd spent so much time mastering had finally come in handy.

These men were definitely professionals, but I managed to hit each of them in the face several times. The parking lot was a chaotic scene, two different factions mired in combat. In the middle of the mayhem, I saw one of the bastards pull out his gun and point it at Tankhun. *Fuck!*

I shoved Tankhun into his van. I pulled out my sidearm, pistol-whipping the bastard holding the door in the face. As soon as he collapsed, I slammed the door shut and gave the driver a signal to get the hell out of here. Then I held my gun out and pulled the trigger as the man opened fire at Tankhun's car.

Bang! Bang! Bang! More gunshots, and the smell of dirt flying everywhere. Tankhun's car finally managed to pull out, once I stopped the men trying to pry the door open with my gun.

The situation was different for Kinn, whose car refused to leave. I showered the thugs with bullets. I wasn't sure if I'd killed any of them—I didn't care. I rushed over to Kinn's van and saw him refusing to get in the car. He had taken out his gun to fire back at them.

"Fucking get in the car!" I shouted at him, launching myself at the gang of goons. They didn't back down, even though most of them were injured and some had escaped to their vans already.

"I'm not a coward like Khun!" Kinn yelled back, fighting just as hard as I was.

I came to the horrifying realization that I didn't give a damn if I killed any of these guys. I shot all of them that I could hit. If I couldn't shoot them, I used brute force. I yanked one guy's hair because he was going after Kinn, then hit him in the neck with the butt of my gun with all my strength.

"Get in the car. You're not helping," I said. All the while, our bodies kept moving, kept fighting.

"I can take care of myself," Kinn replied before punching one of them, making the guy cough up blood.

"You talk big," I remarked. Seeing him act so cocky, I couldn't help it. *See? Because you stayed, they've targeted you.* This was fucking exhausting!

"I'm big in other places, too. Wanna see?" he said with a smirk before dodging a kick and slamming the man's head against the car door.

"Fuck off!" I shouted, stomping one of the bastards hard. I supposed I was imagining it was Kinn, because it was a particularly violent kick. How did Kinn manage to have a dirty mind in a moment like this?

As we fought, gunshots echoed at erratic intervals, along with pained groans and shouts—not from our side, but theirs. There were only a few of them left standing, but they still didn't give up trying to get to Kinn.

I saw one of them retreat to his van and aim his gun at Kinn. I quickly pushed Kinn down, out of the line of fire. I was fuming. These fuckers didn't know when to quit!

Moving away from Kinn, I fearlessly walked straight into the barrage of bullets, firing at the men retreating to their car. I didn't give a damn about my life—I was too busy seething with rage. Why were they still shooting? Even after I gave them hell, they refused to back down. They wanted Kinn so badly it was pissing me off. I was exhausted from all the fighting—and I was furious.

Bang! Bang! Bang!

"Porsche! Porsche, stop!" Kinn shouted from behind me.

"Mr. Kinn! Don't!" one of Kinn's men cried out, trying to stop him from approaching me.

I was too preoccupied to pay attention to Kinn. These fuckers wouldn't stop spraying bullets at us.

In less than a minute of exchanging gunfire, I felt a shock of heat in my right arm. I was hit with such force that my gun fell from my hand. My arm went numb and my rage-ravaged mind didn't even register that I had collapsed to the ground.

"Shit!"

Bang! Bang! Bang! Another three gunshots rang out before the enemy van left. As soon as the van was gone, Kinn approached me, fiercely glaring down at me.

"What the fuck were you thinking?!" Kinn shouted, all other noise drowned out by his voice. "Who do you think you are, walking into the line of fire like that? Huh?!"

Well, I'd said it before—I wasn't afraid of anything. Even now, I wanted to go after them and finish them off.

Big hurried over and quickly examined his boss. "Mr. Kinn. Are you okay?"

Kinn shook him off and turned to me.

"Are *you* okay?" Kinn asked me, his voice softening even though anger still lingered in his eyes. A bruised and battered Arm came over to pick me up. I hadn't fallen from injury, but from the force of the bullet hitting my arm. I could still walk. I held my bleeding arm as the numbness began to transform into shooting, stinging pain.

"I'm fine," I insisted, even though my arm was bleeding everywhere. Shit, I was lucky it was my right arm, or else it would've ruined my tattoo. Then I'd really have to hunt them down. I'd blast their fucking brains out!

"Get in the car. Hospital, now!" Kinn snarled. I sighed and followed him obediently. I saw another one of Kinn's family's vans pull into the parking lot to collect the injured thugs.

Kinn and I stayed silent the entire drive to the hospital. When we got there, he dropped me and the other injured bodyguards off to get patched up. He said a car would come pick us up later.

My injury wasn't a big deal. I could feel that it was just a graze. Some of the others didn't even get shot but still had it worse than me—they'd been beaten badly enough to bleed internally, and had to be admitted to the hospital. Meanwhile, I only needed my wound cleaned and bandaged. The doctor insisted that I keep it clean and take an anti-inflammatory, and said that if the pain got too bad,

I'd have to come back. They found me to be in perfect health otherwise, so they sent me home—surprised that I didn't seem to be in pain at all.

The main hall bustled with people as I stepped inside the house. Mr. Korn immediately came up to me, shifting his gaze to my bandaged right arm. "Hey, kid, what happened to you?"

I had taken off my suit jacket, leaving me only in my shirt, which had one of its sleeves cut off at the hospital.

Kinn, who was sitting with his legs crossed on the sofa, turned to me. "Are you crazy?"

"I'm fine," I said.

But Kinn wasn't done berating me. "You think you're so tough, huh?"

"All right, all right, that's enough. None of our men died," Mr. Korn said calmly. "They used guns this time?"

That piqued my curiosity. They hadn't used guns before?

"Sir, it was obvious that they were only shooting to scare us. But we shot to kill," Big said, glaring at me like I'd done something wrong.

"One fatality, numerous injuries. Actually, opening fire was a great idea for once. I'm getting tired of all the posturing," Mr. Korn said.

They must have just been playing mind games with each other, I realized—like a cold war. Even if there had been assaults, none of them were fatal.

"But this time, we killed one of them," Big went on. "They'll be coming back. Mr. Kant won't be pleased."

Mr. Korn huffed. "How do you know it's Kant?"

The hall fell silent.

"Usually, Kant doesn't use guns," Mr. Korn continued. "These men had guns. Don't you think other parties are involved?"

Big went quiet, hanging his head. I saw him gulp nervously.

"Whoever they are, they'll be coming back for revenge. Anyone with injuries, go rest up—especially you, Porsche," Mr. Korn said, turning to me. "Don't be so reckless next time." He didn't seem mad at me; he was looking at me with consideration and concern.

"Yes, sir," I said. I left the hall and headed back to my room.

I considered Mr. Korn's words and Big's strange behavior. Why did they keep playing mind games with their enemies instead of striking directly? And what exactly was it that started this nonstop conflict?

"Hey. Tryin' to make the history books or something? Showin' off like that," Pete said, inviting himself into my room. I'd forgotten that I hadn't locked the door. I never did back at my own home—force of habit.

"Hey," I said. He pulled up a wooden chair to sit next to me. I sat on the edge of the bed.

Pete's eyes scrutinized my expression. "Same straight face, same big talk. You're doing fine!" he said with an irreverent grin.

"Hey, do we not usually open fire?" I asked him.

"We do, once in a while. But lately it's just been mind games. This is the first time in four months that shots were fired," Pete said, leaning back comfortably in his chair.

"So usually when they attack, it's just a fistfight?" I asked, frowning. I recalled P'Chan telling me not to use my gun unless I had to. I thought he'd meant not to bring it out randomly—I didn't think he meant not to use it on the enemy.

"Something like that, yeah. And abducting the bosses and tortur-ing them... Oh! They did fire at us recently, but it was more like a warning shot, not a gunfight. And as for killing, we only use fatal means on debtors," Pete said.

"Why?"

"Mr. Korn says he doesn't want any more blood on his hands. If it's not strictly necessary, then we don't kill anyone. He also knows that there are—"

"Oh, my sweetie pie!" Arm called out as he barged in. "Are you all right?!" He had some cuts on his brow and his lips, but overall, he looked fine.

"Stop," I groaned.

Arm came to sit next to me and inspected my arm. "You're so cool! You know that?"

I ignored Arm and asked Pete to continue. "What were you saying?"

"Work here long enough and you'll learn. Take your meds. I'll come re-dress your bandage later," Pete said, dropping a bag of medicine on my lap. My wound throbbed, so I took a pill and washed it down with water.

"I'm gonna rest for a bit and go home. Am I free for the rest of the day?" I asked Arm. My shift was supposed to end at midnight, but it wasn't that late in the evening yet.

"You should stay here tonight," Pete said. "Do you think you're good to drive?"

I reclined on the futon. No pillow, no blanket. I wasn't planning to stay overnight anyway.

"Yeah. I want to see my brother," I told him, feeling a bit sleepy as the pain medication kicked in.

"You can see him later. I'll drop you off," Pete said.

Not long after, everything faded to black. I didn't care if Pete or Arm stayed in my room. All I knew was that I'd exhausted all my energy, and I was too tired to stay awake any longer.

I groaned as I felt cold dampness press against my right side. My wound was exposed; the bandage from earlier was gone.

"Trying to be a hero, now look at you," a quiet voice came.

My heavy lids opened slowly into a squint. "The hell are you here for?" I rasped out as the image of Kinn came into focus in my blurry vision. No matter how badly I wanted to get up and confront him, my body felt too heavy.

Kinn, dressed in comfortable clothes, rested on the edge of the bed as he fiddled with my arm. "Hold still. I'm nearly done."

"Go away," I croaked, trying to force my voice out to get this shithead to leave. For all I knew, he'd snuck in here to fuck up my arm even more.

"Is it infected? You seem to have caught a fever," Kinn continued. "Fuck, Porsche. I thought you wanted to stay alive, to take care of your little brother. Why did you get so reckless, you hothead...?" Something warm pressed softly against my forehead.

"Get out of here," I muttered.

"Shut up. Save your mouth for something more useful," he said, a smug smile on his handsome face. I couldn't see him clearly; my vision was still blurry.

"Save it for what?" I asked, not knowing what had gotten into me.

Kinn looked cocky. "Wouldn't you like to know," he said.

A moment later, I felt him bandaging my arm back up. I felt softness supporting my head, helping me sleep more comfortably. I didn't even notice when I drifted back into deep slumber.

"He's talking in his sleep?" Kinn mumbled.

"Hey, Porsche!" came Tankhun's voice as the door opened. The broad figure loomed over the futon, inching his face closer, then quickly straightened up.

"What the hell are you doing here?" Tankhun asked loudly, prompting Kinn to press his finger against his lips.

"He's asleep."

"No! Nooooo! Wake up! You gotta wake up!" Tankhun shouted. Porsche frowned, but he didn't open his eyes.

"Damn it, Tankhun! I told you to be quiet."

"No! He has to wake up! We have plans!"

"He looks like shit. Do you really think he can go out right now? Don't be an idiot!"

"I have to stay in tonight? Damn it!" Tankhun whined. "So what about you? What are *you* doing here?" Tankhun squinted at his brother accusingly.

"That's my business," Kinn said.

"Come on, tell meee!" Tankhun begged.

Kinn shot up from the bed and walked out of Porsche's room. Tankhun trailed after him, pestering him with questions.

I opened my eyes to the sight of Pete sitting on the edge of my bed with his phone in his hands. He turned to me before speaking up.

"What's up, Sleeping Beauty?"

I got up, supporting myself with my elbows. My head had been resting on a pillow, I realized, and there was a blanket covering me.

"These yours?" I asked, my voice hoarse. Pete sat still, ignoring my question.

"Thanks," I mumbled.

Pete looked up from his phone and pointed at a bowl of rice porridge on the nightstand. "Eat up," he said, "so you can take your pain meds and go back to sleep."

"Go to bed, Pete," I said. "I'm fine on my own."

"I want to keep an eye on you tonight," he said. "Don't want you developing a fever."

I was surprised by his kindness. If I hadn't met Pete and Arm, my employment here would have been much more difficult.

"I'm fine. I'm just sleepy from the pills," I said. I wasn't lying. I felt completely fine—apart from the stinging pain in my arm. I looked down at my arm and found it had been freshly bandaged, more neatly than at the hospital.

"Thanks," I told Pete. He looked confused. I nodded to the bandage.

"Ohhh..." Pete gave me a sly look. That got me wondering... I had a weird dream earlier. Kinn had come in here to annoy me, and then he'd done something to my arm. Then Tankhun came in, shouting his head off. Even in my dreams, they couldn't leave me alone!

My throat felt dry, so I lifted myself up to drink some water. Then I grabbed the bowl and started eating.

Kinn... What a fucking asshole! What kind of person spent all day coming up with new ways to mess with me? I couldn't even escape him in my dreams. It was ridiculous.

Apart from his strange words to me in my dream, I also remembered what had happened at the shooting range: when he'd challenged me with that stupid stripping game. I was still conflicted about it—wondering if he really was gay or just messing around. And I couldn't ask Pete...

"Hey man," I said. Pete looked up at me and frowned. "You wanna go to the range when we're free?" I continued, speaking with my mouth full.

Pete laughed. "You're not done with it, huh? Sure. It's free for bodyguards, anyway," he said, then looked back down at a game on his phone.

"Let's have a shooting match next time. Shot for shot. If your score is lower than mine, you lose," I said, then hesitated. Pete grumbled, like he wasn't paying attention. "But there's a catch. If you lose, you have to strip off your clothes," I said. As soon as I finished the sentence, Pete's head snapped up. He looked absolutely flabbergasted.

"What the hell?!"

"Hmm... How do you feel about that?" I asked weakly, pressing my lips together in a thin line.

Pete still looked startled. "Why do you want me to strip? Are you crazy?" He held up his hands to cover his body.

"Don't you guys do that here...?" I muttered, confused. The way Kinn had brought it up, I figured it was a normal occurrence for bodyguards here to play this game, whether to show off their muscles or to humiliate their colleagues.

"Nobody here is into fucked-up games like that," Pete said. He paused for a moment, narrowing his eyes at me with interest. "Why, did someone ask you to?"

"No one! I'm just curious," I quickly replied.

"Ehh, I don't buy it. Who was it? Who wanted to see your perfect, chiseled body, huh?" Pete raised his finger to point at me. I turned my shoulder toward him and gobbled down the rest of my porridge.

"I'm done. You can leave," I said.

"Heh... Did you cast a love spell on someone? Sounds like they can't get enough." Pete moved closer to me, as if to pressure me into answering.

"Pete, you little shit! Get out!" I elbowed him.

"I'm staying here tonight. I already brought my pillow and blanket," Pete said, pointing to a spot on the floor opposite my futon.

"No, I'm fine on my own," I insisted.

Pete ignored me. "Are you going to classes tomorrow?" he asked, lying down on the floor and pulling his blanket over himself.

"Yeah," I said.

"Sure you're feeling up to it?"

"Why are you so worried about me? I'm fine." I was starting to get annoyed. I was tougher than people thought. And the bullet wound was just a graze!

"Can I go with you?" Pete asked.

"Where?"

"Well, the university... I have a day off tomorrow, and I wanna go see some college girls. Please, please, please?" He got up, resting his chin on my bed frame as he begged.

"You don't go to college?" I thought we were the same age. Shouldn't he be attending university as well?

"I only went to high school. I was a professional boxer for a while after I graduated, then I started working here. Please, please, *please* take me with you!"

With him pleading like this, I guessed he probably didn't have that many opportunities to make friends with people his age. Even Arm seemed a little bit older than us. I agreed to take him with me; he'd been so nice to me, I couldn't say no.

I took my medication and turned the lights off, hoping to get more sleep. It was almost midnight; there was no point going back to my place. So I texted Chay for a bit, telling him that I wouldn't be coming home tonight. We'd get to see each other again on Monday.

Ever since I'd started working here, I rarely got to see my brother. I worked through the night until morning. When I got home, Chay was already at school. Sometimes I even got drunk and spent the night here—and now that I thought about it, when I *had* stayed over, it always seemed to be in Kinn's room...

Damn. Kinn *was* gay, wasn't he?

KINN
PORSCHE

13

Premonition

"THIS MAN IS THEIR family's current favorite," a deep-voiced man said as the teenager in front of him lit a cigarette, "especially for Mr. Kinn, sir."

"He seems fearless, very self-assured... So, how does Kinn feel about him?" the teenager asked, a wisp of white smoke escaping his full lips and diffusing throughout the room.

"It's exactly what you think," the man answered, pursing his lips together and averting his gaze as if the thought bothered him.

"He has good taste this time, don't you think?" the young man said, his voice slightly raspy.

"Well, he's *your* type, isn't he? A straight man?" the man in the suit replied, glancing in concern at the young man in front of him. This teenager had all the appearance of a perfectly decent and friendly individual; however, hidden under the surface was a cruel, heartless bastard.

"The ones I managed to fuck before him were usually annoying," he sneered, tapping the end of his cigarette on a glass ashtray. He knew the kinds of guys Kinn preferred, the ones he made arrangements with for his nighttime activities, and he liked to contact them first and defile them before they ever met Anakinn—it was always easy enough to persuade them to have sex if enough money was on the table. The fact that he could orchestrate this behind Kinn's back gave him immense satisfaction. If Kinn ever discovered he'd been having his sloppy seconds this entire time, he'd be furious.

"What are you planning to do next?" the man in the suit inquired.

"Kinn wants him, right?" the young man asked, sounding triumphant.

"In my opinion, yes, he wants him," the older man replied, his brow furrowing as if to emphasize his conviction.

"Even if Kinn isn't interested, I still want him. You know my preferences, yes?" He was attracted to men and preferred taking the dominant role—however, petite, feminine men never appealed to him; he preferred men with robust, masculine bodies.

His lips curved into a twisted grin as he recalled the first time he saw the man. From the moment he laid eyes on him, he was intrigued by his tough, arrogant demeanor.

"Just tell me what you'd like me to do," the man in the black suit replied, seeming irritated by what he'd just heard. He sighed and shot another glance at the young man across from him.

"Keep a close eye on him—see what he's up to," the young man said. "I want you to observe Kinn's attitude toward him, too. The more Kinn wants that man, the more I want him for myself." Anakinn's desire for something fueled his need to have it first.

He would do anything to gain the upper hand on Anakinn. His resentment for what Kinn did to him was carved deep into his heart, and he had sworn to do anything that would make Kinn and his family suffer.

"Yes, sir," the man acknowledged wearily. Although he could not really see the appeal of this new man, he saw it as an opportunity to finally distance his boss from that bastard Kinn. He despised him.

"Now, let's talk business. I've arranged the route for our next delivery. Just let me know when you're ready."

"Hmm... Check for some alternate routes. I want to deliver a larger shipment than last time, considering the police seem to be slacking off lately."

They continued discussing their clandestine business plans for a while before leaving the meeting place, which they rented out specifically for these occasions. Here, they gave each other updates on their mutual enemies and discussed various covert business operations.

PORSCHE

"**D**AMN IT, PORSCHE! You're creeping me out! Get off me!" Tem yelled, flinching away as I rested my chin on his shoulder and breathed down his neck.

"It's only for a second," I replied nonchalantly. We sat on a wooden bench on the ground floor of our college building, and I was testing out a theory. Tem lurched away from me, looking terrified.

"Jom, something's wrong with Porsche!" Tem complained loudly to Jom, who was munching on a skewered sausage.

"Get off!" Tem cried again, trying to push my face off his shoulder.

"Ha ha, you've got it bad, Porsche! What's bothering you?" Pete asked from the opposite side of the bench. He'd decided to come with me to university today. He was so adamant about blending in that he wore the same white shirt and black slacks students had to wear.

"I'm not... I just want to know how it makes you feel, Tem," I replied, shoving Tem's hand away from my face. Tem quickly got up and moved to sit next to Pete instead. The two were already well acquainted, having gotten drunk and danced together during

Tankhun's impromptu Hae Nak procession the other night. When I'd informed my friends that Pete wanted to come along to check out college girls, they hadn't needed any further introduction.

"Asshole! How do *you* feel when someone sucks your neck? It's the same thing!" Tem exclaimed, his expression changing from horrified to sarcastic as he gestured at my neck.

"Hey!" I quickly covered the bandages on my neck with my hand. I'd put three bandages on each side to cover up all the bruises. Damn you, Kinn!

"Who gave you all those hickeys?" Jom asked, pointing the skewer at me.

"What hickeys? I only put these bandages on because they look cool," I said, feigning annoyance at my friends. I nervously bounced my left leg under the table, my mood beginning to sour.

Tem frowned at me. "Cut the bullshit, Porsche. What's wrong with you? You've been in such a bad mood lately."

"It's nothing," I said. I tried to suppress my reaction, but Pete kept giving me knowing smiles.

"What the hell is your problem?" I asked Pete.

"What's *your* problem? Come on, spit it out. You're acting strange, and it's making us worry," Pete said, looking intensely at me as if searching for something. Both of my friends asked Pete what he meant, and he quickly told them that I had groped Arm's crotch and challenged him to play a strange game.

"Just shut up!" I scolded him.

"Since when do you swing that way?" Jom asked. "You know you don't need to be ashamed or anything, right? We're really open-minded about that kind of stuff. Tem even pointed out that your man Mr. Kinn was hot."

I balked at the mention of Kinn. "I do *not* swing that way, you shithead! I like girls! I like big tits!" I snapped.

"Tem, did you say you think Mr. Kinn is hot? Ooh, my boss would be..." Pete turned to look at Tem, who furiously waved his hands in denial.

"Let's get to class! It's about time!" I interrupted before Pete could finish his sentence, still pissed off at Kinn and his repulsive behavior. Just hearing his name infuriated me.

I turned to talk to Pete. "And you can have a look around campus or something. If you get hungry, the cafeteria is over there. I'll call you when my class is over."

"Why does your building have so few girls?" Pete commented as he looked around.

"What do you expect from Sports Science? It's basically like an all-boys school over here. If you want to check out hot chicks, you need to go to Comm Arts over there," Jom said, gesturing to a building on the other side of the university.

"Are you sure they're hot? How do I get there?" Pete asked, suddenly brimming with enthusiasm.

After Jom gave Pete directions to the Communication Arts building, we were finally able to head to our classroom. Pete yelled after me, reminding me to call him when I got out of class.

I didn't get why Pete had to pester me like this. The injury on my arm wasn't bothering me much, since Pete kept waking me up through the night to take my pain medication. I'd insisted he not tell Tem and Jom what happened to me because I didn't feel like answering their questions. Fortunately, I was able to hide my injury under a long-sleeved shirt.

I called Pete after class as promised and told him to return to my building. Pete looked cheerful as he got off the university's free shuttle bus—I bet he liked the Comm Arts girls.

"So, how were they?" Jom asked.

"I got two girls' numbers! They've both got great tits!" Pete exclaimed, moving his hands around to give a demonstration. Tem and Jom excitedly asked if they could see their profile pictures. I even leaned in to take a peek for myself.

I hadn't slept with a girl in ages. Maybe it was time for me to go out and find someone to hook up with. My sexual frustration was starting to accumulate—I really needed to let off some steam. Although I had found a modicum of release with the aid of Japanese porn, nothing compared to being with a real girl.

"Do you want to go home now?" I asked Pete. "I can give you a ride." Today, I'd ridden my motorcycle to school with Pete as my passenger. He had insisted on being the driver at first, but I refused, assuring him that I could handle the bike.

"Let's grab something to eat at the mall," Pete replied, looking at me with pleading eyes. I frowned at Pete's somewhat childish request.

"Fuck the mall. You can eat at the cafeteria if you're hungry," I said bluntly.

"Come on, it's my day off! I want to check out some of the shops, too. Pretty please?"

If Pete wasn't built like a boxer, I would have beat him up for whining like that.

"Yeah, let's go!" Tem agreed. "I'm hungry too."

I sighed wearily at my friend, who was also whining like a spoiled brat. Eventually, I gave in to their demands, and we headed to the mall to grab some food. Pete and I took my bike while Tem and Jom went by car.

At the mall, I quietly walked behind the three of them. I wasn't really a mall guy; I preferred being outdoors. I didn't come here unless I specifically needed to buy something—going to the mall just to window-shop was out of the question. But since my friends insisted on coming, here I was.

"What should we get?" Pete asked Tem and Jom, then saw me lagging behind them. "Hey, hurry up!" Pete came over to drag me by the collar so I could keep up the pace.

"Aren't you glad we finally have time away from that house? No Mr. Tankhun—no Mr. Kinn... It's a relief, even just for a moment," Pete joked.

I agreed with him for the most part, but I preferred heading straight home on my days off. Coming to a place like this in my free time seemed like a waste of energy.

"Let's eat here. I'm too tired to walk around," I said, pointing at a random restaurant nearby that looked like a decent place. I wasn't familiar with the mall's offerings, since I usually ate at my local curry and rice shop.[25]

Pete, Tem, and Jom went to check out the menu on the board in front of the restaurant to decide what to buy. It appeared to be a buffet-style restaurant called Momo Paradise that served Japanese sukiyaki and hot pot. It cost almost one thousand baht per person, and I typically only spent a hundred baht for lunch...but I decided to just enjoy it, considering I was the one who pointed out this place.

"Pete? What are you doing here?" asked a familiar voice. I immediately tensed up and turned around to look at him.

"Hello, Mr. Kinn. What a coincidence!" Pete smiled broadly as he greeted his boss, who was also wearing our university's uniform.

---

25 A curry and rice shop, or ran khao kaeng, is a restaurant that serves a selection of curries and savory dishes over rice. Curry and rice shops are local Thai staples.

Kinn was with three of his friends, whom I vaguely recognized. I looked away and frowned as he approached with a smirk on his face.

"What are you doing here?" Kinn repeated.

"It's my day off, so I asked Porsche if I could visit the university with him. I wanted to check out the college girls," Pete replied with a chuckle.

My friends greeted Kinn and his gang with a wai gesture, considering they were juniors, but I chose not to show them the same respect.

"Tay, is this the place you wanted to eat at?" Kinn turned to ask his friend, who nodded in agreement. "I just met my bodyguards here. Let's eat together. My treat."

I frowned deeply at him, but my friends quickly thanked Kinn in unison. Those greedy bastards would never turn down free food. I had no desire to spend time with Kinn, so I turned to leave, intending to find somewhere else to eat on my own.

"Where are you going?" Kinn asked, stepping in my path.

"None of your business," I said, glaring at him.

"Hey, don't you want to eat with us?" Jom asked.

"No, but you guys can eat here if you want," I replied, trying not to meet Kinn's gaze.

"Come on, let's all eat together," Kinn said casually. "It's my treat, you know..." His smug drawl was starting to piss me off.

"That's why I don't want it," I said with a huff. I didn't know what else Kinn could come up with to rattle my cage, considering I still hadn't figured out his previous actions. I was so fucking tired of his shit.

"I thought you liked extorting money from me. This time, I'm treating you out of the goodness of my heart...with the most expensive course. What do you say?" Kinn asked, raising his eyebrow slightly as he leaned in close.

I quickly took a step backward, cursing at Kinn's penchant for invading my personal space.

"I won't eat here!" I snapped.

"Come on, Porsche. Let's eat here. Come on, come on, come on!" Pete said, rushing to my side and physically forcing me into the restaurant.

I tried to resist him, but there wasn't much I could do. All eyes in the restaurant turned toward us as soon as we entered. I blamed it on Kinn and his pretty friends for being too attractive—I wondered what the hell their parents ate that made them have such handsome children. They could practically pass as K-pop idols.

Pete kept a firm grip on me as a waitress showed us to our table. He didn't let go until he'd successfully pushed me into a seat and sat beside me.

"Nuh-uh! Don't even think about it. If you don't sit down and eat properly, I'll trap you here," Pete warned as I tried to get up, lifting his leg and laying it firmly across my lap.

I huffed, pushing his leg off of me. He was just too cunning—I had to give up. Kinn took the seat opposite me while the rest of us filled the remaining available seats. It was pretty straightforward: my friends and I sat on one side of the table, while Kinn and his friends sat on the other.

Kinn's friend took the menu from the waitress and quickly placed an order while Kinn alternated between looking down at his phone and glancing at me. I avoided looking at him, doing my best not to pay him any attention. *Damn, I was just enjoying a day out with my friends. Why did I have to run into Kinn and deal with his bullshit?*

"Did you take your pills today?" Kinn asked me.

I glanced up at Tem and Jom to see if they had heard him, but they were engaged in a lively conversation with Kinn's friends.

I didn't know why my friends were so friendly with them today when they had hated them that day at the market.

"Fuck off!" I snapped, bracing my arms tightly over my chest as I leaned back in my seat.

Kinn smirked triumphantly, as he always did after successfully striking a nerve. *What a dick!*

"Order up!" the waitress announced, skillfully stacking trays of sliced pork and beef on the table. Our friends promptly grabbed vegetables and tofu, and soon our table was covered with a variety of hot pot ingredients waiting to be cooked in the rich, dark brown sukiyaki broth.

"Try some?" Kinn said, gesturing toward the pot with his chin.

Pete added the vegetables to the soup and carefully read the cooking instructions on the paper placemat. The soup smelled so good, it made my mouth water. I watched as Kinn and the others deftly dipped meat in the hot soup while Pete and I just sat there awkwardly.

"Hey, why aren't you eating? Do you not eat beef?" Kinn asked, putting a piece of cooked meat into my bowl.

"I have hands. I don't need your help." I scowled at Kinn, picking up the slice of beef with chopsticks and placing it in Pete's bowl instead. Pete grinned at me before continuing to munch on his food. I eyed him sideways. Another fucking weirdo.

Seeing that everyone was busy eating, I decided it was my turn to try dipping the beef in the hot soup. Once I'd left it in long enough to cook the meat, I took it out of the pot and started looking for sauce to dip it in. But there was none.

I looked around the table, wondering if I needed to get my own sauce from the condiment stand, and realized nobody else at the table had dipping sauce, either. My eyes widened in shock as

I watched them casually dip the cooked meat in raw eggs before eating. *What the hell?*

"Japanese sukiyaki is eaten with raw egg," Kinn explained, using his chopsticks to mix the raw egg in his bowl before handing it to me. "Give it a try. The texture isn't too slimy...I'm sure you can swallow it," he said suggestively.

Pete choked on his food and started coughing. I glanced at him curiously before returning my gaze to Kinn.

"No," I declared, opting to eat the meat without dipping it in anything. It already tasted great, and I didn't want to risk upsetting my stomach with raw eggs.

"Why not?" Kinn said, placing the bowl of raw egg back in front of himself. "Do you like swallowing other slippery things? Because I could give you those as well..."

He persisted in irritating me throughout our meal, which I found odd. He usually acted stoic and cold. He just wasn't behaving like himself today.

"Leave me alone," I replied as I chewed my food, not really paying attention to what he had just said.

"This is delicious!" Pete said with his mouth full. I agreed with him—it was so damn tasty that my bad mood started to fade away. I guess this food was expensive for a reason!

"Do you not eat vegetables at all?" Kinn asked, noticing that I had finished my third tray of beef without touching any greens.

"No!" I replied irritably.

"What a baby," he snickered.

I took a deep breath, trying not to get worked up by his comment. Kinn was the type of guy who got more annoying the more I argued back. I decided to ignore him to see if he would stop harassing me.

"Do you want to try some mochi?" Kinn asked.

I had no idea why he kept trying to make conversation with me. I glanced up at him, annoyed that wouldn't let me eat in peace.

"What's mochi? Isn't it a dessert?" I asked, wondering if he was trying to trick me. I knew that mochi[26] was a famous souvenir sweet you could get from the Nakhon Sawan province.

"Huh? It's not that type of mochi. It's a Japanese rice cake. Here, try it," Kinn chuckled, shaking his head in disbelief. He picked the soft dough from the pot and put it on my plate before eating one himself. I looked at him in suspicion, but in the end I took a bite, not bothering to argue with him anymore. It looked interesting enough to try.

"How is it?" Kinn asked.

"It's fine," I replied frankly. It was just some sticky dough boiled in soup.

"Are you sure it's edible?" Kinn repeated, looking straight at me.

I glared at him, frowning in confusion. "Yes! It's edible!" I snapped, not knowing why he kept asking.

"If you say so," Kinn said with a snicker.

"What the hell are you getting at?" I said, glaring at him before getting back to my meal.

I noticed Kinn and Pete chuckling with each other sporadically. Those two were probably up to something. Pete kept smirking at me; I wanted to confront him and demand to know what his problem was. He eventually collected himself and urged me to finish eating. Kinn's family and bodyguards really liked provoking me, even when I was off duty!

"P'Kinn!"

We all turned to look as a young man came over to our table.

---

26 Mochi from Nakhon Sawan province in Thailand is made with wheat flour or cake flour. The typical filling is mung bean paste, but it can also be filled with sesame paste, chocolate, or strawberry jam. It is not the same as Japanese mochi made from rice flour.

He was about the same height as Kinn—and just as handsome. He approached us with a big smile on his face.

"Hey, Vegas," Kinn returned the greeting, his lips lifting into a small smile.

The young man put his hands together in a wai gesture and greeted Kinn's friends as well. "Hello, P'Tay, P'Time, and P'Mew," he said.

"What's my favorite boy doing here?" Tay smiled sweetly at the newcomer, prompting Time to immediately force his boyfriend to turn away. Their behavior was puzzling, but I decided to ignore it.

"I'm meeting some friends here," said the man Kinn called Vegas.

I recognized him. He'd been a guest at Kinn's house a while ago—the same day I threatened to pop that one kid's eyes out.

"What brings all of you here? Are you guys celebrating something?" Vegas said, looking at the busy table. His smile broadened when he noticed me.

"There's no special occasion. We're just here to grab a bite. Have you eaten anything yet? Want to join us?" Kinn kindly asked his younger cousin.

"Well...let me sit with you guys for a bit," Vegas said. "I'm supposed to be meeting up with some friends here."

Kinn nodded, shifting in his seat to create some space. As he settled down, Vegas positioned himself across from me. He glanced at me once more, still smiling.

"It's okay if you want to eat with us first," Kinn said.

"I'm all right, P'Kinn. I'll just wait for my friends," Vegas replied.

"He's fortunate it was Mr. Kinn he ran into. If it were Mr. Tankhun, he'd be drenched in this boiling broth," Pete whispered to me.

"Why?" I asked.

"The Major Clan and the Minor Clan are at odds. Mr. Kinn is the only one who's friendly with them," Pete explained.

"So, this guy is from the Minor Clan?"

"Mr. Vegas is Mr. Macau's older brother. The boy you threatened to slap, remember?"

I nodded, vaguely recalling Kinn yelling some sort of accusation that I hurt his family. So this was the kid's brother.

"Hey," Vegas said, interrupting my hushed conversation with Pete.

I straightened up, nodding at him slightly without saying anything. Hopefully he wasn't mad about the incident with his younger brother. Kinn had cursed at me profusely for threatening Macau, and I figured that Macau's actual brother would be even more pissed.

"P'Kinn, is this the guy who wanted to smack Macau?" Vegas asked. I glanced at them and saw Kinn nodding in affirmation. Vegas turned to me. "Why didn't you smack him for real?" he said. "You should give him an extra slap or two for me!"

Vegas sounded playful. He was polite—smiling and joking with me without a hint of anger.

"How is Macau, anyway?" Kinn asked his cousin while adding another piece of boiled mochi into my bowl. Why did Kinn keep giving me food?! I noticed Vegas silently observing Kinn's actions, which I found unnerving.

"That's enough. I'm...full," I said, remembering that Kinn had said I could speak freely with him, but that I had to be polite to his guests and people from the Minor Clan.

"Oh, please, go ahead and eat more. Did I make you uncomfortable?" Vegas asked me.

I shook my head. It felt like there was a glass wall between the three of us and the rest of the group. Kinn's friends were chatting away cheerfully with Tem and Jom, while our section of the table felt tense.

"Hey, Porsche! I've been meaning to ask you for a while—what happened to your neck?" Time asked while staring at my neck, shattering the invisible wall. It was no surprise he knew my name; Kinn sure yelled at me a lot while his friends were around. Time and I had met on several occasions; he was there when I almost burned Kinn's room down.

"He said the bandages make him look cool," Tem answered for me. A tiny smile appeared on his face, like he thought it was hilarious.

Kinn smiled at Tem's answer, too, although he was the reason I needed bandages in the first place. He leaned back into the booth, crossing his arms loosely over his chest. I could tell he was stifling a laugh. *This is all because of you, you son of a bitch!*

"Is it a new trend?" Mew asked.

I refused to answer. Kinn seemed to be really enjoying himself. I frowned at him before realizing that everyone at the table was looking at us.

"They must make you look hot," Vegas said.

I hated being the center of attention. I swiftly got up and left the restaurant.

"Where are you going?" Pete yelled after me.

"I'm done eating," I said bluntly, not looking back.

"Hey! You can't leave me like this! Please excuse me, Mr. Kinn, and thank you for treating me."

I heard Pete's voice in the distance before he caught up with me. I headed to my motorcycle without another word. I fired up the engine, and Pete quickly hopped onto the passenger seat behind me.

Pete leaned forward to speak to me as we rode my bike. "It's bad manners to leave in a rush like that, Porsche."

"Whatever. Do you want me to drop you off at the house?" I asked.

"No! Can I sleep over at your place tonight?" Pete said, shaking my shoulders. "Let's play some games. I don't wanna go back there yet."

"No. Why don't you go back to your place?"

"My place is in another province. Come on, I want to play the computer game you told me about."

I heaved out a sigh. Why did Pete keep begging to follow me around everywhere today? I just wanted to go home and relax. Instead, I had this enormous burden coming home with me. I wondered if Tankhun's troublesome behavior was starting to rub off on Pete.

"How will you get to work tomorrow? I won't wake up early to drive you there," I warned him. I had class tomorrow morning, too.

"That's okay. I'll take a taxi tomorrow."

When we finally made it home, I collapsed on the sofa. Today had left me just as exhausted as the days I worked as a bodyguard. I thought I'd get to spend my day off in peace, but I ended up dealing with Kinn at the mall instead.

Pete entered the living room with my meds and a bottle of water. As soon as he'd stepped inside my house, he'd gone straight to the kitchen to raid my refrigerator. At least he was thoughtful enough to bring me my medicine and water.

"Take your medicine," he said. "And let me change that bandage for you." He opened my backpack without asking for permission and took out the first aid kit.

I frowned at him. "You don't have to be so...considerate," I said. I knew Pete was a nice guy, but he could be a bit much.

"Just let me help." He rolled up my sleeve and soaked some cotton balls in rubbing alcohol.

I quickly checked the front porch—to my relief, there was no sign of Chay's school shoes. I could let Pete help clean my wound and change the bandage without worrying about my little brother seeing me. If Chay saw my injury, I'd need to give him a very lengthy explanation.

Thud, thud, thud.

The sound of someone running down the stairs made me shake my arm from Pete's hold and pull down my sleeve.

"You're back—wait, what happened?!" Chay's smile immediately faltered. I thought my reaction was quick enough, but Chay had noticed I was hurt. He glared at me accusingly, walking over to stand by my side with his hands on his hips. Pete looked startled, gaping at my brother in confusion as Chay rolled up my sleeve.

"I was clumsy," was my weak explanation. "I was taking a walk and some branches cut my arm."

The room went dead silent. Chay continued to glare at me. He was not going to buy my bullshit. I sighed, avoiding making eye contact with him and pointedly looking out the window.

"Who is this guy?" Pete finally asked when he clearly couldn't stand the tension any longer.

"This is my little brother Porchay. Chay, meet Pete. Pete, wai to my little brother, will you?" I introduced them, attempting to lighten the mood with a joke, but it didn't seem to work.

"Hello," Pete said, giving my brother a little wave. However, Chay's sole focus was on me. He looked absolutely furious.

"Damn, that's definitely your brother. He looks *exactly* like you when he's mad," Pete whispered.

Heaving a heavy sigh, I turned to Chay. "I thought you weren't home," I said. "I didn't see your school shoes."

"I'm airing them out at the back of the house. Don't try to change the subject, hia. Tell me what happened!" Chay demanded, forcefully seating himself on the sofa between Pete and me. He pushed my sleeve further up my arm to take a good look at the wound.

"Well...a bullet grazed my arm. It's nothing, really," I replied feebly, accepting my fate.

"A bullet? You were *shot*?!" Chay shouted.

"Keep it down, my ears hurt," I said, trying to keep my voice even.

"Didn't you promise me you wouldn't get hurt?" Chay protested. "I won't let you do this job anymore!"

"I'm fine," I said calmly, not daring to look Chay in the eye.

Chay kept yelling at me, commanding me to quit the bodyguard gig. Pete left us to it, opting to sit at the dining table in the kitchen instead.

During the gunfight, I'd completely forgotten about my brother. I didn't consider how he would feel if something horrible happened to me. The only thing in my mind was rage—those men just kept on coming at us, and my anger made me lose control.

It was only now that I realized the gravity of the situation, seeing the devastation in Chay's eyes. I needed to think before I acted from now on. I was incredibly lucky that I got away with just a graze. If they'd killed me, Chay would've dug up my grave just to yell at me.

"I won't let you stay there. You have to quit *now*!" Chay insisted.

"I promise you, Chay, I won't get hurt next time. I'm so sorry," I whispered, turning to face my little brother and gently stroking his hair.

Chay tightly pursed his lips, but he resumed cleaning my wound for me in place of Pete.

"I don't believe you. I know something worse is gonna happen," Chay murmured, his hands trembling as he tended to my injury.

"Why? Nothing's gonna happen," I said. "I'll be fine, Chay. Just trust me."

Chay didn't let up. "It was just a graze this time. But what will you do if you get shot for real?"

"I'm tougher than I look. You can't get rid of me *that* easily. You know that." I kept trying to assuage his fears, acknowledging that I had made a mistake.

"I just have a bad feeling about all this. I'm worried for you, brother," Chay said, giving me a stern look, though his eyes remained vulnerable.

"You're overthinking things," I said, nudging his head.

"I'm not! I even had a strange dream about it..." Chay gripped my arm hard, begging me to believe him.

"What did you dream about?" I asked.

"You were crying..." Chay mumbled. He looked even more worried, as if he was recalling the image in his head.

"Pfft! A guy like me, crying? You've been home alone for too long. Your imagination is running wild," I deflected.

Chay pursed his lips again, still troubled. Finally, he sighed, looking defeated as he gently placed new gauze over my wound.

"Please just quit. I'm really worried... My dream was so real. You kept crying, and there was nothing I could do," Chay said, his voice quavering. I hugged him and pulled him into a playful headlock, mussing up his hair.

"Hey, stop being so dramatic," I teased. "Aren't you embarrassed acting like this in front of my friend?" I glanced at Pete, who waved and smiled brightly, like he was glad we'd finally noticed him.

I was unhappy with myself for making Porchay worry about me again. I wasn't sure what the future had in store, and I understood why my little brother was worried sick. Perhaps Chay had that nightmare because he kept dwelling on my dangerous job. He was probably just overthinking it...

KINN
PORSCHE

Falling into Place

ETE TOOK A TAXI HOME in the early morning. Last night, we'd played games until two or three in the morning, with Chay joining in from time to time. He'd finally stopped nagging me about quitting my job. It seemed like he understood my reasons for staying, but maybe he just saw that I was tired and didn't want to bother me. I apologized and promised him I'd be okay, because I wanted to cheer him up.

"You guys want to play basketball? P'Ohm's inviting us for a game," Jom said as the three of us came down from the Sports Science building, looking forward to after-class activities.

"Nah, not interested. I've got a long swim practice tomorrow, so I need to conserve my energy," said Tem, who was part of the swim team. He'd been selected to represent our college in a university sports competition, so he had to train hard right now. I'd gone to the tryouts just for fun, and to cheer Tem on. I had no intention of competing on the swim team right now, since I didn't have the free time to practice.

"Oh, right, I have soccer tryouts tomorrow," said Jom. "Porsche, why don't you go to judo practice? It'll make P'Beam happy."

I was required to participate in the judo competition. I often skipped practice because I'd been so busy lately, but P'Beam didn't seem to mind. I'd told him from the beginning that I could join the team, but that I probably wouldn't be able to attend practice regularly. Thankfully, he hadn't complained much.

"I'll go. But right now, I want to go back to sleep," I said.

My arm still twinged occasionally, so I wasn't sure how well I could handle heavy impact. However, I was confident it would heal before the competition.

Since the three of us didn't have any other plans, Tem eagerly asked us to have a meal together at the market stalls behind the university.

"Let's go check out the food stalls," he said, pleading with his eyes.

"Yeah. I'm hungry, too. Hang around for a while, Porsche. Stay and have a meal with us," Jom said, trying to stop me from fishing my motorcycle key out of my pocket.

"Stay with me, pleeeease! I'm lonely."

I sighed deeply, wondering why everyone around me kept begging me to do things for them. I didn't want to say no to Tem, though—he lived in the dorms all by himself, and I hadn't had much time to spend with him lately.

"Hi there!" a tall figure called, turning around to look at us as we walked past.

I said nothing, smiling faintly and nodding my head as the guy walked toward us with a wide smile. It was Kinn's cousin—we'd met him at the restaurant in the mall.

"That's the guy from yesterday. His name is Ve...Ve-something," Jom whispered to Tem behind me.

"Veha?" Tem replied, trying to remember his name. He didn't seem very confident.

"Hello, Veha!" Jom greeted him loudly, not bothering to listen to Tem's objections.

"Vegas. My name is Vegas," the man replied.

Embarrassed, Jom extended his hand to lightly pat Vegas's shoulder. "Right, Vegas. I told you his name is Vegas," he said, trying to save face by passing the blame to Tem, who frowned and furrowed his brow in displeasure.

"We meet again," Vegas said, smiling at me.

I raised my eyebrows and looked at him with suspicion. Judging from the uniform I'd seen him wearing yesterday, he wasn't a student here, and yet here he was in front of the Sports Science building. I was confident he wasn't a third-year or fourth-year student, either.

"I'm just here to meet my friend who goes here," Vegas explained. Jom and Tem were still bickering with each other behind me.

"And you are…?" Vegas asked, raising a brow.

"Porsche," I answered flatly.

"I'm Tem, and you can call him a douchebag," Tem introduced himself to Vegas.

"It's Jom. My name is Jom," Jom complained loudly. Vegas laughed out loud.

"So, you study Sports Science, Mr. Porsche?" he asked, turning away from my friends to look at me again.

He was friendly and polite, and he didn't seem to be a threat. I decided answering him wouldn't hurt. "Yes."

"What a coincidence! I'm lost," Vegas said.

"Where are you headed? I can show you the way," I offered, seeing as we were familiar with each other. More importantly, I almost slapped his younger brother, but he'd let that slide. I felt like it was reasonable for me to show him some courtesy.

"I'm looking for P'Beam. He's a third-year student here. Do you know him, Mr. Porsche?"

Vegas's politeness made me itch a little. It had been ages since someone addressed me so respectfully.

"You don't have to call me 'mister,' you know. Just call me Porsche," I said. Vegas kept looking at me with a smile plastered on his face. "So, you're looking for P'Beam?" I continued. "He's probably in the gym. Walk along the side of this building and turn left. You'll see him there." I pointed down the path. There was only one third-year named Beam, and I knew him well.

"You said his name so respectfully. Which year are you in university?" Jom asked, nosy.

"I'm a second," Vegas replied. "It looks like we're in the same year, huh?"

This Minor Clan guy was incredibly different from the men of the Major Clan. Vegas was friendly and spoke politely, unlike Kinn, who was an asshole, and Tankhun, who was a lunatic. I couldn't believe they were cousins.

"Right, we're sophomores, too," Tem answered, smiling back at Vegas.

Vegas's phone rang, so he excused himself to answer the call. Now that I'd helped Vegas find P'Beam, I turned to talk to my friends about the food stalls behind the university.

"Where are you guys going?" Vegas asked, returning to our group after disappearing for a while.

"We're going to find something to eat," Tem said.

"Oh, I'm hungry, too," Vegas quickly replied. I looked at him skeptically. "P'Beam ditched me," he added. "He said he had a practice session."

I felt a pang of guilt hearing that P'Beam was practicing hard while I was slacking off to go eat.

"You can come with us. The more the merrier," Tem said. I frowned at him slightly. Vegas was a rich kid like Kinn. He might not be comfortable eating street food.

"Well then, I'll go with you guys," Vegas told Tem. He then turned to me. "Why are you looking at me like that, Porsche?"

"We're going to eat at a cheap place. Is that okay?" I asked, raising my eyebrow.

"Sure, I'm just like anyone else. I can eat wherever," he said, giving me a pleasant smile.

I couldn't believe it. This guy should get a DNA test, because there was no way he was related to Kinn. The difference was night and day.

"Let's go, then. I'm hungry!" Jom exclaimed, walking ahead of us. We were too lazy to drive and look for a parking spot, so we parked near the building and rode the university shuttle bus. Vegas sat casually with my friends and chatted energetically with them. He turned to speak to me now and then, and I responded with a mix of smiles and polite answers. His impeccable manners and friendly demeanor made me feel like I constantly had to be on my best behavior.

"Let's get something from Aunt Sally's. Their fried pork and rice is amazing." Tem went up to the street food vendor and requested four menus for us. "Wanna order now?"

"That's quite a unique name," Vegas noted, looking puzzled.

"Oh, we made it up. It's short for salmonella."

Tem, Jom, and I laughed when we saw Vegas's confused expression.

"Is it really that bad?" Vegas looked over at the stall.

I followed his eyes and saw Aunt Sally in the middle of wiping the cutting board with a dirty rag and going straight to the pork afterward. I chuckled.

"But it's delicious!" Jom gave a thumbs-up. Vegas smiled sheepishly, trying not to look at the auntie who was currently violating food safety practices.

"Are you okay with eating here?" I asked Vegas.

He looked up from the menu and chuckled. "Yeah. I wouldn't want to miss out on Auntie's secret recipe."

He ordered and ate in a very unassuming manner, which was a relief. Kinn's cousin was nothing like him. It was good to know that Vegas was the black sheep of the family. He was not at all snobby, didn't give me orders, and didn't see me as Kinn's subordinate. On the contrary, he treated me like a friend.

After eating together, we all went our separate ways. Vegas flaunted his wealth a little by paying for our food, saying he wanted to express gratitude for allowing him to join us. He was so kind that Jom and Tem couldn't stop praising him. I appreciated him, too. If people were nice to me, I returned their kindness; if they were rude to me, I was rude right back.

The next day, I attended class as usual. In the afternoon, I went to practice with P'Beam, who practically bowed to me when he saw me enter the gym.

After a tiring day, more tiring work awaited. I stood and chanted Buddha's name in my mind for a long time, trying to gather my wits to face that bastard Tankhun. Before I could even walk into the house, Tankhun shouted at me from the stairs.

"Porsche! Finally, you're here! Yay!" Tankhun jumped and grabbed my injured arm with full force, making me wince in pain.

"Sorry, sorry, I forgot you got shot. Let's go out together today," said Tankhun.

"Yes, sir," I replied, rubbing my arm.

"Where are we going?" Tankhun asked with sparkling eyes.

"Umm... Where do *you* want to go, Mr. Tankhun?" I asked. He barely gave me a second to catch my breath. *I just got here, and you're already making me pay for my sins?*

"I'm bored of that ladyboy's club. Let's go somewhere else. I want to go somewhere more exciting!"

"Ummm...how about Khaosan Road?"[27] I mentioned the first place that came to my mind when I thought of busy nightlife.

"Yes, yes, yes!" Tankhun excitedly agreed. "I've heard about it, but I've never been!"

Was this guy raised in total isolation? He acted like a newborn baby deer stumbling into the outside world for the first time.

Mr. Korn emerged from the conference room. "What's with all the noise? Quiet down, I'm working!"

I quickly raised my hands in a wai gesture to greet him. He acknowledged me with a nod before returning to the meeting room, closing the door behind him.

"Hmph... Those Minor Clan idiots!" Tankhun exclaimed, not even paying attention to what his father had said. His voice was still just as loud. He even emphasized the words, making the bodyguards around him flinch.

"Mr. Tankhun, please try to be quieter," I pleaded.

"Porsche...I have a job for you." Tankhun lowered his voice and beckoned me to lean in closer, as if there was some secret he wanted to share.

"Yes...?" I replied, leaning in.

"Today, Vegas and Macau are coming over for a meal. When they let their guard down, grab them," Tankhun said and walked to a desk. He opened a drawer and pulled out a length of rope.

"Then, use this rope and tie them to the mango tree behind the house," he continued. "Wait for about three days before you let them go. Just let them shrivel up completely out there."

---

27   Khaosan Road is a short street in central Bangkok, famously known as a "backpacker ghetto." The street is filled with cheap hostels, bars, and street vendors that sell food and souvenirs.

I frowned, not understanding Tankhun's instructions at all. I was so perplexed that he had to shove the rope in my face. I reluctantly took it. What the hell was this idiot thinking?!

"Well..." I said, looking from Tankhun's face to the item in my hand.

"Get it done, okay? Good luck!"

He didn't wait for me to ask any questions. He just whistled and moseyed up to the second floor.

Damn it! I let out a sigh. Why did I have to do this? This was so fucking stupid!

I kept the rope in my hand, but I had no intention of following Tankhun's order. It was idiotic and unreasonable. How could you just go around tying people up like that? They were people! You couldn't just hang them out to dry like laundry and wait to collect them later.

I sighed again, planning to go to the garden to smoke a cigarette and relax. I hadn't been here for ten minutes, and Tankhun had already given me a headache. Damn!

"What's up?" Pete greeted me. "You're back already?"

Pete stood next to Vegas, both smoking cigarettes. I was a bit surprised to see Vegas smoking out here with the bodyguards.

"Oh, Porsche... Hi!" Vegas greeted me with a warm smile, as usual.

"Please excuse me," Pete said to Vegas, bowing his head slightly. Then, he walked over to me with a smile and lightly patted my shoulder. "I'm going to see Mr. Kinn."

"Are you working today?" Vegas asked before taking a drag.

"Yes, sir," I replied, lighting my cigarette and placing the rope I was holding on a nearby table.

Vegas pointed at the rope. "What's that for?"

"To hang myself with," I said dryly. Honestly, I was tempted. I was so fed up with Tankhun!

"Ha! You *are* kidding, right?" he said with a throaty chuckle. "I'd be so sad if you were gone."

I frowned slightly. Vegas's words just now seemed a bit strange.

"What are you doing here?" a familiar voice called out.

I froze for a moment, my expression instantly turning into a scowl.

Vegas smiled at his cousin. "P'Kinn, I came out here to smoke," he said.

I glanced at Kinn and saw that he was still in his school uniform, sporting his usual cocky expression.

"Food's ready. Father told me to call you. Get in there already," Kinn said, putting his hands in his pockets. He didn't look at me at all—he just stared at Vegas.

"Sure. Porsche, I'll see you later. If I pass by your university, I'll say hi," Vegas said, throwing his cigarette butt into the trash can. He turned to smile at me briefly before walking past Kinn. I nodded in response, then turned around immediately because I didn't want to look at Kinn's face.

"Since when are you close to Vegas?"

I felt a chill run down my spine when I realized that Kinn had moved in behind me.

"Fuck off!" I snapped, taking a step forward to put some space between us.

"Turn around and talk to me," Kinn said, stepping closer behind me. I growled. "Or are you scared?" he prodded.

His taunting words made me take a deep breath and turn to look at him immediately. "I'm not scared of you!" I barked, pulling away so that I wasn't too close.

"Hmph. Someone like you..." Kinn scoffed.

I scowled and stared at him angrily. He was probably just trying to provoke me. I tried to walk past him to leave, but he grabbed my arm. Pain shot through me immediately.

"Ouch!" I shook my arm away from his hand. He looked a little stunned.

"I forgot you were injured," he said, guiltily looking at my arm.

"I don't know if it'll ever heal. First Khun, now you, always grabbing my arm," I growled.

"And how is it healing?" he asked, gently lifting my sleeve.

I stood there in surprise for a moment before shaking Kinn off again. I didn't know why the hell he had to keep getting up in my business.

"What's your problem, you nosy fuck?" I glared at him. I was tired! I was *so* fucking tired of Kinn and his constant meddling.

"P'Kinn... Let's go," Vegas called Kinn. The two of us turned to look at him. He was standing at a distance, smiling slightly.

"Oh, you're still here?"

"I saw that you weren't following, so I came to get you," Vegas said, smiling at Kinn. He then glanced at me and smiled even wider. Vegas was taking the annoying bastard away at last.

"Okay, let's go." Kinn turned around and was about to walk away when he leaned in and whispered in my ear, "Don't forget to take your medicine."

I pushed his shoulder away. His face was way too close.

"Asshole!" I hissed. Kinn smiled in satisfaction before walking back into the house.

I hated being a bodyguard in this awful house. The sons were deranged. If I ever got the chance, I should offer my bodyguard services to the Minor Clan. Vegas was friendly, polite, and levelheaded, unlike the kids here. It would be a breeze, and I wouldn't have to worry about that bastard Kinn. Maybe I should beg Vegas to bail me out—we'd make a good partnership.

I was nervous and my mind was muddled. I needed to get the hell out of here. Tankhun was now hurling a string of curses at me.

"Why didn't you tie them up?! How could you let them run around loose?!" Tankhun's shouting filled his room.

"Mr. Tankhun, when would I have had the chance?! His father *and* his bodyguard were here," I wearily explained. If Tankhun could come to his senses—even just a little—his life would be so much better.

"Still, you should have found a chance to do it. Damn it! No one ever meets my expectations," Tankhun snarled, kicking his couch. The rest of his lackeys lowered their heads. I stared at him and gently shook my head. I was so tired of this fucker!

"Mr. Tankhun, that's enough. Go take a shower so we can go out," I said.

Tankhun started to throw things at us, mainly the papers on his desk. I didn't know why he was so enraged. What had the Minor Clan done to make him this furious?

"Next time, you have to make him cry, or I'll make *you* cry!" Tankhun shouted.

I sighed and looked at him quizzically. He angrily stomped to his bedroom and slid the glass door shut so forcefully that the other bodyguards flinched.

"Ugh. I'm so damn tired," I grumbled. I looked at the shut glass door and put my hands on my hips.

Pol patted my shoulder. "Hang in there. Mr. Tankhun loses his shit every time the Minor Clan visits."

"Did he ever order you to tie them up?" I asked Pol, Arm, and P'Jess, who promptly nodded in unison.

"That's normal. Mr. Tankhun always tells us to tie them up, scatter crooked nails on the ground, or smack them in the head. Fuck, man, who'd even *dare*? They always come with a full squad of bodyguards," Arm said with an exhausted shake of his head.

We disbanded to prepare for our night out. Not long after, we were back in one of the family's luxurious vans. Tankhun scowled in silence throughout our journey, which spared us from the earache of his shouting.

When we hit Khaosan Road, his eyes sparkled in excitement.

"Any recommendations? I want to get drunk, but I want something unusual," Tankhun said.

I tried to think of something unusual. *The most unusual thing in my life is* you, *Tankhun!* Eventually, though, I came up with something he'd definitely never tried before.

I led him to a less crowded club with folk songs playing inside. This apparently was unusual enough for Tankhun, since he looked ecstatic.

"Ya dong,"[28] P'Jess mumbled, immediately leaping in front of the bar to place an order. Tankhun intently eyed the row of jars and ordered the bartender to let him try every single one.

"Take it slowly, Mr. Tankhun," Pol cautioned as Tankhun downed shot after shot of mah gra teub rong.[29] Tankhun popped a pickled grape into his mouth right after, wincing slightly at the sourness before smiling again. As Tankhun started to get drunk, he got up and swayed to the music. All we could do was stay close and keep an eye on him.

"There are tons of other clubs around. Would you be interested in any of those?" I asked Tankhun. I wanted to move on to a livelier

---

28 Ya dong is Thailand's equivalent of moonshine, a clear spirit infused with different native botanicals that is typically consumed by the working class. It is also often sold as an herbal remedy.

29 Mah gra teub rong (translated to English as "prancing stallion") is a ya dong infused with mah gra teub rong herb (ficus foveolata).

place. The upbeat music in this joint wasn't bad, but there weren't a lot of customers.

"Yes! Let's go!" Tankhun pushed my shoulder and walked us out of the club. The other bodyguards—who were also getting tipsy—followed us down the street, dancing to the music emanating from every club we passed.

Not long after, one shop in particular caught Tankhun's attention, probably due to its vibrant decorations. He rushed up to the place, which turned out to be a hair braiding booth. Tankhun was fascinated by the dreadlocks and cornrows made with bright hair extensions. A man passed us on his way out with his hair braided in purple strands. Tankhun's eyes lit up, praising the hairstyle excitedly.

"Hey, all of you! Let's get our hair done like that," Tankhun ordered us.

We quickly shook our heads in refusal, making him frown.

"If you don't do it, I'll tear this place down!"

The shop owner recoiled at Tankhun's outburst and looked at us as if to ask what this moron's problem was.

"Mr. Tankhun, we need to look professional for our job," P'Jess explained.

"You work for me. What's the problem? I want to see your hair in bright colors. It's cheerful!" Tankhun crossed his arms, so stubborn that we sighed in frustration.

"Mr. Tankhun, please... We're too old for this," Arm muttered.

"Do it or shave your head tomorrow morning!" Tankhun demanded.

Tankhun was so conceited I wanted to kick his ass. The bodyguards unwillingly had braids put in except for me—I said that my university wouldn't allow it. Arm and Pol shot me jealous glances. *You're on your own, guys.*

I barely held in my laughter at the results. Arm's braids were green, Pol's were yellow, and P'Jess's were red. I really felt bad for P'Jess, who was the oldest out of all of us. I wondered if the poor bastard was married, and if he was, whether his family knew the physical and mental torture his job put him through. Tankhun had picked different colors at random, and his hair was a jumble of multicolored braids.

Our group continued down the street. Passersby gave us funny looks, like we were a gang of punks roaming the street. I sighed. I really felt for the rest of them.

I took Tankhun into a club teeming with Thais and foreigners alike, ordering a bucket cocktail for him to try. This would get him hammered for sure. I was able to keep myself from getting too wasted, even though Tankhun demanded round after round of bottoms-up shots. In stark contrast to me, Tankhun looked absolutely plastered, like a kid who had just discovered the joys of alcoholic beverages.

Seeing there was nothing to worry about, I stepped outside, grabbed some chick's hand, and led her away. I didn't even know her name, but she'd been dancing next to me and had rubbed up on me suggestively multiple times. She looked pretty good and had a nice body, and it'd been ages since I'd gotten laid—I couldn't pass up this opportunity.

I pushed her pliant body into the men's bathroom and locked us in a stall. People were constantly walking in and out, but no one seemed to care. There was more than one couple hooking up in here, after all.

I quickly buried my face in the curve of her pale neck, sucking and nipping hard at her skin. In a place like this, we had to be quick and quiet. Besides, trying to stay silent while we went at it added to the excitement. Sex was usually pretty noisy, but we wouldn't let people outside know what was happening in here. My hand slid under her dress to fondle her breast, our lips never parting. Then, she pulled away a bit, hesitating when she moved to my neck.

"Can I take this off?" she asked, reaching for my bandage. I stopped her immediately. I didn't want her to see the red hickeys underneath. *Damn you, Kinn.*

"No need. Can I fuck you now?" I asked, reaching down to unzip my pants. I was horny as hell and needed to get some damned relief. I shoved her little hand into my underwear to feel my hard-on. *This feels good...*

I lifted one of her legs and fished around in my pocket for a condom. Every night I worked at Madam Yok's place or went out clubbing, I always had one on hand. I was tearing the wrapper when the chick's phone rang.

Rrrrrring!

She stopped kissing me. "Hold on," she said. She dug the phone out of her jeans to take a look. Her expression filled with dread. "Be quiet. My husband is calling."

Impatient, I dropped her leg and silently stared at her panicked face.

"Babe, you're here?! I'm in the restroom, be out in a minute!" she replied before turning to look apologetically at me.

"Sorry, sweetie, my husband's here."

I sighed, disheartened, and watched as my dick went limp and my balls started to ache. I was frustrated that I couldn't get the release I desperately wanted. The woman tidied her dress and walked out of the toilet after apologizing to me one last time.

I locked the door of the stall again once she left. My desire was fading, and it wasn't like I could jerk off while the guy next door was puking his guts out. Plus, someone was calling my name. My arousal had deflated completely.

"Porsche! Are you in here?" Arm yelled. "Mr. Tankhun is totally wasted. We need to head back!"

"Yeah," I replied.

"Hurry up. Mr. Tankhun is making himself sick."

I yanked my hair violently in frustration. This was gonna drive me crazy!

I stayed in the stall until I'd calmed down, then went out into the club to carry Tankhun to the van.

Back at the house, Tankhun was still so drunk that we had to carry him inside by his legs and arms. I really wanted to wake his father up to show him how awful his eldest son looked right now.

"We're done cleaning him up. You can go get some rest. I think everything else is taken care of," Pol said as he tucked a blanket around Tankhun's chest.

Tankhun was out cold, lying as still as a log—I was afraid he'd drunk himself to death. I put my fingers against his nose to make sure he was still breathing, which made Arm laugh.

Seeing that there was nothing left for me to do, I made my way toward the garden, thinking of having a smoke before going home to play games with my friends. However, as I was leaving the house, Pete walked up to me. It looked like he had gone out and returned in a hurry.

Pete shoved a brown paper bag into my hand. "Hey, can you take this to Mr. Kinn for me?" he said in a rush. "I'm about to pee my fuckin' pants. Hurry!"

His restlessness made me understand immediately. Pete sped into the house like he really needed to take a piss. But...what did he just give me? What was so important that I had to give it to that jerk Kinn myself? What a fucking pain. I didn't want to see that bastard's face!

"It's urgent!" Pete shouted in the distance before I lost sight of him.

I looked at the bag in my hand, then to the second floor, taking a deep breath before heading up to Kinn's room. I might as well get it over with.

None of Kinn's bodyguards were around when I arrived at his door. It was already two in the morning, so maybe they were taking a break. I wondered what that asshole wanted in the middle of the night. Did he need sleeping pills? Was that why Pete kept telling me to hurry?

I held my breath, opening the door without knocking like always. I never knocked on Kinn's door and never planned to. However, I soon realized this was a mistake. I came to a screeching halt, frozen in shock at what I saw. Time stopped, and two pairs of eyes stared at me in stunned silence.

That jerk Kinn was in his bathrobe, sitting on a sofa with a petite and completely naked guy on his lap. They were tangled in an embrace, and Kinn's face was buried in the other guy's chest. It was obvious what they had been doing before I'd interrupted them.

In that moment, all my restless thoughts and doubts ceased. My hands went weak, and the brown paper bag dropped onto the floor. I looked down to where the bag fell and saw a blue wrapper tumble out. I knew the brand very well...

Condoms!

I jolted in horror and slowly looked up at Kinn, who smirked at me and said nothing.

"Try to knock next time," said the guy in his lap. He looked familiar—like someone I'd seen on TV.

"Umm...Pete asked me to bring this," I said, pointing to the stuff on the floor. Not knowing what to do, I fled the room with a pounding heart, startled and perturbed by what I'd seen.

I rushed downstairs to the garden, feeling the blood drain from my face.

"So, how was it?" Pete asked, smiling and taking a puff of his cigarette.

"Shit, Pete!" I blurted when I saw him laughing.

"I hope that answers things," Pete said half-jokingly.

Pete had finally answered the question that had nagged at me for days: did Kinn do those things to me because he was gay, or just because he liked to irritate me? Everything was clear to me now. My mind went blank...

"You could have just told me," I said, still in shock.

"You wouldn't have believed me, man!" Pete laughed.

I hated this. Pete clearly wanted me to get an eyeful.

"How could you even know what my question was?" I asked.

"Dude, come on. You asked just about every single soul in this place... Plus, I know more than you think." Pete's gaze moved to my neck.

I gulped, my hair standing on end. All the times Kinn sucked and kissed my neck and said weird things to me—it wasn't to piss me off?! Kinn was gay! Fucking hell! *Porsche, you dumbass! That* was why he was fine with me wearing just my boxers around him. Fuck, I was such an idiot. Why didn't I figure this out before? Shit!

"So..." I prompted Pete.

"Mr. Kinn likes men," Pete said in a teasing tone, giggling. I didn't know what else Pete knew, but this was enough to stun me. *Kinn, you bastard! You wanted to fuck me this entire time?! Fuck!*

I couldn't stop thinking about it. The image of Kinn and his lover kept flashing through my head. *Damn it!* Had I unknowingly put myself in compromising positions with Kinn? I kept thinking about that day I got drunk and slept on his bed. The kiss that night was one thing, but the next morning, Kinn had made me touch his crotch.

I could still remember exactly how it felt. His dick was hard—but I thought it was normal for a guy to have morning wood. Shit! Was Kinn into me?

Still, maybe I was self-absorbed to think that Kinn had the hots for me personally. His partners were probably models and celebrities... Oh, hell. I just realized those "friends" visiting Kinn every night were his lovers—men who looked like they'd been through war after a night with Kinn.

Kinn was a real psycho. Couldn't he tell that I was straight? He'd teased me relentlessly, but did he do that with every man in his vicinity? Pete must have experienced some of it...

Damn it, Kinn had me more paranoid than ever!

I rode my motorcycle back to Kinn's house after class. I took the scenic route, stretching out the time it took to get there, but despite my best efforts, I finally reached the gates of hell.

I was turning into the alley when a black car swerved from the opposite lane and cut in front of me. I braked immediately, but my wheel skidded across the pavement. Luckily, I kept a hold of both myself and the motorcycle, managing not to crash to the ground.

"Learn how to fucking drive!" I yelled, kicking out my bike's kickstand and taking off my helmet. I raked my hair angrily before storming toward the car.

A young man in a black shirt and pants rushed out to check the front of his car. "Is my car okay?!"

"Your car is fine. You should be asking if *I'm* okay!" I shouted. This guy clearly had no common sense. He was the one who'd cut into my lane.

"Why weren't you more careful?" he asked, walking over to stare directly at me.

"It was your fault, asswipe!" I put my hands on my waist. "What kind of shitty driving was that? If I was going any faster, I'd be saying hi to the devil in hell!"

"Let's talk at the police station, then." Suddenly, the guy came up to me, grabbed my arm, and dragged me toward his car. I was a little confused before I forcefully shook off his grip.

"Why the hell do we need to go to the cops? Your car is obviously fine."

"It sounded like you wanted to hurt me, so we're going to the police station. Get in!" he snapped, snatching my injured arm. This time, he squeezed and held tight, and I couldn't escape.

"What the hell? Let me go!" My brows furrowed as I struggled against him. The way he kept trying to force me into his car felt kind of shady.

"Get in!" he growled. His face was intimidating, and he started pulling me with him using both hands. He forcefully dragged me to his car, screaming louder at me. "Get in the car! Don't make me hurt you!"

"Let me go!" I kicked his side hard, but before I could throw my fist into his face, a voice interrupted:

"Porsche, is everything all right?!"

It was Pete. The bastard who was trying to haul me into his car stopped and stared at him.

"This son of a bitch cut into my lane and tried to drag me into his car," I told Pete, furious. "He's saying he'll take me to the police station!"

Pete, with a popsicle in his hand, walked up to the guy and glared at him. I noticed some staff from a nearby convenience store and some other onlookers gathering around. Some of them even held their phones up to take pictures.

"What the hell is your problem?!" Pete asked harshly.

"Damn it! Fine, I'll let you go. Ride better next time," the man said irritably before getting into his car and driving off.

That bastard was crazy! I should've been the one telling him to drive better. He'd cut into *my* lane and tried to drag me into his car! I suspected it was intentional and not an accident, but maybe I was overthinking things.

"What are you doing here, by the way?" I asked Pete, who was sucking on his popsicle and craning his neck to look at the black car as it sped away.

"Right, I was getting something to eat at the mini mart when I heard a bunch of noise. So, I came outside to take a look," Pete answered, showing me a bag from the convenience store.

"How did you get here?" I asked him. He was dressed in casual attire. He was probably on the same shift as me.

"On foot. The store is right around the corner. Are you okay?" he asked as he gave me a once-over.

"I'm fine. Get on!" I revved the engine and let Pete sit behind me. I rode straight into the alley and turned to the giant house.

"You sure you're good?" Pete repeated once I'd parked my motor-cycle in the garage.

"Yep, I'm good."

"Then I'll go get changed," he said, walking along the side of the house to the back where our rooms were. I sighed, running my hands through my hair and checking my reflection in my side mirror before turning around to enter my own personal hell.

"Oops!"

I walked right into a slim figure with a happy smile. He would have looked handsome if it wasn't for that shitty hairdo. He'd come to annoy me from the front porch.

"I'm so happy you're here!" Tankhun said. He stroked my motorcycle and walked around it to check out each side. "Wow, you ride such a cool motorcycle!"

I sighed quietly. "Yes. Mr. Tankhun, are you sober?" I asked plainly, but he ignored my question.

"Cool. *So* cool! I wanna be cool. Teach me how to ride, Porsche. Please, please, please?" He put his long legs across my motorcycle, looking at me with pleading eyes. This was going to be a problem. I was rather possessive of my motorcycle. What would I do if this moron tipped my bike over?

"Khun! Come here, you little shit!" Mr. Korn's voice came to my rescue. Tankhun made a moody face before stepping away from my motorcycle. He turned and signaled me with his hand, beckoning me to follow. *Ugh.* Would I ever get time to relax before my shift?

"What's up, Father?!" Tankhun exclaimed, resting his hands on his waist and staring at his father in annoyance. Mr. Korn sat at a table by the garden with Arm, Pol, and P'Jess, who were all staring at the ground.

"What have you done to them?!" Mr. Korn shouted, but Tankhun didn't even flinch.

"It's cool, right, Father? Gangster style. Yo!" Tankhun covered his mouth and cackled. I bit my lip to hold in my own laughter.

"Damn it, I'm getting a headache. Who told you to get this hairstyle? You too, Khun. Your hair hurts to look at. I thought you were a parrot!" Mr. Korn pressed his fingers to his temples and wearily shook his head.

"Why, Father? People will know we're together. *Four dudes, four dudes, four dudes. We come together, four dudes!*"[30] Tankhun cheerfully sang. If I were Mr. Korn, I'd write Tankhun out of my will!

"And to think you all let him do it! You especially, Jess. You're not young anymore. Think of your wife and sons," Mr. Korn said.

"It's cool, right? I'll take you to get your hair done, too, Father. Yeah? Orange looks nice..." Tankhun clung to his father's arm and put his colorfully braided hair against his father's head.

"Hmph! Fix your hair, all of you. There's a big party this Sunday, and I won't let you look like that for it. It's embarrassing," Mr. Korn said, shaking himself off from a giggling Tankhun before glancing at me.

"How did you manage to get out of it, Porsche?" Mr. Korn asked.

I smiled. I felt sorry for Mr. Korn, but I also found it hilarious. It was a shame that Mr. Korn's handsome son was a total moron.

"My university forbids it, sir," I said.

"Way to go, kiddo... Anyway, take those things out, all of you. You look like a damned flock of parrots. It's making me dizzy."

"Father, Father, Father! I want to ride a motorcycle. Porsche rides one. It's so cool!" Tankhun pleaded and tugged at his father's arm. Mr. Korn glanced at me again.

"You'll get hurt," he said.

"Please, please, please! I'll just ride around the yard. Let Porsche teach me!" Tankhun begged, rubbing his colorful head on Mr. Korn's arm.

"Do whatever you want, but don't leave the property," Mr. Korn weakly replied.

"Are you worried?" Tankhun asked.

---

30 Seeh Khon (Four Dudes) is a song from the Thai comedy movie Yam Yasothorn.

"I'm embarrassed! Go, do whatever you want to do. Teach him, Porsche. It's better than letting him watch TV all day and abuse his bodyguards."

I smiled and softly nodded at Mr. Korn.

"What's that, Father?!" The speaker was a tall, slim man of Chinese descent. He bore a resemblance to Tankhun and Kinn.

"Father, who is he?" Tankhun pointed to the man, who burst out laughing at Tankhun's hairstyle.

"Oh shit, your hair!" the man wheezed in laughter.

"Fuck off! Don't mess with me, you son of a bitch!" Tankhun stood with his hands on his hips and swore at the newcomer, who stopped laughing and frowned.

"Khun, why did you just call your mother a bitch?" Mr. Korn looked up to chide Tankhun.

"Tell him whose son he really is, Father! His brothers both have Western traits. He's the only chink," Tankhun spat.

"We have the same mother, you dickhead!"

With that, I finally realized that this man was Kim, the youngest son of the family. I'd never had the chance to meet him.

"I don't believe you! Son of a bitch! Bastard, bastard, bastard! Kim is a son of a bitch, son of a bitch! Booo!" Tankhun ran around the garden as Kim chased him, cursing all the while. Then, he grabbed my wrist and pulled me to the garage.

"Don't come near me. I'll fucking clobber you!" Kim yelled, pointing at Tankhun before disappearing into the garden.

"Okay, okay, I'll teach you how to ride," I told Tankhun. I couldn't be bothered to argue with him, and it wasn't like I could defy his orders anyway. I picked up the helmet and pushed my motorcycle out of the garage.

"Mr. Tankhun, you ignite the engine here, and the accelerator is here," I told him. "Don't push it too hard. Balance yourself like you're riding a normal bicycle."

Tankhun sat on my bike. He paid attention to everything I said, so I let him ride. Luckily, the yard was so big he could just ride around in a circle.

"This is easy!" he shouted.

"Go slowly. It has high horsepower," I said, following after him. I wasn't worried about him—I was worried about my motorcycle! That bike was my baby. I'd kick his ass if he tipped it over!

"Hey, Kinn. Am I cool?" Tankhun said, making me look up. Kinn was leaning against a pole by the front door, watching Tankhun ride my bike around. I quickly shifted my eyes back to Tankhun. I didn't dare make eye contact with Kinn.

"What the hell are you doing?" Kinn asked his elder brother.

"I'm doing the laundry. What does it look like?" Tankhun retorted, still riding around and beginning to accelerate. I stopped trailing behind him and just stood and watched him instead. Kinn, Kim, Mr. Korn, and my fellow bodyguards joined the crowd.

"Can I do a wheelie, Father?" Tankhun asked. His father shook his head in disapproval.

It looked like Tankhun was having too much fun. I nervously watched my bike, not noticing that Kinn had come to stand next to me. He was right behind my back in mere seconds, startling me. I quickly took a step away from him.

"Is your arm feeling better?" he asked, but I pretended not to hear him.

"Mr. Tankhun, that's the turn signal!" I shouted as Kinn shifted closer to me.

"What's the matter? Are you avoiding me?" Kinn pressed.

I kept ignoring him. I still couldn't get those images out of my head. Being near him felt dangerous, and I had no idea what kind of face he was making right now.

"How do I stop? How do I brake?!" Tankhun hollered.

"It brakes like a regular bicycle, Mr. Tankhun!" I shouted back. Everyone around us giggled. The most amused seemed to be Kim, who laughed and swore at Tankhun from time to time.

"How come you aren't talking back? Have you gone mute? Normally, you'd be slinging curses at me by now," Kinn chuckled in my ear.

"Go ride a balance bike, dumbass!" Kim roared.

"Kim is a son of a bitch!" Tankhun jeered at Kim as he rode. Kim took off his slippers, ready to throw them at Tankhun.

"Let me see your arm," Kinn said, moving to hold my arm. My hair stood on end knowing that he was gay and liked to touch me. I tried to brush him off, but he grasped my arm tightly. It hurt.

"Let go," I said, attempting to pry his hand away from my arm. He refused to listen to me and raised my sleeve, looking surprised by what he saw beneath.

"Why is it so red?" he demanded.

It's because of you all! You keep grabbing me by the arm! Also, that asshole cutting into my lane earlier had dug his fingers right into my wound.

"Is this because I grabbed you yesterday?" Kinn asked softly.

"Mm-hmm," I grumbled. I wanted to put all the blame on him so he'd stop touching me. It was disgusting!

"I'll take care of this," Kinn said, leaning in. I drew back immediately, but he still held my arm.

"Leave me alone!" I exclaimed and pulled my arm back, but he wouldn't let go. I glanced around. No one was looking at us—they were all laughing at Tankhun.

"Where's the brake? Where?!"

"Good afternoon, P'Kinn." Vegas greeted Kinn. I turned to look at him.

"Hey, Vegas," Kinn called and shifted his attention to his cousin. I finally got a chance to pull my arm back. Vegas gave me a big smile.

"What are you guys up to? It seems fun." Vegas looked around and put his hands together in a wai gesture at Mr. Korn, who happened to turn around and notice him.

"Tankhun is learning how to ride a motorcycle. What are you up to, coming all the way here?" Mr. Korn replied. I stepped back a little, but Kinn blocked me; I was stuck here.

"I'm bringing you the document for this coming Sunday, Be[31] Korn," Vegas said as he gave Kinn and me a questioning look. He frowned when he saw Kinn and I acting like kids: when I moved left, Kinn blocked my path to the left. When I moved right, he blocked my right. It had been going on like this for a while, and it was starting to piss me off.

"Well, there's no need to come by yourself. You could've let your men bring it here," Kinn said to his cousin as he continued to engage me in psychological warfare. No matter what way I tried to escape, Kinn blocked me.

"Shit, Kinn!" I swore. I didn't want him to embarrass himself in front of the Minor Clan.

"I'm just passing through... You and Porsche seem quite close, P'Kinn," Vegas grinned while keeping his eyes on Kinn and me.

---

31   "Be" refers to an older brother of one's father in the Teochew dialect.

"I'd like to get close to him..." Kinn whispered. I didn't know if Vegas heard him, but I did. I looked up to see him holding in his laughter.

"Move. Your brother can't stop the motorcycle. I need to take a look!" I hissed. Vegas still had his eyes on us, and Kinn had no intention of stopping his relentless teasing. If his father hadn't been there, I would have trampled him. I hadn't pushed Kinn away yet when I heard Tankhun yell.

"Grrrr...Vegas! Why the hell are you here?!" Tankhun increased his speed and fixed his discontented gaze at Vegas.

"Hello, P'Khun. Hey... Wait, P'Khun! Aahh!"

"Mr. Tankhun, don't!"

"Go to hell!"

Boom! Thud!

Everyone stood in shock, including Kinn and me. We gazed at the water fountain in the middle of the garden. A chuckle escaped Kim, and then everyone joined in on the laughter.

Tankhun had turned the motorbike to hit Vegas, who had dodged him. Tankhun then lost control of the bike. The motorcycle hit the side of the fountain and Tankhun toppled into the pond.

My bike now leaned against the fountain with the engine still running. No matter how sad I was at seeing my baby in such a state, I couldn't stop laughing at Tankhun with his head dunked in the water.

"Ha ha ha! What goes around comes around," Kim said, laughing uncontrollably. Kinn burst into laughter, too. I had never seen this side of him—I was surprised there was some part of Kinn that seemed normal. It turned out he could smile and laugh just like his brothers. Mr. Korn, too, had to wipe his tears of laughter away. Pol and Arm rushed to pull Tankhun out of the water.

"Kim, you dickhead! Shut up! You're supposed to support me!" Tankhun shouted at his younger brother before glaring harshly at Vegas, who was laughing just as hard as the others.

"Right, I forgot," Kim said. "Vegas, why on earth would you laugh at my brother? I'm the only one who's allowed to. Ha ha ha!" Kim began to laugh again.

"P'Khun, if you'd like to learn how to swim instead of riding a motorbike, you could've said something," Vegas jibed. "Are you hurt? Should we check for a concussion?"

Tankhun couldn't hold back his rage, and his father had to intervene.

"That's enough. Inside, all of you. Vegas, stay and have a meal with me." Mr. Korn led everyone into the house along with Tankhun, who kept screaming, "Why did you invite him?!"

"Yes, Be," Vegas said. "By the way, Porsche, I passed by your university today. I bought fried pork and rice for you from Aunt Sally's shop. I heard you like it." Vegas held the bag out to me.

Kinn did not follow his father into the house, staying to stare at Vegas and me.

"Oh, thanks." I took the bag and cracked a smile. Vegas was really nice. This house usually served spicy food and vegetables that I didn't like; Vegas somehow knew what I needed.

"Get inside already," Kinn said, his voice ice-cold. I saw Vegas smirk and walk into the house.

I sighed. Today had been so chaotic, and it never seemed to end. I took my motorcycle—thankfully still in one piece—back to the garage before walking to the staff mess hall. I could finally relax. I was so exhausted!

KINN
PORSCHE

15

Instinct

"YOU IMBECILE!" A shout echoed through a rented house in the suburbs. "You couldn't even get him in the car?!"

"I didn't know he'd be going so slow on that bike. I thought I could cut him off and grab him. How was I supposed to know that little shit would ride so damn leisurely?" responded a man on the opposite side of the room. His eyes mirrored the rage of the man who was accusing him. He wanted to mangle that little shit with his car and drag him away, but he couldn't fathom why the hell his target was so slow. "Isn't there a better way than this stupid plan of yours?!"

Both men were right in each other's faces—it wouldn't be long before the fight got physical.

"Your boss has his people following him around! How was I supposed to get him?" he shot back with a humorless chuckle. Both men grabbed each other's collars, and the others in the room had to pull them apart.

"Both of you are so loud that I can hear it from the front yard. Are you fighting again?" The speaker was a tall, dignified man with a deep voice. He was dressed in casual attire, and his presence caused all bickering inside the house to cease immediately.

Everyone greeted him with a wai gesture. "Hello, boss."

The boss strolled to a sofa and languidly sat down before lighting a cigarette. "You piece of shit," he said in an ice-cold voice, smiling cunningly. Shivers went down the spine of everyone who heard him.

"I have no idea what the hell these guys were up to," a man in a black shirt said to the boss, sounding agitated. "Perhaps they were waiting for Mr. Kinn to capture him first."

"Shh, calm down. Porsche is not a piece of cake. You can't just mess with him. It's not that easy," the boss said, blowing out the smoke and watching as it spread through the room. "Listen to me—if you're too slow, Mr. Kinn will get to him first!

"I won't wait until that happens. I *will* get a taste of Porsche before that bastard Kinn does. The more Kinn wants him, the more *I* want him." He put on a scornful smile as he thought of the strong, handsome man who was both his enemy and the center of his desire.

"Then do something! The sooner you can separate Porsche from Mr. Kinn, the better. Or better yet, kill him," the man in the black shirt said with a pout. He despised that man more than anything. He wanted to distance Porsche from his boss and get him out of his sight.

"The reason you're rushing me... Do you have another motive? Something more than mere hatred?" the boss asked as he squinted at the man in front of him, searching for a hidden agenda.

"Hmph. See what happens if you spare him. You can see how skilled he is. The day we attempted to snipe him at the shooting range—didn't he kill your people?" asked the man.

The day at the shooting range had only been intended as an intimidation tactic. His boss only wanted to see the much-talked-about bodyguard rumored to possess exceptional skills.

"He was skillful indeed. Handsome as well. I'm not surprised that Kinn likes him so much. Don't you think the same?" the boss said. His lips curved up slightly into a smirk as he looked at the man before him. Now he had an inkling of why this man wanted to get rid of Porsche so much.

"If we spare him, your business will suffer," the man protested. "And if he is that close to Mr. Kinn, you can forget about the concessions and the new trade route. Mr. Kinn and Mr. Korn trust him."

He currently didn't have access to any of the documents. Seeing how Mr. Tankhun and Mr. Kinn asked for Porsche all the time, he knew it would be more difficult for him to intervene if they became more closely acquainted in the future.

"I know... And you keep talking business, but I bet seeing Kinn openly show how much he wants Porsche makes you resentful, hmm?" the boss said with a chuckle, making the other man glare daggers at him.

He, too, desired Porsche. That man was very attractive. Moreover, the fact that Kinn wanted Porsche himself only fueled his desire. He was also aware that the man in front of him considered Kinn to be more than just his boss.

"You better hurry up. I'm warning you."

"Mmm... I want Porsche so badly. It delights me to know that Kinn won't be his first!"

This man was known for repeatedly targeting Kinn's partners. He did not necessarily intend to cause Kinn any grievous harm, but that didn't mean he'd never thought about it. Right now, it was more enjoyable to stab him in the back.

PORSCHE

"YOU DON'T WANT to go out today, Mr. Tankhun?" I asked, exhausted. Tankhun was not in a good mood today. He was mad at me for not locking Vegas in a storeroom yesterday when he'd explicitly ordered me to. Who in their right mind would do that? Besides, Vegas was nice to me. Damn!

"I'm not going anywhere! I wanna watch TV! I'm in a bad mood!"

We all put on a straight face, waiting for Tankhun to pick out some idiotic romcom.

"But going out is more fun than watching TV..." I tried to convince Tankhun after seeing my colleagues' sunken faces. Pol looked like he was about to cry, and Arm kept poking my back.

"I'm tired, and my headache hasn't gone away yet! I hit my head on the edge of the fountain yesterday. Didn't you see?" Tankhun replied. Why couldn't he have just hit his head harder and fucking died?

"But I was planning to take you to Thonglor[32] tonight. I'm sure it'll be even more fun!" I persisted, trying everything I could not to be stuck here watching another shitty TV show.

"No! I'm watching TV today. I won't be swayed by you, Porsche. You're ungrateful. Vegas came alone without any lackeys! The least you could have done was smack him." Tankhun kept nagging me, the indignant idiot.

Vegas would just be confused if I suddenly smacked him out of the blue. That would be my reaction if it happened to me, anyway. Tankhun was such a moron.

"But Mr. Tankhun, Mr. Vegas didn't do anything wrong. There was no reason for me to hit him," I said truthfully.

Tankhun immediately turned to furiously glare at me, grabbing my wrist and forcing me to follow him outside his room. What the hell?!

"Where are you taking me?" I asked. Tankhun dragged me to the second floor, then opened the door to Kinn's room and dragged me inside.

---

32 Thonglor is an upscale, hip district in central Bangkok with a lot of bars and restaurants.

"What?" Kinn asked, looking up from his computer to glare at both of us in confusion. Pete, who was standing next to Kinn's bed, also looked perplexed.

"You take him back!" Tankhun flung my hand away, making me stagger a little.

"Oh? Is he no fun anymore?" Kinn glanced at me and cracked a smile. I quickly turned away and looked at Tankhun, baffled.

"He's fun to have around! But he defied me. He didn't smack Vegas in the head when I told him to," Tankhun said. "I want to watch TV now, and Pete is more into TV than Porsche is!"

Pete glared at Tankhun in shock and shook his head.

"Pfft, it's up to you. I happen to...want him." Kinn glanced at me when he paused, which gave me goosebumps.

Shit! "But Mr. Tankhun, don't you want to hang out with me?" I blurted out. Being with Tankhun drove me crazy, but it was safer than being with Kinn. I didn't even want to go near that bastard. I just couldn't catch a break around here!

"Right, Mr. Tankhun. Didn't you say things were more exciting with Porsche?" Pete suddenly cut in. He looked at Kinn pleadingly.

"Damn! If I want to go out, I'll ask you, but now I'm mad at you! Give me my walkie-talkie back!" Tankhun yelled, holding out his hand. I shook my head. Fuck! I couldn't stay with Kinn!

"Pete, you go back to your boss. I want to know how exciting things are with Porsche," Kinn said with a smile.

Pete hesitated, pressing his lips together before walking toward Tankhun. "I'm doing this for you, Mr. Kinn," Pete mumbled under his breath.

"Give me the walkie-talkie, now!" Tankhun demanded. When I didn't move to give it to him, he snatched it from my pocket.

"Mr. Tankhun! Next time Mr. Vegas comes, I'll smack him in the face!" I promised, trying to placate Tankhun. I needed to get away from this place. I did *not* want to stay here! I was dying to leave this house now that I knew Kinn wanted to fuck me!

"It's too late!" Tankhun yelled. "Let's go, Pete! I'll throw a party to welcome you back. Let's watch TV all night!" Tankhun grabbed Pete, who looked like he wanted to die, and stormed out of the room.

The door slammed shut with a bang. I nervously shifted back and forth on my feet, my hair standing on end as Kinn stared at me. What if he wanted to jump every man that got close to him? What would I do?! I was one of his bodyguards. Oh, fuck, would he try to *rape* me?!

"What's wrong?" Kinn smiled and turned back to his computer.

I stayed silent. Since Kinn hadn't asked me to do anything for him, I figured I could just wait outside—it was safer that way. I wanted to stay far away from him for as long as I could.

"Where are you going?!" Kinn demanded as I touched the doorknob.

"...I'll be outside," I said without turning to him.

"Why?"

"I...I'm tired! I want to sit down," I mumbled.

"Sit here on the sofa. No need to leave," Kinn replied.

"I thought I wasn't allowed to sit on your sofa," I said, still facing the door. A shiver crept down my spine as I sensed Kinn moving toward me.

"What are you so afraid of? You've sat on it *and* slept on it before," Kinn said. I felt his cold voice ghost over the nape of my neck, giving me goosebumps. I turned to face him and pushed him away. Why did he love standing so close to my back? It gave me the creeps.

"What the hell is your problem?" Kinn asked, stumbling a little from being pushed. He frowned as he watched me.

"I'll sit outside." I opened the door, but his hand shot out to close it.

"I didn't say you could leave." Kinn fixed his gaze on me.

I silently stared at him as he approached. When he walked toward me, I slowly stepped back, but Kinn didn't let up until my back hit the wall. I avoided eye contact and tried to figure out a way to escape, but Kinn put both his hands on the wall, trapping me between his arms.

"What the hell? Let me go!" I exclaimed, my heart pounding in fear. What would I do if Kinn made a move on me?

Kinn shifted closer, our faces almost touching. "What's your problem? Why won't you look at me?" Kinn whispered, giving me more goosebumps.

Wait! Why was I afraid of him? If he tried anything, I could just kick his ass. Easy!

"Let me go! I'll hit you if you try anything!" I tried to push him off with both hands.

Kinn laughed. "Are you afraid of me?"

I shut my eyes tightly, lowered my head, and continued shoving at his broad chest. He was ridiculously strong—what did this guy eat?

Kinn stood his ground as I pushed him, even as the veins in my arms started to pop from the exertion.

"Afraid of what? Move! Or I'll kick your ass!" I yelled. I felt Kinn's warm breath on my cheek.

I wasn't sure why—maybe it was my injury—but I couldn't use all my strength to push Kinn, which was probably why he wasn't budging.

Suddenly, Kinn grabbed my wrist, dragged me to the sofa, and swiftly pushed me down onto it.

"Shit! What are you doing?" I shouted and tried to get up, but Kinn pressed me back down with his arm.

"Sit still. Or do you want me to sit on you?" Kinn scolded me until I stopped resisting. He towered over me, pushing me down as he had done many times before. One of his hands pressed firmly against my shoulder as he turned to rummage for something from the drawer of the coffee table.

I tried to pry his hand off of me. "Let go!"

"Stay still. What do you think I'm going to do?" Kinn said before letting go of my shoulder and placing a first aid box on the table. Once freed, I started to stand, but Kinn yanked my wrist, pulling me back to sit on the sofa.

"If you get up again, I'll tie you to the couch." Kinn was serious, glaring at me with fierce eyes. I sat back down. However, I shifted away from him as he sat down next to me.

"What are you doing?" I pushed myself toward the edge of the sofa. I felt like a girl about to lose her virginity! I promised myself I would kick Kinn right in the face if he tried anything.

"Come closer," Kinn ordered, taking my wounded right arm in his hand and pulling it hard, making me slide over to him.

"That hurts, asshole!"

"Stay still and it won't hurt. It's so damned exhausting trying to fix your wound!" Kinn shook his head. He held my arm with one hand while opening the first aid box with the other. He took out cotton balls and disinfectant.

"What are you doing?" I asked.

"Don't move. I need to re-dress your wound," Kinn replied.

"No need! I can take care of it!" I shouted.

"I'm going to do it. You know what will happen if you resist, right?!" Kinn pointed at me before letting go of both of my hands to open the medicine bottles. "Don't you dare get up again, or I'll soak your arm in rubbing alcohol!" Kinn laid one of his legs across my lap to prevent me from getting up. I tried to push it off, but he kept it in place.

"Let go of me!" I growled.

"Shit, Porsche! I just want to re-dress your wound. Don't be such a pussy!" Kinn sighed, pushing my sleeve up my arm.

I hated this, but I was powerless to do anything. Grunting in dissatisfaction, I allowed Kinn to clean around my wound with a cotton swab; the alcohol felt cold on my skin. If I screamed, I had no doubt he'd pour it all over my arm.

"Has your injury not healed at all?" Kinn asked, soaking a cotton ball in an iodine solution and daubing it on the wound.

"Of course it hasn't! How can it heal if you keep grabbing my arm?" I frowned as he gently tended to my wound.

Kinn focused on dressing my arm and asked me from time to time if it hurt, but I didn't answer. Somehow, I couldn't tear my eyes away from his godlike face. He had a thin nose, piercing eyes, and full lips, which matched his face and hairstyle perfectly. I felt sorry for all the girls out there. How could he be gay when he was this handsome?

"What are you staring at?"

I quickly averted my gaze, pretending to look at my arm where Kinn was neatly bandaging it. But why had he spoken to me so softly just now? I'd never heard him speak like that. My heart skipped a beat—maybe because I was seeing a side of him that I had never seen before.

"C'mon, are you done?" I grumbled. Kinn looked up at me and smiled.

"You are?" I continued. "That was fast..."

Kinn's smile turned teasing.

I paused slightly and then pulled my arm back. I pushed Kinn's leg off my lap, attempting to get up again, but before I even had the chance to steady myself, Kinn grabbed my waist and pressed me flat on my back.

"Fuck!" I shouted as I thrashed against Kinn. He straddled my body and pressed down with all his weight, the way he was clearly so fond of.

"I'm not finished yet. Why are you trying to get up?" Kinn demanded. Our faces were mere inches apart.

"Let me go, damn it! Let me go!" I yelled, struggling to push myself up. Kinn smirked before grabbing my wounded arm and pressing it firmly against my chest. Time seemed to grind to a halt. The urge to resist faded instantly as I stared blankly ahead. Kinn slowly pressed his lips next to the gauze, gently kissing my arm.

"Get well soon," he said, raising his head. He smiled, then pulled himself away from me. I remained motionless, stunned by his actions.

"I'm done." Kinn slowly put the equipment back in the box.

I started returning to my senses. Half-sitting, half-lying on the sofa, I raised my foot and kicked Kinn's hip with all my strength.

"What the fuck were you doing?!" I exclaimed. If Kinn had done that to a woman, there was no doubt he'd score. But when it came to men—especially a man like me? I wanted to punch him. Damn it!

I stormed out of Kinn's room as Kinn cussed me out, demanding to know why I kicked him when he'd just treated my wound. *Fuck you! I didn't ask you to, you bastard!*

I stalked to the garden to smoke a cigarette.

"Hah! Why are you making that face?" Pete asked, laughing out loud at the terrified expression on my face. My heart still pounded like crazy. I supposed it was because of Kinn's underhanded behavior.

"Your bastard of a boss!" I snarled. If he messed with me again, I'd kill the fucker.

Pete laughed again. "You look paranoid, Porsche. Are you afraid of Mr. Kinn?" he teased me.

"Damn it! Fuck you, Kinn! I hope you become infertile!" I shouted.

"Nice try, Porsche, but Kinn isn't getting anyone pregnant anyway!" Pete wheezed with laughter until his body bent in half.

"Oh damn! I'm completely paranoid now because of you!" I pointed an accusatory finger at Pete.

"Oh, Mr. Kinn won't force you. He wouldn't do anything without consent..." Pete trailed off, glancing at me. I raised my foot and kicked him hard in the leg with a loud *thud*.

What a pain in the ass! And Kinn would definitely force himself on someone—he'd held me down several times already!

"I don't believe you!" I yelled.

"Heh. Mr. Kinn is just flirting with you. Try to resist his charms," Pete replied. I slapped him in the head. He was so annoying!

"How about you? Have you fallen for his charms yet?" I demanded, wanting to know if Kinn treated everyone the same way. If that were true, I'd be in big trouble!

"Look at my face!" Pete exclaimed. "Mr. Kinn would puke. But you—you're handsome, and you've got a great body..."

I chased Pete around the garden until he raised both his hands in surrender. That annoying bastard! He asked for it.

So, had no one else around Kinn been treated like this, or was Pete an exception? Pete's face really wasn't that bad. Damn! Why did Kinn single me out? Why me?

"Damn it! Why me, Kinn?!" I cursed, standing with my hands on my hips, unable to get Kinn out of my head.

"By the way, you're cute when you're drunk!" Pete teased me with a giggle. I chased after him again. I had no idea what Pete's problem was, but he was irritating me like his life depended on it.

What was I going to do? I wouldn't let Kinn fuck me. I would guard my ass with my life!

Kinn didn't summon me for anything else the rest of the night. It looked like he had already gone to bed. I hoped he died in his sleep! I sat in front of his room for a while and went to hang out with Pete, Pol, Paul, and Arm from time to time. The night passed uneventfully.

The next day, Kinn was back to his usual self. He treated me like his personal servant, asking me to fetch documents, snacks, and anything else he wanted. I tried to avoid it by delegating tasks to his lackeys, being alone with him as little as possible. Sometimes, he would walk up to me, and I would run out of the room, not letting him get close to me. I often heard faint laughter as I left, and he didn't sound angry. *Damn it!* Why did I have to be so scared of him? *If he comes too close, just kick his ass, Porsche!*

[SUNDAY]

Nearly everyone in the household had gathered at a swanky hotel in the middle of the city. Mr. Korn was holding a dinner party in the luxurious banquet hall on the hotel's first floor. Kinn said it was a reception for a bunch of new foreign clients who would soon be partners in the family business.

There was a variety of food and drink available, including expensive imported alcohol. Everyone was dressed up in formal attire, me included. I wore my bodyguard uniform: white shirt, black suit jacket, black slacks, and dress shoes. Today's event was especially fancy, so I'd decided to style my hair a little—which made Pete, Arm, and Pol tease me non-stop.

"Holy shit, Porsche... Styling your hair makes you so handsome! The girls here can't take their eyes off of you," Pol teased me. I cocked my eyebrows at him twice to emphasize his point. I felt the same way—I could tell the businessmen's daughters were eyeing me up.

"Not just the ladies, but some of the young men can't seem to look away either, you know?" Pete added, looking at a slender young gentleman who was also staring at me.

"No, thanks," I replied immediately. *I'm sorry, man, you're not my type.*

"Not that guy, *that* guy," Pete said. I looked over the guy's shoulder and saw Kinn glaring at me with a stern look on his face. He waved me over, so I had to leave my group of friends and walk straight to him.

"What?" I asked him in a low voice. Kinn was talking to a group of foreign business associates. Mr. Korn, Kim, and Khun were also there—Khun had finally taken the colored strands out of his hair.

"Follow me closely, and don't cause any trouble," Kinn said in a stern voice. What was I doing to cause trouble? I'd just been watching him. Pete told me to keep my distance and walk around the room.

"Yeah," I said, slightly irritated.

I distanced myself a bit from Kinn's group. I walked along, keeping a reasonable space between myself and Kinn, as he instructed.

Pete had mentioned we couldn't eat anything yet. We had to wait until after the event for food that Mr. Korn had ordered specifically for us bodyguards. Right now, our job was to keep an eye on things. I was hoping someone would pull out a gun and shoot Kinn—now that'd make this tedious event more exciting!

"Porsche, you're looking handsome today," a familiar voice came from close by. I turned around and smiled in response.

"Hello," I greeted Vegas politely. His suit intimidated me a little—it looked just as fancy as Kinn's.

"Have you eaten yet?" Vegas asked, cheerful as usual.

"Oh... I've already eaten a little bit," I replied, keeping my voice and expression neutral. I had snuck some chocolate from Kinn's room earlier in the evening.

"Would you like to try this?" Vegas asked. "I'll set some aside for you." Vegas lifted his shrimp cocktail glass. I declined immediately, knowing that if I ate something at the event, Kinn would rake me over the coals.

"Why? Did P'Kinn forbid you?"

I nodded. Kinn hadn't explicitly forbidden me from eating at the event, but he'd told me again and again in his room and in the car to not cause any trouble. He even pulled me aside a minute ago to repeat the same order. Did he see me as some kind of shit-stirrer or what?!

"Hia! Dad is calling!" came a voice accompanied by a hateful glance in my direction. It was that Macau guy—I remembered him vividly.

"Be there in a sec... Porsche, will you still be around later? I'll stop by to talk to you," Vegas said.

"Yes," I replied. Vegas grinned at me and walked away with his younger brother.

Today, the Major Clan and the Minor Clan were all smiles, greeting the reception guests warmly. However, the overall atmosphere of the event seemed kind of fake. They only ate a little bit of food and barely sipped their drinks. It was uncomfortable to watch.

"What were you talking to Vegas about?" I turned around, surprised to find Kinn there. He frowned, watching as Vegas walked away.

"Mind your own business," I snapped.

"Watch yourself. I told you not to get close to the Minor Clan and—"

"And not cause any trouble. You've got it drilled into my head now," I said before Kinn could finish.

He smiled, satisfied. "Good. And keep your eyes on me, not other people," Kinn said, before going back to cheerfully greeting guests at the event. I scowled at him. Who did he think he was, a precious little panda that I had to constantly monitor? I wasn't a zookeeper!

After Kinn left, a waiter walked over to me with a tray that held a glass of whiskey. "Sir, someone sent this for you."

I frowned slightly and scanned the room, but I didn't see anyone looking at me. I hesitated. Should I take it? Was it appropriate?

"Err... I think..." I glanced at Kinn. He was currently shaking hands and greeting an elderly guest. The waiter picked up the glass from the tray and offered it to me again.

"Please take it, sir. One drink won't hurt."

I looked down at the whiskey, reluctant to take it. The waiter must have known that I was on duty. I really wanted to try the expensive booze, though...

"Please take it, sir, as a matter of courtesy," the waiter repeated with a pleading look on his face.

"All right, then." I turned slightly to face the wall and downed the shot in one gulp. It was only half a glass, so it shouldn't hurt.

"Ahh..." The alcohol was strong. I squinted at the pungent smell and cringed as it burned my throat. It tasted good, though.

"Please give them my thanks," I said, placing the glass back on the tray and searching the room for any woman who might be looking at me. I didn't find one. The only person watching me was Kinn, who glanced at me now and then.

It was a relief he didn't catch me drinking that shot. Otherwise, he would have run over and smacked me right in the middle of this fancy event. Then there was Vegas, who looked at me and smiled, waving his hand. I smiled back politely. That guy was ridiculously well-mannered...

I watched Kinn for a while before the same waiter came back with more whiskey.

"Here you go again," he said, handing me the glass. I pointed at myself in surprise.

"Who's sending these over? Can you tell me?" I asked, looking through the crowd again.

"He didn't mention his name, but please take it. I'll cover you." The waiter, who knew his job too well, shoved the glass into my hand and stood in front of me, blocking me from everyone's view.

"Is this really okay? If my boss finds out, he's gonna kill me." I felt a little guilty after drinking that first glass. I couldn't care less about Kinn, but I didn't want to disrespect Mr. Korn.

"He would be disheartened," the waiter whispered to me.

I snuck a glance at Kinn again. He was busy talking to someone, so I downed the glass of whiskey in one go. It wasn't a moral failing to have a drink occasionally. Just two glasses should be fine, right? I didn't get drunk that easily, so I should be able to handle a couple shots of whiskey.

I placed the empty glass on the tray. "Don't bring me another glass next time," I told the waiter. "Just tell them I said thanks." The waiter nodded and walked away. I looked at the departing figure with a frown before shifting my gaze back to Kinn.

I walked closer to Kinn and started moving around him in circles. Kinn turned to smile at me in satisfaction. I pretended to be working. Otherwise, he might not pay me at the end of the month.

Kinn suddenly slipped away from the group. "Are you hungry?" he whispered to me in a low voice.

At that moment, I was hit by a wave of dizziness. I stared at Kinn, furrowing my brows as I started seeing double. It kept getting worse until I shook my head slightly.

"Are you okay?" Kinn looked at me, confused.

"I'm fine. The lights are too bright. I got a little dizzy." The spotlight from the stage was shining right in my face, so I guess my eyes didn't adjust quickly enough.

"I thought you were going to faint from hunger," Kinn said with a smirk.

I was starting to feel better. The dizziness was gone, and my vision returned to normal. So, I turned to Kinn with a smug look on my face.

"If I'm hungry, will you let me eat?" I asked quietly, raising an eyebrow.

"No, I'm just telling you to hang in there. Wait a little longer, okay?" Kinn teased before nudging his brother to resume their conversation.

I cursed him silently before resuming my walk around the room. However, as soon as I lifted my foot to move forward, the dizziness from earlier came back. I barely kept my balance this time. I was able to catch the edge of the table next to me before I fell. I was lucky—no one noticed. But Pete must have seen it, since he was rushing toward me.

"Are you okay?" Pete asked, walking over and grabbing my arm. As soon as I was able to steady myself, I waved my hand.

"Nah, I'm okay. Just a little dizzy from the lights." The sensation of the world spinning came and went, and it was starting to fade away again. I knew with absolute certainty that I was not drunk, because being drunk did *not* feel like this. And even if I was, two glasses couldn't have made me this dizzy. Could it be some mysterious illness?

"Do you want to sit down and rest?" Pete asked, concerned.

"No, no, I'll just go to the restroom. Keep an eye on Kinn for me. I'll be back in a bit," I told Pete, and quickly walked to the bathroom.

The dizziness went away, but another feeling replaced it. A burning sensation coursed through my body, making me feel restless and uneasy. As soon as I locked myself in a bathroom stall, I put the toilet seat down and sat on it. The dizziness returned, accompanied by a strange sort of...arousal.

I reached into my pants and felt my erection. I didn't know when I'd gotten so hard. I took a deep, heavy breath, overwhelmed by the tightness and the throbbing pain throughout my body. The stall door in front of me began to blur, and a hazy confusion clouded my senses.

The sensations gradually intensified, and I started to see images repeat in my head: first, the girl I almost hooked up with at the club. But then, the image shifted to Kinn, to the night we got drunk and he kissed me. It'd felt insanely good. I bit my lip hard, trying not to think about it.

Sweat seeped out of my body; I was so hot, it felt like my body was on fire. It took incredible effort not to loosen my belt and alleviate the discomfort.

Before I could do anything, a forceful knock on the bathroom door startled me, making me jump. I wanted to scream out in anger, but just thinking about making a sound made me so lightheaded that I could barely see what was in front of me.

"Who's in there? Come out!"

"Let's break the door."

I heard two people speaking, but I couldn't understand them. My mind felt numb, and my hands were losing strength, but the sensations in my body remained intense. Before long, they pried the stall door open. I vaguely remembered trying to struggle free, but I was quickly dragged out of the restroom.

My mind shattered, and I didn't have the strength to resist. Overwhelming desire surged through my body. At that moment, I wanted nothing other than sexual relief.

I was carried up an elevator and hauled into some room. After a while, my body was forcefully tossed onto a large bed. Then, I heard unintelligible voices.

"Is the boss going to come up now? Looks like he can't handle it anymore."

"What did you give him?"

"The first glass was to make him woozy. The second glass was a love drug... That was too easy. Just tempted him with alcohol, and he fell for it."

"Why didn't you use a sedative? That would've been easier."

"Come on. The boss wants to have fun. If he's unconscious, what's the point?"

"Then we should have captured him fully conscious. That'd be way more fun."

"You don't know shit. This guy is too much to handle. If we captured him without drugging him first, he'd have killed us. Doing it this way will be more enjoyable for our boss."

I ignored their conversation. My body contorted as arousal coursed through me, nearly bringing me to orgasm. I reached down to loosen my belt, but a hand firmly grabbed my arm, preventing me from touching myself. This frustrated me even further. Damn it!

My brain couldn't process anything. I did not know what to do. What was wrong with me? Why did I feel so hot and uncomfortable?

"Be patient. My boss wants to have his way with you," said the person holding my arm.

I could only vaguely grasp the meaning of that sentence. I tried to stay conscious, but my mind was too muddled. My gut told me I was in danger. Who was this "boss"? Have *what* way with me? Had I been drugged? *What should I do...?*

I didn't know how much time passed as I lay thrashing on the bed. Then my hands were freed from their restraints, and I felt someone pressing against me. I tried to focus, seeing a sleek black suit and a face leaning close, the tip of someone's nose brushing against my cheek.

The smell of a classy cologne filled my senses. I scrunched up my nose at the somewhat familiar scent. The face of the man on top of me was blurry, but it resembled someone who had been stuck in my head this entire time...

"Kinn?" I rasped.

Smack!

"Ow!" I exclaimed, my face jerking from the forceful slap. My skin tingled in response.

"You're with me now. You are not allowed to speak his name!" I heard an ice-cold voice speak, but I could not identify who it was.

I tried to compose a sentence. If this person wasn't Kinn, who was he? But right now, I could barely comprehend anything. The more pain I felt, the more responsive my body became.

"Those hickeys on your neck... He gave them to you, right? No worries, I'll cover them up."

I felt him nuzzle my neck with the hard tip of his nose. Then, he bit and sucked at my skin until I felt pain and pleasure all at once.

I immediately responded to the sensation, my head replaying the time when Kinn did this to me. I bit my lip, inevitably yielding to the kisses and bites on my neck, and the lips sliding over to caress my own.

KINN

"HAVE YOU FOUND HIM?" I asked Pete. Something happened every time I went out with that damned bodyguard of mine, and it was aggravating. He'd been missing for half an hour already.

Pete ran toward me and handed me a black mobile phone. "I can't find Porsche," he panted, "not even in the smoking room. But I found this in the bathroom."

Pete, Arm, and Pol seemed as worried and frustrated as I was. Why did Porsche love to cause me so much trouble? I insisted time and time again that he behave himself, and I tried to keep him in my sight, but he'd slipped away from me in the end.

I couldn't seem to get Porsche out of my head. Even now, he was frustrating me. Ever since his little stunt at the shootout the other day, I'd been worried for his safety. I was afraid that the allies of Porsche's victims would seek vengeance and try to kill him. And now Porsche had vanished without a trace!

"There is no sign of Porsche, Mr. Kinn," one of my bodyguards said.

I told a few of my men to spread out and look for Porsche. It was very suspicious to find his cell phone abandoned in the bathroom. I had a bad feeling that something terrible might have happened to him. Two scenarios came to mind: either he'd been jumped, or the Minor Clan had swayed him to their side. Porsche seemed close to Vegas lately. Porsche was exceedingly talented, and the Minor

Clan surely must have noticed. However, I was afraid that my first suspicion was more likely.

"They finally let us check the security footage from the lobby, sir," Pete said as he ran back to inform me. I immediately followed him to the hotel lobby.

"It seems all the security cameras malfunctioned. The technician is trying to recover the files right now."

This information made me suspect foul play. It was ridiculous to think all the CCTV cameras in this hotel malfunctioned at the same time. I glared intensely at Pete, afraid that Porsche might be badly injured—or worse!

"Let me have a look!" said Arm, Tankhun's bodyguard. Arm was proficient in IT systems and ran the CCTV system at our house.

Arm moved in to examine the monitor and typed something on the keyboard. I looked around the area, smiling at the guests still passing in and out of the party through the front gate. The event was still in progress, but I'd excused myself to search for Porsche. If I found out he'd disappeared just to slack off, I'd give him the punishment of his life. That man caused us so much trouble!

"I found two working cameras!" Arm announced. Static-filled images gradually materialized on the once-blackened screen; they were shots of this floor and the inside of an elevator.

"Rewind to half an hour ago now!" I ordered.

Arm quickly complied. I did not expect to find anything because it was footage from inside the hotel. If someone dragged Porsche outside, they'd be long gone by now.

"Shit! What the hell?" Arm stared at the screen in shock. I was also perplexed by what played onscreen. A group of men dressed in black dragged Porsche—who appeared to be unconscious—from the first floor into an elevator. Footage from inside the elevator showed one of the men pressing a button and carrying him out as soon as they reached the eighth floor.

All of us rushed to the elevator and pressed the button to call it. I stood there restlessly as we waited for the elevator to arrive, uncertain about Porsche's fate.

"Mr. Kinn, your father is asking for you!" Big yelled at me, but I ignored him. He hurried over to me. "Where are you going, Mr. Kinn?" he asked cautiously.

I remained silent, keeping my gaze fixed on the floor number ticking down on the elevator's screen, impatiently waiting for it to reach the first floor.

"Your father really did ask for you. Please come with me," Big insisted, grabbing my arm and attempting to pull me back into the party.

"Let go of me and get lost!" I loudly told him off. My anger and frustration had built up to the point of agitation. I was worried about Porsche—I needed to know if something had happened to him.

I told myself I only cared about him because I wanted to have a taste of him. Porsche was attractive and he had a great body, but it wasn't like I *liked* him. I just couldn't get his annoying, scowling face out of my head!

"Mr. Kinn!"

I ignored Big. Pete and my other men came to block his path, pointing at him threateningly before following me into the elevator. Pete pressed the button to the eighth floor, looking as concerned for Porsche as I was.

"Do you think he'll be all right?" Arm asked, looking uneasy as he paced back and forth across the elevator. Pete glanced at me slightly and then told Arm to stop. That calmed Arm down a bit.

I stared intensely at each floor's number as the elevator ascended, wishing we could have flown straight to the eighth floor. As the elevator doors finally opened, I saw some men in black suits running away through the fire escape.

We immediately followed them because it was incredibly suspicious. However, Pete and I abruptly stopped our chase as we noticed a door to one of the rooms was left open. Without a second thought, we barged in.

"*Oww...*"

I quickly recognized the voice of the man groaning in pain. Relief flooded through me to know Porsche was still alive. I strode inside the suite, finding Porsche on a large bed. He was dressed only in his boxers, and his bare chest was covered in hickeys. I frowned as I watched him thrash around in agony.

"Porsche! What happened?" I gasped. I thought I'd find him beaten up or trampled on, but this was...

"H...help..." Porsche cried hoarsely, his eyes fluttering open to look at me standing at the foot of the bed. I sat down on the mattress and used both of my hands to help pull him up. My eyes scanned Porsche's body and found it covered with slap marks, bites, and hickeys. I sat there in stunned silence, not knowing how to react.

"Is... Is that you, Kinn?" he asked, biting his lip.

"Yes! It's me. Who did this to you?" I replied, my heart in my mouth. I couldn't bear to see him like this.

"I... I don't know. They drugged me... Help..." Porsche answered, his voice trembling with suppressed emotion. I glanced at Porsche's boxers. The front was tented up and damp with clear fluid. My eyes widened; I was unable to comprehend that those bastards had drugged Porsche.

"Leave us, Pete," I told my bodyguard. He looked pitifully at his friend, pursing his lips tightly before walking out of the room and closing the door behind him.

"Did they do anything to you?" I asked, still holding his arms to keep him sitting upright.

"Help," Porsche cried weakly; his head fell forward until he rested his forehead on my shoulder. The sound of his shaking breath was loud against my ears, stirring something within me.

"F...find me a hooker...or a girl somewhere. I can't hold back," Porsche pleaded, looking at me with lustful eyes. His soft moan made me swallow as I tried hard not to react to the temptation in front of me.

"And where would I find them?" I asked before taking another deep breath to control myself.

Porsche lifted his hand to lightly pound at my chest. "Please? Or just take me to a massage parlor... Y'know, *that* kind of massage parlor," Porsche begged, his quivering voice pleasing to my ears. I bit my lip angrily, thinking they must have given him a very potent drug.

"Just...masturbate. I'll wait outside," I finally answered. Despite how turned on I was seeing Porsche in this state, I did not want to have sex with him without his consent. While I could admit that I liked to take liberties with him, I had never attempted to force myself on him.

"I...I can't. It's not enough," Porsche protested, sounding even more distressed. Then, he pressed himself against me slightly, nearly pushing me to my breaking point.

"What do you want me to do? I'm the only one here, and I don't—*oof!*"

Porsche threw his arms around my neck and pulled me down for a kiss, cutting me off midsentence. I was stunned for a moment before I closed my eyes and kissed him back. One of my hands went to cradle Porsche's face, tilting it slightly so I could suck and bite at his red, pouty bottom lip.

"Mmm..."

The sound of Porsche's throaty moan aroused me even more. The moment he opened his mouth to gasp for air, I slipped my tongue inside, tangling it with his and exploring his mouth.

Porsche moaned as we continued sucking each other's tongues, neither of us wanting to stop. I couldn't deny it—Porsche was a good kisser.

I broke the kiss, nuzzling my nose against his cheek and pressing my lips there instead. I alternated between kissing and licking his cheek before moving down to the curve of his neck, which was covered in hickeys. Anger flared inside of me as I noticed fresh marks covering all the ones I had left on Porsche's skin. Eager to reclaim my territory, I began forcefully sucking and biting his neck until Porsche hissed in pain.

"Hey, that hurts!" he cried, lightly smacking the back of my neck. I encouraged him to lie down on the mattress, and he complied without resisting. My tongue returned to lap at the skin on his neck, this time targeting his prominent Adam's apple. I licked and sucked at the skin, leaving a new trail of bite marks along the way.

Porsche turned his face upward, willingly accepting my advances. The drug those men had given him must have been powerful, because he started to grope me through my suit. I stopped kissing his neck for a moment so I could start removing my clothes, smirking as Porsche panted and looked up at me.

"I don't want to do this with someone unwilling," I said, raking my eyes over the man beneath me. I didn't want to stop, but I needed Porsche's unequivocal agreement. I wanted to be sure that I wasn't doing anything against his will, even when his body obviously showed his desire.

"I...I don't know, but I can't stand it anymore," Porsche groaned, twisting his body around. It turned me on so much that I almost forgot how he'd gotten into this position.

"If you want to have sex with me, I will. But if not, tell me to stop," I said, shucking my jacket and tossing it to the floor. I was about to unbutton my shirt when Porsche gasped his reply:

"Um... Do it."

I smirked at how husky his voice sounded and finally shrugged my shirt off, tossing it to land somewhere near my jacket. Bending down, I kissed Porsche deeply. Our tongues once again entwined in a sensual dance, neither of us letting go of the other. My hand moved across his chiseled chest and squeezed it hard; I found a perky, pink nipple and rubbed it firmly with my fingers.

Porsche's moans and groans were fuel to the flames of my desire. I kissed down the column of his neck to his chest, his body arching up deliciously at the touch. My mouth closed around his nipple and I sucked it hard, swirling my tongue around it before moving my mouth to lavish attention on the other one.

Porsche's sinewy body fascinated me. No matter where I lapped or sucked, it would pull delicious moans from him. I couldn't wait any longer—I had to get inside of him.

I unbuckled my belt and opened the clasp of my pants while kissing down his torso. Porsche's muscular abs really did something to me, and I couldn't help sucking more marks on them. Then, my hands went to his slender waist, squeezing and rubbing it gently before pulling his boxers all the way down to his knees.

I stopped kissing his skin, pulling away to look at Porsche's cock. It looked painfully hard, the head glistening with precum. Groaning in delight at the sight, I wrapped my hand around his shaft.

Porsche startled and grabbed my shoulder tightly as I kissed down his stomach and stroked his length at the same time. His belly tensed with the rhythm of my hand, and he tossed his head from side to side as arousal flowed through his body.

"Ah...I...I can't," he groaned, digging his nails into the meat of my shoulder. The pain turned me on even more. I straightened up on the bed, jerking him off faster and fumbling with my other hand to free my own erection. I stared intensely at him, jacking myself to the same rhythm, wondering if Porsche knew just how much he'd turned me on.

"*Fuck*, I'm... I'm gonna come," Porsche whined, tensing up for a moment before coming all over my hand and his own stomach. I continued to jerk myself off, my dick becoming painfully hard at the sight of Porsche panting in exertion. This man was too fucking sexy...

"Did he fuck you?" I asked, my voice trembling a little.

"N...No. There's a condom in my pants pocket," Porsche replied, gesturing haphazardly at the floor.

I furrowed my brows slightly and said, "Your condom won't fit me. It's too small."

Porsche's dick looked somewhat above average, but it was still smaller than mine. I bent over to pick up my discarded suit jacket and fumbled for my wallet. After finding a condom, I tore open the packet with my teeth.

"I won't fuck you raw," Porsche said. "Put a condom on me."

I frowned at Porsche. Did *he* think he would be the one fucking *me*?

"Hah. Sorry about that, Porsche. You can't fuck me—I always top." I quickly turned Porsche onto his stomach. He hadn't even started yelling at me yet before I rolled the condom down my cock.

"No! I don't want that... Let...let me fuck you."

I chuckled at Porsche's desperate plea and raised his hips so he was on his knees. I placed my body between his legs and used my knee to nudge them further apart.

My finger gently stroked the cleft of his ass, prodding at his hole. I sighed in relief to find it still untouched before smearing what was left of Porsche's cum on my fingers around the tight pucker. He flinched away immediately, but in his feeble state, he couldn't do much more than that.

"K-Kinn, please...don't."

Porsche begged me to stop, but it was too late. He was the one who agreed to have sex with me in the first place, and I just could not let this opportunity pass. Porsche clawed at the bedsheets as I pressed my finger against his hole. He was so damn tight; my fingertip could barely slip inside. I bit my lip hard, concentrating on working him open.

"This already feels so good... Don't tense up, Porsche," I whispered, bending down to gently kiss his back while I steadied his hip. Porsche turned his face to the side, his brows knitting tightly together as I nibbled at his neck. I took a moment to steal another kiss from his lips before finally pushing my finger in all the way to the knuckle, moving it around to stretch him.

I alternated between sucking Porche's bottom lip and thrusting my tongue inside his mouth. Porsche continued to wince in pain but eagerly reciprocated my kiss until I pushed a second finger inside of him.

"Ow, Kinn! That hurts!" Porsche whined, unsuccessfully trying to push me off of him. "Enough...Kinn." The way he moaned my name was so damn hot.

I let go of his hip so I could use my other hand to jerk him off again. Porsche's dick had stayed hard this entire time, but stroking it would distract him from the pain of penetration. I pushed in slowly and forcefully until both of my fingers were inside his tight hole.

As I continued to stretch him, Porsche buried his face into the mattress, biting the bedsheet hard to stifle his cries. The sight nearly sent me over the edge. I pulled my fingers out immediately, ready to bury myself inside of him.

"N-no... Kinn, don't," Porsche protested, shaking his head frantically.

I bit my lip hard as I slowly rubbed my erection against his hole, giving him a taste of what was to come. I wanted Porsche to know that his first time would hurt. From how tight he was and his obvious inexperience, I was certain that I was the first person to fuck this man.

I straightened myself and spat on my dick, spreading the saliva until it was just slick enough. There was no time to look for lube, so this would have to do. I knew that first times could be challenging, and Porsche would be in for a world of pain. However, I could not hold myself back any longer. With some difficulty, I began to press the head of my cock into him.

"Don't tense up... Just relax," I said, gently massaging Porsche's ass to comfort him as I took my time pushing inside.

"It... It hurts... I don't want this anymore," Porsche said.

"Hey, don't clench down like that! I barely got the tip in. You're gonna make me come," I hissed, sharply inhaling as a jolt of pleasure shot through me. It already felt so good; I just wanted to slam into Porsche and fuck him hard. However, I still had some sympathy for him, so I resorted to slicking up my dick with more spit in the hopes of easing his pain. I tried one more time to force my way in.

"Ow! That hurts! Stop!" Porsche cried, arching up as I kept pushing in.

"Try to relax. It won't hurt if you relax," I whispered in his ear, leaning down to kiss his cheek and playfully bite his earlobe.

Porsche shuddered violently as I finally buried myself to the hilt.

"Agh! Damn it, Kinn!" Porsche roared, pounding his fist against the mattress before turning to bite down harshly on my bottom lip. It really stung, but I found myself enjoying the sensation of pain; it made me want to thrust into him even harder. *Fuck, he really turns me on!*

"Porsche, you're so fucking tight that you almost hurt me," I growled after pulling my lips free. Porsche's ass was so hot and tight—I couldn't stop myself from moaning.

Porsche thrashed around, still biting the bedsheet to muffle his cries. After pausing for a while, I started moving again. Never able to control myself in the throes of passion, I lifted myself up from Porsche's back and started pounding into him in earnest.

The force of my thrusts made Porsche's body slide forward across the mattress, almost making my cock slip out. I quickly braced my arm around his torso, pulling him back onto my dick and fucking into him deep. Porsche closed his eyes tightly as I fucked him senseless. I couldn't stop.

"Fuck, Porsche! You feel so good," I grunted, throwing my head back at how good it felt to be inside him. The tattoo covering his arm caught my eye, and it made me snap my hips forward even faster. I usually preferred lovers with flawless skin, but the tattoo on Porsche's arm was so fucking sexy. Damn, this man would be the death of me!

The smack of flesh against flesh and the sounds of passionate moaning echoed through the room. Porsche seemed to relax a little, starting to make keening noises of his own.

"Kinn... It hurts..." Porsche bit back a moan, turning his head back to glare at me, eyes glistening. He did not seem to notice that this action spurred me on, making me thrust more forcefully inside of him.

My hand reverently caressed his skin, paying special attention to his tattooed arm, before moving to tightly grip his waist. Porsche kept falling forward as I fucked him passionately, and I had to pull him back up into a kneeling position several times.

"Are you close?" I asked breathily as his ass began to rapidly clench around me. My pace became erratic and I pushed into him hard as I chased my release.

"Y-yeah... I'm close."

I slowed down, changing the angle before driving deep and fast into Porsche. He gasped, moaning incomprehensible syllables as his body moved with each of my thrusts.

"Mmm, yeah... So tight." I thrust forward, hitting Porsche's prostate until he jolted up from the bed. Smirking, I kept hitting that spot until he thrashed.

Porsche's body tensed up before he spilled his release. I hadn't even touched his cock. I fucked into Porsche's ass until I tumbled over the edge with him.

"Oh, *fuck*," I groaned, thrusting in a few more times before my hips stilled. It felt amazing. Porsche's ass was so tight, and his walls kept pulsing around my cock until I couldn't bear it any longer. I quickly pulled out and peeled off the condom before rolling a fresh one onto my dick.

I turned Porsche onto his back and bent down to kiss him again. Porsche's body remained still.

He shook his head. "L-let... Let me go."

"You haven't had enough. See? You're hard again." I grabbed his hardening length to emphasize my point. Porsche's face contorted, but before he could utter another complaint, I continued to pursue our intimate act.

The reason why we were in this situation tonight was lost on me—I even found myself thanking the person who drugged Porsche. Whatever it was, it was working wonderfully! We would probably be here all night; I didn't think we were going to stop anytime soon.

I'd finally gotten a taste of Porsche, and it was so much better than I had ever imagined.

THE STORY CONTINUES IN
KinnPorsche
VOLUME 2

CHARACTER
&
NAME GUIDE

Characters

The identity of certain characters may be a spoiler; use this guide with caution on your first read of the novel.

MAIN CHARACTERS

'Kinn' Anakinn Theerapanyakul

GIVEN NAME: A-na-kinn

NICKNAME: Kinn

SURNAME: Thee-ra-pan-ya-kul

The second son and de facto heir of a notorious mafia family. Has a habit of getting rough with his partners.

'Porsche' Pachara Kittisawasd

GIVEN NAME: Pa-cha-ra

NICKNAME: Porsche

SURNAME: Kit-ti-sa-wasd

A normal college student who is extremely skilled at martial arts. Since their parents died, he takes care of his younger brother.

SUPPORTING CHARACTERS

'PORCHAY' PITCHAYA KITTISAWASD: Porsche's beloved younger brother.

UNCLE THEE: The younger brother of Porsche's late father. Has a severe gambling problem.

TEM AND JOM: Porsche's best friends and fellow university students.

MADAM YOK: Porsche's former employer and owner of the Root Club.

KORN THEERAPANYAKUL: Kinn's father and the current head of the main branch of the Theerapanyakul mafia family, aka the Major Clan.

'KHUN' TANKHUN THEERAPANYAKUL: Kinn's eldest brother.

'KIM' KIMHAN THEERAPANYAKUL: Kinn's youngest brother.

'VEGAS' KORAWIT THEERAPANYAKUL: The eldest son of the Minor Clan.

'MACAU': The youngest son of the Minor Clan.

ZEK-KANT: Korn's younger brother and head of the Minor Clan.

TAY AND TIME: Kinn's friends.

'BIG': Kinn's former lead bodyguard, before Porsche took over his position.

'PETE': Tankhun's lead bodyguard, who temporarily switched positions with Porsche.

'POL', 'P'JESS' AND 'ARM': Tankhun's other bodyguards.

'NONT': Kim's lead bodyguard.

'CHAN': Korn's secretary.

Names Guide

Thai names follow the western pattern of a given name followed by a family name. Thais are also given a nickname, which is more commonly used when Thais refer to their family, friends, and close acquaintances in their daily life. Thai nicknames can be anything the parents find appealing, a nickname their friends prefer to call them, or even nonsensical words in foreign languages.

In Thailand, it is unusual for people to use someone's surname in casual conversation, unless specifically required. To formally refer to a person, given names are preferred.

Thai honorifics

P'/PHI (IPA pronounciation: /pʰiː˥˩/): A gender-neutral honorific term used to address older siblings, friends, and acquaintances. It can be used as a prefix (P'[name]), a pronoun, or informally used to address unknown people (e.g. store clerks, or shopkeepers).

N'/NONG (IPA pronunciation: /nɔːŋ˥˩/): Used to address younger people, in the same manner as "Phi."

Teochew honorifics

The Thai Chinese are the largest minority group in Thailand, integrated through several waves of immigration. Of these, just over half are Teochew, from the Chaoshan region. Families with Teochew roots may still occasionally use the Teochew dialect, especially when referring to other family members. Some of the terms that appear in this novel are as follows:

HIA: Elder brother

BE: Older brother of one's father

ZEK: Younger brother of one's father

GOU: Older or younger sister of one's father

AGONG: Grandfather